# Readers love *Bound by Guilt*
## by SANDRA BARD

"I thought this book was a very good example of how to do 'from enemies to lovers' chemistry and do it well."
—Reviews by Jessewave

"I really enjoyed this story. It was complicated… Not at all a traditional romance… In their own ways they save each other, even as they grow enough, to begin to save themselves."
—Gay List Book Reviews

"There's a lot of emotion swirling around here— emotions that are not always pretty… but the writing is intriguing and, I thought, as a first novel, Sandra Bard hit it out of the park."
—Joyfully Jay

By SANDRA BARD

Bound by Guilt
Finding His Feet

Published by DREAMSPINNER PRESS
www.dreamspinnerpress.com

# FINDING HIS FEET

## SANDRA BARD

Published by
DREAMSPINNER PRESS

5032 Capital Circle SW, Suite 2, PMB# 279, Tallahassee, FL 32305-7886 USA
www.dreamspinnerpress.com

Finding His Feet
© 2016 Sandra Bard.

Cover Art
© 2016 Stef Masciandaro.
http://www.stefmasc.com
Cover content is for illustrative purposes only and any person depicted on the cover is a model.

ISBN: 978-1-63477-337-9
Digital ISBN: 978-1-63477-338-6
Library of Congress Control Number: 2016901602
Published July 2016
v. 1.0

Printed in the United States of America
(∞)
This paper meets the requirements of
ANSI/NISO Z39.48-1992 (Permanence of Paper).

*To everyone who put up with me while I was writing this book.*

# Acknowledgments

I WOULD like to name a couple of people who helped me with this book: Kushanthi, who read the book while I was still struggling with the plot and gave me valuable feedback; my sister, Ishi, who continuously asked me if I was done; and to all my other family members, who know that I write… something. Perhaps I should also thank the computer people who fixed my laptop so I could finish this book.

# Author's Note

I WROTE this story for close to a year. I got stuck halfway through, not because I didn't have an idea but because I had far too many ideas.

I was born into a country torn by close to thirty years of civil war, and for the first twenty or so years of my life, all I knew was war. And as a result, I didn't want this story to be about that.

But I always wanted to write a story about armors: each armor would have a specific ability and color, and I spent time mapping out each of them, all ninety-seven of them. There were two options for me to choose from where armor could be used, and I was already writing a sci-fi series and didn't want to start another. Hence this story.

It was also during that time that I did a lot of traveling, and I chose to travel by train, mostly because it was the only option available short of stealing a car and a driver at gunpoint. My life became a series of stations, diesel engines, and black smoke on my clothes. I would pull out my tablet and start typing away while I swayed back and forth on the rust buckets that had been old before I was born. While I traveled through different landscapes, from the cold hill country with mountains covered in plantations, to the beaches where the sea ate at the coastal dams and the shotgun-shelled houses were being slowly claimed by the sea, this story took form and grew step-by-step.

I think at one point I told my office mates that I just couldn't get my characters off the train: I was referring to my endless traveling that was slowly wearing me down, since I was dying to sit down in front of a proper laptop and do some hardcore editing.

But in my travels I met some wonderful people who told me stories of how they survived hardships during the war, from one lady who made her own wedding dress at night and got married in her backyard during the curfew, to a man who lost his only daughter to fever because there was no way for him to go out and get medicine.

This story, in essence, is everything and nothing, because I didn't even try to write about what I had learned and heard. It was just about the feelings it inspired.

I wanted to highlight the abilities of the armor, but more than that, I wanted to concentrate on the human spirit. That people survive, no matter what, and find ways to bounce back from unimaginable disasters.

It is about hope.

# CHAPTER 1

*The last defense*

*THERE WAS the time she lost her partner.*

Vorani tried to lift the heaviest of the blocks trapping Kaden's legs. She braced her shoulder against the flat side of what had been a support column for the building and concentrated on her armor power levels. Her armor was a classic offense model, with more weapons than plating, giving her speed and firepower but not much physical strength.

Kaden tilted his chin up as the overhead structure creaked and groaned. "Vor, I want you to leave me."

Vorani rolled her eyes at the request. "We're in this together, remember?"

"You agreed to work with me, not die with me." Kaden's eyes were clear despite the pain he must have been feeling. "Please, you have to go."

"I can't leave you." The building shook around them. The fighting was still going on outside, and due to the explosions and the impacts from the heavy artillery, the surrounding buildings were becoming more unstable.

Theirs had been a mission to sabotage one of the enemy cells hidden close to the border. Vorani had kept watch while Kaden took off his armor so he could slip through the narrow ventilation shaft to infiltrate the base. The enemy had attacked while they were still inside, and Kaden had not managed to crawl free before the place had collapsed around them.

"Don't die for me." Kaden lifted his hand to reach for Vorani. Vorani wondered if he was in love with her; as work partners they'd never spoken about it, but in her heart, she knew, in the way a woman always knows, that he harbored some feeling for her—even if all she felt for him was friendship.

"I'm not dying for you," she gritted out. "I'm making you live."

Just then a scream rang out and Vorani looked over her shoulder. Luckily for them the building had been empty, but this was a civilian-occupied area. They could both hear it, the scream of distress of someone young and scared—and very much alive.

"Go," Kaden told her. "It's what we trained for."

"To protect people," Vorani said as she clutched Kaden's hand. "Not to watch each other die."

"Give me my armor and leave," Kaden told her desperately.

Vorani looked at Kaden's armor, one of the famous, hard to become compatible with, black armors, one of five in existence and the only one in the field. She pulled the leg and chest pieces toward Kaden and gave them to him, wondering which of them was being stupid. "You can't put it on with your—" lower legs trapped under the rubble.

"We are all that stands for the freedom of the people," Kaden told her, reminding her of her oath, the one they took when they first accepted the armors. "Go do your duty, Vor. I'll be waiting."

Vorani stood up, wiping a tear from her face, and turned toward the sound. She could see the sunlight streaming through the gaps in the concrete and thought it ironic that Kaden was trapped not five feet from freedom. "I'll come back for you." She wasn't sure if he heard it over the sound of screaming. Then she clenched her wrists where the controls for her armor were sited and mentally commanded power to her feet so she could run toward those who needed saving.

As she dived through an opening in the building, she turned around for one last look. The whole structure groaned, and even as she watched, the middle caved in, leaving behind a cloud of dust.

"...AND THAT was how I lost my partner and realized my true duty was to the people who need my protection." Vorani finished her story as her enthralled audience, fifty new recruits, looked up at her, eyes shining, mouths open, waiting for her next words. She turned to her left and nodded to the stage manager to let him know the next item should be lined up. Her speech was almost over. "And remember this, you are all here voluntarily, some to take up the armor that will give you the power to protect the innocent, others to support the armored units. It will not be without sacrifice. Now, my own loss is not something I wish to—"

He could take it no more. Vorani was a good speaker, and her story probably had a moral to it, but she was using the tragedy for her own benefit to win over the audience and gain herself some sympathy. And he was in a hurry.

He pushed past the stage manager, and the man squawked in protest. "Excuse me, coming through, move." He could see the moment Vorani's face went from serene acceptance to outright horror as he strode onto the stage, his armored boots hitting the wooden panels with a muted thud.

"Hey," he said to the audience, giving a small wave to emphasize his point. The audience broke into a loud, excited whisper. Kaden knew his armor drew attention: unlike Vorani's muted dark blue, his was a matte black; some called it a different shade of gray, but to him it was a very dark black, so black it didn't reflect any light—like a void. It stood out in the drab, khaki surroundings of the stage, like a negative beacon. "Former partner here... my name is Kaden, and as you can see, I'm not dead. We just decided not to work together after that incident."

Vorani looked as if she was about to explode, and Kaden decided to act quickly. "Now, excuse me—I need to borrow Senior Expert Maxis for a little while. I promise I'll return her to you to continue this fairy tale."

"Kaden," Vorani hissed, but unfortunately she was still wearing her mic and her voice carried across the open hall. She collected herself and looked at the audience with a grimace that could pass for a smile in the low light. "Students, this is Senior Expert Kaden Pace who has come to—" She broke off and looked at him, searching for something to say. "Perhaps you'd like to share some of your wisdom with the new entrants? They'd love to hear a few words of encouragement from you."

Kaden looked down from the stage and smirked. As usual, the main building had been expanded outward with hastily erected tent material to accommodate the sudden influx of people. "Go home. You're here because you think wearing an armor is going to make you a hero. Well, it doesn't. You're here because we lost fifty-seven armored warriors this year"—four of them wearing original armor, something the new recruits needn't be told until they were actually assigned their gear—"which means there's always more space for cannon fodder. Half of you will quit anyway before your five years of training is up, and the rest of you will be—"

"Kaden." Vorani didn't even bother to try and keep up the pretense; she was anything but subtle as she gripped him by the upper arm and pushed him off the stage. She slammed an open palm on his back to vent her frustration, and the force of her blow made him stagger for a second. He had to take several quick steps forward to keep his balance. "What the fuck"—she tore the mic off her chest and placed it on the small table in the corner—"was that? What were you doing spouting all that nonsense, scaring off the kids?"

"Someone needed to tell them."

"Well, it didn't need to be you."

"Why not? They need to know. Or you could tell them a couple more facts, instead of brainwashing them with made-up stories."

"What would I be telling them?"

"That the building I was in was brought down by our Army… that they didn't wait for us to clear out before they fired on us. The enemy cell we went into was a part of the resistance. There were more sympathizers in it than Harians."

"We don't know for sure who fired on that building. Anyway, you took too much time getting the info," Vorani said earnestly. "You knew we were on the clock."

"Maybe you need to tell the truth." Kaden looked away for a second. He wasn't there to fight or review facts about what had gone wrong with their last mission. He'd done that already, numerous times, both in his head and on paper. "I was good enough to tell you what to do before."

Then Kaden realized just how wrong that sounded. He and Vorani had had fun before; they'd joined the training about the same time, both chosen to be original armored warriors, had been friends then lovers for a very brief time and finally partners, a duo who supported each other on the field—but now they were total strangers trying to be civil. Kaden had never called the shots in their partnership. It had always been Vorani.

Perhaps their relationship was more than that. Kaden was a war orphan, foisted from orphanage to orphanage until he had reached the right age to be recruited by the Army. By then he had been far more interested in trying to find his brother, whom he had been separated from, than fighting for his country. Whatever righteous anger he had felt at the thought of his parents' death at the hands of Harian remote drones had fizzled down to nothing in the wake of long food lines and cold showers. In fact, the reason he'd decided to stay in the Army had been the free food.

He had never thought to rise up the ranks in the Army—that was for people with ambition and goals and family influences. Kaden had resigned himself to a life of boot polishing and spoon counting when Vorani had burst into his life. She had both her parents and a plethora of siblings and a house to live in. Because of her patriotism, she joined as soon as she reached the right age. He had run into her at camp on the very first day; Vorani had been annoyed that she'd been set back almost a year and was complaining loudly about it. The recruitment for young cadets was done once a year; born in October, Vorani had to wait almost six months before her enrollment.

It seemed strange that a daughter from a middle-class family, in clothes that actually fit her, would take to the poor boy in mismatched shoes, but it had started out as a rather solid friendship. It had been Vorani's dream to become an armored warrior, and not just any armored warrior, but one who wore an original. To Kaden, the armored warriors were the elite of the elite in the Army, the people who got to wear the almost-mythical body plating that supposedly protected them from everything. True, they were the ones fighting in the front lines, but their gear seemingly made them invincible; they were allowed special privileges because of their invaluable contribution to the war. Unlike Vorani, he had no desire to go out and kill Harians, but he also wasn't completely brain-dead. From what he'd seen and heard, he understood that only a select few could wear the armor, and from that, the original suits were even more distinctive.

Original armor picked the wearer, not the other way around. Back then, Kaden hadn't understood all the talk about genetics and compatibility, only that he was never going to be lucky enough to be chosen.

But Vorani had pressured him to get tested, and somewhere along the way, as he'd gone through arrays of fitting rooms, rattling around in the different metal parts, he'd fallen in love with the process. When Vorani had been found to be compatible with an original armor, Kaden had wanted to belong to the same group. Not to mention there had been a rumor the Army was going to send anyone who was not ready to join the armored unit back to the orphanages for another three years. Vorani had stood by him as he'd gone through fitting after fitting. Ultimately, Kaden had made up his mind to build up his body strength so he could at least wear a more modern pile of metal, when he'd finally clicked.

Each rejection had been painful, some more than others. Every time he'd tried on a suit, piece by piece, he'd wondered if it would be the one. But as the final headgear assembled over him, he would be disappointed. Sometimes there would be a dead silence as he stood there in the dark, the visor's night vision function failing to operate. Sometimes it was wrenching pain inside his head as if a hand had reached in and twisted his brain for a couple of seconds. Once, it had been a blinding headache and nonstop vomiting for two hours.

He'd been ready to give up on it when the black armor had "clicked." For some, the click was an actual sound in the back of their head, like two parts snapping together. For Kaden it had been a smooth transition from one person to two—he imagined it was similar to a sword sliding into a scabbard created just for it. From then on, he always had an extra presence in the back of his mind.

All he was, in a way, was due to Vorani, who'd stood by him and spurred him on. Though he'd stated that he'd once given her instructions, that was a lie. Even in bed, she'd been the one to dictate how he should act. That, more than their sexual incompatibility, and along with her insistence of keeping it secret, had been what caused their parting. Vorani had realized that sleeping with Kaden was hurting their friendship, and she called it off. Thinking back, she'd called the shots for a majority of their relationship. Kaden waited for her to point out just how hollow his earlier words were.

Vorani, luckily, didn't even bother to answer, just gave him one of her patented looks that spoke of her disappointment. "What do you want, Kaden?"

"Why am I not back on active duty?" It hurt him to ask, but he needed to know. As was the policy of the armored warriors, it was not just Medical that had to clear an injured warrior back to duty, but that person's direct superior as well. In his case, it was Vorani, who had been promoted while he'd been "lounging around" in a hospital bed.

"Because I don't think you are ready," Vorani told him sharply before turning around as if to walk back to the stage.

"Wait." Kaden reached for her but stopped just short of touching her. "Is this because I refused to be your partner anymore?" He had to ask.

Vorani's sharp bark of laughter was like a slap across the face. "You really do think highly of yourself, don't you?"

"What else am I to think?" Kaden stepped back with a scowl, arms across his chest. "I cleared the obstacle course in full armor, and the shrink test, and when I went to the office to see if I had an assignment, they told me I hadn't been cleared."

"I'll tell you why you haven't been cleared," Vorani told Kaden, and he knew he'd pushed her a little too far. "You refused to take a physical in camp."

"Why should I?" Kaden said, puzzled. He ignored the cold feeling of dread in his middle to stare back at her defiantly. "It's not one of the requirements. I've been cleared by Dr. Lane and that counts as a medical. There's no need for me to repeat it."

Dr. Melanie Lane had been his doctor at the Warrior Hospital, and since it was technically a part of the Armored Warrior Division, a medical examination in the hospital was the same as one in camp. Even the same doctors performed it at both locations.

Vorani nodded at that. "I spoke to Melanie and she told me some bullshit about patient privacy and stuff." She scowled and looked away. "The last I heard, your medical records were still in transit."

"You called Melanie?" The cold in his middle grew.

"She was your doctor while you were recovering," Vorani pointed out reasonably. "She was the only person who saw you for six months while you were in the hospital."

Kaden was lucky that the other doctor who assisted in his surgery had been transferred to another combat zone and most nurses at the hospital had rotated out by the time he'd been discharged.

"I tried to visit, but Melanie was quite insistent I stay put. You'd think she was hiding something."

There had been a time when Kaden refused visitors, not letting anyone even call him because he hadn't wanted them to see him in his pathetic state. He'd been recovering from having a building fall on him; he'd had little time to deal with well-wishers, bringing him baskets of fruit. However, Vorani's statement hit a little too close to home, and he tried to distract her. "Did you think I was fucking her?"

"That would have been the least of my problems." Vorani didn't even flinch at his underhanded attempt to distract her from the main point. "And what made you think I would care? Besides, I would have found that more believable if Dr. Lane had a dick."

"It's still an invasion of privacy."

"I didn't call her to talk about you. I wanted to know the hospital's power capacity. To make sure the storage units for the fertility clinic were operational."

"Oh."

"It would have been better if you'd simply agreed to have a child."

Kaden felt as if that had come out of nowhere. He knew very little about the history of the mobile weapon he wore, but every Army recruit was given a crash course about it. From what Kaden remembered of those lectures, years later, it had been an invention by the eccentric Dr. Orche, who had meant the armors to be a gift to be passed down through family lines. Perhaps the Orches—Laure and Langvil, father and son— had designed everything with the intention of it being used by a specific group of people. Some speculated that since Langvil joined the research a good fourteen years after his father, perhaps he had had little control over the very first models. It had been Langvil's notes that had helped develop the second generation of armors. The new armor didn't have the same weakness, but it was too late for those who were compatible with the prototypes.

Being compatible with any original armor was genetic, and the government was "encouraging" original armor-attuned warriors to reproduce, even going so far as to collect their sperm and egg samples and provide them with surrogate mothers, where needed. He had his sperm stored as was mandatory for all Army recruits, but the last thing Kaden wanted was to have a child. He was on the verge of doing something stupid, but none of it involved a future generation.

"Well, these days I'm having all the fun without the strings," Kaden said as lightly as possible.

"Your sex life is not my concern, although I hear you've been going to the alleyway outside more often than before. Submit your blood work just in case. I hear those hookers have all types of STDs."

"Then why not just clear me for—"

"I am still your superior," she said sharply. "You were my partner before you became my responsibility, and my intuition tells me something is wrong."

"Well, your intuition has been wrong before." Kaden could see the conversation taking a turn he didn't want, and he decided to retreat while he could. "Look, I know you have to go back to the audience." He gestured toward the stage, where the sound of restless voices could be heard. "I'll leave you to it. Sorry for having disturbed you."

Vorani looked as if she was about to cave in, but at the last moment her eyes fired up. "You know what, Kaden, wait a little," she said as she gestured over her head toward someone in the background. "Pali, carry on. What's the next item?"

Pali, as tall and dark as her armor was silver, stepped forward at the sound of the question. "The second-year cadets have arranged a demonstration."

"Get it started," Vorani instructed her subordinate. "I'm stepping out for a bit." Then she grabbed Kaden by the upper arm, blocking the laser-flare ports in his armor, and dragged him out the back of the tent, where the welcome event was being held.

"I know you're busy and probably should go on—" Kaden had been counting on it, in fact. He had planned on ambushing Vorani on stage because she was busy and would approve his request without thinking too hard. Why hadn't he kept his mouth shut instead of spewing forth his bitterness, not just for the students to hear but also for the rest of the senior armored warriors who had been attending the ceremony?

"I think this is the first time we've had a face-to-face conversation since the last battle," she said seriously, and Kaden's heart sank. Her eyes were earnest, and the way she looked at him as if he was the most important thing in the world made his knees weak. He looked around hurriedly to see if there was a chance of them being interrupted, but it was Welcome Day, the most important day, when all those youngsters who had joined the glorious Joscalian Army to protect the country from the evil Harians were welcomed to their camp. For security reasons, all the camps around the country celebrated Welcome Day on slightly different dates but with the same enthusiasm. Realistically, it was the first day when twelve- to fifteen-year-olds were separated from their parents and introduced to the harsh reality of what it meant to join the Army, and everyone had places to be and things to do. No one slowed down or even looked at the two of them.

Kaden couldn't think of any reason to call somebody over to them. "If that is all you're going to say, I'll be going, then." As much as he wanted to stand and argue with Vorani, he was treading on dangerous ground and knew it was best to withdraw before she discovered just what Dr. Lane had been kind enough to cover up for him.

"What's all this about?" Vorani looked at him levelly—no anger, no sadness, but calm and collected and ready to sort things out.

"Nothing, really," Kaden said, backing out. "I wanted to ask to be released for field duty, that's all."

"Why didn't you ask me that while I was in my office?"

*Because, frankly, it would have led to a conversation just like this.*

"We never speak one-on-one anymore," Vorani continued, undaunted by his inability to say anything.

"Really." Kaden looked around for an escape route. "We talk almost every day at dinner."

"In public, with everyone a foot away from us, and you ask me if I like the soup." Vorani managed to pack a lot of contempt into her voice. "Kaden, you broke up our partnership over the phone."

"I was in hospital then...." He trailed off weakly, knowing his excuse was a very poor one.

"You refused visitors."

"Are we going to go over that again?"

"No, we're not," Vorani said with a tired smile. "I suppose I'm no longer your partner and therefore not supposed to look after you."

"Then okay me for fieldwork."

"I'm not going to do that until you tell me what is wrong."

Kaden tried one last time to provoke Vorani. "Is this your way of getting revenge for me dissolving our partnership?"

She simply shook her head and looked at him. "Why are you in the armor, Kaden?"

Kaden felt cold sweat break out on his forehead and spread over his entire body, even on parts that he deliberately refused to think of. "What?" he managed to force out through his constricting throat.

"You don't take your armor off. I've never seen you without it since you came out of hospital. Maybe I should call you in to meet one of the counselors."

"I take it off," Kaden protested. "I have needs, you know, and this thing doesn't have convenient openings." He managed to make a vague vulgar gesture he knew Vorani, a twenty-year veteran on the force, would understand easily.

Vorani rolled her eyes in response. "No need to be crude, Kaden. I'm glad you don't shit in your armor."

"There's no crime in wearing it," Kaden said, feeling the need to emphasize it.

"There's a word for people like you."

"Ex-partner?"

"For people who don't take off their armor after a traumatic event," Vorani continued without pause. "There're two types of people, those who don't go near their gear because they think they'll be asked to fight. And the type who think it's the best protection against—"

"I'm not like that." Kaden cut her off before she could complete her sentence.

Vorani looked at his face for a second and nodded. "I can see that."

Kaden turned away, letting his shoulders relax. "I'm going to go back to my barracks," he said without any inflection. He'd tried and he'd failed.

"I'll think about what you said," she said softly.

"Think on it." Kaden didn't turn around, presenting Vorani with his back. "Do you want me around the new recruits?"

# CHAPTER 2

THE COMMON area was where the newest recruits bedded down and would live for at least the next two years. It was an open dorm large enough to hold thirty bunk beds, with a corner reserved for a few recreational games, though right then, the area appeared to be empty of all furniture apart from a couple of chairs. He spotted four of his fellow armored warriors as he approached the entrance: Alden, his batchmate, whom he usually got on well with, though they'd trained separately, and his partner, Elisha, who was famous for her fondness of playing tricks on people. They were up to something because they were lugging large buckets of water.

The other duo present, Finzer and Claina, appeared drained by all the energy the first pair was exhibiting. Claina leaned against a wall support, while Finzer slumped on a chair with his back to the door. Kaden entered the common area just in time to see Alden upend a bucket of water over Elisha's head. Kaden supposed that Elisha was used to Alden's antics since she had been partnered with him for as long as Kaden had been with Vorani. Elisha laughed good-naturedly and stepped back, shaking her head to dispel some of the water. She grasped the front of her chest plate, pulled it off, and placed it on the table. Unlike the black armor Kaden wore, her model called for physical removal of each individual piece.

Kaden was sure there were only about twenty such original armors in existence. Hers was one of the older models, passed down her family for two generations. He could see gash marks and the infamous hole in the hip plate that had been patched up. It was that armor-piercing missile shot that had killed Elisha's mother, though Elisha never spoke of it. Unlike his, hers wasn't self-repairing.

It was easy to see the progression from the detachable chest plates to the final models, such as the black armor he wore. Kaden wondered if he could point out to Vorani that keeping him out of the field meant not using a very powerful weapon.

Deep in thought, he wasn't even aware he'd been spotted until a rush of water fell on his head as well, and he looked up to see Claina with another bucket in hand. He supposed he should be grateful that Claina, who wasn't as social as Elisha, was joining in with them. Kaden laughed obligingly and folded his armor back up to his waist, wading into the fray. He didn't want to act like an asshole. Like the others, his underarmor was waterproof but not temperature controlled, and he shivered a little as he sat down next to Finzer, who was also looking a little blue around the edges. He wasn't wearing his armor at all, and Kaden knew it was due to practicality. New armor was notoriously hard to wear full-time.

"What's this about?"

"Cleaning before the fresh meat arrives," Finzer said with an open grin. The new recruits were always split up into smaller groups and assigned to each dorm. The senior cadets who finished their training graduated to one of the upper dorms. Even the senior officers joined in the fun of cleaning the recruits' dorms in memory of their first years in the armored unit, although they seemed to be making an extra effort that year. Most likely because there were more senior officers in camp; the fighting in the borders had come to a temporary standstill.

"Uh." Kaden, unimpressed by all the water, shook his head. "I can't see how this is helping. Why can't we do it the way we always do?"

"Switching on the sprinklers, that's too easy," Finzer retorted. "How did it go?"

Kaden knew what he was asking about. "She said no."

"Damn, that's what you get for having your former partner as your senior officer," Finzer said without heat. "They always try to protect you from the worst."

"Well, keeping me here isn't helping," Kaden grumbled. "Another four months and I'll have been off the active-duty list for an entire year."

"Oh," said Finzer, understanding his worry.

Everyone knew what happened when the one-year mark was up. The administration forced armored warriors to retire or turned them into desk jockeys. At the very beginning, some families whose sons and daughters had been killed in action had tried to claim the armors, as their family lines were most likely to be genetically compatible with the gear. The families had argued that since no one else could wear them, surely they could keep them as mementoes of their loved ones, not to mention the prestige they could gain from holding on to them. But the Army's claim had prevailed. Why should a nonfighter get good armor when there was always a shortage of usable gear?

"I think the rule is mostly for the new suits," Finzer said as if reading Kaden's mind. "You know how hard it is to match yours in particular."

"True," Kaden agreed. The black armor he wore had only been compatible with one other warrior a long time ago. Unlike some, Kaden hadn't tried to find out what happened to the previous wearer of his armor—not wanting to be pressured by a dead man's ghost. The man had no offspring, and the armor then sat disused in storage until Kaden came along.

Kaden sighed and settled back. There was nothing to do except sit with his fellow warriors as they did juvenile stunts or go back to his room and look at the ceiling. It was too early to see if there were any hookers, or streetwalkers, as they sometimes called themselves, at the gate. Any military camp offered a good business setting for sex workers, and there were always one or two milling around. Kaden would usually pick one of them for a quick hand job or a blow job when he needed to ground himself, but it didn't feel enough, and with his noncombat pay, his savings were sinking to dangerous levels.

There were other reasons to cut back on sex. The prostitutes he'd been with had never asked why he wanted to be "serviced" while he was in armor, but from Vorani's comment, his reluctance to take it off had been noted, and he didn't want the gatekeeper to check that he always went out in full gear. Once matched, the armor was his to wear at all times until it was given away freely or until he died, but only a handful wore their gear all the time, especially inside the camp. Some, like Claina, only wore theirs in combat. For Kaden to wear his armor to pick up a hooker was probably equivalent to taking a nuclear bomb to a two-year-old's birthday party.

"It took me three months after the time I got injured before they let me out," Finzer offered after a while.

"I know," Kaden said under his breath, feeling frustrated with how little he'd accomplished that day. He had taken to reading lately, but there was a dearth of reading material. The library consisted of a lot of military strategy, history of the war between the Joscalians and Harians, and the most recent addition, the history of space travel—which consisted of two useless pages. Kaden would have given anything to read a good love story about two idiots who couldn't make up their fucking minds.

"They are holding people back because there's no need to push them to the field. There's been a break in fighting since the big battle in Ganden—" Finzer hesitated when he realized it was the last skirmish Kaden had been in. "I mean, everyone needs a rest. Even the Harians behind the drones are only human. They need to rest as well."

"I hear it's the peace talks." Claina moved toward them, bucket still in hand. "They're talking about sending a group over here as ambassadors and us sending a group of ours as hostages."

Unlike most, Claina rarely joined in their conversations, which Kaden always thought was a trait left over from the time she was ostracized for her coloring, before she joined the Armored Warrior Division.

Unlike the rest of them, she had light brown hair and light eyes. Kaden, in contrast had dark hair, black eyes, and olive-colored skin, like other Joscalians. Claina was pretty, and Kaden remembered with a pang of nostalgia that they'd been voted the best-looking cadets of his batch during his third year. Claina was chosen for her "outstanding overall looks" while he had been told his skin set off his bone structure to perfection. The girls and some of the guys had stated they liked his brooding, serious expression. There had been a time when such trivial things mattered, before he'd been thrown headfirst into actual combat. And now, after years of fighting, everything he'd worked for was evaporating.

"I don't see myself going over there to talk *peace*," Finzer spat, stressing *peace* as if it made his body cringe. "Not even if they ordered me."

"But I hear you moved your wife and kid to a farm on the outskirts," Alden said mildly, and Finzer flushed and looked away.

"I'm just protecting the next generation of fighters." Finzer sounded impassioned, though he didn't look all too happy quoting government propaganda.

"I for one would be happy if my kid didn't grow up to be the next weapon," Alden said firmly.

They all knew the government's interest in armored warriors reproducing was to have more fighters for the future and not a sudden concern over the fall in the birthrate, as publicly claimed. The war between Joscal and the newly independent state of Haria had been going on for 130 years, and both sides expected it to last a hundred more. The Joscalian Army fought with all they had, sacrificing countless soldiers, not just armored units, for the sake of maintaining their border, while the Harians hid behind their remote drones. It was common knowledge that over a hundred million Joscalians had died in the first ten years of the war alone, and nowhere in the country was safe to bring up children.

Kaden snorted and looked away. He didn't have kids… so not his concern.

"They're even talking about sending a joint team to salvage what they can from Ground Zero," Elisha added, sounding amused. Ground Zero was the starting point of the second phase of the war, when Haria had bombed the peaceful Joscalian island of Compen. Situated on the border between Joscal and Haria, it was coveted, and now officially out of bounds to both countries since the incident. "From what I hear, there's not much to salvage, anyway. They're even talking about letting some refugees settle near Compen Beach Town, but the island is still off-limits."

"Makes sense." Kaden nodded. "No one's going to hand over that island unless they're sure there's nothing worth taking."

"So everything's in the planning stage, which is why there's this long calm," Claina concluded.

"It's called a cease-fire," Elisha told her sharply.

Kaden wasn't sure he believed it. "Or they're planning the biggest counterattack ever, and we need to be ready."

"There is that."

"From what I hear, our side is the one resisting the change in borders," Alden added thoughtfully.

"Well, it is our country," Finzer said firmly. "All of it."

There was the sound of quick steps and everyone turned to the entrance to see a junior office helper walk in.

"Instructor Kaden Pace," the helper said.

"Instructor… when did you become an instructor?" Finzer asked the same question Kaden was about to ask.

"I'm not." Kaden got up and moved to the messenger. He took the message pad from the cadet and frowned. It read *To: Instructor Kaden Pace.* "Huh."

"What does it say?" Elisha called, and Kaden realized everyone in the room had ceased whatever they were doing, which wasn't much, to see what was about to happen.

"That…." Kaden frowned as he read the rest of the message. "I've got a mission."

"That's great," Finzer said, and the others added their voices.

Though Kaden wasn't exactly best friends with the rest, he spoke to them and hung around with them on a regular basis. Recruited at roughly the same time, they had been in a few skirmishes together.

"But it's an observation mission. Two cadets, Bradley and Wayland Olgesh, who are in training. I'm supposed to watch over them until they achieve their Second Level Competency Grading." Kaden frowned.

*What the fuck was that?* Then he remembered that was the same exam he'd taken in his third year of training, then called the Level Clearance 2. He'd been so young then; it had been close to twenty-three years ago, and he'd struggled over the obstacles and the stupid mission he'd been assigned. In a way, he'd expected battlefield missions to be as easy as his very first training operation, so simple to complete under the guidance of his now long-dead mentor.

"Hey, I remember those missions," Elisha chipped in enthusiastically. "Mine was to guard a supply train from Morgan to Jalen." Kaden remembered that she had not been a part of their camp during training but had transferred from Morgan after her marriage. "Nothing happened the entire way, not even raiders, but my mentor, Lavinia, was there. Felt better knowing she was watching my back." She sighed. "She's retired now, and I think one of last year's cadets matched up to her armor."

"Mine was to take a bunch of senior citizens from one of those old hospitals being evacuated to another," Finzer said quickly, probably to break the depressing memories. No one wanted to talk about a time when their armor was going to be taken away. "I was glad Alden was there, because there was this particularly feisty old gal who kept pinching my bottom."

"Your armor doesn't expose your bottom," Kaden blurted out, caught up in the moment despite himself.

"Well, it did, for that mission."

The messenger cleared his throat pointedly, and Kaden looked at the pad in his hand. "This isn't a real mission. I'm playing babysitter for two kids who're going to go get their nature badge or something." The administration never paired kids together unless there was a good reason. The kids were most likely too young to be married, so siblings, probably twins. Wonderful. He was stuck with a pair of boys—double the trouble.

Finzer looked up thoughtfully. "This means both of them have original armor?"

Kaden could see the implication. It wasn't unheard of for siblings from the same family to wear original armor, but in every instance, it had been one sibling taking over the original armor of the other sibling when they couldn't fight anymore, which in most cases meant the first one had died. Kaden couldn't really recall if there were instances of two siblings being compatible with original armors at the same time. Perhaps there had been people a while back, but not during his service.

He hesitated and then cleared his throat. "Can two people be compatible with the same set of armor at the same time?" They would all know he was referring to the new armor.

Claina was the first to answer. "Apparently, they can't. Something to do with it being attuned to individual brain waves or something."

Alden snorted. "Remember the time that kid in Gasin tried on his father's armor when the guy went home for the holidays? He's been in a coma since then. The doctors say that even if the kid recovers, there won't be much left of him. Seems it doesn't make a difference that they were related. If the armor isn't given freely, then the rejection is ten times as bad as when trying on an incompatible armor."

Kaden had heard the news, but he hadn't analyzed it in depth as Alden seemed to have done. "So, no for these two sharing the same armor?"

"I've trained one of them—Bradley—for a short while. Good kid, very focused, but has some authority issues. Doesn't like being told what to do," Claina spoke finally. Kaden had an idea that she was holding back something, but he didn't think it was out of malice, if the look of amusement on her face was anything to go by. "The other one—Wayland—has the original armor, which can manipulate something. Metal, I think, you know, like Vishnu can."

Everyone knew Vishnu's armor gave him the ability to push small metal objects away from him at times, though how it was done was never really explained. Not all the original armors had abilities (or perhaps the wearers hadn't discovered them); some were simply protective covering to be worn. The secrets of each armor were known only to the person or people who created them; even the technicians who handled them only understood how to do basic repairs. When people had first argued that armor was too dangerous to be used in combat, the Army had pointed out that it was their only hope to keep the borders safe. Statistics showed that the Harians had been winning the war until the armored warriors were introduced.

"You will be monitoring their performance and evaluating them to make sure they're ready to go to the next level. It's a big responsibility," Elisha told him gently.

All Kaden knew was that he might not get a shot at a real mission until he'd completed everything Vorani had to throw at him. At least this would keep him out in the field.

"So, what's their mission?" Finzer asked.

"They have to retrieve an armor," Kaden read.

It didn't look all too bad, a very quick, easy mission. Not that the people in charge ever assigned complicated, dangerous ones to kids who were about to finish the second level. "Dead armored warrior. They need someone to pick up his gear from the base near his family home and bring it back here." Dead warriors were displayed to the public in their armor—at least those who had enough of the body to show. There was a joke in the armored unit that for a proper burial, all anyone needed was the head and the suit. But the gear was far too valuable to be buried and was removed before the cremation. It was stored at the base closest to where the deceased was buried—in this case the base closest to the dead warrior's family home—and someone from the base he was posted at would go and pick it up after a period of mourning.

"Poor guy, whoever he was." Elisha moved up to Kaden to look at the message. "If his armor's being returned in a box, he probably didn't have any family able to take it up after him."

Kaden tried to make light of the situation. "Maybe no one wanted to."

Claina shrugged. "Same thing. There's a myth that armors don't become compatible if the wearer doesn't want them."

"So, who died?" Alden changed the subject, gesturing toward the pad with impatience.

Kaden looked up. "Some guy called MacCrave." Everyone looked blank, so not one of theirs. They didn't know everybody in the camp. The current base had a total of five thousand military personnel at all times. Kaden barely knew one tenth of them in person. "Well, at least it'll be easy for your cadets. Just go and report to the base and arrange for it to be brought back. The only tough part will be deciding what transport to use." Elisha was a senior instructor who had trained a lot of cadets and had children of her own, two of whom were currently in training. "Not bad, should be easy. They'll get some practice."

Kaden could feel a smattering of resentment and the start of a tension headache. It had to have been Vorani, assigning him to this mission—he couldn't complain about it, but this was not what he wanted. He could hardly go and rage at her, because that would prove he was an asshole. He would have rather been assigned to an actual fighting unit; he'd heard there were some skirmishes in the front line, and he needed to be able to go there and be useful. But he was stuck doing odd jobs.

"Think of it this way," Finzer said quietly. "If you do this well, you might be allowed to join the main fight."

"I'll take it under advisement," Kaden said heavily. He turned to the messenger and managed a smile, which probably resembled a snarl. "I accept this mission," he said before he reached for the pen and signed his name at the bottom of the document. "When do I have to get ready to escort these brats?"

"In two days' time," the messenger said before turning to go. "But Senior Expert Maxis will be contacting you soon for a meeting."

"Thanks," Kaden called out to the retreating messenger. Now he at least had something to do. Perhaps he could go and test his battle reflexes on the training course in preparation for the mission.


THE TRAINING field was arranged the same as it had always been, but that didn't make the obstacles any easier to overcome. Kaden looked at the timer and took a deep breath. He could do it. He hadn't done the main obstacle course since before his accident, and he was about to remedy that. Although he had cleared the indoor training course, this was the one that really counted. And if he couldn't complete a simple course, then he wasn't fit for active duty, no matter what.

The first step over the line triggered the timer. He started out at a run, scaled the twelve-foot wall, and fell to the other side easily, ignoring the hanging rope that he was supposed to use to slide down. He didn't need to worry about the impact to his legs; his armor took care of it and the landing was surprisingly easy—more so than before the accident. As he strode forward, something snagged his armor where his ankle plating locked. Kaden scowled in frustration—he had landed on a patch of barbed wire and the wires had wrapped around his ankle, holding him in place. If he'd used the rope, he'd have landed on it a little more gently, but when he'd dropped, he'd squashed them, triggering some sort of trap.

Kaden decided he didn't have to put up with the time-wasting bullshit of bending down and untangling the wires. There was a reason his armor had the plating it did: it was able to take a lot of beating. He needed to save his lasers, just about the only weapons in his armor, for later, in case he needed it. He pushed forward using his thighs and the armor moved, cutting through the wire as he waded across it, like twigs breaking under pressure. The sharp edges tore at the metal plating but didn't get a proper grip, and Kaden didn't worry too much. With luck, by the time he'd reached the end of the course, the plating would have "healed."

He was through in a couple of seconds, mentally cheering himself— *oh shit, pit*, he thought before he hit the bottom of the trench that ran through the training field. The pit was generally said to be everywhere and nowhere. Theories about the seemingly self-moving ditch abounded: from the Army using magical means to move it, to prisoners of war being brought out at night just to dig and move dirt. He really didn't care either way. All he knew was that he needed to get out of the five-foot-deep, two-foot-wide gash in the earth he'd fallen into.

He heard the whistling sound just in time to look and groan. There was a secondary trap, a huge boulder released from an overhead crevice. Kaden had two options: dodge or face it full on. Of course, there was always a third option: he could die.

He mentally checked his weapons status. They were half-charged, enough to blast the boulder to dust, but as he stood there bracing, it seemed as if time had slowed. He could see the large boulder falling on him, and he wondered what it would feel like to let it crush him. When the building had fallen, he'd felt very little pain, but the pressure had been enormous. He'd struggled to free his legs, caught under the beams that had fallen across him. He'd first felt the skin break. Then he'd heard the calf bones crack, toes break, ankles bend as the pressure increased, distant screams a muted buzzing in the background.

Then Vorani had run out. And that's when Kaden knew he was going to die. He had lain there, his armor clutched in his hand, knowing he didn't have the leverage to put it on. There wasn't much use in putting his helmet on when the rest of his body was going to get crushed. He'd simply given up. As his mind had relaxed, he'd stopped resisting the mental uplink the armor had forged since the first time he'd worn it. He'd opened his mind to the armor controls fully for the first time in his life and accepted that he needed to be folded into it. He'd accepted what it had offered, companionship in his last moments after being abandoned by his partner. He'd always assumed he would die alone, but at that moment all he'd felt had been overwhelming loneliness and the need to be with someone.

He'd always felt the link with his armor, like a flicker at the corner of his eye or nudge at the back of his mind. When he'd finally realized he was always going to have that feeling of something knocking to be let in, he'd slammed the door shut. He'd never had what some warriors had, that almost-mythical connection that allowed them to know where the armor was with their eyes closed. Once he'd accepted he was going to die, he couldn't fight his armor forever, even if that meant giving up on it. There had been a whisper in his mind—*Sorry*—and he could feel the self-repairing plates trying to fuse around him. Logically he knew he must have put on his armor, but what he remembered was different, almost dreamlike—no doubt his mind bowing to his inevitable death. The chest plating rolled over him, and the rest had poured like molten liquid. Through the gaps in the rubble, the boots had squeezed close to his crushed lower legs even as he scrambled to pull his lower body free. The building was collapsing, but if he could—

He snapped back to the present with a painful jolt to find himself at the bottom of the pit, arms above his head in a defensive position, the boulder just inches from his hands, and he hadn't even activated the firing mechanism. For a moment his body seized. *Finally*, he thought when the boulder hit him, and he braced himself for pain and the inevitable—

The boulder crumpled into dust. He blinked. Dust obscured his vision and Kaden blinked again as the goggles automatically extended to protect his eyes.

There were stories of the first armored warriors found inside their self-repairing armor, not a scratch on the surface, while they'd bled to death inside the metal plating.

Never had he heard of armor that took over control from the wearer, but that's exactly what had just happened.

He didn't have time to be freaked out by the fact his armor had taken things into its own hands, so to speak. He needed to keep moving.

Kaden pulled himself up to the lip of the pit and scrambled to dry ground, not even bothering to dodge the metal spears headed his way. He caught one in his hand and threw it away; the rest bounced off his armor, leaving scratches he knew would be gone shortly. He broke into a run, letting the projectiles brush against him until he came to the water's edge. The stream was close to fifteen feet wide and eight feet deep in the center, if he remembered correctly from last time, and unfortunately his armor didn't give him the ability to walk on water.

A simple large body of water would be too easy; there would be traps. There were armors that allowed for wearers to swim or at least breathe under water for a short time. His was not one of them. Kaden decided to wade in cautiously, hoping the ground sloped and didn't drop off all of a sudden. The cold water lapped at his knees. He reached the first obstacle, a series of tilted wooden panels that rose from the water. He considered blasting them aside, but he had an inkling he might need to scale them rather than destroy them, to reach the other side.

Kaden hooked his fingers over the edge of the first one and climbed onto it, his shoulder muscles straining. The armor added another fifty to sixty pounds to his body weight, but after years of living in the suit, it didn't feel like much. He might not have worn it constantly before the accident, but twenty-three years of combat experience meant a large number of hours in his gear, both in and outside of the field, and he'd gotten used to the weight. His boots had hooks at the edges and spikes at the bottom for better grip. Kaden found the right handhold and climbed up the first board only to discover it was glowing softly in the middle.

An explosive charge underneath. Vorani had speculated that the black armor Kaden wore was built for stealth. It self-repaired, moved silently, and allowed for fast movement, but it came at a price: the black armor had less plating and lacked most of the weapons and detection tech that other suits came with. Right then, Kaden would have traded some of that stealth for something to detect explosive devices from a safe distance.

Again he felt the strange mixture of dread and excitement as he looked at the glow—how big a charge, he wondered. Enough to blow up a sizable chunk of the wooden stage, at least. *No need to get up every morning, no need to pretend to be anything, not whole, not hurt, not, not....*

His arms straightened and he flung himself off the board to another, caught the edge of it, and repeated the maneuver. The third board broke under his weight, and he hit the water with a loud splash, loud enough to cover the sound of the first explosion. The second explosion buffeted him and he slammed against the base of the concrete column holding the boards in place. He felt the pressure of the water and the thump of the concrete but no pain—the courses were not designed to kill people. The Army left that in the hands of the enemy. He spluttered as water rose in a large wave over his head, seeping into his mouth and nose.

The weight of the armor he had shaken off as immaterial earlier felt like a thousand pounds as water flooded the small openings in his suit. The explosions rocked his body, and each wave of water battered him against the central column. Water collected in the middle, entered through the gaps, and pushed him down like a gentle but firm hand.

Kaden knew the procedure. He knew what was in the handbook since he'd read it a lot in the past few weeks.

*Take the armor off when in a water situation, especially if you're wearing a non-water-combat armor, attach the armor to yourself if possible (suggestions: rope, chain, locking a small piece of armor to yourself), and throw it out of the water first. Next, you should follow as fast as possible.*

Kaden could take off his armor, fold it into a block, throw it out of the water, haul himself out, and roll over it in less than fifteen seconds. He'd timed himself. But chances were there would be observers, and he didn't want to do it.

The second option was to sink with the armor and see how long he could hold his breath while walking on the bottom. He'd get mired in the mud and the progress would be slow, and he would more than likely run out of air before he reached the other end—not that he knew what to do when he got there.

Kaden was tempted to just sink, go under, forget everything, and for a second, he wondered if he should simply let go and fall—but they would more than likely pull him out if he didn't come up soon enough. Then they might strip his armor off him. There were instances when armor had been removed from unconscious combatants, mostly the new gear, but the result was the same. Some warriors injured while wearing their armor refused to get back into it. It was something Kaden was never going to do. But sometimes the Army decided warriors were incompetent and not fit to be in the armored unit if they'd been injured due to their own negligence. A deciding factor in that was how they'd used their gear and their physical status. They were gently persuaded to step down, and their equipment was assigned to more capable soldiers.

What worried Kaden most was, should he drown in the training course, that the Army might strip off the suit for all to see what he had lost, and take his armor away from him forever.

That and the possible humiliation of being the first person to drown on a training obstacle course made Kaden spring into action. He dug his fingers into the middle pillar and started climbing, using the hooks on his boots and his fingers to dig holds. It was slow going, but he made it out of the water, the climb becoming easier as the water drained out of him inch by inch. He finally reached the top platform. Once he was up, he was tempted to lie on his back and gasp for breath, let his shoulder muscles relax and feel his fingers unclench, but it was all too easy, and he still had half the course to complete. He stood up and started off in a run, leaping off the platform.

He caught the ropes hanging overhead and slid the last few yards until he reached the end of the course. He folded back his helmet as he walked toward Vorani, who was standing there with her gaggle of newcomers and two female warriors in armor, probably junior assistants, there to help her manage the crowd. They were too old to be cadets but they were dressed in the trainee uniform.

"So, kids, I charge for the show," he quipped as he stopped before them. The water was still slowly draining from his armor, and he could *feel* the scratches in it repairing, even if he couldn't actually see them.

The "kids" looked suitably awed, and even Vorani nodded at him, face blank. "You beat your personal best," she told him flatly. "And I see your armor compatibility has gone up. How much is it now?"

Kaden hadn't checked in a while. He looked at his left-hand display, and his eyes widened in surprise: 91 percent. The compatibility measurement came with every original armor, showing how much the wearer had synced both physically and mentally with their suits. While 100 percent was never achieved, at least 40 percent compatibility was needed for it to be mobile.

"Why didn't you take it off?" the taller girl to the left of Vorani asked. Kaden froze. "When you fell into the moat, couldn't you have taken it off and saved yourself?"

"Because...." Kaden took a deep breath to steady himself. "That's only possible if you're in the training course. In real life, if you're in water, you're either being swept away or swimming, and unless you took off your armor before getting into water, the chances are you're in the water involuntarily. Take your armor off and you'll lose it. There could be an enemy or ten waiting for you to be separated from your only defense, so they can kill you."

The girl nodded thoughtfully. "But what if there is no column for you to climb?"

"You improvise," Kaden snapped, feeling a little annoyed by the persistent questioning. It wasn't as if he had all the answers. He glared at her and realized with surprise that she wore a new armor.

The new armor, also known as modified armor, was patterned after the original armor, though the technicians had never perfected the neural link that created the mental connection between the wearer and the suit in the originals. That knowledge was lost along with everything else on Compen Island, Ground Zero. The result was an extremely heavy pile of metal plating that only the very strong could move in. The modified armor had more built-in weapons and none of the compatibility issues of the original, but it was limited by the strength of the person inside. The amount of body strength required to walk around in modified suits was astounding. Unlike the original armor, which weighed probably twice as much but supported itself by melding with the mind of the soldier, the new kind needed to be carried. Most new armored warriors were men for the simple reason they had the required strength. To mount a gun was possible, but extra ammo meant more weight, and there was a fine line between practicality and stupidity.

It had none of the quirks of the original armor, such as being self-supporting and semisentient, but all the inconveniences, even if they were better than nothing when fighting Harian drones. But what surprised Kaden was the fact the girl who wore it was slender and shorter than him, not at all the proverbial bodybuilder-type warrior usually assigned to such armor.

Feeling thrown off-balance, Kaden looked at the second girl.

The younger girl wore dark gray armor with a metallic sheen and strange markings on the shoulders and knees, with several patches near the chest, side, and left calf—an original armor that had seen some wear. Since those who had read what was left of Dr. Orche's research had proven beyond doubt that blood relatives of the original armor bearers were the most compatible, it was most probably something of a family heirloom.

"What would you do in water?" Vorani was looking at him expectantly.

"Just swim," he said weakly. "Or walk under water—the armor is good enough for that."

Vorani nodded, ready to move on. "Your ankle got caught in the wire. Did it punch through the armor?"

Kaden shook his head.

"But—" The younger girl was cut off by the older girl, who shook her head pointedly.

"Vorani?" he said with a frown. Vorani never did anything without a reason, not even bringing cadets to a training course.

"Kaden, I want you to meet the two you'll be escorting—Bradley and Wayland Olgesh."

"Can we talk?" Kaden told Vorani with a stilted smile that indicated they should step away from the rest.

"The Olgesh family has a lot of influence," Vorani said as soon as they were out of hearing range of the new recruits. "Their father is the advisor to the president and some say might be the next defense minister."

"That's nice, but that information has nothing to do with me."

"I picked you because you wouldn't be awed by the names," Vorani said wryly.

Kaden stopped short of rolling his eyes. "The names threw me off. Why are they named after boys?"

"Traditional family names. It's common enough in their part of the country." Vorani shrugged. "Look, they're new here. Transferred out from Magden because Bradley had some issues with the people there."

"Bradley is the older cadet in the new armor?" Kaden asked just to confirm his understanding.

"Yes, and she'll be in charge of planning the mission."

"Right." Kaden thought that sounded wonderful. Not.

"Look, I'm assigning something that must be completed. They both need to do this, and it's not going to be all that difficult."

"Is that why there's two of them?"

"Bradley was held back a year, and she agreed to wait an additional year so she could take the exam with her sister."

"That's not very reassuring."

"Bradley's more than capable of looking after things. Let her manage it," Vorani said easily. "You just sit with them for the duration, and come and file a short report saying it's done. And stay out of Bradley's way. This is part of her assessment as well."

"What is?"

"Taking care of the basics of such a journey."

Kaden was running out of reasons to protest. "Those two really weren't what I was expecting."

"What were you expecting?"

Kaden tried to think and realized he'd imagined very little about who his assignment was going to be. "Uh… twin boys."

# CHAPTER 3

BRADLEY AND Wayland were neither twins nor boys.

The extremely thin file (Kaden was sure most of the important documents were removed from it) he had read the previous day had given him very little information about them.

Bradley, the older of the two girls, was eighteen, the same age Kaden had been when he'd started actual combat. She was tall, though not as tall as Kaden's six feet two, a good-looking girl (which the file didn't mention, but Kaden had eyes) with long black hair combed back into a sensible ponytail. Her new armor was blue with a dash of gray on the edges, a semimodern model that gave more coverage to the arms and legs but at the same time managed to look sleek.

The note from Vorani mentioned that she would make a good leader but probably wouldn't take orders very well, whatever that meant, and that Kaden should let her take charge unless he could see the situation was dire. Since it was a simple mission, he decided he just needed to sit back and let her lead.

Wayland, the younger girl, wore the original armor, which was metallic gray of a lighter shade than her sister's trimming, with green dashes on the shoulder and knees. She was smaller than her sister at five six, with shorter hair as well, but it was obvious at first glance they were related. They both had sharp features, black, piercing eyes, and firm mouths. Their faces were triangular, with large eyes set off by a small nose and mouth, balanced by large ears that would have looked ridiculous on most but suited them well.

Wayland had an expressive face with sparkling eyes and a ready smile, while Bradley looked exactly like a still photograph, emotionless, which masked her beauty, giving her an unapproachable look. The file had mentioned Wayland as the mouthier of the two, but it was Bradley who was in charge of the group, and she made it clear from the start.

She watched Kaden saunter toward the train station, with a look of displeasure on her face. "You're late."

"I was under the impression we were leaving on the 0800 train," Kaden said as he walked up to her with a smirk on his face. She had to learn to unwind and relax. Kaden wasn't going to throw a wrench into her plans, but she needed to know her leadership was arbitrary and he was the senior officer present.

Bradley gave him a flat, unimpressed look and adjusted the box under her right arm with a grunt of acknowledgment. Kaden decided to let it go. He was an observer, there to see how they would carry out their mission, not to react to what they did or even to advise them. Bradley would handle their funds and the route; they were ready.

"Is that all you have?" Bradley looked at his small carry-on with surprise.

Kaden shrugged. "I travel light." And he didn't need to pack a lot for a two-day journey by train.

Bradley bristled at his tone. "Hope you remembered to pack your socks."

The hysterical laughter that burst out of him surprised all of them, and Kaden fought to bring himself under control. "That's probably the last thing I need."

"I wish my armor had inside padding," Wayland complained loudly, and Kaden smirked at Bradley.

Kaden watched the travel cloak she wore flutter up in the faint breeze and adjusted his own cloak so it would not fly open. His travel cloak was light blue, made of a lightweight material, long enough to fall to the ground. There was a hood as well, but he wore it pulled back since he wasn't wearing his helmet. He could call his helmet through his neural link if needed, as could Wayland, unlike Bradley. The travel cloak was basically a long sheet of material that could be fixed around the neck of the wearer, with a simple clasp and encircled the whole body. There were no other fastenings but a whole lot of overlapping material that formed a slit from the neck to the ground on the side, so that should the wearer move, it would not impede their movements. It was waterproof and fireproof, not that it was going to be of much use on their journey, but Kaden liked it and would have donned one even if Bradley hadn't insisted they all wear them. Wearing armor in public made people uneasy; the travel cloak over it, no matter how flimsy, seemed to reassure them.

The train was the most obvious choice of transport since there was a station close to their base and had a direct route to Koresa, where former armored warrior MacCrave had been based. If they were to take the bus, they'd have had to change buses three times since there was no direct route, and there was never enough legroom with the armor. Training missions were far too unimportant to warrant an official vehicle, and they just didn't have the funds to hire one for the entire journey.

They walked onto the inner platform at 0745. Kaden had traveled on the train before and he'd never purchased a ticket—such things were overlooked with armored warriors, but Bradley, a stickler for rules of any kind, bought second-class tickets for all of them.

Kaden wandered off to sit on one of the side benches while the two girls stood at parade rest on the platform, backs straight, their packs on their shoulders. Looking at them made Kaden's shoulders ache in sympathy. He leaned back, stretched out his legs, and closed his eyes. Bradley, he knew, was glaring at him, as if expecting him to keep staring at her for cues. He wasn't going to give them marks for wasting energy. They just needed to get their job done and not act like a couple of textbook rookies. After a couple of minutes, Wayland broke formation, and much to the irritation of her sister, stomped up to Kaden and sat next to him.

She was holding the box Bradley had been carrying earlier, and Kaden could see it was addressed to a Mrs. G. MacCrave.

"What's in the box?" he asked when she'd settled next to him, looking defiantly at her sister. Bradley twitched but remained standing, obviously too fresh and full of energy to give in to the temptation of sitting down.

"The last effects of Warrior MacCrave," Wayland said casually, flipping the lid open.

"Wayland!" Bradley sounded scandalized. "You can't."

"But you opened it when you got it."

Bradley colored. "That was to make sure they weren't setting us up with something else." She moved a couple of steps closer to them, though she didn't sit down.

Kaden ignored her to look into the box and felt a flutter of sadness as he looked at the last possessions of the dead guy. A marker pen, an old calendar with a couple of pages torn out, a card in an envelope, a couple of sweets, and a transparent adhesive tape.

"They cleared out his belongings a while ago," Bradley explained in her stilted voice. "These were the last of the things left behind."

Kaden could see little point in it, but he pulled out the card and flipped it open. It was garish, red and yellow with a couple of butterflies on the side. More suited for a woman than for the stern-faced, middle-aged man Kaden remembered from the photo in the file. MacCrave had been his senior by over twenty years and hadn't been in the same unit, so Kaden had never exchanged words with him. "Happy birthday" read the inside. In smaller letters, at the bottom, "25th September." A couple of seconds later, he heard the weak tones of "Happy Birthday To You" playing from the card, a high-pitched sound that grated on his ears. He flipped it shut and shoved it back into the envelope with a scowl.

"Was his birthday on the twenty-fifth of September?" he asked no one in particular.

"It was April 27," Bradley informed them. She frowned when they stared at her. "I looked it up. Protocol says I have to know all the background information related to the mission, and I read everything there was."

"That's—" Kaden didn't know what to say. Someone had sent a birthday card on the wrong day; it happened, but Bradley seemed the type to make sure there were no stones unturned. He was about to tell her not to get that anal about such a mission, when the rumble of the train approaching the platform stopped him.

There had been talk of electric trains, but they had never been introduced to their part of the country. Electric trains were expensive— and the war between Joscal and Haria was expensive. Diesel trains were adequate, and anyway, the Army was happy with those shuddering hulks of metal, which were cheaper and didn't depend on an uninterrupted power supply. For the government, the risk of introducing something so fragile and easily targeted by the enemies to the border, outweighed the benefits. Railway tracks were easier to repair and maintain than—Kaden had no idea what to call the things an electric train ran on—power lines? Most border towns didn't have power lines connecting them to the main grid because the fighting had damaged relays; hence the still-popular diesel trains. Kaden had seen people get hit by trains, some deliberately and some by accident; it was a quick and inexpensive way to die. In either case there was almost nothing left to pick up afterward. He wondered how fast the train was approaching the station and whether his armor could withstand the force of a train ramming into it.

It was so tempting to find out—a scientific experiment, in fact.

He abruptly came to himself and realized he was staring blindly at a young man hunched over, sitting on the bench next to them. Brilliant blue eyes looked at him from under the bill of a sports cap, and he drew back startled—a Harian, or at least someone with Harian ancestry.

The boy, aware of Kaden's stare, looked away, and Kaden stood up, more to keep his mind distracted than anything else. Bradley was already making sounds of impatience that he wasn't moving fast enough to board the train.

Second class meant a carriage with a seat for each person, but only first class had seat numbers and prebooking. People could sit where they wanted to in any of the six-seater carriages. The train was crowded; their station was a little out of the way, but a place for people to pass through on their way to better destinations. Movement between compartments was only allowed when the train wasn't moving, and as usual there was a rush to find a place to sit.

Bradley picked a carriage at random and opened the door, happy to discover it was relatively empty. There were three people inside: a man, a woman, and a small girl. They all got to their feet the moment they noticed the armored warriors and started to move out.

"No need," Bradley said quickly. "We just need to sit—"

Kaden could have told her not to bother. The people respected them far too much to sit with them. As the family moved out, the woman caught Wayland's armor-encased hand and bowed. "Thank you."

Wayland looked floored for a second before she smiled. Kaden had had moments like that in his youth, awed that these people—adults—were thanking him. That his actions mattered and that he was doing something worthwhile. Kaden wondered if he should tell Wayland not to get too used to it; armored warriors who got used to praise became unimaginable assholes. Then they died.

They sat easily in the empty carriage despite their full armor, the girls sitting across from him. He supposed he should start thinking of them as cadets or future fellow warriors, but they were so young and eager and untainted by death and war and—

Just as the carriage door was about to slide shut, there was the sound of running feet and a flurry of clothes and dusty boots. The newcomer was about the same height as Bradley, with close-cropped hair and deep blue eyes—the young man from the platform. He'd pushed back the cap, or it'd fallen off in his rush to get into the train. The shadow was gone from his face, and in addition to his eyes, it was obvious by the fairness of his skin that he had Harian blood in him. It wasn't uncommon. There had been a time when Haria and Joscal had been one big country and people had intermarried. Kaden's own mother had confessed to a Harian relative, though he'd never seen any physical evidence of that genetic "stain"—at least not while she was alive, and definitely not in himself. Kaden supposed there were crossbreeds around; after all, it wasn't as if they could all pack up and leave for another country. But most Joscalians found it hard to tolerate even a hint of Harian ancestry given their hatred for Harians in general. Those of mixed heritage kept a low profile in society, trying hard not to be noticed.

The newcomer looked around at the carriage and grinned infectiously at them. "Hello, hope you don't…." He *really* looked at them as he turned around after sliding the door shut, at the armor peeking from under their robes, and froze. As soon as the boy stopped smiling and focused his attention on them, Kaden realized the "boy" had old eyes, eyes that had seen a lot of hardship and action, more suited for a veteran soldier than a carefree cadet. "Armored warriors, oh…." He started to pull the door open as the whistle blew and the train jerked forward.

"There's no need to go." Kaden spoke softly, more to annoy Bradley than because he wanted the company. "There's plenty of room."

"No, I…." The "boy" stopped and looked at them. "I don't think so—" He pulled out his cap and started to put it on as he turned to go. "I think I can make it to the next carriage if I hurry."

"You should stay," Wayland offered, and Kaden bit back a grin as Bradley grumbled under her breath. "It's dangerous to jump between railcars even if you open the door."

"I saw you on the platform," Wayland spoke suddenly. "You were reading a data pad on the bench by the newsstand."

The boy didn't look too comfortable about the mention of owning foreign tools. "I got it from a wholesale importer, one of the old models." Kaden didn't bother telling him they didn't arrest people for buying off the black market. The things on sale in the normal shops were shit anyway.

"What took you so long to get on the train?" Kaden suddenly asked, more to keep the boy from leaving the carriage than anything else. He winced internally even as he spoke because the question came out abrupt and intrusive.

The newcomer faltered for a second and then shrugged. "I had to figure out which carriage to get into."

"My sister is fifteen and if you touch her, I will break your fucking arm," Bradley said in her normal tone, which was unfriendly going on freezing, and the boy stepped back looking genuinely alarmed. He probably believed in the media image of armored warriors that showed them as savior angels who couldn't even swear to save their lives.

"I'll sit with your father," he said as the train pulled out. He stumbled and fell heavily onto Kaden, who was seated comfortably, legs spread.

Kaden hadn't expected the boy to give in to their invitation and sit in their carriage—the train must be really crowded. Or perhaps the boy was really, really interested in sitting with them. He scanned the newcomer quickly: nondescript clothes that didn't hide the shape of his body, no explosives strapped to his chest. There was a chance he was carrying some explosive in his backpack, but he lacked the zealot gleam of a suicide bomber, and years of experience had taught Kaden something about people. The boy might have another purpose for sitting with them, but he didn't look as if he wanted to kill them. Anyway, it was safer to keep him with three armored warriors than have him sit with the civilians.

The boy managed to sit half on Kaden's lap, arms and legs everywhere. Kaden snapped his legs together, and the boy fell to the side with a curse, making Wayland giggle.

"I'm not their father," Kaden said defensively as he tried to act unoffended. He supposed he was old enough to be Wayland's father and perhaps Bradley's as well. A couple of colleagues had kids and some of them were in their early twenties and in training with him. His colleagues had started young, and Kaden supposed he looked older than he felt. Still, it didn't mean he remotely resembled the girls in any way, and it wasn't just the difference in skin tone.

Up close, their companion in the carriage wasn't so much a boy as a young man in his early to late twenties, light skinned. Kaden saw a dusting of freckles on his cheeks, tempting lips, and a faint sheen of sweat on his neck, and looked away to assess what the others were doing.

"He's our instructor." Wayland's tone suggested she was amused by the probable insult.

"Important mission?" the man asked Wayland, smiling at her eagerly.

"Yes," Bradley snapped quickly, though Kaden didn't think the young man was flirting with Wayland, simply being nice to a young girl while asking some rather probing questions.

Kaden frowned. The man was far too inquisitive for a casual observer, and the entire conversation sounded forced. He'd opened his mouth to tell him to back off when an unnerving thought crossed his mind. But the chances the man was a spy for the enemy was ridiculous. He could be a newspaper reporter or an underground radio-show host, or someone who wanted to boast that he'd come across some important people. Their mission wasn't a critical one, just something foisted onto him because he had annoyed Vorani. If the girls were to blab about it to someone who might spread the news, well, his duty was to only observe how the cadets acted in public, not advise them on how to behave. Even if the man learned that they were out to bring back an armor, there was nothing he could do about it. The armor was safe in the Koresa Army base for the time being, and if the girls revealed too much about their route, Kaden could suggest a change of plans or ask for an extra escort on the way back.

"I saw the three of you traveling together and assumed...." The newcomer trailed off and then tried again. "Don't you get assigned vehicles if you're going on a mission or something? Not that it's any of my business."

"It's not," Bradley said sharply, and Kaden supposed she at least seemed to understand the importance of not giving out too much information to a civilian. At the same time, he felt a hint of irritation at her just for being so standoffish. He'd been a rather easygoing cadet, not so full of himself as Bradley was.

"I'm... sorry," the man said with a shrug. "I'll switch compartments at the next station."

Which was about half an hour into the future. The Army outpost was a little farther away from other towns.

Kaden wished he'd read the complete file on the cadets. He wasn't allowed to unless there were extenuating circumstances, such as a preexisting medical condition—though why they'd be in the Army in the first place if that was the case was beyond him. Files were mostly sealed in case the information influenced the examiners negatively. He didn't need the file to see they were from a well-to-do family. Rich, with servants, and not used to public transport, from the way they had wiped the seats before sitting down, their arms close to their bodies as if afraid they'd catch something.

They sat quietly, Kaden reading the book he'd brought along, with an occasional glance out the windows to see if there was anything worth looking at. Bradley seemed as if she wanted to do the same but was reluctant to move in case the newcomer looked at Wayland. Wayland simply appeared bored at the silence in the carriage.

Kaden wished the man hadn't gotten in with them. They could have gone over the mission plan or reviewed their equipment—not that there was much. They had the standard armor tracker with the ability to track an armor up to one kilometer away, some ration bars, water, and a change of underarmor suits. No one had issued a communication unit for them since there was little need for it. In case of an emergency, they had instructions to use the radio either in the train or at different stations. He supposed one of the cadets could have a cell phone on them, though—he looked at Bradley and decided they did not. It was against regulations to bring a cell phone on a mission in case someone used it to track their position—or more likely, it distracted one of them. Armored warriors would sometimes smuggle a small unit while on simple missions and the higher-ups turned a blind eye, but he couldn't see Bradley, with all her stiffness, taking the risk of being found out and disqualified from the exam.

The man shifted a little, moving when he accidently touched Kaden's armored knee, and finally opened his bag. Everyone, including Kaden, tensed.

The man pulled out a food container, which he popped open. The smell of bacon and eggs filled the air. There was fresh bread in it, and Kaden's mouth watered. Wayland stared at the man with wide eyes, and from the way Bradley was staring too, it was obvious she'd forgotten to pack any food for them.

Not that they really needed any—the journey was only about twelve hours long, not enough for anyone to starve to death, and Kaden had eaten breakfast before setting out, but the food they were served in camp never smelled as appetizing.

The man took out a sandwich and bit into it. The bread was toasted golden brown on the sides, and as his teeth broke the crust, there was the sound of a crispy crunch; fresh tomato and a piece of lettuce peeked out. Saliva collected in Kaden's mouth, and he looked out the window.

There was nothing to see but bushes, trees, green grass, brown grass, roads, vehicles—the sound of another bite from the sandwich filled the carriage, and damn, why hadn't he packed himself something to eat? Kaden wondered if he should get up and look for the restaurant compartment (for first-class passengers only, but exceptions were made for armored warriors) at the next stop, when the man shuffled his feet and coughed.

"Um, I've got a lot of food—my aunt packed it for me. Would you like some?"

"Yes, please," Wayland said quickly before Bradley could overrule her, and Kaden felt his own resolve waver. He didn't eat food from strangers, but as far as he could remember, he had never been offered any before. He looked at the man and sighed.

"Yes, thank you, it looks wonderful." He supposed it could be poisoned, and then hoped that if so, it was fast acting.

"Tastes great too," said the man, holding out the box.

Kaden folded back his armor to reveal his fingers, and he pulled out a sandwich. Wayland got up and walked over to take one.

Bradley shook her head despite looking at what Wayland was munching on longingly. "I had a big breakfast," she said, and from the look Wayland gave her, it was a lie. Maybe Bradley was waiting for them to fall to the floor so she could be proved right about the dangers of accepting food from a stranger.

"Too bad," the man said. "My aunt runs a restaurant in town, The Foo-Dream."

Kaden had been there several times before the accident but not since his return, and he didn't think cadets were allowed to eat out. "New management?" Kaden had to ask. He didn't remember the food being this good.

"As of this week," the man said proudly. "I came around to help her set it up and now I'm going home." He looked at them and smiled apologetically. "I hope one day I'll be able to make food just like hers."

"Well, that's some ambition," Bradley said sarcastically. Kaden wondered where that had come from.

But the man seemed to have picked up on the hostility. Most young men of this age were in the Army unless they had some bizarre medical condition. "I'm also into... not fighting."

"Ah, a pacifist," Bradley said in a tone that said "one of those people."

"No, I just want the fighting to stop," he said patiently. "Doesn't everyone?"

"Well, it doesn't happen by simply talking about it," Kaden intervened smoothly. The man hadn't said anything new or controversial; it was a common enough theme. Just that some people, especially those in the Army, took it the wrong way. "At least you're supplying us with food. Thank you very much."

It was as if the wind had been knocked out of the man by the unexpected turn of the conversation, and he turned to Kaden with a bright smile. "I'm Shun. It doesn't seem nice to share food but not introduce myself."

It seemed he had passed some sort of test. Kaden felt himself smile in return. "Kaden," he said, holding out his free hand, and Shun smiled so brilliantly he felt his heart stutter. "Bradley"—Kaden pointed to her— "and this is Wayland." There was only a little danger with revealing the first names of everyone—it wasn't a state secret. And it was too late. The girls had called out to each other by their real names while Shun was present.

There was no talk about Shun leaving their carriage at the next station, though several people got off. His food tasted delicious, and Kaden felt, for the first time in a long time, a smidge of interest when Shun's shoulder accidently brushed his. The hookers were nice, but they hardly felt like real people, whereas Shun seemed to light up the entire compartment.

"Um, where are you going to?" Shun asked after they'd pulled out of the next station. It seemed rude to ask Shun to leave after they'd eaten his food. "I'm getting off at Shilean, and if you're getting off there as well, you can come with me to grab a bite to eat. My mom cooks the best—"

"We're going to Koresa," Wayland said quickly. "But I know there are buses to Koresa from there. Maybe we can get off there and...." She looked pleadingly at her sister, and having taken another bite from the sandwich, even Kaden was tempted to press the point.

Kaden sighed. Well, they might change their return plans and come back through the coastal road, just to be on the safe side. The armors were most vulnerable when no one was wearing them in transit. Transporting MacCrave's armor should be easy enough, but it wouldn't hurt for him to take some precautions in case the information got into the hands of the wrong people.

Bradley was quick to veto the idea. "No, we have a schedule to keep." She had a point.

"Then please." Shun held out the box of sandwiches to Bradley, and this time she grabbed one quickly as if afraid someone might take it.

It was safe enough since neither Kaden nor Wayland had collapsed after eating Shun's food.

"Thank you," she said after a short while. From the way she stuffed it into her mouth, it was clear she also appreciated it.

"Are you going there on official business?" Shun asked in the silence. "I mean… are you getting off at Shilean? Not that you… have to tell me or anything…." He flinched as if he'd said the wrong thing.

Kaden assumed Shun was trying to find more information.

"Official business," Bradley said after a couple of seconds. Her upbringing probably did not allow for her to be outright rude to someone who had given her free food.

"Well… okay." Shun looked embarrassed by the brush-off. "Um… well, I just…."

Yes, it was going to be a stimulating conversation. Kaden decided to step in. "You've got another four hours to Shilean, and we've eaten your food. Perhaps we can buy you lunch at the next stop."

Bradley coughed and snapped out, "Expenses don't cover food for another person," then had the grace to look embarrassed. "I suppose it won't hurt."

Kaden had been meaning to buy Shun some food with his own money, not use their expense account, but he remained silent.

"I wouldn't want to impose on you in any way," Shun said hastily. "You must be on an important mission if you have funds."

"It's the opposite," Wayland groaned. "If it were important, we'd have unlimited funds."

"Any mission is important." Shun managed to sound conciliatory. "Have you been on a lot of missions?"

Wayland pouted. "This is our first. It's actually an exam."

"What happens if you fail?"

Not the question Kaden expected—he assumed Shun would ask more about the actual mission parameters.

"We have to retake it next year," Wayland explained. "Until then I think we dig ditches or scrub toilets or something."

Shun nodded as if he'd understood something profound. "Ah." He turned to Kaden. "I suppose you're going with them as their supervisor."

"Something like that," Kaden admitted. He could see that Shun was curious about their mission, but it was not his place to tell him to stop asking questions.

"Well." Shun settled back and returned his food box to his bag. "I think I'll catch some sleep now. I was up most of last night working the tables."

He closed his eyes, and a couple of minutes later, his head listed onto Kaden's shoulder. When he threatened to fall over because of the swaying of the train, Kaden quickly held him in place. He hadn't re-covered his fingers with armor, and he could feel the warmth of Shun's body clearly—he smelled clean, with a hint of warm bread and soap, and Kaden felt a stirring in his lower body from something so simple.

Kaden closed his eyes and slowly drew back the armor from his shoulder and left side so that Shun would not feel the hardness of the metal against his head.

He was surprised by how quickly Shun had integrated himself into their group. He didn't seem to be in awe of them but had tried hard to talk to them and fit into their midst. Most people fell into three groups: those who worshiped the armored warriors from afar, those who were afraid of them, and the third group, who regarded them as celebrities, real-life superheroes who saved the day and had extra abilities, whom they stalked as much as possible given the military restrictions. They were said to have fan bases, where people fantasized about having sex with armored warriors, not very selective of who it was. Kaden didn't think most people even realized there were two types of armor in operation.

He toyed with the idea of asking Shun if he was willing to have a quick grope in the bathroom—then remembered his last experience in a train washroom, which hadn't gone too well. Still, if Shun was amenable to a hookup, there were ways and places. If Shun was even interested in him, or men in general, of course—

Wayland asked, "What do you think—?"

The entire carriage jerked. The brakes screeched loudly, and Kaden balanced himself, flinging out his free arm so Shun wouldn't go flying off to the other side.

"What was that?" Wayland asked, jumping to her feet.

Kaden continued to sit as Shun stirred on his shoulder. He didn't remove his arm as Shun sat up groggily and looked around. "I'm sorry. I didn't mean to sleep on you."

"It's fine," Kaden said shortly as the train gave another lurch and came to a complete stop.

"Which station are we at?" Shun sat up straighter and reached for his bag. "How long was I sleeping?"

"Not long, and we haven't reached a station yet. Must be something in the middle of the track—" Kaden tried to remember if they were near anything that required the train to stop. "Construction, repairs, or perhaps some military convoy."

There were always impromptu railway repairs, and the military was prone to secret maneuvers that people on unimportant missions—people such as them—never heard of. He sometimes wondered if the Harians were equally disorganized when it came to their war effort.

Shun didn't seem convinced. "I hope so," he said, looking around with a worried expression. "There's been stories."

"Of what?" Wayland demanded hurriedly. Her eyes were wide with excitement, and Kaden could see her impatience for something to happen.

"Of train raiders," Shun told them. "You must have seen it on the news."

Kaden, who had removed himself from everything since the accident, shook his head. "What about these raiders?"

Bradley nodded knowingly. "They have someone on board who'll pull the emergency brakes when the train is near an empty area. I guess it's preplanned and then they board the train, steal everything, and ride out before the authorities come."

Kaden blinked in surprised. "I really didn't think such a thing could happen in this—"

Wayland perked up as if she'd thought of something. "Maybe this is just a mechanical fault of some sort."

"There's a war going on," Bradley said, sounding so much like a government announcement that Kaden wondered if she'd done a stint in broadcasting. "They need to realize this isn't helping anyone, especially not the war effort."

"Not everyone who robs a train is against the war effort," Shun said softly. "People need jobs, and there's restrictions on food and other things."

Kaden agreed with him silently. There were power cuts and trade restrictions and food shortages, but their country was at war; it was expected. He remembered his mother stealing tomatoes from the neighbor's garden when there'd been food restrictions—and that had been back when he was a child. They hadn't been rich enough to buy food on the black market. All those years of war hadn't helped the country's economy much.

"I fail to see how being a criminal helps anyone," Bradley commented dryly. "They're just a bunch of people who don't want to find a job or join the Army."

Shun huffed. "Not really. There are people who are too old or too sick or just not cut out for fighting." He looked ready to say more.

Kaden's father hadn't joined the Army either, an old back injury and his own reluctance kept him from being drafted. While Kaden agreed with Bradley about the train robbers, he could also see Shun had an argument ready, and it wasn't the time for them to get into a philosophical discussion. "Let's deal with one problem at a time and figure out why our train stopped."

Wayland hesitated at that. "What if there really are train raiders?"

Bradley got to her feet. "I'll go look. You stay here and look after our things."

"Why don't you ask Instructor Pace to look after it," said Wayland, moving the box from her lap to the seat. "I'm coming too."

Bradley turned to Kaden with a raised eyebrow, as if expecting him to make a comment.

"It's probably not train raiders," Kaden said firmly.

Just then, the public announcement system in the train coughed to life and rumbled a barely coherent message, asking everyone to stay seated and informing them the train was surrounded.

All three looked at Kaden, and he shrugged. "I was wrong."

Bradley accepted the statement. "We have surprise on our side; they probably don't expect armored warriors on the train."

Wayland turned to Kaden with wide eyes, ignoring her sister altogether. "But where're the raiders? Shouldn't they be all over the place?"

Kaden assessed the situation. "They probably want to disable communication in the train first, and then make sure it doesn't move away, so engine room first and then gathering things from the passengers."

"They did say the train was surrounded." Shun turned to Kaden, looking for his opinion.

"How long is the train?" Kaden asked Shun, trying to remember what he'd seen when he boarded it. He could have asked the cadets, but he wanted an excuse to speak to Shun. As a civilian, Shun wasn't used to combat, and Kaden needed to know if he could keep a level head during a crisis.

"Not that long, maybe six passenger compartments and the engine." Shun sounded calm enough.

Kaden fought the urge to stick his head out the open window—it was not the right time to get it blown off—and instead peered carefully around the edge of the sill. There seemed to be other people more foolhardy than he was, sticking their entire bodies out but not getting off. It could have been because the train was too far from any place resembling civilization or because they could see something that discouraged them from getting off. "Stay away from the middle passage of the train. It's not like the raiders came with a platoon of people."

"I don't get it." Wayland sounded petulant, but Bradley looked at Kaden with understanding.

"Two people on either side of the train?" she surmised. "One person at the engine, and two to move down the corridor and rob people, probably guns…."

Everyone had guns. One thing about there being a war: it was easier to get hold of weapons than food. Kaden could see proof of the leadership and strategic planning skills mentioned in Bradley's file.

"One outside on the ground," Kaden added after careful consideration. "I'd have someone on the roof to keep watch—there doesn't seem to be higher ground around here—and probably more than two people working the inside. You can keep a train in one place for only so long, and speed is essential—"

"Why are you all just sitting here and talking about people getting robbed at gunpoint so calmly?" Wayland snapped, looking furious. "We have to help them."

Kaden closed his eyes and listened. It was very quiet apart from the sound of shutters going up and the buzz of general conversation drifting in through the open window. "No hurry, no danger yet." People opened compartment doors and windows, but no screams of pain or distress followed.

"They'll hit first class first." Shun spoke in a soft voice. "Then work themselves back."

"Seems like it." Bradley walked up to the compartment door. "There's no one in this part of the train yet. Everyone should be in the front—engines, I think." She opened her pack, pulled out her helmet, and put it on. Next she slowly undid her travel cloak, folded it, and put it on her seat. "I'm going to check it out."

"Is your armor on defensive?" Kaden had to ask. As much as he wanted to put an end to his babysitting job, he didn't want his charges dead.

"It's got 80 percent plating," Bradley told him flatly, and Kaden could see her disappointment in him.

He should have looked up her stats.

His eyes widened—80 percent plating was as high as an armor could go in defensive without becoming far too heavy to carry. Even if Bradley's armor had been designed just for her, it was extremely heavy.

He had been underestimating her, but it was still his duty to keep her safe. "Keep your neck covered."

"I'm going too." Wayland stood up.

"No." Bradley's refusal left no room for argument. "I don't want you—"

"Well, it's my mission too," Wayland whined. "I want to come."

"Not a good idea." Kaden stepped in before the situation deteriorated into the two sisters fighting. He supposed he could simply command her to stay, but there didn't seem to be any real need to do that yet. "They might have sent people to the back of the train as well." Or to the middle. "You might want to stay here as our backup." It would keep Wayland in the compartment.

"Fine," Wayland grumbled.

"Keep Shun with you," Kaden instructed as he stood up and put aside his travel cloak. It didn't hamper his movements much, but he preferred to have nothing around him in case there was a fight.

He waited until Bradley was out of the compartment before pushing their shutter open the entire way. "Don't go out," he said to the two inside.

A quick peek through the window revealed nothing out of the ordinary. Then he thrust his head out, looked up, and found a ledge above the shutters. He created handholds as he climbed out, pushing his fingers to make holes in the metal so he could climb to the roof of the train.

*A person on the roof,* he thought and looked over the ledge. A sentry would probably be on one corner, close to the back end since the front was already occupied by raiders.

Kaden crouched low once he was on the roof and stared at either end of the train. He spotted the watcher, who was conveniently looking away from him. Kaden used it to his advantage. His armor wasn't as loaded with weapons as some suits were—frankly, in a fight, black armor seemed the most useless, but what he had was better than nothing. He directed his shoulder gun, aimed, fired, and watched the man fall over the side with a muted thud. He hadn't shot to kill, but the burst of energy released from his armor was enough to knock most people unconscious, and the fall was still a fall even if it wasn't that high. Luckily all of it was done in near silence—the shoulder gun was only audible to someone standing close to him, and the man had conveniently fallen in the undergrowth, which had muffled the sound.

He stood up slowly, hoping there was no one around. However, to be on the safe side, he called up the helmet. It slid silently over his head. He didn't like wearing the helmet and usually left it off until the last moment. It made him feel like a horse wearing blinders, cutting off his side vision. It settled low over his brow, and he waited a second as he adjusted to the feel of something enclosing his neck. Then he walked over to the place where the first man he'd shot had fallen over, looked down, and knocked out the other person who'd come to investigate, using his laser on shock mode. He stood on the roof of the train, waiting, counting seconds, but it seemed there were no new additions. His initial assessment of two people on the outside was correct.

Once that was done, he looked around for the first time, taking in their surroundings.

They were on a flat area, which had probably seen some fighting in the past. The train track did not run as close to the border as it did in some places. The war was supposedly a border war, but it was hard to find any place in the country that hadn't felt the effects of it. Craters of old explosions and the husks of what had been houses littered the landscape. From the way wilderness overran the dilapidated houses, war had touched this place close to a decade ago. Or maybe more. It was certainly remote enough for an ambush. A tarmac road ran alongside the track, pitted and broken in places, with grass and other forms of greenery breaking through the paving. What interested Kaden was the off-road vehicle parked there, as battered and broken as the road itself, but obviously still mobile, with new tires on all its wheels. Farther back, Kaden could see the flattened undergrowth the jeep had driven over to reach its current location.

He at least knew how they'd come, and he could guess as to how many had arrived. He looked around to see if there were any more vehicles and spotted a bike in the distance but nothing else. He did a quick mental calculation. The off-road four-wheel drive could probably hold five people, maybe six, and two more for the bike. If they were planning on going with their companion from the train, there were a total of eight or maybe nine robbers on board.

Was there anything worth stealing on the train apart from what the passengers had on them? There didn't seem to be anyone boarding the train from the back—perhaps they'd already done so, but the majority would be in the engine compartment and first class. He hoped Bradley was as efficient as she looked. Subduing people in close quarters in an armored suit should be easy, but it really wasn't in practice. For the people who folded easily at the sight of those weapons, it was a simple process of pointing and telling them to stand still. But for those who resisted, warriors had to figure out the force needed to incapacitate without killing them while wearing something strong enough to blow a hole through a brick wall with a single blow.

Kaden was just about to head for the front of the train when he heard a single gunshot. He hurried toward the engine at a run, leaping over the gaps between the carriages without breaking stride. He jumped down to the walkway outside the engine compartment and looked inside to see Bradley nearly rip the arm off a tall woman dressed in low-riding jeans, a blue shirt, and boots. She punched the woman in the face with an armored fist, snarling, her anger making her appear more alive than before.

Kaden wondered why she was using excessive force to subdue an unarmed raider, when he realized there was a bleeding man, in the uniform of a railway employee, sprawled on the floor.

"Bradley," he said sharply as she raised her hand for another strike. The woman, whom he assumed was the shooter, sagged; there was no fight left in her. "Is there only one?"

He walked over to the fallen man and stooped over him, taking care to keep clear of the blood pooling on the engine floor and dripping out through the rivet holes. It was a *fast*-growing pool of blood, something that didn't bode well for the victim.

"There's more," she said with a scowl. "I should—" She indicated over her shoulder to the rest of the train.

"You should," Kaden told her cautiously, wondering if it was her usual fighting style or if she had lost her temper. "Remember to pull your punches. It's not training. They aren't wearing armor." Technically they weren't even supposed to hit anyone other than Harians when they were in armor, but there were exceptions. The rules had improved in the past thirty years, making it easier for armored warriors to deal with internal problems as well as Harian-related issues. The police had handled internal unrest until the uprisings in the seventies, when the government had deployed the Army to subdue out-of-control civilians.

"I'm... yes." Bradley let the raider drop and rushed off.

Kaden sighed. He supposed he should follow her and see how she handled the situation, make sure she didn't kill anyone, but people who were stupid enough to raid a train full of civilians needed to get their butts kicked. And Kaden had an injured civilian to look after, something Bradley hadn't done, but should have.

The Joscal Railway Company uniform the injured man wore reminded Kaden that there were other railway employees somewhere about. Surely it took more than one man to run a train. Kaden should have remembered that in the first place, but these days he kept making stupid mistakes and missing out on small details. The man was alive, though just barely, losing blood too fast. Kaden took a deep breath and pulled back the armor from his hands so he could lift the man's shirt and press it against the wound. The man groaned in pain, but Kaden continued to apply pressure to the bullet hole as he looked around for possible help, and spotted the radio under the engine driver's seat.

He reached for it with his free hand and pressed the button to call central dispatch. As he relayed the situation on the train to them, he heard the sound of an armor blast, the high-pitched whine followed by the sound of shattering glass, and broke the call.

The man moaned lightly and his eyes fluttered open, revealing bright blue irises, and as the man tipped his head back, under his cap the hair was light brown, like Shun's. Another person with Harian blood.

"He's alive." Bradley sounded surprised, and Kaden looked at her sharply as she walked back in.

"You didn't check?" he said coldly.

"I thought he was dead. She shot him." Bradley had the grace to sound apologetic.

"And you lost your head," he admonished her gently.

Bradley stood over him, hands clenched. "The reason she shot him was because he had blue eyes. She said something about the Harian scum and—really she was robbing a train. They aren't allowed to have an opinion about it."

"Hm." Kaden looked around for something to tie the compression down with, and Bradley knelt beside him, her armored knee touching the blood.

"My basic trainer was Instructor Claina, and she took a lot of flak from people when she was out of armor because of her coloring," she remarked, almost as if trying to explain her anger to Kaden. "I took out the others," she added as an afterthought.

Kaden always wondered why the armored warriors who actively fought against the Harians seemed to have less hatred toward them than the actual civilians. Was it because they saw less of the Harians and more of the drones the Harians used, or was it because the armored warriors had their share of mixed-blood warriors in their ranks, enough to have grown used to seeing light-colored hair or skin? The Army was a great place for equal employment opportunities regardless of gender or skin color.

"Did you kill them?" Kaden asked without inflection. If she had, it would go in her report, but it was not his place to judge if they killed someone in combat. Kaden had done his share of killing.

"I tied them all up and kept them in the first-class restaurant," Bradley told him with a grim smile, and Kaden realized there was no blood on her—anywhere.

"Good." He stood up. "How many in total?"

"Six including her." Bradley smirked. "I took them out before they knew it."

Kaden ignored her boasting. He was familiar with the adrenaline rush that came with going up against the enemy. Bradley was confident in her armor, having taken out civilians playing at being criminals. "I took out two, that makes it eight. There's a chance we missed one more person." He looked at her and smiled. "Go ask one of the people you tied up."

One person shot was no big deal, Kaden thought as he used the injured man's belt to bandage the wound. It was an acceptable loss. One against all the people in the train was well within mission parameters.

Just as he'd finished, Bradley burst into the engine room. "They say the last one went to second class."

They turned to face each other and then, as one, started to run toward their compartment along the corridor. Kaden knew there were close to six carriages on the train, each carriage divided into a smaller compartment with dividers; it was illogical to assume the last raider was going to be in their compartment.

But he was.

Kaden didn't crowd the doorway because Bradley had come to a stop outside, but he walked over to look inside. The last raider was a man, perhaps a little younger than Kaden, his face scarred by what looked like a shrapnel wound and his eyes steady. Kaden would have given anything for an over-the-top overzealous fanatic, rather than someone who was taking in the situation calmly.

Shun was in a corner of the compartment, his hands drawn around himself protectively. The raider was behind him, a well-oiled gun that looked like a high-velocity, large-caliber... *something* pressed to his head. Kaden didn't know all his guns by name. It hadn't been a part of his training. No one expected armored warriors to shoot with guns. Basic training took care to teach them which end to point and that was it.

What was wrong with the situation was Wayland, who stood to the side, her eyes conveying shock, unmoving but uninjured. Kaden cursed under his breath. He had seen this with cadets who weren't used to combat: she'd frozen.

"If you come in, I'll shoot the Harian and I'll shoot the girl in the face." The raider sounded very calm and collected.

Kaden groaned mentally. The only real open spot in their armor was the face, and a full-frontal face shot had killed a few people he knew of.

Bradley tried to move past Kaden. "Wayland, snap out of it—"

"We don't have any money," Kaden said softly. "And your companions have been captured."

"Then I'll have to settle for a hostage."

"My sister is not for—"

Kaden could have simply smashed his head against the wall and been done with it at how *stupidly* Bradley was behaving. She'd just given away how important Wayland was, and that was never a good thing when the enemy had the upper hand.

"I don't want to take someone in armor as a hostage," the raider said, speaking softly. "I'll take the Harian."

And because at that moment Kaden had been looking at Shun, he saw the flash of fear on Shun's face and felt his mind come to a grinding halt. He had worked so well with Vorani because he'd come to accept her worldview, in numbers rather than people, because he was an orphan with very few connections. Just a few minutes ago he had been thinking of the possible death of the train worker as an acceptable loss, a calculated possibility, but with Shun he realized he couldn't let it go. True, he might not know Shun very well, not even his last name, but having sat in the same compartment with the man for hours and eaten his food, Kaden felt responsible for him.

He took a deep breath. "I doubt he's a Harian," he said trying to keep his voice level as Bradley spoke over him.

"He's as much a citizen as—"

"Don't tell me about Harians," the raider snarled. "They're the reason we don't have enough jobs, why our children are starving—"

"Please, give me a break," muttered Bradley, her hands clenched into fists. Unlike Kaden's armor, her modified suit didn't cover her hands, and she wore thick gloves for more flexibility—something Kaden noticed in the middle of everything because he was looking around, thinking furiously. He needed to get Shun to safety and get Wayland to move.

"It's true," the raider insisted, and Kaden saw the shift then, from calculating thief to fanatic. Maybe the man needed a reason to ease his guilt for robbing trains, but regardless, there was a weakness.

"Keep him talking," Kaden whispered, taking a careful step back. He couldn't disappear from view; it was too obvious, but if he could make the man lose concentration enough to loosen his grip on the gun....

Bradley understood quickly. "What have you got against the Harian?"

"You know what," the man raged.

*Can you disable him without killing him?* thought Kaden to the armor as he looked at the gun and felt the suit make adjustments to his helmet scope-vision through his neural connection.

"We took them in when their fucking island was sinking into the sea and see how they paid us back? Took over a part of our country and wanted a separate state. Now they're fighting over our border, which is ours from the start and—"

"It was over a hundred years ago," Shun said mildly, and Kaden's focus wavered as he looked at Shun. Despite Shun's steady words, Kaden could see his hands were shaking and he looked pale. "Your government took in those people as refugees."

Kaden hoped the intruder hadn't noticed Shun's reference to Joscal as *your* government, implying Shun wasn't a part of it.

The man was too wrapped up in his own argument to think logically. "Who refused to leave, who used our resources and fucked our women and"—Kaden could see spittle flying—"then wanted a part of the land?"

Kaden hoped Shun was in on their plan to keep the raider occupied. Well, if he was, he really sounded invested in the argument.

"The only reason the Harians wanted a part of the country was because they were sick of being treated like second-class citizens. Couldn't get proper jobs, couldn't go to proper school, couldn't even own their own homes. Of course there was going to be a revolution. There was going to be a—"

"If they were so fucking unhappy with how we treated them, they should have gone back to their own country," the raider snarled.

"Couldn't because it was under the sea," Shun snapped back.

For a moment Kaden was sure the raider was going to shoot Shun in the head, hostage be damned, when a break came in the form of the sound of sirens—the police. Central dispatch must have alerted them to the situation on the train. The raider looked out the window in surprise. Just as quickly the raider snapped his attention back into the compartment, but his momentary distraction proved to be his undoing. At that moment the world seemed to jolt as Kaden's armor let loose a bolt of charged energy that hit the raider full on the head. He toppled over with a gasp, and Kaden decided to act as if he had planned that shot, that his armor hadn't taken over.

"Shun," asked Kaden turning his attention to Shun, knowing that Bradley would take care of Wayland. "Are you hurt?"

"No, no," said Shun with a shake of his head, though he looked none too steady on his feet and sagged toward Kaden.

Kaden had put a hand around Shun and steadied him against his chest when he heard the first slap.

Bradley used the fastest method to get Wayland out of her stupor. "Snap out of it, Wayland. How could you not do anything when he was about to shoot Shun? He'd have shot you as well."

Wayland seemed to have unfrozen and she snapped back defensively, clutching a reddening cheek. "He just burst in. What was I supposed to do, shoot him?"

"Yes," Bradley shouted back.

"I didn't want to kill him."

"Well, he'd have killed you."

"But I…."

Kaden sighed and helped Shun sit down. He'd seen people like Wayland, too soft and useless in a fight. Some got better; some never got used to it. But as a wearer of an original armor, Wayland didn't have the luxury of quitting. She was going to have to man up and learn to kill because that was what the Army needed her to do in the end.

He could hear the police boarding the train.

"Bradley, go show them where everyone is," he said, his punishment to her for leaving the injured man behind when she ran after the raider. He also wanted her to ease up on Wayland, but shouting at her wasn't going to help.

Bradley nodded, her lips pushed back in a snarl, though he couldn't figure out if the anger was directed at him or at Wayland. "We'll talk when I get back," she said and moved out.

"It was horrible," Wayland told Kaden once her sister left. "They wanted to shoot him because he had light-colored hair." She stared at him, probably waiting for him to berate her for freezing, and Kaden looked away, knowing it wouldn't help matters.

"Bigots." Kaden knelt down and secured the raider's hands with a piece of leather.

"It's nothing," Shun said bitterly. "I've had worse when I was going to school. Everyone wanted a piece of the kid who looked like a Harian. Even the teachers wouldn't touch my book, and my mother finally—" He broke off with a wry grin. "I finished at a very exclusive school for people like me."

"I thought the prejudice would be less now." Kaden stood up. He had always fought at the borders; he hadn't thought of what the people in the middle went through.

"It's not." Shun settled back to his seat. "I always curse my father. You know, it's his blood that's causing me all these problems."

"Your father's a Harian?" Kaden winced at Wayland's unashamed curiosity.

Shun shrugged. "Didn't know him at all." He knelt and picked up a box from the floor of the compartment. Kaden recognized it as the one that contained all that remained of the late Warrior MacCrave. "Here, dropped this earlier."

"Don't even remember it falling," said Wayland, taking it from him.

"Hope there was nothing to break."

Wayland shrugged. "Nothing, just a card and some stuff."

"Funny you need three people to take a card," Shun said as he sat on the seat, and Kaden noticed his hands were still shaking.

"It's some dead guy's belongings," Wayland told him.

"Some dead guy—"

Shun paled and for a moment Kaden thought he was going to faint. He kept an arm on Shun's shoulder and squeezed lightly.

"Hey, you all right?"

"An armored warrior is dead." Shun seemed to collect himself as he spoke. "I knew a few of them when they came to the… the Foo-Dream. We had some regulars. Just didn't want to find out one of the guys I'd played darts with is dead."

"I don't think MacCrave was the type to play darts anywhere," Kaden told him kindly. "He was based at another camp and died in some accident on an away mission." The government made sure to house their armored warriors in different places, never keeping them in one place all together; wouldn't do to have the best die in one nuclear attack.

Not that MacCrave had died for a worthy cause. Kaden had asked around the camp when he'd gotten the mission, and the story was MacCrave had died with his dick in his hand and his armor on the side table in a whorehouse. Not that it should be mentioned to the widow, so the story was he'd died during an undercover job. Kaden supposed most of the action took place under the bedcovers.

"So, you're going to give back his things," Shun repeated softly.

"And collect his armor," Wayland added.

"Why would you—" Shun broke off as the police came in to take the last raider, and they all remained silent as Kaden went to give them a statement.

# CHAPTER 4

"THAT'S THE first time the police haven't questioned me after an incident," Shun said after the train started to move.

The police had sent a new engine driver, and they were finally on their way, only two hours behind schedule.

Bradley seemed to find a problem with the statement. "You didn't do anything."

"I have Harian blood," Shun pointed out. "I'm on the wrong side of the border." Then he gave a wry grin. "I don't think there's a right side."

"That's bullshit. We have plenty of people who look like you in our division."

It was an exaggeration; they didn't have *plenty* of people with Harian heritage, but it was nice that Wayland was making an effort.

"Wearing the armor gives you the right to belong," Shun told her with surprising patience for someone correcting such an obvious misconception. "Otherwise, people like us don't belong anywhere."

"What do you mean?" Wayland seemed to be truly oblivious to the situation within the country. "Things aren't that bad for the people here."

Kaden kept quiet. After the World Unification Council or WUC—pronounced wook for short—had called them out on it eleven years ago, the government had put a stop to the national media depicting Harians as evil. But Wayland was too young to remember a time before that, and she was a little shielded from reality.

"It's not that bad if you live in an out-of-the-way town," Shun told them.

Shun was now leaning against Kaden's shoulder; one of his hands rested lightly by Kaden's knee—not that Kaden could feel the touch through the armor. He was tempted to pull back the armor a little, take off the top half—nothing serious, just half a thought, but it was the first erotic impulse in a long time.

To be without his armor with someone, to just let go for a moment....

"So," said Shun as the awkward silence grew, "are you sure you can't get off with me at Shilean? My offer is still open, and you can get a bus to Koresa. It's faster, and there's free food."

Shun pressed firmly against Kaden, and Kaden wondered if the offer could be extended for something more.

"We've lost time as it is." Bradley didn't sound as stiff as before and really seemed to regret turning down the offer. "We need to be at the camp before eleven when the gate closes."

Kaden supposed they could stay in Shilean and head off early morning, but he wasn't sure of their accommodations there, and Shun might not have room to let them stay at his place. And deviating from a mission because of food was bad form.

"How about on the way back, then?" Shun asked.

"We'll have the armor then," Wayland said morosely. "I don't think we'll be able to move around when we're lugging that along."

Kaden didn't bother silencing Wayland; he really didn't think Shun was an enemy spy.

"You already have armor," Shun pointed out.

"The dead guy's armor," Wayland explained to him. "We have to take it back."

"Why don't you have it with you?"

"Good question," Wayland said looking at Kaden. "Why not?"

"Because a dead armored warrior's body is displayed in full gear." If there was nothing left to show, the Army flaunted the empty shell. Though God knew how they'd put Kaden in his since it was controlled by his thoughts. Kaden made a mental note to look up how former black-armored warriors had been prepared for burial.

*I can always ask for a closed casket*, he thought grimly. *Or die in a corner where they'll never find me.*

He looked up to see three faces looking at him curiously and realized they hadn't understood his explanation. "MacCrave was buried in a family plot, so the Army moved his body there in full armor." *Is there someone whose job is to put dead warriors back into their armors?* Kaden wondered absentmindedly, then spoke again. "And once the funeral was over, before the burial, the armor was removed and taken by the Koresa command post. And we're on our way to collect it."

"And you give it to another person?"

"If it's compatible, yes," Kaden told Shun.

Shun looked so eager Kaden decided to crush his dream, if he had any, of becoming an armored warrior before it took form. While Shun might be a pacifist, being accepted by an armor would translate to acceptance by everyone, and that might mean more to him after almost being killed for having the wrong hair color.

"It's not the height or anything like that. All old armors, what we call the originals, are meant to fit the fighter and grow with them. But most old suits were designed to learn with the original wearer, and it's the bloodlines that matter. If your parent or even an aunt or uncle wore one, the chances are the same armor would accept you." There was more to it, but Kaden didn't know how to explain in five minutes what he had learned during five years of basic training. "But you have to start young so the compatibility grows with you."

"I heard it's all in the head," Wayland said and got a dirty look from Bradley.

Kaden wondered what that was about. He hurried to intervene before the girls could snipe at each other. "Could be. There are records of soldiers who were too scared to return to the field. The old records say their compatibility fell below the minimum requirement. Apparently it also happens for some who spend a long time out of their armor, but I don't know how true that is." There was always talk around the camp. Didn't mean it was all true.

"What about you?" Shun asked. "How many in your family were in the Army?"

"No one in my family ever wore an armor. I just tested for it and came up compatible."

Shun leaned forward. "Does that happen often?"

"Now we test all new recruits with all the armors in storage," Kaden told him. "Our camp gets a lot of new recruits, hence the need to bring this armor back."

They hadn't tested everyone twenty years back, but with the shortage of compatible people, the military was getting desperate.

"So." Shun leaned against Kaden and ran a finger over his armored chest. "What does the black armor do? I've never seen this type before."

Kaden wondered if it was by accident that Shun's finger had run over where his nipple would be. He shivered a little inside from the imagined feeling, though he hadn't actually felt the touch. "Well." He hesitated and turned to the other two. "Pop quiz, what do you remember from what you've learned?"

"It's hard to be compatible with," Wayland said after some time. "But you're right. I really don't know what it can do."

"I know there's five of them in existence," Bradley added. "And... and... it self-regenerates."

"But so do some other armors," Wayland pointed out, then looked at Kaden. "I know self-regenerative armors are rare, but there are some, aren't there?"

"True," Kaden agreed, then decided to tell them what little he knew of the armor he was wearing. "This has the fastest regenerative rate. But it also has almost no weapons apart from these—" He tapped his shoulders. "—so many speculate that they were incomplete armors."

"So where do you get power for your weapons?" Shun asked.

Kaden hoped it was just curiosity, but what he was revealing wasn't exactly secret anyway. "Mostly solar." He was aware of the danger of giving away too much information.

"That means you can run out of power?"

"Well, in the lasers and all," Kaden admitted. "But it won't affect the movements."

Shun frowned. "I thought armors froze when they ran out of power."

"Guess I haven't used mine much." Kaden gave a wry grin, aware that saying his gear had unlimited power was not going to sit well. He had a hunch his body powered the armor, that the longer he stayed in it, the more the energy built up. New armors occasionally ran out of juice—it wasn't possible to keep an unlimited supply—but the originals never ran out of core power even if the weapons ran dry.

When the Harians got wind of the armor project, they'd bombed the entire island. The original armors he and Wayland wore were some of the few retrieved from the steaming rubble of a subbasement under Dr. Orche's labs, and many called them the prototypes. No one wanted to take apart the existing armor—the first few attempts had been unsuccessful, to say the least, and technicians had destroyed ten before they realized Dr. Orche's genius couldn't be replicated. The Army put a stop to outright experimentation on original armor, since everyone wanted battle-ready armor, not piles of crap.

"But what you wear," Shun said, turning to Bradley, "can be fitted to anyone?"

"Yes, but this one was made for me. At least, some of the arm and leg parts," Bradley explained. "That's why there's few of these. It's expensive to make, but on the plus side, if you're the right size, you can recycle parts from other armors. None of those pesky compatibility issues. But there's a much longer training period for this type."

Shun leaned forward. "How old were you when you started training?"

Bradley seemed willing to talk about herself then. "Physical training when I was twelve. I was fitted with the first armor when I was fifteen."

"So, did MacCrave have kids?" Shun asked with a frown. "They must want to take over their father's armor."

Kaden supposed the turn in conversation was because Shun had resigned himself to never acquiring a suit of his own.

"He's got two sons," Bradley said, and Kaden remembered she'd looked into the file. "They weren't really interested in taking over their father's occupation, or weren't compatible or something. Either way, no one wants to wear it."

"So you're going to collect it?"

"It belongs to our base," Bradley said stubbornly.

"I suppose." Shun relaxed against Kaden.

Kaden felt a tightness in his groin, and the armor plate didn't help. He sighed and slipped a hand around Shun's shoulder and was welcomed with a small smile.

Shun murmured, "Tell me when we're close to Shilean." And with that, he closed his eyes and slept.

THE REST of their journey after Shilean was anticlimactic, but Kaden admitted the view was worth the long journey as the train circled the mountains near the border. The bus route used a more direct tunnel under the mountain, but the trains still followed the old tracks over it. Kaden kept his mind on the view, and admitted to himself that he was disappointed that Shun had departed with only a brief farewell to them.

Koresa was a town with a resolved border, which meant the hundred-foot border-dividing fence was clearly visible from a distance. It loomed over them the moment they got off at the platform, and Wayland and Bradley kept looking at it with wide-eyed curiosity. The bright floodlights that lit the area around the fence bleached everything of color, giving it a surreal appearance.

They were waiting for their pickup from the camp because Koresa didn't have any form of public transport. There weren't enough civilians living there; the town was just too small to warrant it. When Bradley called the camp using the secure line at the station, they were told it could take up to half an hour for their ride to arrive even though the camp was not far away. That left them with time to stare at the fence in silence.

Beyond the fence was no-man's-land: the area between Haria and Joscal as decreed by WUC. The resolved boundary stretched from Gilaw to Dontun, where the borders again became unclear, since those two countries hadn't reached a conclusion on where each one ended.

Though Koresa had seen a lot of fighting before the fence went up, the fact it had a defined boundary meant it was one of the more peaceful towns, but being so close to the border meant it wasn't exactly a very popular town to retire to. The armies on both sides maintained a mile-wide strip of bare land between them. WUC had helped clear everything in the middle of the no-man's-land: trees, houses, rocks, anything, leaving the entire area a flat, featureless desert so that anyone sneaking in or out would be obvious.

All three of them moved to the edge of the platform to stare at the fence in fascination—there were no buildings nearby on Joscal's side of the border either, probably because of the constant patrolling by the border guards, and the bright floodlights prevented people from building houses too close to the fence. Kaden supposed the fence was electrified when needed. Land mines were probably buried in the no-man's-land to dissuade people from crossing over.

Kaden was surprised both sisters were standing. The journey had taken close to fourteen hours, and Wayland was only fifteen years old. She had to be tired, but Bradley must have been exhausted; she'd been walking around with heavy metal plating strapped to her, with no proper ventilation or air circulation.

Kaden almost suggested they walk to the camp—they'd walked farther in basic training—but he held back, waiting for Bradley to make the suggestion if she felt like it. As she remained silent, he did speak in the end. "The two of you go and stay in the camp," he said without inflection. "I'm going to get a place in town."

"Really." Bradley looked surprised. "Why?"

"I need a little time to unwind, and you need to be away from me," he told her patiently. "I'll meet you tomorrow at the camp."

"Fine," said Bradley with a suspicious frown. "Have you made reservations wherever you're staying?"

Places Kaden usually stayed in didn't have landlines, let alone something like a reservation system. "Yes."

"Tell me where you're staying, in case we need to contact you at night."

Although he could see the logic in her argument, he wasn't about to comply with her wishes. "Look, I need a little privacy."

"It's not like we're going to come banging on your door," Bradley said with a scowl, crossing her arms over her chest.

Kaden opened his mouth to protest and was interrupted by someone clearing their throat. He turned to see one of the border guards coming toward them, probably drawn by their armor and the fact they were standing there arguing.

"Can I be of service to you?" the man asked as he drew closer.

"Yes," Kaden snapped. "Where would you recommend for a quiet night and some good food? My fellow warriors will be staying at the camp."

"But you said—" Wayland started to protest and shut her mouth when Bradley elbowed her.

"With company or not?" The border guard gave Kaden a knowing wink.

"By myself," Kaden stressed. He didn't feel like sleeping in a whorehouse no matter what.

"There's the Sleeping Mice," the guard said with a nod. "Not too expensive, good food."

"Huh," said Kaden to Bradley. "I'll be staying with the mice."

"How do you know if it has any vacancies?" Bradley asked the guard.

"In this town, all the time," the guard said with a wry smile. "It's not a proper inn, just a house with rooms to hire, and the owner also picks up guests from the station when needed. I can call him now and ask him to pick you up."

"No, the camp said they'd send us a driver," Bradley told him. "We can drop Instructor Kaden off on the way."

Kaden wasn't sure as to how well received the idea of an instructor going off and leaving the students he was observing was going to be. "Actually, I think it might be a better idea to call for a pickup."

"There's something moving," Wayland gasped, and Kaden turned his head to see where she was looking.

She was pointing into the no-man's-land on the other side of the fence.

"Must be an animal," Bradley speculated, and Kaden agreed.

He squinted against the glare of the floodlights and spotted a small brown something move. An animal, most likely. A medium-sized dog, maybe—and then the shape stood up, and Kaden's eyes widened. A child of about five years old, dressed in brown rags, with skinny, bare feet covered in dust and pale yellow hair shining in the light like a beacon.

"A Harian." Bradley turned to the border guard for an explanation.

"There's always a few there," the guard shrugged. "Beggars and a few poor kids looking for scraps to eat. The people sometimes toss their garbage through the holes in the fence, and they pick it up."

Bradley looked worried. "Isn't the fence electrified?"

"Between you and me, we don't have the power to do that." The man shrugged. "If there's an attack, we'll switch it on, but why waste power now? It's not like they can climb the fence."

Wayland eyed the fence speculatively. "No one's ever done it?"

"Not in the twenty years or so since the fence was put up." The guard sounded extremely confident. "Now I suppose anyone wanting to cross would have to go over to one of the places where the border isn't set."

"Wait." Bradley sounded surprised. "You mean Harians still cross over to Joscal?"

"And our people cross over to there every day," Kaden told her. The girl might be intelligent, but she lacked general knowledge. "There's always someone not happy with how the country is run, and some of them actually have relatives and family on the other side."

"I didn't know that," Wayland exclaimed.

"You wouldn't know it by looking at this," the guard looked amused and pleased to have someone to impress. "But before the fence, people used to cross over a lot in Koresa. There were some poor families living close to the border from the other side, and they'd come over to sell things at the market—but the armored warriors sent to clear the border put a stop to that before the fence went up."

"I guess we can't have them coming over here," Bradley commented without much heat, and when Kaden looked at her, she appeared thoughtful, not vindictive.

He supposed he had more reason to hate them than she did, but he found it hard to work up any rage toward the faceless drones that had caused a building to be brought down on him. Kaden moved to a bench on the side, intending to sit, when the screech of brakes stopped him midmotion.

"Our ride's here." Wayland turned with a spring to her steps. "I just hope they have showers."

"I'm sure they do." Bradley looked tired as she picked up her bag from the ground. "I hope they have a port where I can plug this thing in and charge it. I'm running low on power and my legs are starting to stiffen."

Kaden agreed. Armor was great, but it wasn't comfortable, and from what he'd heard, the new armors got harder to move the more they ran out of power.

They watched as the driver got out of the open-top jeep and came running up the steps. She leaped over the turnstiles and looked around as her feet hit the platform. At the sight of them, she hurried over, hands clenched. "Instructor Pace, I'm sorry, but the armor you came to pick up was stolen from our base not an hour ago."

# CHAPTER 5

"Look, it's not something small," said Kaden to the base captain, Pierce Layman, original armored warrior, armor color yellow, twenty-five-year combat veteran. "How did you lose it, put it out to dry on your clothesline?"

Captain Pierce kept a blank face. "A boy came, said he was MacCrave's son and wanted to try on the armor. On record, MacCrave had two sons, and the photo on the ID was passable. He had the standard identification, so we took him to the armor room per procedure and let him try it on. The room was secure, and we had a medic on standby—sometimes armor rejection can be painful." The last was added for the benefit of Wayland, who looked puzzled. "It's standard procedure."

"Then?" Bradley prompted.

"Then he turned around and punched a hole in the wall and ran off."

"Huh," said Bradley, clearly not comprehending what had happened. Kaden understood her confusion.

"It was green armor," Pierce explained. "Not—" He gestured to Wayland's silver-gray suit. "Not the elemental green but more light green. I'd say luminous, but it wasn't. I can show you a color swatch—"

"What is its base ability?" Kaden asked in a low voice so as not to reveal his annoyance at such irrelevant information. He could always look at a photo later on.

"We thought it was gas resistance. It has a filter that falls over the mouth. But when the boy donned it, he released a gas," Pierce answered. "Paralysis. Our medic tells me it can kill in large doses."

"Did you know the armor could do that?" Kaden asked.

"No."

He knew there were armor abilities that were not on file, the wearers discovering something new that even the previous wearer didn't know about. But such discoveries usually took time and practice and familiarity.

"He knew about it," said Kaden, trying to remember what MacCrave had specialized in. He turned to Bradley. "Your research of his file—was there any mention of it?"

"No," she said. "The only note was it came with breathing filters—protection against gas attacks."

Pierce breathed out noisily. "Works both ways."

"How did he know of an ability no one else knew about?" Wayland asked in the silence.

Kaden turned to Pierce. "I take it he wasn't really MacCrave's son?"

"Not his legal one, anyway," Pierce confessed. "The identification came across as false, but it's not like we run every ID we come across through the database. We ran the photo but he doesn't show up anywhere. No registration paper, no driving license, nothing."

"So, a spy?" Bradley asked.

"Or a border jumper," Kaden added. Then he froze as another thought occurred to him. "Can we see his picture?"

"Of course." Pierce signaled the communication officer to bring a data pad.

Kaden took it and looked at the photo, but he'd already had an inkling he was going to know the person, and he was right. Shun's face stared back at him, eyes wide, hair as black as any Joscalian.

He and Bradley shared a quick look of understanding. Kaden supposed he could come clean and admit that Shun had learned the information from them, but that might cost him the right to operate in the field and ultimately, in his armor. He looked to Bradley who quickly shielded the photo from Wayland's view. She was likely thinking of the dangers of failing the exam, of being held back another year, or perhaps being separated from her sister, who wasn't ready to go out and fight on her own. But he knew he couldn't stay quiet about their involvement with Shun either.

He met Bradley's eyes. "Let me call Vorani and sort out a few things."

Vorani might prove to be a better person to do that than Pierce, who was itching to pass the blame. The armor had been stolen from right under his nose and he was partially responsible for it. Pierce might try to shift the blame toward Kaden, but Vorani would have no such compulsion since her career was not threatened.

Bradley nodded in understanding. "We won't talk to anyone."

Pierce snorted in irritation, probably because he understood that they were withholding information. "What next?"

"You have a tracker on the armor, don't you?" Kaden asked. Every armor was tracked, even the ones they were currently wearing.

"Yes, and we activated it," Pierce told him and then hesitated.

Kaden waited a few seconds, but it was obvious Pierce needed prompting. "And?"

"The armor is heading toward the outskirts of Compen Beach Town."

Compen, the out-of-the-way island where the original armor had been born and the space program had died. The place where Harians had openly declared war on them. A shell of an island, where people lived in the beach town even though it was technically off-limits to everyone. A place to lie low.

"Will he reach Compen?" Kaden asked.

The communication officer shook her head. "That armor isn't going to reach Compen. The island is closed off to everyone."

"The chances he'll reach Haria?"

"That side of the border is closed, monitored by WUC, and anyway, he'll have to cross the branch of the Syde River where it empties into the sea. Again, monitored by WUC."

"Can't we block him before he reaches the beach town?"

"We can't keep him out if he wants to. It's not like we have a perimeter."

"Is there anything we need to worry about in Compen Beach Town?" Kaden asked. "Any new projects, any salvaging?"

Pierce shook his head. "With the peace talks, we're not going near that place, which makes it problematic when it comes to chasing the armor."

"So why Compen Beach Town?" Kaden thought aloud.

"We withdrew our troops recently because of the peace talks. There are a few refugees and lowlifes but nothing major."

"So, he's going into hiding, not attacking, and hopefully, not about to sell the armor to the Harians."

The communication officer pulled up a map book. "If he wants to get that armor across the border, he'd have had a better chance breaching the fence here than at Compen Beach Town. The island is as secure as a fortress."

"We could wait," Kaden said softly. Then he remembered it wasn't his place to decide. He turned to Bradley. "It's your call."

Bradley looked at all of them: the communications officer, Kaden, Captain Pierce, Wayland, and a stray technician standing by the door. She took a deep breath. "I guess we'd better go after it, then." She looked down at her hands and sighed.

Kaden spoke next. "But I think we need a full night's rest before we start off, and rushing in the dark is hardly likely to help. I'd also like to see all the data available on Compen Beach Town."

Captain Pierce looked thoughtful as he turned to Bradley. "This might be too much as a first mission for someone as inexperienced as you."

Bradley looked neither angry nor annoyed. "Perhaps. But I have to finish my first mission, and it was to bring back the armor."

"There won't be a black mark against you if you don't," Kaden told her with a gentleness that belied his inner turmoil.

"I know it's just my very first mission, nothing important." Bradley stuck her chin out, lower lip trembling. "I need to do this. How hard can it be? We have three armors between us and he has only one, which he acquired a couple of hours ago. It takes time for people to become compatible."

"But it has a gas attack," Wayland pointed out, no longer looking as childish as before.

"There has to have been some data on it," Bradley fumed through gritted teeth. "Someone must have known, MacCrave's wife perhaps, or someone."

Kaden had a suspicion that MacCrave and his wife might not have been very close if Shun, claiming to be his son, had managed to fit into the armor and use it. "Or perhaps a girlfriend or a mistress," he suggested.

"We're looking into it now," Captain Pierce told him. He gave a wry grin. "You can't go stumbling in the dark, and there's a couple of hours before light. I've assigned rooms for you... perhaps—"

Kaden turned away when someone burst into the room, holding a beeping data pad. The technician was old, perhaps close to retirement age, and had definitely seen some action before he'd been roped into doing office work. His left leg had been amputated above the knee, made obvious by the crude prosthetic he wore. The prosthetic was not even close to his flesh tone and was obviously only good for giving the man support. He also had a walking stick strapped to his arm to help him move, and it was all so cumbersome and ugly, Kaden had to look away.

"What is it?" Bradley demanded. "Has the armor—"

"No, there's a signal in this room," the man announced.

"A tracking signal." Kaden stood up and looked around. "Is someone listening in on us?"

"Nothing like that. It's simply a makeshift location beacon." The man moved closer to the center of the room and waved his locator over the table. He zeroed in on the box they'd been carrying. "It's here."

Bradley, who was the closest, upended the contents and pulled out the birthday card. The beeper went wild. She made to open it, but Captain Pierce put a stop to her actions with a firm, "Let the tech handle it. We don't want to destroy any evidence we have."

Bradley relinquished it with reluctance and looked at them all defiantly. "I didn't know what it was before I brought it here."

Captain Pierce looked tired. "No one's accusing you of anything. It's late, and we're talking in circles now. As Cadet Bradley said, let's meet in the morning. We have a supply truck heading past Compen Beach at 1000 hours. We'll drop you off at the turnoff to the beach town, but it's technically a no-man's-land, so anyone going there will be on their own."

"Fine," said Kaden, getting up. He could not insist on going to the Sleeping Mice now. He needed to drop a quick message to Vorani about their meeting with Shun, edited very carefully to minimize the part where Shun had learned everything about the availability of MacCrave's armor from them. "Where do we sleep?"

"We've allocated a single room for you," Captain Peirce told him. "Senior Expert Maxis called ahead and insisted on it. There's food in the kitchen, though it'll be cold, but we have almost unlimited hot water in officer's quarters."

"Thank you," said Kaden, meaning it. He walked out of the room, avoiding looking at the technician who was pulling back the inside of the birthday card with a pair of tweezers.

Once he was outside, Kaden paused to let Wayland and Bradley troop past him and turned to Captain Pierce.

Captain Pierce didn't blink. "Ask," he simply said.

Kaden shrugged. "What's there to ask?"

"Why we didn't do a full credential check before letting him get into that armor." Captain Pierce sounded jaded. "I'll tell you why—because we were desperate to let someone who was a blood relative try it on."

"He had two sons...."

"Who were both apparently destined for 'greater things.'" Sarcasm rolled off him in waves. "He knew it for a while. He could have just signed up for the breeding program and made sure there was someone to take over the armor."

That damn thing again, Kaden thought, and his expression must have reflected his disgust at the idea. "Look, I know the government calls it some fancy name, but at least you admit that it's a breeding program."

"Now he's dead, and it's a waste of potential if you ask me."

Kaden disliked the senior officer's attitude that anyone who could fit into armor should take up arms and fight. Potential, that was all they were, not people, not individuals, just cannon fodder. Kaden knew he should let it go this time, but he couldn't help but bite out, "I suppose you're all for passing on the armors—"

"Oh, don't be like that," Pierce said with forced cheerfulness. "I don't mean to say we need to breed children to fight, but without the next generation, who will continue our work?"

Kaden turned to go. "I'll retire to my room now. Thank you."

"Are you sure you don't want a drink for the night?"

"Not when I have to go to Compen Beach Town tomorrow." Kaden knew when to be polite. He stepped out. He even closed the door to the briefing room behind him without a sound.


KADEN HAD his shower sitting down on one of the stools the room had come with, the secure communicator the base had provided for him sitting on the other stool out of the water's range. Though it was after midnight, Vorani answered on the first ring, looking bright-eyed and freshly groomed.

"You're calling me in the shower," she said in a flat voice.

"Saves time," Kaden told her. He'd aimed the camera so only his upper body was visible; he wasn't a pervert. "You must have heard what happened." He had sent her a report as soon as he'd reached the room, and she must have also received the report from the Koresa command post.

"This Shun person," Vorani said, jumping to the main topic. "What did he strike you as?"

"A nice guy, knew his food," Kaden answered quickly. "Not dangerous in any way."

"But he still stole an armor and planted a transmitter on your group." Vorani made it sound like it was Kaden's incompetence that had led to their problems. Well, he might have been somewhat responsible, but he certainly didn't want to discuss that just then.

Kaden reached for the shower gel. "The transmitter must have been on the birthday card from the beginning. How come our base didn't pick it up?"

"Because it only became active once it was out of the base," Vorani told him with a worried look. "We went through the camera footage from the train station, and we have him. He'd been on the platform every single day for the past month with his data pad, perhaps waiting for a mail carrier or someone like you, transporting the card."

Kaden knew better than to point fingers at people, so he let Vorani's earlier accusation slide. "But do you know anything about him? Have you spoken to MacCrave's wife?"

"They separated a while ago, but she preferred to stay married to him for the benefits. She seemed glad to see the last of him. Wasn't the loving husband in any way."

"So, could have had a girlfriend," Kaden speculated.

"How are the girls doing?" Vorani asked, changing tack.

"Fine." Kaden blinked to get rid of the soapsuds flowing over his eyes and to deal with the sudden change of topic.

"How's Bradley?"

"A little more professional than you were at her age." Kaden wasn't trying to be professional. He might not like the way Bradley behaved toward him, but it didn't mean he was going to fail her or cause her trouble.

"Well, she was the competitive one. She and her sister get on all right?"

"Why do I feel as if you're not telling me something?" Kaden said as he reached for the conditioner. There was water, so why not enjoy it.

"The family armor Wayland is wearing was originally worn by Warrior Amanda Olgesh-Smith. I think she was before your time, and she wasn't posted at our base. Anyway, Bradley tried it but was only 3 percent compatible with it, too low to even move it, and along came Wayland who tried it on and had 48 percent compatibility from the start."

"So, big sister resents not getting the armor, that she's stuck with a modified armor while her younger sister gets an original."

"Something like that," Vorani nodded. "She resents Wayland for that, but still, as a big sister she tries to make up for it and for what she thinks is her shortcoming for not being compatible with the family armor. She's bound to make impulsive decisions. The first year here she almost died, overtaxing herself, training to become strong enough to fit into that hulk of metal she moves around in."

"She's driven. Watch out for her. Hold her back if needed," Kaden said with a nod. "Got it."

"If there's anything else...."

He shook his head. "I need to eat something and get some sleep. I'll catch you later."

But Vorani didn't cut the connection once it was obvious that Kaden had nothing more to report. "Kaden, when you go to Compen Beach Town, just try not to stir up too much trouble. Our troops are withdrawing, but it's still being monitored, and there's talk of another joint salvage operation heading to Compen. If the Harians catch you there and think we jumped the gun, we'll be in big trouble."

"I'll be careful," Kaden promised her. "We'll be out of there before you know it."

"And you have to make sure there are no international mishaps," she added with a wry smile. "WUC is waiting for us to slip up so they can slap our wrists and make us sit still at the peace summit, in shackles."

Finally, Vorani recognized him for the experienced warrior he was. She knew he was capable of taking charge of two cadets and completing the task without a hitch. Still, he felt obliged to say something. "I'm not the village idiot, you know."

"Priority is getting the armor," Vorani continued. "Shoot the boy in the head if you want to. Just don't waste too much time on him."

Kaden would have agreed with that plan two days ago, but after having met Shun, all he could muster was a vague nod and a grimace. He wasn't sure he wanted to kill Shun without hearing him out, no matter how obvious his crime was.

Vorani switched off the connection, but Kaden still made sure to toss a spare T-shirt over the camera before he pulled the towel from the wall hook. He dried himself and reached for his armor stacked next to the wall. He was only going to bed; he didn't need underarmor for short stints in the suit. The spray of water had given his armor a gleam, as if dark fire moved inside it, and he held it out to the light. He never got tired of looking at it.

Then he started getting dressed.


KADEN HAD a quick breakfast and walked into the camp gym to find Bradley lifting weights. She was dressed in a sleeveless, tight, black tank top and a pair of knee-length black leggings. She was more slender than expected and at the same time more muscular.

Kaden walked over to her, making no effort to muffle the sound of his metal boots against the cement floor. She looked up, her eyes bloodshot, her mouth strained.

"Did you sleep at all?"

"I should ask you the same," Bradley replied, snapping the weight back into place and sitting up. The lighting in the room made it obvious that she was a modified armor warrior.

The undersuit the warriors wore under their armor offered limited protection. Bradley's shoulders were scarred where the armor had rubbed against her skin until the scars had become calluses. Kaden could see marks on her arms, elbows, wrists, and on her legs, knees, and ankles, and he bet there were scars under her clothes around her ribs and waist. Probably around her crotch as well. They were typically found on every single place where the armor plates overlapped, where the strain on the body was the greatest.

That was the modified armor: a dead metal weight that bogged the wearer down and sometimes slowed them or crippled them. Those who wore it for a long time apparently developed back problems from lugging it around. In battle it could turn to a death trap, people moving around in damaged armor with no idea it was compromised, or simply running out of power midbattle.

In contrast, Kaden's own armor responded to his needs without him even thinking of it. *I need you*, he thought to his armor and it seemed as if a sigh had spread across his body, a silent acknowledgment. He knew his armor like a second skin, every scratch and dent as it grew back. He was aware of it as he stood there, the weight balanced just right, never a scar on him outside of battle. "Are you still sure about going after the armor?"

"We are responsible for pointing Shun this way," Bradley told him. "I intend to fix it."

"There are other armors. We can afford to lose one," Kaden said, not really meaning it.

In response Bradley touched her scarred shoulder. "Really don't think so. And what if he takes it over the border to the Harians, and uh… they decode its secrets?" There was little possibility of Shun doing so from the vicinity of Compen, but there was no guarantee he'd stay there for good.

Kaden knew Haria hadn't been able to get their hands on a single original armor for the duration of the war. It was the Joscalians' secret to keep, theirs to guard.

"The suit needs to be brought back. That doesn't mean you and your sister are the best—"

"She won't freeze again," Bradley promised. Then she hesitated and sighed. "I… had the people here ask after the engine driver who got shot yesterday—they say he's going to make it."

Kaden looked at her in surprise. He wondered if she was pretending to care, or if the remorse was genuine, and then he felt ashamed of his thoughts. Kaden himself had forgotten all about the guy who'd been shot on the train. "We're leaving soon. Is Wayland ready?"

Bradley got to her feet and stretched her neck. Kaden could see the muscles in her body ripple—even without the armor, she would be a formidable fighter. "I'll go check," she said as she moved toward the exit.

"Get something to eat," he told her back. "And maybe get some sleep while we're on the way." This was Bradley's first time out and about in her armor. She might have pulled all-nighters studying for the theory component exams, but he knew just how different the physical strain of not sleeping was in actual battle conditions. "You aren't made of metal, you know."

She stopped but didn't turn around. "And what about you, Instructor Pace. Did you sleep in that armor?"

Then she was gone, leaving Kaden standing in the gym in silence.

# CHAPTER 6

COMPEN HAD never been a real island town; it had been the Joscalian-Harian research center located in the middle of the sea and an education institute established in the seventeen-year lull when both countries were tired of the war and had called a halt. There had been skirmishes, but most believed the war had come to an end, and the two countries were happy about where their borders were.

There was the Joint Space-Launch Facility, which had been run by the person considered to be the greatest mind the world had ever produced, Dr. Langvil Orche. Harian by birth, Orche was educated in Danal, Koramal's capital city and center for science, when his parents moved there during their later years. He eventually settled in Joscal to set up his research center.

He had been well received by most. At universities he gave speeches, which many attended but few really understood. He also worked part-time at the local university, where his courses were only popular with those who wanted to develop neural networks and understood complex five-dimensional mathematics. No one mentioned he had been born a woman.

If Dr. Orche sometimes spoke for the antiwar movement and urged the governments of Joscal and Haria to form a peace treaty, he was ignored; he was a harmless enough person who didn't cause too much trouble. It was then he got it into his head to develop something to end the war, something that would stop the fighting completely. Many believed he was working on a weapon that could read the minds of the enemy, a remote bot similar to the ones Harians used but with more discrimination when it came to killing. Harian drones sometimes went out of control and killed their own units, which was not a good thing for the Harian Army.

Dr. Orche was working on the armor, of course, taking over the work of his father, Laure Orche, who had started his research on the same subject but had been killed several years earlier in a bomb attack over a civilian area. Dr. Laure, had been trying to find a way of developing self-repairing body armor that would protect the wearer, and he had had so many ideas of what their capabilities should be. His change of residency to the joint island university to share his work with other like-minded people had been met with skepticism and suspicion by people from both sides of the border.

He had developed different types of armor, small batches of them with different capabilities. The story was he had then demonstrated the armor capabilities to the government defense officers, one of whom had been a Harian spy. The Harians had fired a powerful thermonuclear bomb at the research facility—which had taken out the city center with it.

Close to fifty thousand people died that day, and Dr. Orche was just one of them. With him died the secret of producing neural interfaces for armors and the knowledge of producing the different types of suit. There had been nothing left of the research facility until finally, a few armors were unearthed from military bases where they'd been sent as samples. A few more were discovered in the basement of the research facility, so deep underground they were only discovered five years after the initial bomb blast.

The attack on the research facility was seen as an act of hostility, and the war that had been going through a quiet period revived again. Compen Beach Town became a dead city, out of bounds to all.

It was currently an unofficial no-man's-land, torn between the Joscalian government not wanting to let go of the area in case there were hidden treasures in the research center or the surrounding area, and the Harians, who were salivating to get their hands on it. The Harian government once filed a claim to WUC that they owned half of what was in Compen because Dr. Orche and some of their scientists in the labs at that time were their citizens. The resulting battle lasted about ten years before WUC finally declared Compen off-limits to both sides. Both countries circled the island like wolves over a kill, not wanting to make the first move, but testing each other.

Compen Beach Town was situated along the stretch of beach that ran from the Syde River inlet for a couple of miles. The thin strip of a town had flourished because of the economy the research center brought with it. Though not directly affected by the bomb, apart from some structural damage and a negligible loss of life, the town had ground to a halt afterward. It was not considered a people-friendly place, but unfortunately it was their destination.

The three of them dismounted from the cargo hold without a word as the vehicle they were in slowed down and rolled off the side of the road. As one they started to move over small fences toward Compen Beach Town. Since it was abandoned no one *should* live there, but there were people around. Scavengers; civilians from both sides displaced by the war, with nowhere to go; criminals in hiding; soldiers running away from their responsibilities—they all wound up on the beach. The Joscalian Army and WUC forces supposedly swept the town once in a while, picking up a few criminals, but for the most part the inhabitants cleared out and then came back once the searches were over.

The town was confined to a wide headland, only a beach road running alongside. There weren't many entry points because of its location. They had to move fast, find Shun, and leave with the armor. Kaden looked at the locator once for confirmation, and then they were over the ramp and slithering on their bellies toward the closest building.

He supposed there were observers, scavengers from the town, but they traveled light and if they moved quickly, would be out without too much trouble. No one was expecting them, so they had the element of surprise on their side, but Kaden could think of a half-dozen WUC laws they were violating just by being there. By the time they'd reached the first large building, Kaden was just glad of the cover it offered, even if it smelled strongly of urine.

"We can't stay here," Bradley said, pointing to a building to their right. "Let's move before someone comes."

"No one close by," Wayland stated with confidence.

"How can you tell?" Bradley snapped. "You always said you couldn't sense people—too much vibration."

"No vehicles here, not many people." Wayland turned to Kaden. "Through my armor, I can feel the vibration on the earth when people walk and stuff. No one around."

"Useful," said Kaden, looking to Bradley. That was convenient, but not as useful as their locator. "Which way is the armor?"

Bradley made a face and pointed to the left, away from the buildings toward open ground. "That way, maybe another eight hundred meters." Then she added the obvious: "He's sticking close to the edge of the beach city."

"There might be good reason for that," Kaden said.

They started out in the direction of the empty space, trying hard not to look too closely at what they were walking through. The bomb had been close to eighty years ago, a memory softened by time but not forgotten. Students still learned about it at school—hell, even Kaden had, and he'd seen the photos of the island—but no one talked about the beach town. With nothing to keep the population going, they'd shut down everything and moved off. The university quarters on the mainland, the houses for the research staff, shopping malls, banks, department stores, high-rise towers that had acted like hotels for tourists, the trade centers—it was all abandoned.

He could see furniture inside houses, garden flowers that had grown wild, traces of fabric at broken windows, and the rusted remains of a small bicycle left on what had been a driveway.

*They lived*, Kaden told himself as they walked after Bradley. The people in the outskirts had lived, mostly, apart from those who'd gone to work on the island that day, but still, they'd made it.

"Instructor Pace," said Wayland, coming up to him.

"Creepy, isn't it?" Kaden gave a wry grin. "Nothing like what they show in school."

"No," Wayland agreed. "See, my dad made me a swing like that once."

Kaden didn't look. "They are all adults now, older than me, even." And probably dead, but that wasn't worth mentioning.

"I guess."

But Wayland didn't seem convinced, and when she edged closer to him, he didn't dissuade her. He wondered if he should suggest she stay behind, but he realized leaving her alone in the midst of such decay would be even worse than taking her farther into the dead city.

"We're close," Bradley snapped, her body tense, and Kaden looked at Wayland.

"Can you sense anything?"

"Which way?" Wayland asked.

For a moment Kaden was sure Bradley wouldn't answer, but finally she pointed to a collection of buildings half a kilometer in front of them.

"As far as I can make out, it's some sort of barn."

"Well, then, he's not moving much," said Wayland thoughtfully. "But there are people moving to the far left." She shrugged, unconcerned. "Don't know if they saw us or if they're simply going for a walk."

"Right," said Bradley dismissively. "We go in and take the armor and we back out, quickly."

Kaden hoped she had a more refined plan. He took off his supply pack and kept it aside, then pulled out the gas mask and put it on. "You'll need to be a little more specific."

"The barn is old; it's got holes," Bradley said without even looking at him. "You go from the right, I'll go from the left, and Wayland will go from above—"

"Why above?" Wayland protested before Bradley had stopped speaking.

"Instructor Pace, can you take out a side of the barn like you did that rock in the obstacle course?" Bradley asked, ignoring Wayland.

"Yes," Kaden said in a low voice. He didn't know why he felt the need to whisper; it just felt right.

"Do it with a lot of noise and flash. That'll distract him and keep him busy. You also have the advantage of speed. You can stay out of range if the gas mask doesn't work."

Kaden nodded. "I can be bait."

"I'm going to come from the right, a little after you—"

"And catch him."

"No, I'm also bait." Bradley pulled out her gas mask. "Wayland will be on the roof of the barn by then and can drop the net over him while he's distracted." She turned to Wayland. "The net is metal, so I hope you can handle it."

Captain Pierce had given them the net. It released a large electric charge that knocked out armored warriors for a short time. A very short time, sometimes, and there were a few armors resistant to electricity, but they were hoping Shun's suit wasn't one of those. Given that they hadn't known about the gas, there were no doubt other things they didn't know about.

It was an okay plan and would keep Wayland out of the way should she freeze, and hopefully keep Shun alive.

"Ready," said Kaden, standing up and letting the helmet extend from his neckpiece over his head.

"Give us time to get into position," Bradley said.

Kaden realized that, weighed down by her armor, Bradley should be the slowest of the three, though she'd never shown it.

She went on. "I'm also going to stash our stuff." That included their armor tracker and rations. They hadn't been issued an emergency radio in case WUC detected a transmission from inside an off-limits area. "Don't want some scavenger to steal it."

"How do I get up there?" Wayland asked, looking at the barn. "Who knows if the roof is strong enough?"

"You can walk onto it from the other building." Bradley no longer seemed worried about sending her sister into danger. Out of the three of them, Wayland was the most protected, since there had yet to be an armor that could fly—unless Shun's armor floated on gas, but that was improbable.

Bradley withdrew the net from its folded pouch and gave it to her sister. "You can climb it using that broken window, and then make your own footholds the way Instructor Pace did at the course."

Kaden wondered if her protective-sister act on the train had been just to keep Wayland from getting all the glory. Damn Vorani for telling him what had been in their files—now he was overthinking it.

"All right." Wayland didn't sound too enthusiastic. "Do you think a fall from the roof will kill me?"

Kaden studied the drop. "You're in armor; you won't even feel it." He was only partially lying. She would feel it, but she would be safe.

Wayland looked mollified. "I hate heights." But she walked to the building pointed out and started climbing in quick, smooth moves without hesitation.

"She'll be fine," Bradley said with a look at Kaden.

Not that Kaden was worried or anything. "Well, I hope she doesn't get detected by who knows what on that green armor."

Bradley dismissed his fears with a shake of her head. "Her armor does this… thing where it's undetectable."

Kaden tried to remember everything he'd read about Wayland's suit's capabilities. "That wasn't on her file, was it?"

"Her armor manipulates metal and is made of metal. So there's this thing she does, I'm not really sure about it, but it's like she makes it invisible to scanners. People can still see it if they look at it visually, so it only works with distance sensors."

That was an interesting bit of information. He nodded, eager to get the show on the road. "Gas masks on."

Bradley pulled hers on. "Make some noise in one minute. That'll be enough time for both of us to get into position." And then she was gone.

Kaden was impressed. She was young and untrained, but he could see the potential in her. He'd have thought of a plan similar to that if he were working in a group. He moved silently toward the barn, skirting the other structures, working on building up the charge in his armor.

*A loud noise, huh? I can do that.*

Once Kaden was at the wall made of rusted metal plating, he picked up a rock and threw it at the wall, where it made a hollow sound. Then he knocked on it several times. He grinned. If he was going to be the distraction, he was going to do it with finesse.

Shun was probably hiding, tense, not wanting to move. "Roy, is that you?"

So Shun was inside for sure. Now that he had heard the noise, he would be looking in the direction of the wall—

Kaden let the charge loose.

The large flash of light should have blinded Shun as the wall blew to bits, and the shock factor should hold him in place. Kaden walked in and cursed.

Shun stood in the middle of the barn, shocked but not blinded, his visor having descended at the right time. His armor was iridescent green unlike the matte green of Wayland's armor's decorations. It had a very luminous sheen, and beyond doubt was not meant for stealth. As Shun faced Kaden, further plates of the armor flowed seamlessly over his arms and legs and the breathing mask extended below the visor.

Kaden had little time to admire the suit since the flash had, much to his dismay, blinded Bradley, whose armor hadn't extended its visor when needed. She jumped back, her hand still pressed over her eyes, and in that instant, Shun bolted out the side of the barn.

Kaden leaped over the fallen debris, brushed by Bradley, and gave pursuit. He had to catch Shun.

Shun turned around and directed a mist of gas toward him, but the gas mask proved to be effective. Kaden carefully monitored his breathing as he approached Shun from the side. He didn't bother speaking as he circled Shun—that only happened in movies—and waited for his next move. Shun had two options: run or fight. He was better off running, but Kaden was faster. Either Shun ran toward the beach—a dead end—or inland, where Kaden would cut off his retreat.

Kaden moved to block Shun before he even took a step in that direction. He had always been able to predict the movement of an opponent in a one-on-one fight.

This was his first time in a combat situation since the accident, and he could tell his armor's compatibility had improved. The reaction time between his mental commands and the response was instantaneous. He didn't approach Shun straightaway; for all he knew the gas attack went with some other lethal weapon, and there was only so much an armor could do when it came to protecting its wearer against another.

Shun looked back inland and seemed to consider his options. Kaden could see his mind work—Kaden was herding him out of the city, so perhaps there was a large task force collected behind them.

Shun surged forward and attacked.

Kaden blocked the first punch, catching it in the center of his palm. His glove's metal strained, then made adjustments for the speed and force of Shun's punch, which hadn't been bad for an untrained thief using armor for the first time. Kaden kicked Shun on the right side and ducked left, following it with another punch and a chop to the neck.

Most armor designs were the same, despite the different abilities and colors. Kaden knew where the weaknesses were.

*Disable, not break*, he thought as he pulled back an energy charge. He didn't want to kill Shun, simply get him out of the armor. If they'd been in the barn, the net would have done its job, but unfortunately they were outside, and it was past midday, by the looks of it. Not a good time for an armored warrior showdown. Too much light; any "accidental" WUC helicopter or low-flying media aircraft overhead could easily spot their movements.

Kaden moved faster and faster—aim, punch, jump back, punch— felt Shun's movements and then gave in to the need to finish the fight quickly. He pulled back quickly, letting Shun come forward, and then leaned back. Shun seized the opportunity, pulling at Kaden's gas mask, and Kaden went with it. He could only hold his breath for a maximum of two minutes—perhaps two and a half if he was lucky, but it was doubtful; he didn't have a diver's lung capacity. He caught Shun's hand and held on tight even as the gas sprayed onto his face. He moved for a headbutt, close enough to Shun to follow through with the move, but at that moment, Shun jerked his own head back and Kaden snapped forward, unable to stop in time.

Shun followed through with a punch to his stomach. Kaden's armor compensated, the plating locked, but the punch had carried a lot of force, enough to lift him up and fold him in two.

Enough to force him to open his mouth and gasp for air and get a lungful of gas.

Before they left the Koresa camp, the base medic told Kaden the gas could kill in large doses, and even as his instincts kicked in and he snapped his mouth shut, he felt the gas tickle the back of his throat and his lungs. It burned, making his eyes water. He sagged. Damn, that was powerful.

He jumped back, giving himself some breathing space as he waited for the gas to disperse, but Shun wasn't about to let him wait. Shun leaped forward to take Kaden down; Kaden brought up his hands to block him—or he tried.

His arms were heavy; he could barely lift them. Paralysis, as the medic had mentioned.

Taking advantage of Kaden's weakness, Shun followed through; his uppercut snapped Kaden's head back. Then he reeled Kaden in close and followed with a vicious punch to the stomach. Groggy from the gas, Kaden's knees gave, and he felt the horror of his body betraying him.

*Help*, he thought desperately as he tried to evade the next blow.

His plates locked; his armor was responding, making up for where he couldn't. And as Shun punched him again, his arms came up and locked onto Shun's left elbow.

Shun tried to pull back, and he looked at Kaden. Kaden's eyes fluttered closed against his will as his head sagged forward.

"How...?" Shun asked as he pulled back, but Kaden's fingers remained locked.

Kaden got a second mouthful of gas for his efforts, but his armor was in control by then, and it seemed to read Kaden's fear that if he didn't take down Shun soon he would probably die.

The armor reeled Shun closer, and Kaden forced himself to think through the fog of gas—he needed to sleep, his body felt so heavy, his eyes kept closing, and he really couldn't think clearly. He just needed to stop Shun's movements and—

The armor swept forward and picked up Shun in a bear hug, locking Shun's arms to his side.

*Head*, Kaden thought, and he head-butted Shun as hard as possible while releasing an energy charge through his palms. When Shun's eyes rolled, Kaden finished him off with a punch that put him under without any protest.

Kaden's armor caught Shun before he fell, and Kaden collapsed under their combined weight as the effects of the gas spread. He managed to stand up—his armor did it for him?—pick Shun up, and stagger to the barn as quickly as possible, which was not very fast. He had a problem locating the barn; he could barely keep his eyes open, and it was by luck that he managed to find the place. His boots got caught on every snag in the ground, and he was aware that he was swaying from side to side, despite his wish to walk straight.

The barn was not the safest place, but it was out of sight, and the other two should be there. He hoped Bradley had recovered from the attack and wondered if he should apologize.

She stood by the opening, her gas mask in hand and her face set in a scowl that eased when she saw him. "I was stupid not to realize the attack could blind me," she said the moment he arrived. "Let's get him out of his armor."

Kaden was again impressed by her no-nonsense attitude, but it worried him too. She was supposed to be headstrong and argumentative, but he saw a lot of control—he just hoped it wasn't suppressed anger. He could leave the character analysis for later. He moved to help her strip Shun of his armor.

Kaden tried to think… something about removing armor. He was missing something. He shook his head to clear it. It gave him a case of tunnel vision that had him staring myopically at the far end of the barn. He put Shun down none too gently and attacked the green wristlet first. Then he froze as Shun's limp hand rolled off Kaden's unresponsive fingers—stupid gas.

Then the boots. Well, he hadn't finished the previous task, but boots were very important to him. Shun's armor didn't fold back everywhere as Kaden's did, and with the wearer unconscious, there wasn't any resistance.

"Hey!"

Wayland whined, and Kaden realized she was still on the roof. He looked up and could see beams of sunlight streaming through holes in the metal roof, illuminating her armor so it shone brighter—all those pretty colors and butterflies—or perhaps it was the effects of the gas.

"We'll get you down next." Bradley briskly pulled off Shun's boot, wrinkling her nose as she did so.

There was no underarmor—Shun had never received one from Supplies as they had. His feet smelled boiled.

*Ah, well*, thought Kaden.

As he pulled off Shun's chest piece, he discovered what he'd forgotten.

Armors were self-protective, some more than the others, and this armor was defensive through and through. He managed to stumble back as Bradley got a face full of gas from the chest piece, a last defense against anyone trying to take the armor by force. Kaden coughed as he jumped back, and Bradley took a couple of steps as well, but from the way she shook her head, it was obvious she was already feeling the effects.

"Fuh-uck, should have... remembered that," Kaden spluttered as Bradley slumped to the ground on the opposite side of the barn.

As luck would have it, just then Shun's eyes fluttered open. He lay still for a moment before sitting up, feeling his forehead, and wincing. "Fucker," he spat, looking at the two of them before focusing on Kaden. "It had to be you."

"It goes both ways," Kaden said as calmly as possible for someone so woozy. "Now come, we have to get out of here."

"You're going to have to carry me and the armor out. Good luck," Shun said with a scowl. "That armor's mine."

"Because you stole it," Bradley told him from the other side of the barn. She was slowly recovering from the gas.

"No, because MacCrave is my father, and... and—" He seemed to search for a reason to justify his actions. "—you told me the armor belonged to the family."

Kaden had suspected that much, but he sighed. "There are better ways of getting an armor. You didn't need to steal it." His speech was clear, though he supposed he was sounding odd due to the gas still muddling his thought processes.

"Really?" Shun said in defiance. "How did you come about yours?"

"I went to the academy, tested, and found I was compatible." Kaden walked up to him in what he hoped was a straight line and held out a hand. "Come, we don't have a lot of people who're truly compatible with armor. We'll get you equipped and enrolled." He wasn't sure of his ability to fight at that point. It seemed the effects of the gas only increased with time.

"So I can fight the Harians?" Shun spat.

"You really think I enlisted to fight the Harians?" Kaden laughed and Shun looked at him wide-eyed. Kaden was surprised by his own willingness to talk. It seemed getting gassed was a little like getting drunk. "Some people might enlist because of family honor and bullshit, but I was a war orphan with no schooling. I couldn't do a job. It was either shovel shit or enlist, and there at least, the food was free."

Shun deflated at that and looked at Bradley, struggling to her feet, with a grim expression of determination. "I suppose you at least want my head on a platter."

"We… all of us… just want the armor," Bradley said.

The mention of the armor seemed to set Shun off again, and he looked at it in disgust. He still wore the upper leg and arm pieces. "Doesn't seem right. It should be—those things are sentient, right?"

"What, the armor…?" Kaden looked at his in alarm. He'd made discreet inquiries about his gear, but it seemed it was the only one that *read* him that accurately, and no one ever "spoke" to their armor the way he did. Surely Shun's armor couldn't possibly be—"No, that's just a myth. The armor responds to the wearer, but that's it. Nothing else. You must have realized the moment you put it on."

"But if the wearer is in control," Shun protested, staring at the armor, "then it was…. Look, it just isn't fair that that thing—the armor—isn't responsible for anything that happens—"

"Being a bastard is sad, but there was no need to steal it," Bradley said wearily, sitting back on the floor. "You caused us a lot of trouble. We need to get out of here."

"If you think name-calling is going to distract me, trust me, I've been called worse. That armor is something I worked hard to get. I'm not letting go of it without a fight."

Kaden had expected that; he hadn't thought Shun would come with them after the hassle, but they didn't have time to argue.

"Why not?" Bradley demanded in a reasonable tone, stopping Kaden just short of punching Shun under the chin and putting him out, perhaps shattering his jaw in the process, but that would be small price to pay for sorting out the trouble. She struggled to stand up but failed and sat down with a thump.

"The mind is the last thing to go." Shun shrugged. "It wasn't what I thought it'd be, but that armor—"

"What did you think it'd be?" Wayland asked from above.

Bradley spoke to Shun as if her sister hadn't spoken. "You are compatible with an armor, an original armor. It's a great honor. You'll probably be recruited as an armored warrior."

The bitterness in her voice made Kaden wince, but Shun seemed distracted by the content rather than the tone.

"So I can kill people?"

"We don't really kill people," Wayland said confidently. "We keep the peace."

"That's just propaganda, and you know it." Shun's voice dripped with contempt.

Kaden laughed as if Shun had just come out with the funniest joke. He laughed so hard he listed to the side. He should just shoot Shun and take the armor, not stand there, talking to him. They were losing the advantage… but Shun was soooo interesting.

"You're too young," Shun said to the cadets. "But ask your instructor. He must have lost count of the number of people he's killed."

Kaden moved forward in case Shun was planning something stupid, and stopped as a wave of dizziness overtook him and the room wavered.

Wayland started to protest. "But—"

Shun continued. "Why would I want to kill the Harians? Or anyone?"

"Keep forgetting you're a pacifist," Bradley said in disgust. "But only when it suits your purpose."

Shun barked a laugh. "I suppose I am." His hair caught the sunlight streaming in, free of whatever he'd rubbed in to darken it so that he could pass as MacCrave's son at the Koresa Army post. It stood out bright yellow.

Kaden looked at Shun and the armor, and he felt an idea click in his head. "Bradley, you accessed MacCrave's file. Tell me about his family, background, appearance."

Bradley frowned at the change of tack and struggled to concentrate. "He was Joscalian, went back three generations. His grandfather was a communication officer in the Army, but his father was an Army doctor, and MacCrave was the second son in the family—" She looked at Shun and sighed. "You get your looks from your mother. She was Harian."

It wasn't a question. Shun didn't answer, looking away. Above them, Wayland gasped.

Bradley frowned. "MacCrave had a Harian mistress."

"No!" Shun looked angry for the first time since they'd pulled off his armor. "My mother wasn't some glorified armored warrior's whore. She was a vegetable seller on the Koresa border before the fucking fence went up."

They all remained silent as Shun continued, anger coloring his voice. "MacCrave was posted on this side of the border in Koresa to monitor the people coming and going, searching them. Should have figured this was his hometown… it happens. Apparently soldiers get posted back to their hometowns, even a shithole like Koresa."

Kaden remembered Koresa had undergone a positive development because of the Army outpost and the introduction of the train line, before which it had been a small town on the border, with barely twenty houses.

"His father was posted there as a doctor," Bradley continued reciting the file. "MacCrave later on married a local girl he'd met while he was living here."

"Well, he certainly didn't marry my mother," Shun spat. "He raped her. Knocked her out with the gas in his armor and raped her—repeatedly."

"Who told you that?" Kaden asked.

"My mother's friend who raised me." Shun seemed to struggle to contain himself. "I have no reason not to believe her. She smuggled me over the border when I was small because she thought I could pass for a full-blooded Joscalian here. I couldn't pass for a full-blooded Harian over there, too dark. Doesn't make a difference. I don't belong in either place."

"He couldn't have raped your mother," Wayland mumbled from above. "He was an armored warrior. He wouldn't have…."

"What, just because he wore a hunk of metal around him? He doesn't all of a sudden become a saint," Shun shouted at her. "What makes you who you are? Your armor doesn't decide it."

"But—" Wayland started.

"Wearing that isn't going to give you the will to ki—"

"Stop it," Kaden snapped when he realized Shun was going to remind Wayland that she had frozen in combat. It had gone on long enough. "Bradley, get your sister down. I'm going to secure the prisoner, and then we're going to move out."

"Yes." Bradley struggled to stand up. "Way, move to this side and get to this wall."

"Take off the rest of the armor," Kaden told Shun from a safe distance, his lasers ready.

In theory, once disconnected from the central chest piece, the armor became dormant, but Kaden never trusted that bullshit. It was probably true with the new armor, but the original armors operated on a different level. For all he knew, Shun's armor sprayed gas from every piece.

Shun shrugged and complied, his gaze fixed on Kaden's weapons.

"No more gas?" Kaden asked to be sure.

"I don't think I have any to waste. There's a small compartment in the chest… needs to be filled with some chemical, I think," Shun offered with a shrug. "It's running low, and I don't think it fills itself." Kaden agreed with that assessment: only lasers self-charged; the rest of the armaments had to be replenished by hand.

Relieved that was finally over, Kaden moved to tie up Shun. The sound of something breaking, a stick perhaps, brought him up short. It shouldn't have mattered, but they were in the wrong place, making far too much noise, and overstaying their welcome. He wheeled around sharply. "Bradley, we're not alone."

At least Bradley didn't ask how he knew that. "Way, can you see anything from there?"

"If I'd been on the ground, I'd have felt them come," Wayland grumbled as she looked up.

Kaden felt a smidge of anger. She wasn't taking it seriously. She was acting as if it was an annoyance to their conversation. He should never have brought the two of them with him.

There were people hanging around the beach town, without armor but armed to the teeth; in other words, dangerous. However, their weapons were going to be, if not primitive, at least not high-tech. Probably no armor-piercing rounds.

Kaden moved to the shadows, letting his armor build up charge. He was going to have to take out the group outside, fast. He turned and almost walked into a wall—*where did that come from?* Shit, he was still under the influence of the gas.

He pried loose an old bar and flexed it. It didn't break—good stuff. He rushed forward, caught Shun by the shoulder and pushed him down, pinning his right hand and pushing the metal bar to the ground. He bent the metal and drove the other end into the earth, trapping Shun's hand between the ground and the bar. He didn't think it would hold for long, but he had to move quickly anyway. "Stay low and don't move."

Shun's face was a mask of outrage, but Kaden was already leaving the building.

He exited the barn from the hole in the side, leaving the two girls squabbling as to why Wayland was stuck above. He immediately caught sight of the first person, a man dressed in dark clothing, in the underbrush to his right. He incapacitated the man with a chop to the neck and kept moving. The next had a metal bar, but his armor was expecting it, and he moved smoothly with the blow, caught the bar, pulled, and hit the person back.

Scrambling came from inside the barn; there were other people inside, but he hoped Wayland could deal with them. Bradley didn't look as if she couldn't handle combat, but she was still drugged. The thought of leaving everything to Wayland didn't reassure him. Instead of doing a full circle, Kaden doubled back and hurried into the barn through the hole. He had to see what—

The explosion rocked him back on his heels; he came to a halt to catch his balance, cursing his luck. He knew that sound—each explosion ingrained into his mind, years of listening for them did that. The sound of a short-distance armor-piercing missile going off in close quarters.

As the dust and smoke cleared, he rushed inside. He'd left Shun on the floor, unprotected and—Wayland lay on the ground. Her electric net hung from the rafters above, snagged on a loose nail. The fall, as predicted, hadn't killed her. The barn was fifteen feet high, and her armor had saved her. However, untrained in how to handle such a fall, she lay stunned on the ground, not moving.

A short man with dirt-crusted clothes held a small launcher, balanced against his shoulder with both hands. It was aimed at Wayland's head. From the way the man held it, legs apart, braced for the shock wave, Kaden knew he'd used it before. The stance was that of someone with military training.

Bradley stood off to the side, curled as if ready to jump, and thrumming with the need to take action. But she was still unsteady on her feet and probably unable to move with her usual grace. There were other people in the barn with them, including a woman whom Kaden assumed had scrambled in through the other side of the barn. She sported two large-barreled guns, and she gripped them with steady hands: she also knew how to use them without any problem. Bradley gave the woman only a cursory glance, her gaze locked on Wayland.

Kaden wondered if he could move fast enough to disable both these newcomers before they fired. He could only shoot one person at a time; his lasers couldn't shoot simultaneously in two different directions. He was still feeling the gas, and his eyes didn't focus at that distance, so he could shoot Wayland by mistake. He could inch closer, and if he could take out the guy with the missile launcher.... But even as he tried, he heard movement behind him.

Kaden looked over his shoulder and sighed. Another armor-piercing missile launcher, this time aimed at him. Where did these people get such weapons? Did these things just wash up on the beach? He briefly toyed with the idea of moving anyway, but a missile to the back of his helmet at this range would probably kill him in a couple of seconds. It would be painful, but only for a short while, and he would be free of the additional burden of pretending to be whole. Kaden could take out most of the people in front of him, though. At least one of the girls would survive the attack, Shun could have his own armor and—

There was a possibility the insurgents might shoot the girls first. Kaden sighed. Far too many variables, and if they shot one of his arms or his lower torso with a missile, he could look forward to days of suffering before an agonizing death.

"I really don't want to kill a child." The man holding down Wayland sounded expressionless. "Everyone take off your armor and keep it down."

"No," Bradley snapped, but as she looked at Wayland, her conviction seemed to falter. "Look, we can talk this out—"

Kaden could see what she was trying to do: stall for time so Wayland could recover enough to move. Wayland's talent was elemental, moving metal, and she could maybe do something, but unfortunately the man threatening them also seemed to have realized it.

"Modified armor won't stand a chance against this," the man said without batting an eye. "I'm not sure if an original armor would. Anyway, certainly not the person inside it. Now, take off the armor."

It was bad that the man knew about the weakness of the two types of armor; most civilians were not good at even spotting the differences unless they were up close.

"Just leave her alone." Bradley started to take her chest plate off. She wore light brown underarmor, slightly padded. The padding usually helped with the bruising, but wearing too much compromised flexibility. She was padded just right, but given the state of her body, it wasn't enough.

"We came to take a prisoner with us." Kaden gestured to Shun. "We'll leave with the armor. We have no interest in you." It was not exactly negotiation tactics, but Kaden didn't care; he didn't want to leave the armor. "There will be problems if you take our gear."

The man didn't talk, just indicated with his head, his hand steady, and the woman moved toward Shun.

For a second, Kaden felt his heart sink: they were going to shoot Shun, and he was responsible for securing him helplessly to the ground like a pinned bug. But the next instant, she kicked at the metal bar, shifting it enough so Shun could pull his hand free.

"I'm glad we decided to come instead of Roy." The man smiled, all teeth. "The armor, as promised."

Shun nodded silently and started to pull his off, piece by piece.

*Damn, he's been working with these people all this time.*

When Kaden looked at them, Bradley was down to her boots, and a woman who had recently joined them was pulling Wayland's armor off. They were a rather large group of people—well armed and prepared, to boot.

The man with the missile launcher stared at Kaden evenly. "Next."

"No."

"Do it." He prodded Wayland with his foot.

Kaden took a deep breath. He could do it, move fast enough to stop him before he pulled the trigger, but if he was even a second slow, Wayland would lose her head, and he wasn't that selfish. He could feel the acceptance build up inside him, the need to—

"When I take off my armor, you have to shoot me in the head," he said as he sat down. The man looked at him, puzzled for a second, then snorted, and Kaden inhaled, wishing he had a whiff of that gas to help him settle his nerves.

The missile-wielding maniac probably thought Kaden was some fanatic who believed armor was life. In this case he was correct, but it still didn't make it better. Kaden folded back his gloves, unlatched them at the wrist, and put them on the floor, next to the chest plate. Then the vambraces—forearm pieces that housed the compatibility gauge and other indicators. Each piece folded back and separated, segment by segment.

Bradley's muted gasp drifted over as Kaden folded down his left boot, then his right, and set them next to the growing pile. He was happy he was sitting down because he couldn't have stood even if his life depended on it. His left leg ended three inches below his knee, and his right ended halfway down to his ankle. The underarmor encased his legs, the material folded neatly and pinned down because the stumps were still sensitive.

The doctors had tried to save his legs but not at the right time. There were reasons, though they were not important, like lack of manpower and Kaden being low on the list of people needing to be treated.

He pushed the armor away. "Let the girls go, but you have to kill me."

The man looked at him without speaking, and Kaden saw something akin to pity in that face. "Instructor Pace... Kaden." Bradley's voice sounded strangled. "Don't—"

Kaden didn't look at her. "Bradley, shut up. Take your sister and go."

The other men had brought a small cart with them and were hastily piling the armor onto it. All four suits.

Kaden could see the remains of metal bars and a few wires poking from the corner of the cart. So this was a scavenger team, who'd struck gold in the form of four armored suits, three of them original models. He closed his eyes and sighed as the men started to retreat. Watching his armor moved away felt as if something was tearing his body to pieces, pulling his hairs out one by one. He could feel it like the physical detachment of a limb, an amputation without anesthesia.

*No!* Kaden thought as the man with the missile launcher turned to the woman with the guns and nodded. She would be the one to kill him. He needed to die—he couldn't survive as a cripple. He would rather die.

He braced himself for the bullet and looked up, eyes forward. Bradley swallowed, looking from Kaden to Wayland, her face drawn.

"Don't shoot him," Bradley begged. "Please Instructor... *Kaden*, you need to—"

The boom that reverberated surprised them all, and Kaden looked down, expecting to see his underarmor oozing red. But he was unhurt, alive.

The woman holding the gun was staring at something behind Kaden with a scowl.

Kaden looked over his shoulder to where the shot had come from and gasped. Shun was standing, gun in hand.

"You got the armor, there's no need to kill him," Shun stated.

The leader, the man with the launcher, hesitated as he looked at the group. "I don't want anyone following us."

"They won't," Shun assured them. "Wayland is hurt and... no one's coming after you."

"Wait." Kaden rose to his knees and crawled toward the man with the missile launcher. "You promised to kill me." It was important he died; he needed to die. The underarmor suit snagged on protrusions from the floor, tearing into his skin—his knees, his palms—but he didn't care. All he cared about was the need to die. He couldn't go back without his armor, and he couldn't live like that either, a secret, a cripple. It wasn't possible. Without the armor Kaden was as good as dead.

The woman stopped and turned around, a speculative look on her face.

Shun spoke, his voice low and gravelly. "Don't kill anyone. You got their gear."

"Why not?" Kaden yelled. His throat felt blocked, perhaps a leftover effect of the gas. "You were going to blow off her head not five minutes ago!"

Bradley stopped him, stepping between Kaden and the woman. "Take the armor. We're not going anywhere."

"Move," Kaden grunted to her, trying to push her aside.

"Instructor Pace, I need you to calm down." Bradley sounded as if she was crying, but Kaden didn't look up. "My sister is hurt, but I can only check on her if you stop trying to get yourself killed."

"Move, dammit," Kaden snarled again. "Go play with your sister."

"I have people," the leader told Bradley, ignoring Kaden. "They tell me there's no military personnel anywhere near the town."

Bradley, the traitor, didn't bother to lie. "Then you have time to get away before we come after you."

"Give me the device you used to track us," the leader demanded. "We'll keep moving."

"We should make sure they can never come after us," the woman spoke.

Bradley talked over Kaden's head. "I'm the only one who can come after you right now. My sister is hurt. Kaden...."

*Won't be taking a step.* Kaden completed the sentence in his head, then aloud. "I won't be coming after you unarmed."

The woman didn't seem convinced. "But you—"

"They'll come after you some time or another." Shun, the other traitor—or was it someone else? Kaden was losing track—joined the conversation. "You have their armor. You've never killed needlessly before. There's no need for bloodshed here. You can't kill one and walk away. You'd have to kill all of them... all of us. And she's a child."

The leader nodded and retreated one step at a time, and Kaden watched his last chance at escape slide away. "Please, you promised...."

Bradley turned around. "Fine. I don't have time for this."

As she came closer, blocking Kaden's view of the retreating armors, Shun walked around to speak to the leader. He supposed it was important. Did Shun know these people? Had he drawn them into a trap when they'd gone after him? He should have realized it was a trap. He should be dead.

"I should be dead," he told Bradley, trying to convince her to see things his way.

Bradley stood over him, very close. "I'm... going to do something about it."

Good, thought Kaden as he started to move, when she turned around. The low kick knocked him back hard, and the punch stunned him so much he felt his eyes flutter shut.

"You aren't thinking clearly," Bradley told him, and she punched him again. "I don't have time for this, so stay still."

The blackness that engulfed him was absolute.

# CHAPTER 7

*THERE WAS the time he helped a stranger....*

Shun couldn't believe it. He blinked, sure it was some optical illusion that had him seeing the black-armored warrior—Kaden, his name was Kaden. But Shun had only met (flirted with) him on the train, and that felt like a lifetime ago as he saw Kaden lying there, unconscious, his legs stopping below the knee.

He skirted the older girl, Bradley, moving toward Allen, who was putting aside his missile launcher so he could help Jane drag the cart with the armors. He stepped up to Allen and spoke in an extremely low voice. "Where's Roy?"

Allen didn't look impressed by Shun's style of questioning. "He's with us."

"What does that mean? Is he hurt or—?" Why had Roy not come to the meeting place, and why had Allen come with missile launchers, prepared?

"He's fine." Allen gave away nothing.

"You aren't going to kill them now, are you?" Shun knew the easiest thing to do was to kill them all.

Allen gave him a thoughtful look. "You have your principles and I have mine. I don't see much point in needless killing—" He hesitated a little. "—and my experts tell me that armors don't work if the wearer is killed."

Shun frowned. He hadn't heard that before. He knew it was the opposite, in fact, but held his tongue. Voicing his doubts might earn everyone, including himself, a bullet to the brain.

Allen must have seen his expression because he smiled with little humor. "It wasn't like that in my time in the Army. He tells me it's a new thing they came up with to stop the armor from falling into the wrong hands if someone dies during battle." He stepped closer until he was speaking directly into Shun's ear. "I don't know whether to believe him or not, but that's my official standpoint. That way, I don't have to put any of you down and the armors stay with me."

Shun tried hard not to flinch as Allen invaded his personal space. "Why?"

"Like I said, why would I kill my people needlessly? And anyway, if what Roy says is false, at least it will keep someone in my group from getting the idea to sell that suit to the Harians." When Shun swung his head up, Allen smirked. "I might have my ideals, but I'm not stupid enough to think everyone in my group abides by them."

Shun supposed he had to buy that as reassurance that no one would be killed. "Will Roy be leaving with you?"

"We got your armor, thank you," Jane told him in a cold voice that promised him she'd shoot him in the guts if he interfered, and he stepped back, letting them go, his mouth dry.

He had to figure out what had happened to Roy. Roy was the closest thing he had to a friend, to whom he'd confided his plans to steal the armor. Roy had understood Shun's need for closure and had been the one who'd come up with the tracker inside the birthday card. Shun didn't have the knowledge for that. For a moment he contemplated simply turning around and moving away.

The younger girl who'd fallen from the roof was alive, and the older girl seemed to have a good right uppercut. Captain Allen had taken everything of value and left. Shun had nothing to do with the military group, and he was outnumbered three to one—well, two and a half to one.

He needed to know for sure if the black-armored warrior's legs were hidden under him, perhaps folded beneath his body somehow, though he couldn't figure out how that would work. Shun moved forward slowly while Bradley was preoccupied with her younger sister. He approached the fallen man—Kaden—and reached out to touch where his legs ended. It was one of the most horrific things he'd seen, not because it was terrible, but because it was so ordinary.

He had seen people maimed by land mines. No one spoke of it, but at the border both sides had taken to burying land mines to prevent people from crossing, and sometimes people, mostly kids scavenging for scraps, would step on one and get blown up. Shun had been one of those scavenger kids, growing up, learning the tricks to avoid mines, throwing stones and then walking on them. He'd seen people with their feet blown off, their legs, their lower bodies decimated, but still alive and coherent enough to talk. He wouldn't wish that on anyone.

But what made the sight he was currently seeing so terrible was just how unexpected it had been. He'd sat next to the good-looking black-armored warrior on the train and had entertained thoughts about what might be hidden under all that hardware—he had not been thinking of the lack of legs.

*Well, not technically legs*, thought Shun as he traced the left leg, which ended just below the knee, and the right that ended a little lower down. He traced the underarmor suit, trying to figure out if it was somehow creating the effect, because he wasn't ready to accept that the man, who'd been moving around so fast that he seemed to blur when he ran, was footless.

Kaden was lying on his back, eyes closed, breathing, and Shun frowned. Surely no matter how hard Bradley had punched him, it wouldn't be enough to knock him out for this long. He reached for the pulse point, carefully, when—

"Step the fuck away from him," Bradley snarled.

Shun looked up, gripping the gun tightly, knowing he wouldn't be using it even if he were to point it her way. He respected her as a fighter although he didn't know her all that well. Perhaps she was the type to attack first and ask questions later—the Army seemed to like that mentality in their people. Still, she had tried to reason with Allen and had kept her head.

"Did you know he didn't have legs… well, feet?"

The question stopped her for a moment, but then she strode forward, pushing aside Shun and his gun as she knelt beside Kaden. She reached with surprisingly gentle hands and turned Kaden until he was lying on his side, and she felt his pulse the way Shun had intended to do. Kaden's face appeared pale despite his dark skin, his black hair framing his face making him appear even paler, and Shun admitted the man looked good, even with the start of an enormous bruise on his left cheek.

He also looked surprisingly young for an armored warrior veteran. The dark skin and the armor probably protected him from the sun and exposure to the elements. It had been the eyes that had looked old, old and tired.

"I didn't hit him that hard," Bradley muttered in frustration as she patted Kaden's cheek gently. "Wake up, Kaden. Instructor Kaden, we need you."

"He did inhale a lot of gas, more than you did." Shun got back to his feet, pushing the safety on as he stuck the gun in the back of his trousers. He'd have to get rid of it later—he had little liking for guns, and having one with him would simply tempt him to use it, perhaps to save himself, as he had behaved with the armor. He hadn't even intended to put that suit on, but once he'd done so, it seemed stupid not to try to get away.

Shun brushed the dirt off his clothes and backed up a little. There wasn't anything else he needed to do. The armor he had taken the time to steal, and had tried to destroy, was gone, and he could see the stupidity of trying to get it back. What worried him was that Roy hadn't shown up as promised. Roy, who was supposed to help him destroy the armor.

He would try to track it later; he knew the person who'd taken it. Captain Allen was a former soldier, retired due to injury, who was very good at rallying the people. Shun did not work with Allen or for him. He preferred to work on his own, checking in only when he needed help. But he'd worked with Roy before, and Shun considered him a good friend. With Roy's radical ideas and pacifist way of life, it was hard to imagine he would ever join Allen's crew willingly. But from what Allen had implied, Roy was with him. Shun would have to rescue him.

"What are you going to do now?" Bradley asked as she knelt beside Kaden. She didn't look at Shun, but she was obviously talking to him.

"I'm… going now."

"Where?"

"I—" At that moment, he didn't know.

"You seemed rather friendly with those people."

Shun didn't like how accusatory Bradley sounded. "I know of them. I don't work with them. In case you forgot, they also took my armor."

"Are you going after the armor?"

Shun hesitated. "I really don't know." He didn't know how, where, or what to do next. It had been so easy: go after the armor, get it, destroy it, and call it even. He needed to think, regroup his mental processes. "My friend, Roy, he was supposed to meet me here. I was waiting for him. Something might have happened to him. I need to go look for him." He turned away from her.

"You can't just walk away from this. You started it. Those people took our armor because of you."

He heard the sound of Bradley getting up, and he turned around quickly, just in time to sidestep her.

"Don't hit me." He didn't think he could walk away from a punch like the one she'd thrown at Kaden. "It's not my fault. In fact, it's your fault for coming where you shouldn't have. Aren't you supposed to stay out of this area, anyway?"

One reason he'd returned to Compen Beach Town to destroy the armor was the lack of military presence in the vicinity. He hadn't counted on armored warriors following him that quickly. When Roy and he had cooked up the plan, Roy had assured him the Army would have to get permission from WUC to enter the beach town, and that would give the group enough time to get rid of the stolen goods.

"Our armors are in enemy hands," Bradley shouted at him. "That hasn't happened before, we've never lost four armors all at once—ever, and now we're going to lose the armor to someone who might sell it over the border."

"Don't be ridiculous—" Shun started to say and broke off as he realized that perhaps what she was saying was true. "Well, it might be for the best. It might even up the power balance."

"You're saying that as if we're winning the war." A new voice joined in, surprising both Shun and Bradley. "We're not the bad guys."

Wayland look at them, her gaze clear. Bradley rolled her eyes, shoulders sagging, though her voice didn't betray any of her feelings. "I see you're awake."

"I think I broke my arm." Wayland moaned, struggling to sit up. "Ow."

"That tends to happen when you fall off the roof," Bradley said none too gently, and Shun decided that the two sisters weren't emotionally expressive. "Anyway, what Way is trying to say is, who knows if getting armor on the other side is going to stop the war?"

Shun considered it. People on both sides of the border were human, with human weaknesses, and really, the armor might not cause so much of a power balance as an inequality. And in the end, he didn't think he was ready to be the person to betray the country he'd grown up in since he was about nine years old. "I don't think they'll give the armor to the enemy. They're not—"

"Even for money?"

Shun thought it over. "You want me to get it back?"

"No." Bradley shook her head. "I want you to help me with Instructor Kaden so I can go after the armor."

"What's in it for me?" The question was second nature to Shun, who'd learned at a young age that nothing came for free and he might as well trade up every time someone asked for a favor. He wondered if she had anything to trade.... Anyway, a part of him knew he was already going to help them. It was not in his nature to let anyone die needlessly. Chances were that these three might die in Compen Beach Town if he left them there. There were other scavengers about, and the three were defenseless, easy prey. Helping them go after the armor went against his belief in nonviolence—unless he had no other choice.

Bradley became quiet as she thought it over for a couple of seconds, then nodded. "What do you need the armor for?"

"It's mine. My father's, actually, and you already know no one else in his family wants it."

All those years of planning to obtain a hunk of metal, and he'd lost it after having it in his possession for a couple of hours—less than a day. He wanted to get it back, but a part of him was disappointed. He'd wanted that armor for revenge—revenge for his mother because she had talked of the green armor with hatred in her eyes, of how it had stood over her while she lay paralyzed. She'd never mentioned the person inside of it. For her, the hatred had been for what she could see on the outside.

But after having gotten ahold of it, Shun realized his revenge was hollow. The man responsible for the crimes was dead, and the armor, for all its worth, was just a lifeless piece of metal.

"Do you want it back?" Bradley asked.

Shun thought for a second; he did want it back. He had tracked that armor for years, finding out about the person who had worn it the hard way, and then, devising a way to track the person to his home, because he had wanted to confront him while he was not wearing the armor. "What are you offering—you can't seriously be giving the armor back to me?"

"Well, if you were going to give it to the enemy, you could have just crossed the border at any time, so I don't think you'll do it now."

"No, I wasn't going to." It hadn't occurred to him at all, though he was technically a Harian by birth.

"Fine, then. If you want the armor, we'll come to some agreement. You can have it in exchange for helping us."

"You're really going to let me walk away with that armor?" Shun wondered if she'd shoot him in the back of the head after he'd helped them.

"If you disappear with yours, I won't say anything," Bradley assured with easy confidence. "You'll have at most a week with it before the Army tracks you down with the tracker. What I meant was, you can walk away with it."

Shun could believe that.

He had wasted so much time trying to find MacCrave. And to think he'd wandered away from his starting place, when the man he'd been searching for had been living close to the town he'd first crawled into through the stupid barbed wire.

It had been before the hundred-foot fence had gone up, before the electric fence was powered, while everything had been under construction. A soldier had actually seen him when he'd emerged from the other side, but she'd turned around and walked on, pretending not to see him instead of reporting him, and Shun had been in the country, just like that.

"You could also join the Army," Bradley offered after a couple of seconds.

She must have thought his silence meant he'd rejected the deal.

"Papers get lost all the time, what with the air bombing and all," she added quickly. "And… and my family has influence. I can use it to move you inland to where there's no fighting. You won't have to face a Harian drone or any soldiers or kill anyone. You can be a bodyguard to some rich minister who wants an armored warrior in his escort party. We can get Instructor Kaden to vouch for you."

"Why in the world would he want to do that?"

"Because otherwise you could tell command he doesn't have legs, and they'll take his armor away from him."

"I didn't know it was a secret."

Bradley rolled her eyes in reply. "Yes, because Instructor Vorani just forgot to tell us that Instructor Kaden doesn't have his lower legs. *Please*. If it wasn't a secret, the whole camp would have known. You saw the way he acted. There was no way *anyone* knew about it. And you can ask him if you want, when he wakes up."

Shun couldn't see much wrong with that argument.

Bradley added, "He did save your life on the train. You owe him that much."

Shun couldn't argue with that logic. Should Allen do a second round and find them within the city, chances are he might shoot them anyway. He, unlike Shun, had been known to kill people. "How do you intend to get the armor back. Call for help?"

"And be on record as the first squad to lose a total of four armors in one day?" Bradley scoffed. "I don't have any way of calling for help. The plan was for us to carry it back to the road and wait for pickup. We had three days before the vehicle that dropped us came back. Is there anywhere we can regroup? My sister can—can track the armor and I can.... I can—" She took a deep breath, collecting herself. "When Instructor Kaden wakes up, he'll be able to help."

"Really?" Shun didn't even bother to hide the skepticism lacing his voice. From what he'd seen, Kaden hadn't looked all there. "Well, anyway, I know a place where we can at least be safe for the time being."

She looked around the barn one last time. "Let me grab the electric net."

Leaving Bradley to retrieve it, Shun walked over to Kaden, who was lying still, and bent down to try and lift him. He grunted with surprise when he realized just how heavy the man was for someone only in their underarmor.

"Help Wayland. I'll take him." Bradley stepped forward and picked up Kaden with surprising ease. Shun felt grateful he'd not been hit by one of her punches—it would have felt like being hit with a tank-piercing round.


KADEN HEARD the rain hit the roof even before he opened his eyes. He stayed still, flat on his back, taking in the new sensations. He was on a bed; he could feel the pain in his jaw, the coldness of the air moving, and the sound of someone breathing next to him.

Kaden didn't want to open his eyes. He could remember everything that had happened so clearly that he was tempted to just lie there forever. *Perhaps it's a dream*, he thought as he mentally called for his armor. He would be aware of it if it was within five meters of him, but all he could feel was darkness. The armor wasn't near him and certainly not on him, so he didn't want to get up. Instead, he felt the urge to keep his eyes closed and will himself back into nothingness, even if it was a short-term solution.

He was aware of the absurdity of his actions—he couldn't just lie there with his eyes closed indefinitely, and he *was* curious about where he was. He opened his eyes and found himself staring at a ceiling—a yellow ceiling with dark brown watermarks. Regardless of the stains, it appeared solid in the strange light, with strange shadows playing on it. He couldn't see much because the room was in semidarkness. He turned his head to the side and found himself looking at Shun, who was staring at him steadily, the bruise on his face appearing as spectacular as the one Kaden felt forming on his own. Next to Shun was the room's only light source, floating in a bowl. From where Kaden was lying, he couldn't make out what it was, but it produced enough light to keep them from being plunged into total darkness.

"I'll explain to you what is happening so there won't be any confusion." Shun spoke in a steady voice. "We're at my place. It's night." As if the lack of light hadn't explained it. "And the girls are in the other room." He sat back and seemed to consider what to say next. "We have an understanding, and… I couldn't exactly leave you the way you were."

"I'm in your room," repeated Kaden, sitting up in stages and ignoring the last sentence. He was, as he'd suspected, naked, and he automatically pulled away the sheet and looked at his legs. The stumps were as he remembered, the damaged, pulled flesh gleaming where the candlelight caught the scars. The skin on his legs was pale compared to the rest of him, as if they weren't a part of him at all. He looked away with a muted curse.

"Bradley will be coming in soon," Shun told him as if to deter him from moving. "If you're suicidal, she'll knock you out and tie you up."

"I'm not going to kill myself." Kaden didn't want to meet Shun's eyes and see the disgust there. He played with the bedspread, pulling it up to cover the ends of his legs. "I had all the chances I wanted when I was in the barracks. I'm just too cowardly to kill myself."

"I'm not going to argue with you on what your idea of cowardly is," Shun said, getting up and walking to him. He pulled out the corner of the sheet and pushed it over Kaden, covering him so it would look decent.

Kaden looked at Shun with a raised eyebrow. He had hidden the state of his legs because he'd been afraid that his armor would be taken away from him, but he wasn't body shy. He was in the Army, and he'd bathed in mixed showers before he'd been promoted to his own room with an attached bathroom.

Shun blushed and looked away. "Bradley is coming soon," he repeated and then shrugged.

Kaden realized he'd forgotten something important about his team. "How's Wayland?"

"Concussion, dislocated elbow, probably a broken finger or two, and a couple of bruised ribs, but she'll live," said Bradley, coming into the room carrying a couple of mismatched bowls balanced on a tray.

The bowls were steaming and smelled so wonderful that Kaden sat up straighter and held out a hand. Bradley was dressed in a large shirt that exposed a lot of scarred leg, and Kaden assumed she was wearing Shun's clothes. He couldn't remember any of them packing a change of clothing.

"You should be hungry. You've been sleeping the whole day," Bradley said as she handed over a bowl. "I didn't hit you that hard." She stared at him a long time, as if to make sure he was not going to swallow his tongue, and Kaden desperately tried to think of something to say.

Luckily for him there was the shuffle of footsteps and Wayland appeared at the doorway, looking beat up—her face one large bruise, her left hand in a sling—but alive and mobile. She walked over to join them with only a hint of a limp. She was also dressed in a shirt that reached midthigh, and Kaden had the idea Shun probably didn't have many clothes to give out in the first place, which was probably why Kaden only had a bedsheet to cover himself.

Wayland perched on the corner of the bed with ease, and Kaden felt glad that Shun had covered him up. Being open-minded was one thing; flashing female cadets was another.

Once the food was distributed, Kaden started to eat, at a loss for anything else to say or do. The first spoonful of broth—well, it was thicker than soup but not quite stew—turned out to be surprisingly good, and he swallowed quickly even though it scorched the roof of his mouth. He looked up at Bradley in surprise. "This is great."

"I didn't cook it. I simply served it into the bowls."

Kaden felt as if someone had turned on a lightbulb in his head. He turned to Shun and attempted a smile, though his cheek protested at the movement. "As good as your sandwiches. You seem to have a talent for cooking."

Shun didn't acknowledge the compliment, simply ducked his head and started to eat. There was an awkward silence as they all ate, and though the food was delicious, Kaden found it hard to swallow around the lump in his throat.

"So, are we your prisoners?" he asked Shun, unable to keep quiet.

"Hardly." Shun shrugged. "I felt partly responsible for your situation, so I invited you to my place. You can stay the night, but I expect you'll be leaving in the morning."

It wasn't a straight-out order, and Kaden felt they could stay should they choose. He couldn't hear anything apart from the rain. No people, no cars. "Where exactly is your place?"

"A small house in Compen Beach Town." Shun grinned. "It wasn't as if anyone was using it."

Kaden turned to Bradley and tried to read the expression on her face, but it remained blank, making him feel uneasy, as if he was missing something. "What's our situation?"

"Well, apart from the loss of our armor, we also lost all our gear. It wasn't where we hid it when I went back, so the chances are those people or someone else took it."

"For the record, no, I didn't take it." Shun sounded insulted. "I didn't have the time, and you saw what I carried back with me when I led you here."

Kaden felt his heart sink at the thought of that. "So, no way of tracking the armor?"

"None." Bradley destroyed any lingering hope with one word. "We are out of food and gear, we're in semihostile territory, and Wayland can't move fast."

She didn't need to mention that Kaden couldn't be moved at all—at least, not easily. Which raised another question. "How did I get here?"

"I carried you," Bradley said. "He helped Wayland." She indicated Shun with her head. "We were lucky no one saw us. I swear, if you pull another stunt like that, I'll shoot your elbows and leave you to rot." The anger was justifiable, and it seemed she held her control by a very thin line.

Kaden didn't know what to say beyond "I'm sorry."

The silence took over again as they continued, or pretended, to eat.

"I don't get it," Wayland said softly. "What happened to your legs?"

"What do you think?" Kaden snapped at her and then immediately felt like a heel. He took a deep breath and leaned against the wall, keeping the bowl on his lap. "They were amputated." That was all too simple. "When the building collapsed on my legs and trapped me, the armor failed to come around my legs completely and my legs got crushed. By the time they dug me out, the armor had healed around my legs—not much, but it was there to hold them steady. They took me to the hospital and...." It was hard to explain the situation to Wayland.

"Couldn't they be saved?" Wayland asked in a small voice. "I thought the military hospitals had the best facilities."

"But never enough people," he told her. Time and the fact he was practically staring at his injuries helped him deal with the anger he felt at her unthinking statement. "We had been fighting for almost two months, nonstop, and the fighting only stopped three days after I got injured. They were bringing in those who were hurt and dying every second. The corridors were lined with people. There were people out in the waiting rooms and along the road leading to the damn hospital." The only reason Kaden had even made it inside had been because he wore armor. "The hospital was overflowing," he said lamely. "The procedure was to treat those who were injured the least first so they can return to the field and fight."

Wayland looked up in surprise. "But—" Then she seemed to change her mind.

"It was obvious my legs were broken. I couldn't have returned to the field even if I wanted to, so I was not a priority for treatment. The armor fixes most things, but it doesn't heal the wearer, and by the time it was my turn, my legs were beyond saving."

Ironically, held together by the armor, his bones had started to heal, but the rot had set in to his flesh, turning his toes black, and the infection that followed....

"The kindest thing the doctors could have done was amputate them both at once, so I wouldn't have to go through it twice." But they hadn't even been able to do that. Two different surgeries, losing parts of himself, slowly.

Wayland wasn't ready to drop the matter. "How come no one knows about it?"

"Dr. Lane did write, but documents get lost all the time," he answered with feigned casualness. In fact, Dr. Lane had misfiled the documents—a common enough occurrence during emergency situations that no one had thought twice about it, and no one had caught it. "And I walked back to camp under my own power. What else was there to say?"

The second set of documents Dr. Lane forwarded were carefully altered to leave out his injury. They were still on the way, rerouted through a distant outpost in Gilaw.

What no one knew was that Dr. Lane and Kaden had grown up in the same orphanage.

"So the armor was the only thing helping you walk?" Bradley inquired.

"It was either that or disability, and I didn't feel like it," he said looking at his bowl, which was empty. Huh, had he eaten all that? "You saw that guy at the post in Koresa. The prosthetics leave a lot to be desired."

Anyway, there were no armored warriors with prosthetics. All the other armors required the wearer to have all four limbs. As far as Kaden knew, his suit was the only one that acted the way it did, compensating for missing parts.

"Let me get refills." Bradley got to her feet. She took the bowl from Kaden without asking, then collected the rest and walked out.

"She's not angry with you," Wayland said the moment Bradley had left the room. "I know angry. She's always pissed off at me." She grinned.

"She has reasons to be angry with me," Kaden said as he felt his eyes close.

Wayland poked his side with a finger. "She was worried about you."

Kaden looked at his hands and wished he still had a bowl, so he would have something to do with them.

"She was so pleased when Instructor Vorani assigned you as our supervisor," Wayland told him, making him feel even worse about the situation they were in. "She thought you were great. The way you took over the training course was so awesome. She was talking about it the entire—"

"She carried me here. She must be very strong," Kaden said.

"She's always been strong." Wayland looked proud. "She walks around in full armor."

They all kept quiet as Bradley walked back with full bowls on the tray.

Kaden took his, surprised to find he could still eat. "So"—he turned to Shun—"there was no aunt running a restaurant. You were just waiting for someone with the transmitter on them to get on the train."

"I was waiting for a military mail delivery," Shun told him. "They always use the train. Free rides for military needs."

Bradley seemed to comprehend the problem. "You didn't know MacCrave was dead."

"I didn't," Shun agreed. "I just wanted to live my own life, told myself I wasn't into revenge. Didn't want to find the guy who raped my mother, and after all those years, I was ready to let it go. First I got a letter from the family friend who'd pushed me over the fence from the Harian side. He said Mother was dead. Then the peace talks were announced, and I knew I had to find my father before the war ended. I wanted to confront him about what he did. It seemed so lame that he was going to be hailed a hero and made to retire with benefits after all he'd done."

"But then you found out he was dead and you had to change plans," Kaden continued for him.

"It was all so easy. I colored my hair black and walked into the armored unit at Koresa. I wasn't even sure the armor was going to fit me—er, be compatible with me, and when it fit, well, you know what it did. I panicked and ran. Then when I came here, I thought what the hell. I was going to destroy it. No one was going to use it to gas people or force them to do things."

"In a barn?" Bradley asked in disbelief.

"On the way I contacted my friend Roy, who's interested in armors. We're both from around here, and it was a convenient spot. He told me to find an out-of-the-way place with cover, and the barn was it."

"Seems like a stupid place," Wayland muttered under her breath.

"Well, I certainly couldn't do it here in my home," Shun deadpanned. "Didn't want to risk bringing down a wall. I was waiting for Roy, and well, you know what happened."

"We have to get them back," Bradley stated. "Do you know where those people could have taken them?"

"Yes and no," Shun replied. "I know of them. Captain Allen is former military. I heard he was asked to retire after he got injured, and when he left, he took with him some of his loyal followers."

"And hardware as well?" Kaden asked dryly. "I can understand some of our guns appear on the black market, but it's harder to imagine our armor-piercing missiles ending up there."

"Why would we have something that would hurt our troops?" Wayland didn't know much about the way the armed forces operated.

Bradley did. "Those missiles are really good against Harian drones from what I hear."

Kaden was reminded that neither Bradley nor Wayland had seen actual combat. He frowned as he thought it over. "But how could Allen have gotten hold of them?"

"The word on the outside is he still has contacts with the suppliers," Shun told him reluctantly. "He's still loyal to Joscal. Probably why he didn't kill you—saw you as fellow soldiers."

"So if we find him and ask for the armors, he'll give them back to us?" Bradley pulled out a chair and fell into it.

"Why would he need the armor? He can't use the originals, at least not while they are linked to us." Kaden wasn't sure anyone in the group knew the answer.

"He might not know that," Shun said after a thoughtful pause. "I didn't know that two people couldn't wear the original armor at the same time. Perhaps he was in the branch of the military that's never heard of that."

Kaden didn't buy that information. "Most Army captains know that stuff."

"He didn't shoot any of us. What else could it be?"

Kaden could see the logic in that reasoning. He nodded and moved on to his next question. "What does he do? How does he feed and arm his people?"

"I hear he gets international contracts from rich people to do stuff," Shun said in a small voice, sounding pained. "Perhaps he thought the armors could be of use to him."

Kaden could see that happening. "Some patriot."

"At least he doesn't commit much violence within the country, from what I know," Shun told him.

Bradley snorted. "The man threatened to blow off Way's head and agreed to shoot Instructor Kaden."

The ensuing awkward silence was finally broken by Kaden clearing his throat. "We need to get the armor back."

Wayland sighed. "I suppose we walk around looking for it. How large can this town be?"

"That's not going to help." Bradley dismissed her out of hand. "You haven't seen the aerial photos. This place is huge—where do we start? They might not even be in Compen Beach Town."

Kaden thought it over. "The chances are, if they have the armor, they'll try to see whether they're compatible with it. I mean, most people would be tempted."

"The modified armor will fit anyone about the right build," Bradley said in frustration. "There could already be someone walking around in my armor."

"Not mine or Wayland's or… Shun's," Kaden told her instead of snapping at her for missing the obvious.

He tried to close his eyes and see if he could feel his armor. There had been days when he'd felt it in the room like another presence, and he'd read stories of people bonding with their armor to the point it had come flying at the mental command of the wearer. But it wasn't to be. He could feel the panic building up in the background and squashed it down forcefully, thinking hard. "You mentioned a friend—Roy? Who is he?"

"He's really good with armor. He's as close to an expert as I've ever come across without being military."

"A very good friend of yours?"

"I contacted him through an armor fan group when I was searching for a way to track MacCrave's suit," Shun admitted, looking a little guilty. "He's intelligent but has some odd theories about armor and…."

"What?" Kaden asked when it became obvious Shun wasn't going to continue.

"He would have liked to study one," Shun concluded in a small voice.

"Well, those people came equipped to take down armors," Bradley said, quick on the uptake. "Your friend must have sent Captain Allen and his goons."

Shun was quick to answer. "Roy would never do that, and Allen doesn't take orders from people. He does what he wants. If anything, Roy's a prisoner."

"We could start from where Roy used to stay," Kaden said finally. "I assume he's a resident of Compen Beach Town?"

"He and his girlfriend live to the northeast in one of the high-rise buildings—used to be the bank, I think." Shun looked out the window, which Kaden could see was heavily barred. Noticing Kaden's glance,

Shun smiled. "Don't take it personally. The family who used to live here was high on security."

"I suppose I'll take a look when it's light. I don't feel like stumbling around in the dark, in the rain," Bradley observed. "But that's still a lot of places to look if the armor isn't there."

"Especially since the beach is that way," Shun said dryly. "And hence the sea."

Kaden became aware of another sound muffled by the patter of the rain: the steady break of the waves beating against the shore. They were close to the beach. He might even be able to see it in the morning.

"What happened to them?" Wayland asked in a small voice, throwing them all off topic. "The family who was living here."

"They evacuated after the bomb blasted the island," Shun told her. "There were a couple of salvage operations to the island to pick up the pieces, but no one ever came back to the town after that. I guess a few people must have come back to take their valuables and all, but not to settle down and reclaim their homes. But they obviously expected to come back, because when I came here, there was a key under the carpet and the house was fully furnished. I simply moved in, did a few repairs, and took over the place. No one else wants this, too open, too close to the edge, but I like it that way. And there's enough houses for the other misfits to go around, so why fight over this one?"

"Where do you get the food?" Kaden asked as he put down his empty bowl. He was full and starting to feel sleepy again.

"I hunt. There are rabbits and a few other animals living here. Some homeowners grew vegetables. This family had a plot, overgrown, but I cleared it up a little. I make trips outside now and then, collect tinned food and stuff for odd jobs. Stock up on things I can't make, like clothes, shoes, and wet wipes." At their blank looks, he shrugged. "There isn't much of a water supply here. It beats toilet paper and stuff."

"I think we should go to sleep now," Bradley said when Wayland bit back a yawn. She looked at Shun and nodded. "I lit the fire like you asked. It's a nice idea."

"It's a luxury," Shun told her with a crooked smile. "You're lucky it rained."

"Your turn next," said Bradley, taking Kaden's bowl from his lax fingers. "I actually soaked our underarmor and put it up to dry, which is the last time I do anything like that. Appreciate the trouble I took."

Kaden felt a wave of gratitude at the gesture. "Thank you." Since the underarmor was waterproof, it didn't absorb sweat either, and that tended to collect inside.

Bradley gave Shun a pointed look. "We're going to sleep."

It was then that Kaden realized the enormity of what had happened. He was going to be left alone with someone he'd just met, with no way of moving, completely dependent on someone else for all his needs. He could feel panic building up in his chest in a crushing weight, and he had to take a deep breath to collect himself.

It didn't help that once the other two had shuffled out, Shun turned to him and smiled, completely oblivious to Kaden's internal turmoil. "Time for your bath."

# CHAPTER 8

SHUN HAD an outhouse, roughly built, leaning against the outer wall of the house. Kaden supposed it had once been a garage, which Shun had transformed by dividing it into two sections.

"Damn, you're heavy—Bradley must be strong," he told Kaden after seating him on the small ledge at the side.

"She is," said Kaden, grateful Shun hadn't tried to ignore the fact he was crippled—ah, he supposed he had to refer to himself in the politically correct term, physically disabled, injured on duty, whatever. If Shun had ignored it completely, it would have been awkward for both of them, but speaking aloud about it helped, strangely.

The toilet was a hole in the ground with a screen around it. "It empties off to the drain down the side," Shun said pointing it out to Kaden. "What can I say? I don't like shitting in empty houses like some people do, and indoor plumbing doesn't work around here. And there's only me, all the time. Today's an exception." He looked to his left. "I'll leave you to it. Do you need any help?"

Kaden removed the bedsheet he'd wrapped himself in while he was being carried across from the house and gave it to Shun. "There, it'll just get wet." Then he dropped off the ledge and got to his knees. He waited a couple of seconds until Shun had moved away.

At least now Kaden was able to breathe out cautiously. There was nothing to do but proceed; he could see little point of trying to drown himself in the toilet bowl.

Kaden closed his eyes tightly for a second and wished the humiliation was easier to bear, but he'd survived worse at the hospital before the doctors had allowed him access to his armor. He had exceptional upper-arm strength, though Bradley had proved to be stronger than she'd looked, despite being slighter built than him.

"Are we using the same water the cadets used?" He wasn't too keen on that idea.

"Nope, I emptied the tub and refilled it."

"Why waste water when you have so little of it?" he asked to distract himself.

In reply, Shun pointed to a separate water tank on the top of the house. "That catches rainwater for drinking. There'll be a couple more rains this month, and I'll have enough to last me some time. Plus, I don't have that many things I can store water in."

The toilet area was illuminated by a small paraffin lamp that Shun had brought out before carrying Kaden out, and in the weak yellow light, the outhouse turned out to be crude but clean and dry—and stocked with wet wipes. While the toilet was just a hole in the ground, Shun had thoughtfully placed a couple of flat bricks on either side so he could sit on them and not the ground.

Shun called out, "Call me when you're done, then we can go ahead and check the water temperature."

Shun was referring to the bathtub in the next partition of the garage. Once the rain had started, Shun's bathtub had been placed directly under the hole in the tarp to collect the water. The bath was heated by lighting a fire under it, and an old rubber mat placed on the bottom prevented the user from burning their butt when they got in.

Kaden finished his business, used the wet wipes and a bucket of water Shun had left to flush the toilet, and pulled himself out toward the bath.

Shun was by his side in an instant. "I told you to call me when you were done," he grated as he struggled to pick up Kaden. Even without his lower legs, Kaden was heavy, and Shun staggered a little before abruptly placing him in the tub. "Shit, sorry, slipped."

The sides of the tub were hot, but the place where the rainwater fell remained cold, and Kaden gasped as his body experienced several different temperatures at the same time. He noticed the trickle of water from the hole in the trap and braced himself. "Rain is letting up. There won't be enough to fill this again. Why don't you get in as well?"

Shun looked away, head down. The paraffin lamp he'd brought flickered in the wind behind its glass cover, obscuring his face in shadows, but Kaden was sure Shun was blushing. "I'll bathe tomorrow."

"Well, you need to be clean if we're sharing the bed," said Kaden, his voice low. If there was a spare room, the cadets—how ironic was it that they were taking care of him?—were in it.

"I'll sleep on the floor."

"It's not that warm." Kaden motioned him closer. He could feel the rain, the darkness illuminated by flickering lamplight, and the entire surreal experience leaching away at his inhibitions. "Is it my legs you're uncomfortable with?"

"Cheap shot," said Shun with a wry grin. "It's not the legs." He leaned into the bath, bracing himself with both hands. "You know it's not the legs, and we both know this isn't just an invitation to share water together."

"Is it because I was trying to catch you half a day ago?"

"And you socked me so hard I have a few loose teeth?" Shun answered with a smile. "No, it isn't that. I really don't think we're on opposite sides right now. We both want to find the people who took the armor."

"Then sex with me shouldn't be too much of a moral dilemma for you." Kaden kept quiet for a moment, surprised by his own boldness. He'd hardly felt anything since he'd lost his legs. He might not have been body conscious, but having his legs amputated seemed to have also amputated his libido, and he'd not even masturbated in a while. The dead-eyed hookers outside the camp, fumbling at his penis, had been as personal as it got. The lust he'd felt for Shun on the train had been easy to dismiss, but now, here, trying to persuade Shun into the bath with him, he wondered about it.

Shun had looked at him on the train: then Kaden had been an armored warrior, but now, without his armor, he was... helpless, and he wanted to shift the balance of power. He supposed he should be angry with Shun for the situation they were in, but for the world, he couldn't blame him. It was all water under the bridge, and although perhaps he should spare a thought to the cadets and what would become of them, right then he didn't care.

He didn't have his feet; he was incomplete. He couldn't imagine a life beyond that. The girls were young and mobile and had an influential father. He was sure they would survive.

Kaden was too emotionally drained to care about anyone, even himself.

He didn't care that Shun was responsible for Kaden losing his armor, he didn't care that he should have planned better, that he should have... should have.... He just wanted to ground himself, feel alive and needed, and Shun offered a better chance than the hookers outside the camp ever did.

Kaden moved swiftly, wrapped a hand around Shun's wrist, and pulled hard. Unbalanced, Shun fell into the water headfirst with a curse, and Kaden tugged him until he was on top of him, tipping Shun's head and kissing him hard. Shun turned with a hand on Kaden's chest and braced himself by placing the other hand under Kaden's body—not that the tub offered much room.

Kaden rolled his eyes. "You're not that heavy," he said easily and pulled Shun down for another kiss.

As they kissed, he became aware of just how painfully out of practice they were. Their noses smashed against each other, their hands slipped, and when the cold water fell on Kaden's legs from above, he hissed in displeasure.

"This isn't the ideal setting," Shun said, breaking the kiss. But he didn't draw away, and from the looks of it, he wasn't averse to the idea of making out with Kaden, who supposed it was hard to come by people to have a quick tryst with in the shell of the beach town.

Kaden groped Shun, cursing when his hand slipped and his elbow touched hot metal. It really wasn't as romantic as it should be.

Shun gave a short laugh and sat up, braced against Kaden's chest. "Are you sure I'm not heavy?"

"I can lift you in full armor, trust me."

"Well, let's clean up and go back to my room. It's a lot more convenient than this."

Kaden nodded. "Is there soap?"

There was a sliver of soap, which Shun used on him, running his hands all over Kaden's body. Shun started with Kaden's chest, placing a kiss on the hard muscle there before soaping it. Next, he moved to Kaden's arms and ribs before leaning down and placing a kiss on his stomach. It wasn't overly erotic, but the act of having someone kissing his navel made the rest of him tingle. Kaden watched as his erection bobbed out of the water, just the tip, and he felt a flush of embarrassment.

But Shun was truly into the spirit of the moment, and he leaned in to kiss the tip of Kaden's penis and then drew back, continuing to soap Kaden's chest in small, steady circles. There was no washcloth; Shun would lather his hands and, after putting the soap away, run them over Kaden.

Shun hesitated when soaping below Kaden's waist, but then he plunged his hand under the water. Warm and slippery, the hand slid over

Kaden's already aroused penis and cupped his balls, then explored farther down. He washed Kaden efficiently and reached for the soap again.

Shun looked at Kaden, took a deep breath, and then let it out all at once. "I'm going to soap your legs," he said softly, and Kaden's erection withered at the mention. "I'm not going to touch the... end, I just wanted you to know."

Kaden nodded and braced himself. "It's better than the sponge baths I got from the nurses at the hospital." He tried to keep smiling while Shun started to soap his legs. After letting him soap his ass, it seemed stupid not to let him touch his legs, but as Shun reached his knees, Kaden realized he didn't want him to go farther down.

"Your turn," he said a little sharper than intended.

Shun complied without protest. He sat back on Kaden and pulled off his shirt, which he wrung out and put on the side of the tub. Next, he struggled with his trousers and pulled them off as well.

"How about the underwear?" Kaden asked with a leer, or as close to a leer as he could. He was still feeling a little shaky from having Shun almost touch the ends of his legs.

Shun shook his head, and Kaden assumed he was blushing again. "Let's leave something for later," Shun said and held out the small piece of soap. "Your turn."

Kaden cupped the minute piece of soap with slippery hands and started to lather up Shun in wide circles over his body. Shun maneuvered himself to face Kaden so he was straddling his lower torso, looking down at him. Shun's wet hair looked darker, framing his face and highlighting his cheekbones. Kaden's erection twitched in interest.

Shun was close to hairless, but his skin had not been treated like Kaden's, whose body hair was removed to make his armor fit easier. Shun was not overly muscular, but it obviously wasn't a body used to idleness. Shun had no extra fat, just muscles and scarred skin. Not as scarred as some warriors, but Kaden had touched some raised patches and was sure there were more. He slipped a hand under Shun's underwear, then cupped his butt and pulled him closer.

Shun groaned and ground onto Kaden, who leaned back against the cooling tub and pulled Shun down for another kiss. They kissed more passionately this time, tongues meeting as they rubbed their bodies together. Kaden's hands sneaked around to the front and cupped Shun's semierection.

"We really need to go in soon," Shun said with a sigh. "I have cold water running down my back, and if you can lean against the tub, it means the fire's gone out."

Kaden realized Shun was right. The light from the lamp was fading, and they needed to get inside soon or remain outside in darkness. The tub was getting cooler and the water losing heat. "Let's go." He started to briskly wash the soap off them.

Once finished, Shun climbed out of the tub and picked up his clothes. He had a clothesline running through the garage and he hung the wet clothes next to the underarmor suits. He changed to a rather old pair of shorts that was hanging from it, then reached for the sheet he'd helped Kaden wrap around himself before coming out of the house.

Shun dried himself briskly with it. "I'm going to pull you up and wrap this sheet around you. I'll dry us properly once we're inside."

Bracing himself for the next part, Kaden pulled himself up and hauled himself out by the strength of his arms alone. His stumps usually hurt a little when he pressed them down after immersing them in water, and he didn't want to try putting pressure on them. Shun caught him under the armpits and pulled him up, staggering a little under the weight. He tried to balance Kaden and reach for the sheet, but Kaden snorted, grabbed the sheet, and draped it over them.

Kaden hated the helplessness brought on by his disability, but he wasn't about to give in to it now. He nodded to Shun. "Let's go in."

Shun blew out the lamp and walked into the house. Inside, he skirted some old furniture in the "sitting room" and headed farther in with Kaden balanced in his arms.

Kaden held on to Shun's trembling shoulders, hoping Shun's strength would last the short walk back to the room. As they walked past a room with a light coming from under the gap between the closed door and the floor, they heard low voices talking over each other. It sounded as if Bradley and Wayland were having some sort of argument, and Kaden wanted no part of that.

Shun got to his bedroom and tipped Kaden onto the bed with a huff.

Kaden hit the bed on his back and gasped—it wasn't the most comfortable bed around, though he'd slept on a few that were worse. The mattress sagged in the middle, and whatever was at the bottom—a board, he supposed—poked at his back. When he pushed himself up to his elbows, Shun was moving around the room, closing the door, and placing a chair against the knob. Next he crossed to the window and pulled down a tarp he probably used as a curtain, and finally he lit another candle.

Taking advantage of Shun's distraction, Kaden hastily dried his stumps with the bedsheet. He wasn't sure if he'd done a proper job of it, but it wasn't as if it would kill him.

"This is an occasion." Shun was still trying to catch his breath, and Kaden didn't think it was all because he'd carried him inside. "I've lit two candles."

"Well, I'm happy to realize I rate more than one candle," Kaden said with a grin even as he thought about just how much of Shun's resources they were using. Food, candles, soap, and clothes. Shun didn't look as if he had a lot to spare.

Shun stood in front of him. Kaden hooked two fingers around the waistband of Shun's shorts and pulled them off in one move, dropping the clothing to the floor.

Shun was semierect, his penis uncut, his pubic hair much lighter than the hair on his head. He waited until Kaden had looked his fill before moving to a small drawer in the side of the room. He pulled it open, and out came a bottle of lube and a condom. Shun looked at the condom and shrugged apologetically. "Think it's expired."

"You won't need it. I haven't been with anyone since the accident, and they checked me at the hospital." Kaden hadn't had full-blown sex anyway, and hand jobs hardly counted; the hookers had insisted he wear a condom when getting a blow job because military personnel had a high rate of STDs.

"I haven't gotten myself checked, but I've always used a condom," Shun said as he threw the lube on the bed next to Kaden. "But if you want, we could just—"

"No!" Kaden came close to telling Shun he didn't care if he had all the venereal diseases known to man, but stopped himself. It was probably not what Shun wanted to hear. "I believe you."

Shun looked at Kaden with narrowed eyes, but lust won and he crawled onto the bed, which creaked ominously.

"Is this strong enough for the two of us?"

"Don't know, never shared it with anyone." Shun straddled Kaden, sitting on his stomach. He leaned in for a kiss, which evolved into a series of soft bites down Kaden's neck. He reached Kaden's chest and lingered a little, teasing a nipple before breaking off breathlessly.

He picked up the lube and passed it to Kaden. "Prep me."

Kaden opened the lube with unsteady hands and reached under him. Shun scooted forward and lifted his butt up obligingly so Kaden could work a finger inside him. The second finger was tighter, but Shun soon relaxed and the third followed quickly. Kaden would have preferred to work on it more, feeling for Shun's prostate, but Shun pulled up and lined up with Kaden's penis, and then there wasn't much to do but go with it.

Shun was warm and tight, and he moved languidly for the first few strokes, never still but adjusting himself minutely until every stroke made him gasp and cling to Kaden. Then he gripped Kaden's shoulders and started to ride him in earnest, his head bent, sweat rolling off his forehead.

Kaden held him by the hips and went for the ride as pleasure rolled off him in waves. He had missed sex; it had been so long, and Shun was perfect in every way. With his drying hair curled around his head and the candle creating a halo around him, Shun appeared as ethereal as a dream as he rode to his orgasm. Shun's passage tightened around Kaden as he came, and Kaden gripped Shun's hips tightly and thrust up three times more before achieving his own climax.

Shun collapsed on Kaden's chest. Kaden held him close, feeling their hearts racing as their bodies shook with the aftermath of their orgasms. After a couple of seconds, Shun got up, picked up the wet sheet, and used it to wipe them both clean. Then, as Kaden watched, he walked around the room, putting out the candles and arranging the clothes in order. Kaden supposed Shun had done it a lot in the darkness, since he walked unerringly to the bed and didn't stumble once before settling in.

They didn't speak when Shun spooned in front of Kaden and Kaden threw an arm over him. Kaden kissed the base of Shun's neck and felt him shiver lightly before closing his eyes.

Kaden wondered just what his role would be the next day, left behind in the house while Bradley and Wayland moved out searching for the armor. Before, he'd have at least felt angry and frustrated, but sex seemed to have ironed out the edges of his emotions, at least for a short time, and Kaden drifted off to sleep.

KADEN WOKE to a loud bang, reached for his armor, and hit warm flesh before he remembered where he was. He sat up while Shun mumbled a little and also sat up, apparently not altogether there.

Bradley stood by the open door; the chair Shun had used to prop up against the knob lay on its side on the floor—that had been the bang. Bradley looked furious.

"Bradley, what—?"

"Wayland's gone." She ignored their state of undress. "I'm going after her."

"You can't go alone," Kaden told her. He struggled to think things through in his sleep-addled mind.

"But I can't carry you everywhere." Just because Bradley stated it without any emotion didn't mean it hurt any less. "I'm sorry, Instructor Kaden, I can't—"

"So now you're going to trample all over this city on your own?" The beach town in the height of its glory had fanned out to cover close to four miles of beach.

"I'll try to follow where she went," Bradley said. "She would definitely head toward the armors, and I'll just follow her."

Kaden looked down at Bradley's feet. She was standing in her underarmor suit, but she didn't have anything on her feet for the simple reason that her armor had been her boots. "You can't go traipsing around on bare feet."

"Wayland did just fine, and I can wrap my feet in something. It'll have to do."

Kaden decided to skip the questions about why Wayland and Bradley had been fighting and why Wayland would have left without informing anyone. He would save those questions for later, after Wayland had been found. "But you'll be stumbling around blind. Do you have any idea where Wayland could have gone?"

"You did say we should head for the building Shun's friend Roy was squatting in," Bradley said after some thought.

"Shun didn't exactly give directions," Kaden pointed out.

Shun, who'd been quiet the entire time, spoke up. "Going anywhere without a plan is stupid. There're a couple of old books in the front room, maps of this place before the bomb. Take a look while we get dressed, and then we'll discuss a search pattern."

Bradley looked frustrated. "Why didn't you tell us this last night?"

"Because stumbling around in an unknown place without any weapons isn't the way to go," Kaden said dryly.

Shun said, "Go find out about this place, and we'll proceed from there."

Kaden knew Shun was simply killing time, giving Bradley a reason to cool down, and he agreed with it wholeheartedly.

It took Bradley fifteen minutes to go through the maps, and then she was back in the bedroom and was considerably calmer.

While Kaden got dressed in his underarmor, still cold from the rinse Bradley had given it the previous day, Bradley leaned against the doorframe and talked.

"We had a fight yesterday. She was mad at me for making her go up on the barn roof, and I was furious at her for not understanding why I did it. In the end, I think she thought it was her fault we lost our armors, so now she's gone to get them back."

The underarmor was a stretchable material that came in two parts—tights for the legs, and the top, which linked together in the middle with a zipper. Once he'd pulled it on, Kaden worked on folding the material around the ends of his legs and pinning it so as to cushion his stumps. He worked without looking up, and no one mentioned it, though he was painfully aware of Shun and Bradley watching.

"No chance she might have gone out to the road to look for help?" Shun, who'd dressed earlier, asked as he passed out coffee in the same bowls they'd had dinner in the previous night.

"She won't do that," Bradley insisted. "Once she gets an idea in her head, she sticks to it, and she really wanted to find the armors on her own."

Kaden froze. That was what he should be doing, should have done the previous night. He had thought of that possibility briefly but dismissed it as a last option. He looked up when he finished adjusting his clothes. "I'm not saying she is stupid, but it seems the logical action to go get help, as Shun just pointed out."

"I wanted her to do just that last night," Bradley snapped in frustration. "Told her I'd go look for the armor and she should go to the command post in Koresa and ask for help. She'd have told me if she was going that way."

"When did she leave?" Kaden asked as he sipped the coffee. It was weak, too watery, but warm, and he supposed Shun had a limited supply.

"I don't know. Early morning," Bradley said in frustration. "She got up and said she had to pee and went out. I fell asleep waiting for her, and when I woke up, it was light and she wasn't back. She must have slipped out then."

"Are you sure she wasn't kidnapped? There's supposed to be scavengers around here." As much as he didn't want to voice it, Kaden had to point out all the possibilities.

Bradley shook her head. "She took her underarmor and the electric net."

"Kaden, if she's going after the armor, she'd have gone to where we agreed to start from. Roy's apartment," Shun said.

Kaden felt a frisson of pleasure as Shun said his name, the first time since their introduction.

"I'm going after her." Bradley stood up. "You'll only slow me down, so I need to go alone."

"We can't leave him," Shun said suddenly. "Captain Allen knows where I live, and if he comes here...."

"That's fine." Kaden wasn't anyone's charity case. "Bradley, go with Shun. Just leave me a gun or something and—"

"How are you going to move?" Bradley said, not cruelly, but it still made Kaden feel as if she'd punched him. "Even if you had a wheelchair, this place doesn't have ramps."

Shun smacked his fist into his open palm. "I have a cart. I use it when I go scrap heap diving. It's slow, but we can drag Kaden on it, and I can point us in the right direction."

Kaden felt a protest build inside him as he considered the humiliation of being dragged around in a scrap cart.

Bradley spoke before he could voice it. "You need to be the one to put on your armor when we find it. And if you stay here alone, we'd have to come back this way to pick you up, and that might take more time than we have."

Kaden could see the logic in the offer, and it wasn't as if his legs were going to grow back anytime soon. He swallowed the last of the coffee and grimaced as it made a scorching trail down his throat. "Let's go."

# CHAPTER 9

THE CART turned out to be small and low to the ground and looked like an old child's toy, but at least it had four wheels and was mobile, which was more important than comfort at that time. Kaden assumed it'd be Bradley and him for the chase, since there was no real need for Shun to accompany them, but it turned out Shun was also going with them.

"Why?" Kaden asked, puzzled. "We'll return the cart on the way back and...."

"I thought with me escorting you, Bradley could move ahead and scout and not worry about leaving you alone. Plus, I want to find out if Roy is all right." But Kaden watched Bradley look at Shun thoughtfully and wondered if they were thinking the same thing. Shun had wanted that armor really badly.

Waves of grief and anger washed over Kaden at the thought of his helplessness. A scream of frustration welled up, but he fought to contain it. In armor, he was a fully functional person, but out of it, he was as good as dead. He swallowed hard and nodded. "Do you have the gun from yesterday?"

"Yeah, but it's not like I'm going to use it on anyone."

Bradley looked skeptical. "Really."

"Not my nature to kill people," Shun offered.

Bradley looked unimpressed. "Pacifist."

"Just give me the gun, then," Kaden said to prevent any hurt feelings.

Shun nodded and went back into the house to retrieve it. While he was gone, Kaden turned to Bradley and spoke in a hushed voice. "Can you take him out if needed?" He hurried to correct himself when she gave him a startled look. "I don't want you to kill him, just knock him out if it looks like he's about to grab our armors and run."

"I'm not the one screwing him," Bradley told him with a frown.

"We still need to arrest him once we get the armor, though," Kaden explained.

"You were ready to let him go just now."

Kaden didn't point out that she'd also been ready to leave him behind. "That was before he decided he wanted to come with us. Makes me wonder if it's all out of the goodness of his heart."

"Fine," said Bradley with a look on her face that said she was thinking of something else. Well, it wasn't as if he could explain everything to her.

They set off much later than they'd expected after Shun took the time to collect some water bottles, a little food, matches, and wet wipes. He locked the house and hid the key under the rock near the sagging front steps, and Kaden got the impression it was something of a routine to him.

"Why don't you take the key?" Bradley asked as she stood beside the cart.

"What if I don't come back? Or can't come back." Shun spoke with aplomb. "I want someone else to be able to use that place."

After that there wasn't much conversation as they set off toward the northeast, over grass-covered roads that were slippery from the previous night's rain. Bradley set off to scout ahead and to clear the path. The cart was low to the ground, with small wheels, and each pothole and grass clump shook it as it was pulled by Shun. Each jolt made Kaden's teeth rattle, and he had a tension headache half an hour into their travel. Kaden tried to help, wrapping some leather strips they'd cut from an old sofa around his hands and guiding the cart through the worst of it, but it was slow going.

Every time the cart would get stuck on something, Shun would pull and Kaden would lean over the edge to push. It would break free, jostling them, once almost toppling Kaden off the cart. He came close to giving up and telling Shun to go on. It was the most helpless he'd ever been, and somewhere inside, Kaden swore he was going to kill the people who'd stolen his armor.

By the time Kaden and Shun had navigated a particularly troublesome nettle patch, he had scratches on his palms and Shun looked equally battered. Kaden was exhausted. They were approaching the main area of the town, with more buildings, less greenery. Though unseen, the sea could be heard clearly. There were wider pavements and no sign of Bradley anywhere. "Where's she?"

"She went ahead," Shun said, indicating a direction vaguely with his hand.

Kaden took a deep breath, closed his eyes, and probed for his armor. Nothing. Well, he tried. "I thought you said Roy's building was more that way," he said pointing south. "It hasn't moved, has it? I think we're closer."

"She'll be back soon," said Shun as he started to pull the cart in the direction Kaden pointed out. He could see sweat rolling off Shun's back.

"We should take a water break," he offered, and Shun nodded before slumping onto the ground next to Kaden's cart.

Kaden felt a wave of gratitude for what Shun was doing for him. "Thank you for dragging my ass around," he muttered, the words dragged out of him with difficulty, as he passed the water bottle to Shun. "You needn't have bothered with it."

"It wasn't as if I was doing anything better."

"What is your job? Do you even have one?"

"I'm a freelancer. I do everything. Before I got it into my head to confront MacCrave, I did odd jobs for people around the towns. The closest town to Compen is Giff—small town, no Army outpost. People are all right, and there's always some odd jobs to be done around their houses. You know, since the most able-bodied people are enlisted."

"Do they ever wonder why you haven't enlisted?" Kaden asked, really wanting to know. Shun passed the water bottle back to Kaden, who took it, freezing for a second when he noticed a dark shadow reflected in the water. He tried to look casual as he closed the bottle and kept it down. Something inside him clenched and then relaxed, and he almost bit back a smile. Finally....

"They think I'm a Harian bastard, my mother slept with someone from the wrong side of the fence, which I am, and we aren't allowed to enlist if we can't prove citizenship."

"Hmm," said Kaden, not really paying much attention to the chatter. "Bradley is taking her time, isn't she?"

"Is she? I thought she scouted ahead for much longer, before."

"But she might be going in the wrong direction," Kaden told him quietly. "Go see if she's anywhere nearby."

Shun hesitated and picked up the handle of the cart.

"All that water went straight to my bladder," Kaden told him without meeting his eyes. "Leave me for a while and I'll follow as much as possible. Come back for me if I haven't caught up with you."

"I don't like the idea of splitting up."

"We haven't seen anyone, and anyway, you said this area doesn't have any scavengers about." They were in an area that had been mostly parking space—large, empty, with nothing worth picking up. Even in cities where people still lived, people didn't spend time in open areas when there were bomb threats and the fear of aerial attacks. And, as Shun had mentioned while they were moving, the town seemed strangely devoid of people recently. Perhaps Captain Allen and his group had cleared out the riffraff.

"Fine." Shun moved away with obvious reluctance. Kaden picked up the water bottle and kept it on the cart, away from harm. Then he crawled out of the cart and reached for the handle, a long metal pole with a crossbar at the end. He gave it a tug and sighed. Well, if he ever needed a weapon he could pick up the entire cart and throw it. Too bad he didn't have the gun—he'd given it to Bradley, who'd practically wrestled it off him. She probably thought he'd shoot himself or something, which was stupid since he'd had more access to weapons back in the camp, and he'd been fine. Almost.

Anyway, there was a distraction around the corner.

There were fewer of them, and they weren't as organized, but the shadow he'd spotted earlier took the form of a group similar to Captain Allen's, though hopefully not as armed. Kaden did a fast-paced crawl until he was in the shade of a sagging metal hut—a security booth, he supposed—and leaned against it. He didn't have to wait long; there were five of them, and they all rushed at him together. Well, at least he didn't have to worry about how many he had to take out all at once. They didn't have guns, but there were knives and some pretty impressive-looking metal bars and one chain that Kaden wouldn't have minded owning.

He waited until they were within hearing range and then smiled. "I don't have any money."

They paused, looked at him, sitting there in the shade, his legs extended before him, harmless if it wasn't for the brown underarmor he wore. For a moment he flirted with the idea of letting them take him out, but none of the weapons looked like they could kill him quickly. Kaden wasn't after a long, painful, suffering death or possible internal injury.

They were all of them young, all of them male, and something about the way they looked at him said they weren't going to walk away. Well, he wouldn't have sent Shun away if he thought they were going to have a picnic together.

"Where's the friend?" one of the group spoke, and Kaden reassessed their genders. At least one of them was female—or something thereof.

"He'll be back soon," Kaden lied, and as he knew it would, it pushed them into action.

Kaden let the first guy with the metal bar come close, then ducked to the side and caught the next guy by the ankle and tipped him. He caught the next swing of the metal bar—the pieces of leather he'd wrapped his palms with doing nothing to lessen the force of the blow—then wrenched it free of the owner, using it to catch the metal chain swinging at his head. He moved quickly, pivoting his body on one arm to avoid the woman swinging the knife, using his lower body to spin around and gain momentum. He threw himself to the ground, landing on his shoulder, but didn't stop rolling, pulling the metal bar with him. The first guy he'd tripped was still getting to his feet, but a metal bar to the back of his head put an end to it. Next, he systematically took out the former owner of the chain and the knife-wielding woman—man—person by breaking their knees and tossing them aside.

Two remained.

"Why are there fewer people around?" Kaden asked as he dug his fingers into the old tarmac and tore out a clump of asphalt.

The man standing with the knife in hand shrugged. "Because there's something bad happening," he said as if it was obvious.

He didn't look threatened by Kaden's improvised weapon; rather, he looked more amused by Kaden's lack of knowledge.

When the explanation didn't come, Kaden smirked at the man, goading him into answering. "Ghosts?"

The man gave Kaden a look that said he clearly thought Kaden was out of his mind. "No, there's some group of people going around killing people."

"Gangs fighting each other?"

"Nah, they use a lot of military hardware. Pick off groups one by one. Many just cleared out—seems easier than sticking around."

"You could run away," Kaden offered. It seemed Captain Allen and his group was systematically clearing the town so they would be the sole occupants. Which seemed out of character for a man who had let them go after he'd stolen their armors. Kaden wondered why he'd changed tactics.

"Do I look like someone who runs away from anything?" the man said, the conversation having given him confidence.

Kaden should have run toward him, but it wasn't an option, so he chose the next best thing: he propelled himself forward with his arms, using his knees to push his body, and leaped at the other assailant. He punched low in the gut, feeling the man's body give, and when he had doubled up, Kaden grabbed him by the chin and pulled him down to his level. It was easy to catch the knife-wielding arm and pin it and then break his wrist. The man, however, managed to wriggle free of Kaden's hold, jumping back a couple of feet, cradling his broken wrist. Kaden watched as the last man also inched closer. He pushed himself to his knees, ready to take them on, when he realized they were running away, skirting Shun who had returned with Bradley and Wayland in tow.

He looked at Bradley, who had an odd expression on her face. "What?"

"You're smiling. Beating up people must make you feel good," she said with a shrug and looked over her shoulder at Wayland, who was trailing behind them with a scowl on her face. "Look who I found." Kaden gave her points for ignoring the scavengers scattered on the tarmac.

"You had your sister worried," Kaden said as he sat back on the ground. He pulled the chain toward him and wrapped it around the metal bar. He was going to keep both; they were good weapons. He pointedly didn't look at either of the girls as he stashed his weapons and started his slow crawl back to the cart.

Shun kept pace with him quietly, hands in the pockets of his pants. All Kaden could see were Shun's fists clenched in his pockets. Shun didn't offer to help at all when Kaden hit a rather rocky patch.

"You're angry with me?"

"You wanted me out of the way so you could—"

Kaden interrupted him before the conversation could drag on. "I wasn't sure, and anyway, there was no need for you to get involved. You have enough problems as it is, without trying to get yourself killed."

"I could have scared them away." Shun indicated the remainder of the pathetic lot lying on the ground, some still groaning.

"How was I going to vent my frustration, then?" said Kaden as he clambered up to the cart. "Well, pull me to the girls, then. Let's see what's bothering them."

They skirted the fallen figures, making a wider detour than needed, and walked to where Bradley and Wayland stood, bodies tense with anger.

"We have to get going," he told them. "We can't be in the open like this."

"Look, Roy's building is close by, so we can check it out," Shun added with a flip of his head.

"If it was that close, why did you...." Wayland trailed off as her face cleared. "You lied to us."

"Wanted to give Roy time to leave if needed. Sorry." Shun didn't look sorry at all.

"Now you seem to think he's not there," Kaden observed.

"You know how I leave my key under a rock when I leave my house?" Shun pointed out. "Roy sticks an old newspaper out of the second floor window when he's in the building."

They all looked at the building he'd indicated. There were no newspapers sticking out from any window.

"Maybe he ran out for supplies and will be back soon," Kaden offered.

"Or taken by force," Bradley added.

"Doesn't hurt to take a look." Shun looked at the sky and frowned. "It'll be midday soon."

"What happens at midday, we turn into pumpkins?" Wayland asked dryly.

"No, but the rumor is there's a spy satellite that goes overhead, and no one wants to be caught outside when that happens."

Wayland looked unimpressed. "What does it do, shoot lasers at people outside?"

"No, but we are in a town that is on the border of an island that's been declared off-limits by WUC, so let's at least stay in the shade," said Kaden as he propelled the cart toward the shadow of Roy's high-rise. There was a building set much closer, but this was the most stable looking and he'd had enough of support columns falling on top of him.

"Wait," said Wayland hesitantly. "What about them?" She was indicating the people who were still sprawled on the ground around them. "We have to help them."

Kaden shook his head. "No, we don't."

Wayland wasn't convinced. "But they're hurt."

"They brought it on themselves," said Bradley. She walked over to the cart and grabbed the handle. "Let's go."

"But it's our duty to help everyone," Wayland protested. "We have to be fair to everybody, friend and foe—" She was seriously quoting the manual, something Kaden didn't think was possible.

"Oh, shut it," Bradley snapped in irritation. She grabbed Wayland's elbow with her free hand and started to drag the cart and Wayland across the overgrown parking lot with ease.

They managed a couple of steps before Wayland broke free and wheeled around. "No, I'm not going. You can go if you want. I'm going to help those people."

The entire group came to a standstill, and Bradley looked at Wayland with contempt. "Really, what makes you think I'm going to—"

"I don't care. You're always telling me what to do."

"Why do I get the feeling this is going to be an all-out family fight," Kaden said to Shun in a light tone. "Let's just go and leave them to it."

"No need," said Bradley, turning to Kaden with a grimace. "I don't have time for this." She turned around and started toward their original destination, the cart dragging behind her in quick jerks. They reached the building, and Bradley kicked the door in without even slowing down, sending it flying off its hinges with a loud bang.

"It was already open," Shun said without any heat as he helped the cart over the remains of the door. "Roy camps out in a back room on the next floor. His workroom is in the front, but he sleeps in the back."

The inside didn't look too impressive: broken glass, a few overturned pieces of furniture, and a load of dust. It could have been any abandoned building anywhere. They all paused, not that Kaden was moving on his own anyway, when they heard footsteps and tensed. Wayland appeared at the doorway looking defiant.

"What, they didn't want to be helped?" Bradley mocked Wayland as only a sibling could.

Wayland crossed her arms and stood back in a way that said she wasn't going to move until she'd said her piece. "Well, if you'd just been a little nicer to them, perhaps they'd have been—"

"Really don't have time for this, Way," Bradley snapped.

"No." Kaden was surprised to hear his own voice echoing in the empty room, and from the looks the others gave him, so were they. "Let's just get this over with. Obviously this disagreement between the two of you is nothing new, so out with it, Wayland. Tell Bradley what you want to say."

"Now that isn't—" Bradley started but stopped short when Kaden held up his hand.

"Let her speak."

"Fine," Wayland snapped. "You never let me do anything, you don't—"

Bradley didn't seem to care very much about letting Wayland speak. "That's because she's an idiot who sees a fairy tale in everything. She really believes that armored warriors are kind, caring—"

"I don't care about what you think we should care about—you don't even have a real armor. All you have is a fake one and—"

"Mine is as real as yours and—"

"You're just jealous you weren't compatible with my armor. You think you'd have made a better warrior than me, but let me tell you something, I'm the one who's compatible, not you."

There was a long pause, during which Kaden felt Shun grab the edge of the cart and pull at it ineffectively while Bradley froze, her arms unmoving. She was still holding on to the cart handle, and it might as well have been sunk into concrete. It didn't even budge.

"Well, fine," she said in a monotone voice, then turned away from Wayland. Kaden expected Wayland to apologize for her hasty (but maybe truthful) comment, and from the way she opened her mouth, it was evident she wanted to say something. But Bradley had shut down, and there seemed to be nothing to say.

Bradley turned to Shun. "What do you think is safer, upstairs or staying here? We obviously need to regroup."

Shun hesitated, clearly thrown by the change of conversation, which gave Wayland the time needed to state her piece.

"That's it?" she said. "You're not going to say anything?"

"You want me to speak?" Bradley said in a calm voice. "After you've made up your mind about what I'm going to tell you, you want me to say something? What do you want me to do, announce that I'm not jealous of you?"

"Well, it's not like it's not true," Wayland snapped, probably annoyed Bradley wasn't giving her the fight she wanted. "You were the one who followed me to training camp. You were the one who first tried on the armor and it didn't like you."

The silence was so ominous Wayland stepped back, and Shun shuffled his feet, moving so Kaden, in his cart, was between Shun and Bradley. Kaden considered the merit of scrambling off the cart and crawling away, dignity be damned, because Bradley looked as if she was about to pick up something and slam it on Wayland's head until something gave. But when Bradley spoke, her voice was strangely reasonable, and she might have been speaking about someone other than her sister. She turned to Kaden—Kaden imagined his face looked bloodless and tense—and gave a small smile.

"I suppose the first bit is obvious," she told him with a raised eyebrow, challenging him to say something to contradict her. "Family wants boys, so named the girls with boys' names, yada yada yada." She barked a laugh. "Well, our family was at its best when my grandfather was fighting in the war, when he was compatible with the armor. But my father, the utter failure, couldn't make it move, so of course he and my mother planned it out that their children would win back the family honor. I grew up hearing about that damn armor every fucking day of my life. They were always telling me how I'd be the one to fight in it—and every fucking birthday was 'Bradley, wait until your twelfth birthday, we're going to have a freaking huge party when you fit into your armor. When you become an armored warrior, we're going to invite the Huntingtons and have an over-the-top party and show off....'" She broke off with a gasp, having run out of air, but continued as soon as she'd breathed in. "Well, you get the idea. Anyway, so I thought, great, I'm going to wear the fucking armor, even if I hated it.

"On my twelfth birthday, I was at the Army outpost where the armor was stored before eight in the morning, with my parents in tow, waiting to fit my damn armor on." Bradley looked at Wayland and sneered. "Saw it for the first time, and it was ugly, had bumps on it, none of that smooth metal to it. It was like a rock, all gray and pitted, and when I tried it on, it was like being inside a fucking metal coffin. The damn thing closed around me and I couldn't breathe. Thought I was going to die. And that was the end of their fucking dream—you should have seen my parents on the way home. It was like someone had died. Mother was crying and Dad was saying over and over again, 'we still have Wayland, we haven't lost everything.'"

She stopped talking with a gasp, and for a long while, no one spoke. Then Kaden realized he should say something. "That's the longest I've heard you speak, ever."

"Well," said Bradley, sounding calmer. "I'm just trying to say I didn't want that armor. I don't want it."

"But then why are you here?" Wayland shouted at her. "I got the armor, the one you don't want. So why are you here with me?"

"Because you can't do it," Bradley shouted back, her voice echoing in the empty room. Kaden looked at Shun and saw with relief that he was scanning the room. The sound was going to attract anyone who was in the area, who was stupid enough to investigate.

"You mean because I am not bloodthirsty like you?"

"No, you dimwit," Bradley said, sounding more frustrated than angry. The long speech probably took a lot out of her. "Because you can't hurt anyone. You couldn't take out that man in the train, you couldn't take out Shun, and you are just not meant for this. Some people are meant for this, and you just aren't."

"Well, I'm not cut out for pruning the family roses," Wayland snarled.

"You have roses in your garden," Kaden said loudly, breaking up the fight. "That's brilliant, but time's up. We've been in the same place for too long, and it's going to take me ages to get up those steps, so we have to move." The steps looked like they were made of concrete and metal, not wood or anything fancy that would have decayed with time—though the railing was sagging.

"Well, that's what I'm here for," said Bradley, letting go of the handle and walking to Kaden. "Hold on tight." She caught Kaden by the underarms, lifted him, and swung him onto her back with ease, so all he could do was hang on to her like a backpack.

"Someone grab the cart," Kaden called out over his shoulder, not willing to let go of Bradley. Normally he wouldn't have anyone else do this, carry him around like a sack. The previous night Shun had struggled, but Bradley handled him with ease, as if he weighed nothing.

"I'm going to take a look," Shun said and ran up the steps before anyone could stop him. They all tensed; Kaden had forgotten Shun was not their friend after having spent the day and night with him. He wondered if he should order either Wayland or Bradley to go after Shun, but a couple of minutes later, Shun came down, breathing hard, a frown on his face. "He's cleared out. His gear is gone. Doesn't look like he struggled."

No one knew what to say to that. "Let's go up anyway," Kaden told Bradley. "We need to regroup and discuss what Wayland saw." And decide where they were headed next. He also wanted to see Roy's place, just in case he'd left something behind. "Let me down if you need to rest," he said as she started up the first flight of steps.

"Please, I can do this in full armor," she snorted as she strode up in long, fluid steps.

"That armor is heavy," Shun said, from behind. "I mean, when I tried on the... armor, it was so heavy, it was hard to walk in it, and I was supposed to be compatible with it."

"There's no compatibility in the type of armor I use," Bradley told him. "At least with the original armor, it compensates and adjusts, or so I hear. With the modified armor, you have to be able to walk with all that on you. I trained every single day for three years after Wayland was recruited, so I could join the armored warriors. I'm one of the strongest people there. I can move as fast as almost anyone in an original armor, in my hunk of metal."

"Lots of training," said Kaden, aware if he were to anger her he might possibly find himself flung down the steps. "All that effort so you could look after your little sister."

"Well, she obviously no longer needs me," said Bradley, making it clear that line of conversation was over. She looked over the other shoulder at Wayland and asked, "Did you find anything when you went off on your own?"

"I think I know where the armor is," Wayland mumbled after a couple of seconds. "At least your armor. I saw someone wearing your armor, a guy, though I think he'll take it off soon. Looked too heavy for him."

After several seconds of silence, when it became apparent that Wayland wasn't going to speak further, Kaden demanded, "Well? Which way?"

"That way." She gestured vaguely. Kaden mentally gave her a couple of negative points. He'd have to teach her how to give proper descriptions and location information.

"How far and how many? What's the place like? Did you check to see if there were any exits or entrances?" he snapped, getting a little tired of the whole ordeal.

"There were many," Wayland muttered after a long pause. "I didn't really count, and they were in a building by the corner, close to the sea, the one with the black outline, and I really don't know much about it."

"That's the most unhelpful description of anything I've ever heard." Bradley traversed another flight of stairs. "You'll need to be a little more specific. Didn't you learn that in Basic?"

They were walking past large empty halls, broken floor tiles, and shattered windows, but it appeared more like age-related damage than actual human violence, and Kaden looked at Shun, who was keeping pace with them easily. "Is this building empty? A lot of people living here?"

"Should be empty." Shun nodded. "No one likes to move in to buildings this open and large. Glass windows make terrible insulation, and there's no water close by." Kaden remembered the town had been removed from the power grid, water lines, and gas supply a long time ago. "Roy hated it—it was Astrid who wanted to live in the sunlight. She was planning on a rooftop garden until we pointed out that it was a stupid idea. What if it was spotted from the air?"

"What happened to the furniture?" Bradley asked, not even a little breathless from all the climbing she was doing. Kaden, clinging to her back, could feel her heartbeat, as steady as when they'd started.

Wayland chipped in, her voice soft, probably quoting from something she'd read before. "They could have taken the furniture when the office buildings were relocated."

"Could be," Kaden answered, not wanting Wayland to feel left out. The group was tense enough without adding more discomfort, and he wasn't sure it would help them later on. "We might be safer on a higher floor."

Bradley turned toward the staircase wordlessly and started climbing.

Kaden looked around for inspiration, not that there was much to notice in the emergency stairways they were using, and then blurted out, "Ever notice that nothing has changed in building design in all this time since the bomb? I mean, paint this place up and it could be anything anywhere in downtown."

Shun had an answer for that. "Roy says that's because everyone is so obsessed with the armor and replicating the process, progress came to a halt in everything else."

"You seem well read on that subject," Bradley said, stopping and adjusting Kaden a little, and Kaden realized she probably wasn't as tireless as she seemed, even if they were progressing at a regular pace.

"I don't read a lot," Shun said with a shrug. "Never picked up much of that, but I do hear what people say, and it seemed the government stopped everything to fund replicate armors and to develop weapons."

"We have made improvements," Wayland said quickly, probably just to be contrary. No one could be stupid enough to actually believe otherwise. "We have a good transport system and—"

"We have old diesel engine trains," Bradley sneered. "I hear Jasin has those electric trains everywhere, not like we do. It's only in the capital, but that's more than we've got." She was referring to their neighboring country on the other side of the sea. "We import all our electronics from there, cell phones, data pads, things we can't even imagine making."

Wayland had a belligerent look on her face. "But it's not like we can make everything even if there was no war."

"We have to import food because most of our labor force is in the Army or busy making ammunition," Shun said softly, probably quoting some antiwar propaganda he had heard. Kaden had heard similar sentiments, and he knew it was true. Before the war, Joscal had been a self-sufficient country, and when the country had taken in Harian refugees, they had done that with confidence.

"It's not like we're a poor country," Wayland said stubbornly.

"The only thing that's ever come out of Joscal was the armor," Shun snapped back.

"I suppose you have no reason to love the armor," Kaden agreed as they continued up the stairs. The building had such high floors the stairs seem to go on forever.

"Roy has a theory the armors weren't invented to fight, that they were meant to be for the space project, like deep-space exploration suits for hostile planets and things."

Kaden had also heard that theory, but if the armors weren't originally designed as weapons... so what? He looked at the long hallways and large open spaces they passed on each floor, wondering what they had contained before. It seemed weird to think that once people had worked in such spaces, done things such as peer out at the town from the windows that overlooked the—

Kaden tapped Bradley's shoulder lightly. "We might be high enough to look over the town."

Bradley looked to where Kaden was pointing, an open door by the landing that led into the building, where the narrow corridor widened into what had been a large office space. There were a couple of office tables and some chairs listing to the side, office furniture probably deemed too damaged to be moved. Kaden let Bradley decide if they should stay on the floor or keep climbing, and she seemed to prefer the first option.

Once they had walked onto the floor, he waited until she'd found a clear space to put him down, then sighed as Wayland joined him a couple of seconds later. She hesitated, then placed the cart she'd been carrying next to him. "Do you want to stay on it, or…? There's glass on the floor—it might not be safe."

"I'm fine." Kaden clambered onto it. Shun walked up to him and grabbed the cart handle. He felt a flash of resentment at the way everyone treated him, as if he'd lost his mental capacity as well as his lower limbs, but he let Shun drag the cart toward what had been an open balcony. It was true. He did want to see the city, but he would have preferred if he had been asked before being dragged across the floor as if he were a doll.

He had regained some of his pride when he'd beaten up a couple of people, but he lost it entirely when Bradley, his student, had picked him up and carried him like a toy.

But Kaden bit back any comments as Shun struggled to maneuver the cart over a set of grooves in the floor—they had once served as window runners, where the glass windows could slide open onto the balcony. The glass was long gone, but the metal, rusted and corroded, stuck to the floor. Wayland stepped in to help, jerking on the handle. As the back wheel rolled off the metal railing, the cart jumped, and Wayland gasped as the entire thing jerked forward. Kaden almost fell over and had to steady himself by slapping his palms on the floor. The sharp metal stung his palm, and he almost jerked his hand up before he caught his balance.

"Instructor Kaden, are you all right?" Wayland sounded worried.

"Just a nick," Kaden said as he shook his hand.

"I'm sorry, Instructor Kaden," Bradley said, much to Kaden's frustration, and he found himself grinding his teeth. "I wasn't paying attention. I should have helped you over."

"You have nothing to be sorry about," he said as he closed his fists, dismissing Wayland, who had come to help. "Just point out the damn building you saw our armor in."

Wayland jerked back as if slapped, looking to Bradley for support. Kaden wondered if anyone other than Bradley had ever spoken to Wayland harshly. Bradley didn't even glance at her, keeping her eyes fixed on the view, while snapping, "So, where is it?"

Wayland walked up to the edge of the balcony, and Kaden noticed the railing had come free in places, suspended over the edge, having come loose from the center fixing. The concrete in the edge was also crumbling piece by piece, and a couple of chunks came off when Bradley ventured to the edge to join Wayland.

"Be careful," Kaden blurted before he snapped his mouth shut. He didn't want to sound like their father.

The view was rather dismal: there were taller buildings in the town but none near the building they were in, and they looked down on a lot of dilapidated structures. The broken windows looked like dead eyes, and despite the midday heat, a cold shiver ran over him.

"That one," said Wayland, pointing to a building to the far left, and instead of looking at the building, Bradley looked to Kaden. "The one with the outline."

"Instructor Kaden, you had the highest compatibility with your armor," said Bradley.

Kaden nodded and closed his eyes as he concentrated on the direction Wayland had pointed. He could feel something like a mental scratch, a pull, and it was coming from the right direction, but it wasn't as if he could pinpoint the exact location. A part of him was aware that it could be wishful thinking on his part, his need for his armor to be there projecting a pull that didn't exist out of textbooks.

"It could be there," he said as he opened his eyes and really looked at the building where the armor was supposed to be. It was ugly and had probably been ugly even when it was new. The short, squat building was about five stories high and sat in the shadow of the other buildings. The outline Wayland had spoken of was a metal strip about a meter thick inlaid into the yellow stonework. There were very few windows, and those that were there were sunk into the sides like arrow slits. The glint of green-black to the right of it meant—

Kaden looked at Shun. "So close to the sea?"

Shun nodded. "No surprise they chose that. That place is built like a fortress and one of the least damaged buildings since the rest give it protection. The sea means easy access to water."

"What do we do now?" Bradley asked as they all stared at the building.

"We do nothing," Kaden said slowly. "You need to go scout out the area."

"I thought you'd say that," Bradley said after a couple of seconds. She started to turn. "No time like the present."

Wayland turned to Bradley. "I'll come with you."

"No," Bradley said sharply. "I'll go alone."

Wayland hesitated. "Can't—" But Bradley pushed past her and started to walk out. She hesitated as she strode past Shun and inclined her head toward him. Shun nodded in understanding, or what passed as understanding, and then she was gone, bounding down the stairs. Kaden felt a stirring of envy at the ease with which she moved and looked away before he came across as a sorry loser.

Wayland stood silently for a moment before throwing her arms up in the air. "I was trying to help. I found where the armor was, and look, Bradley can't tell me I'm acting like a wimp and then accuse me of being a selfish bitch when I do something on my own."

Kaden didn't answer, simply turned his back to her and looked out at the horizon.

"Why does she have to be such an asshole?" Wayland muttered loudly, and Kaden realized she was waiting for him or Shun to either validate her actions or to tell her that she was wrong. He didn't so much as turn his head when he heard Shun move toward Wayland, probably to comfort her.

While Kaden could see her point—she was young and optimistic—he could also see what Bradley was referring to. Bradley tried hard to protect her sister and to keep her out of danger, and really, Kaden didn't think Wayland was cut out to be a warrior. She was too soft, too nice, and there was no room for such people in the war.

He moved closer to the edge of the balcony and looked down. It was a fair drop, would probably kill him instantly—and for a moment he toyed with the idea of leaning forward and letting go. Bradley could deal with the armor, Shun could figure out how to get revenge or justice or whatever for what his dead father had done to his mother, and Wayland could whine as much as she wanted. He'd be free. All he needed to do was lean forward a little, let go of the railing he was holding and—

A hand landed on his shoulder, casual, soft, not holding him back in any way. "See the sea," Shun said as he squatted next to Kaden. "It looks really deep, but there's a shallow sandbar between the mainland and the island. You can kind of guess where it is by the way the color changes. Many speculate that there are hidden labs beneath it."

"Secret labs of Dr. Orche." Kaden grunted in surprise. "I read about a search operation the government carried out after the bombing."

"This area was already off-limits from what I know, and all they could do was aboveground scanning using overhead satellites."

Kaden already knew that. "They couldn't find anything."

"The sea's also very cold. People think it can hide heat emission from an array of generators that's keeping the labs powered. No one's ever seen or even found a clue to support this theory, but people are optimistic, if nothing else."

"Optimistic," Kaden parroted. "Yeah. Don't see much of that in anyone apart from Wayland."

"She's young and hasn't had anything bad happened to her yet." Shun sat down close to Kaden and allowed his legs to hang off the side of the balcony. He remained silent for what seemed like a long time. Kaden would have relaxed into the moment, but he sensed Shun waiting for something or holding back on a comment.

"Out with it."

"Why are your legs of different length?" Shun blurted out.

Kaden looked at Shun so fast he almost gave himself whiplash, but Shun, taking a page from Kaden's book, was gazing at the horizon, not looking at him. But his hand, hovering close to Kaden's shoulder, said he might try to grab Kaden should he slip. Kaden might not have his legs, but he was still a heavy individual and he just might drag Shun with him.

"When... they amputated the legs, they did one first and tried to save the other. But it just made the infection spread higher and when that was cut off, it had to be chopped off farther up." There, he was fine speaking of it, even using different vocabulary to explain the process by which he lost his legs. "Then Dr. Lane wanted to cut back the first leg so the stumps were of equal length, said it would be easier to fit prosthetics and all, but I threw a fit and told her not to come near me. I'd lost...." He was not going to break down. "I'd lost both my legs and—" All he had was a life of nothing in front of him. The government would pay him a disability pay, but it was not for life. Kaden suddenly imagined himself roped to a wheelchair, moving over uneven pavement as he tried to go to his job at the bottling plant, where everyone regarded him with pity. Being a war hero was fine, but once he was half the person he was before, no one would see an armored warrior; they'd see some cripple to be pitied.

"Why don't you go for prosthetics, at least as a backup?"

"Because...." Kaden hesitated. "I'm not the first armored warrior to lose a limb. And every single time they were fitted with prosthetics,

their compatibility dropped to below minimum. The technicians think
the armor feels rejected and therefore stops responding to the user."

"Even simple prosthetics like a... a... missing dick?" Shun
inquired, then flushed under Kaden's glare. "Sorry, bad joke. Just that,
do injured armored warriors always give up the suits?"

Kaden felt as if he was talking about the same thing over and
over again. "If they lose a major part, like a limb and can't move the
corresponding part of the suit, they have to give it up. Neither the armor
nor prosthetics have worked for any of them so far."

"But your armor compensated for you, huh?"

"Something like that." When Dr. Lane had seen that Kaden was
depressed (he'd tried to increase his pain medicine drip to the point it
would have sent him into cardiac arrest) she had suggested that perhaps
he should at least polish his armor. Kaden had accepted the suggestion
for what it was, a distraction. He'd actually refused to look at it, knowing
his fighting days were over. Why torture himself with what he couldn't
have? But as he'd touched his armor, he'd known what needed to be
done. The leg pieces had snapped on effortlessly and enclosed his legs,
giving the illusion of two fully functioning legs. He'd not tried to stand
up for the first hour or so, simply sat on the bed with his legs stuck in
front of him, just breathing in and out to calm his heartbeat.

His stumps were still healing, and despite the illusion of being
complete that his armor provided, he didn't have feet. He shouldn't have
been able to stand up. Then slowly, he'd set one "foot" down and put
weight on it. It had held. He'd deliberately put the other "foot" down
and pushed himself upright, holding on to the bedstead in case the
armor collapsed around him. But it hadn't; the armor had held him aloft,
compensating for the lack of real feet the way only his armor seemed
able to do. He was complete.

"It was all a lie."

Shun laughed at that, a sort of bitter, self-deprecating one. "In case
you haven't noticed, we all do a bit of lying. I make up cover stories for
myself, and sometimes, even I believe in them."

"What are you doing here with us, Shun?" Kaden asked softly.
"Two cadets, who are not exactly getting on well with each other, and
me. You could have made it out on your own and found your armor
faster. We're all just slowing you down."

"Bradley offered me a deal." That was something Kaden hadn't been expecting to hear.

All of a sudden he felt his fascination with the long drop diminish as he turned to Shun and frowned. "Care to elaborate?"

"After all of you… lost your armor and Bradley knocked you out, she promised I'd be able to join the Army and take the armor as my own," Shun explained to him. Kaden had the impression he was getting the short version of the story.

"Why didn't you do that in the first place?"

"And tell them I was a Harian bastard?" Shun snapped. "With my nonregistered, questionable-citizenship status, not a chance. Didn't even know if I was going to get the armor that way, would have destroyed my mother if she'd gotten to know about it and… anyway, I wanted to confront the man. Didn't even know this armor was available for a refitting." He took a long breath. "You might not believe it, but I did try the right way. I wrote to the Army a couple of times reporting MacCrave for what he did to my mother. Nothing ever came of it. I suppose I could have spoken in person at some outpost, but I really didn't know how well they'd take it. Plus, I didn't have any papers, wasn't even born here and… so I turned to people whom I thought would help me."

"And this friend of yours, Roy, you sure he didn't stab you in the back?"

There was no hesitation when Shun spoke. "He wouldn't."

Kaden could see little point in arguing about something he could do nothing to change. "Uh, you seem so sure. How close are you?"

There was a pause as Shun assessed the question. "Are you asking me if I trust him or if I was fucking him?"

"Both."

"I first heard of him when I was feeling around for people who might know of the armor—where certain armored warriors might be based. I wanted the green one, but it seemed stupid to advertise it as such, so I simply asked around for anything. And when I say ask, that's all I did, went to places and talked a little. It wasn't as if I could write fan mail to anyone.

"I heard about a guy who knew about a guy who was really into armor details, and I called him. He was shacking up with his girlfriend in a place down the beach from here, and he was really into Dr. Orche's work, both of the Orches, plus some newer work by a woman. I think a doctor or some scientist.... Francine. I didn't see much significance in his work, but we kept in touch. I crashed at his place a couple of times, and really, he was just interested in knowing how these armors work. He wasn't into hurting anyone."

"Really," Kaden said dryly.

"He was the person who suggested I settle here—I just didn't like the high-rise buildings, too open. I hope he's okay. Him and Astrid." That answered Kaden's question as to whether Shun was fucking the guy. "He'd have gone crazy over your black armor. He didn't think there were any that were deployed."

Kaden had been a pretty low-key person, even before the accident. Not having much offensive power but plenty of regenerative ability due to his armor, he had been used in mostly undercover operations, such as sneaking into enemy buildings—like the last mission that had gone wrong. Not that Kaden was about to bring that up. "I hear they have a lot of these armor fan websites on... er... the Internet," Kaden said, hoping to defuse the tension that had crept into their conversation. It wasn't that he didn't know what it was, just that it was strictly controlled by the government, and even fan sites, as far as he knew, were monitored. There was very little in those apart from pictures of armored warriors in full gear, sometimes hand drawn, but he was surprised sometimes the government even allowed that.

"It's called boosting patriotism," Shun offered, as if reading his mind. "People need to love the Army, otherwise how would they fund the war?"

"Funny." Kaden snorted. "I wasn't feeling the love."

Shun gave him a flat look. "Is that some sort of invitation?" He placed a hand on Kaden's knee and turned around to look over his shoulder at Wayland. "We aren't exactly alone."

Kaden, who had not even been thinking of sex, placed his head on Shun's shoulder and huffed. "Really not the place or the time." He could feel Wayland watching and sat up straight, becoming professional. It was time to deal with reality; he needed to tackle the problem at hand. He indicated with a nod that she should come over.

"What?" Wayland sounded suspicious as she drew closer to them.

"Tell me about the building. How did you find it?"

"I followed my armor," she admitted. "I could feel it."

Kaden didn't even know how to comment on that. "Did you see your armor there?"

"No, I hung around the building—knew you'd eventually catch up to me."

Kaden wondered if Wayland even understood how careless she had been and just how lucky she was that she had gone undetected. He turned to Shun. "Is that Allen's usual hideout?"

Shun shook his head. "Roy would never have picked a building so close to those people. And I thought Allen would move toward the edge of the city, where it'd be easier to run."

"Unless he's running toward the sea," Kaden surmised. "Wayland, when you were there, did you see any boats?"

"I wasn't looking."

Kaden had had it with her childish, negligent attitude, and his expression must have conveyed it.

"I suppose you want me to go to the roof and check," Wayland said, sounding none too pleased. "Perhaps your friend is also on one of the upper floors. I should go and see if there's any sign of what happened to this person who supposedly lived here."

"There might be… it might be… not safe," Kaden said lamely as he realized what he'd been about to say. No matter what, Wayland was a trained fighter; she was, at least in theory, well versed in a lot of things such as searching a place or doing visuals. Still, so far, she had displayed very little of her abilities.

"I'll walk up and take a look around," she said with a shrug. "I didn't see any footsteps on the dust, but who knows. I'll be careful. I scored the highest in my class in hand-to-hand." Kaden must have looked surprised since she smiled. "Bradley coached me."

Kaden wished he'd brought a short-distance communication relay so he could stay in touch with the immediate people in the field. Then he realized the concrete buildings would probably interfere with the feed. "You have a watch on you?"

"How long do I have before I report back?" she asked.

Kaden thought it over. The building was large but mostly empty. There might be a few things left behind. He'd take a trolley over the cart he'd been pulled along in any day, and it would give Wayland time to move on her own and think about what her sister had said. "Report back here in half an hour. See if you can find something more practical for me to move around in."

She looked as if she wanted to say more but in the end nodded. "I'm going to work my way up, a floor at a time."

"Yell and we might hear you."

Shun nodded and got to his feet as she left, then walked behind Kaden. "Do you feel like getting off the ledge now? We've got half an hour, so I can show you the love." He gave an exaggerated leer that made Kaden snort.

Kaden felt his throat tighten even as he laughed and shook his head. "I think this is not the place, and really, if Bradley walks in on us—"

"She'll be the type to keep watch, so we won't get disturbed," Shun said firmly. "Come on, then. You on the ledge is making me feel… edgy."

Kaden gave a wry smile and pushed away from the ledge, using his hands to lever himself off. He scrambled onto his knees and winced, before trying to figure out the best way to move from the balcony to the inside.

"This is going to be an awkward question, and I know you hate it, but… er… can I carry you?" Shun asked.

He decided to ignore the reference to his disability and hoped Shun would understand. "How about the table there?" Kaden suggested, pointing to an abandoned steel office table against the far wall. It was gray and rusted, the sea air getting to it, but it seemed solid enough.

In reply, Shun picked up Kaden awkwardly, hands under his armpits, and Kaden tried to help by sliding a hand over his shoulders. "Mind the metal gutter," he said as Shun stepped over it, almost losing his balance in the process but managing to walk to the table— staggering with Kaden half slipping off because his underarmor was slicker than naked skin. Shun bumped into the table and managed to drop him onto it.

"Sorry," Shun said in a small voice. "That could have gone better."

"Moving the cripple from A to B?" Kaden said, trying to sound grateful for the help. "Not your fault." He arranged himself so his legs hung over the sides and leaned back against the wall. The table groaned but held, and it seemed as if it would stay that way. He shook his head and tried to work through the anger and frustration he was feeling.

"I don't even know what to say," Shun confessed. "Nothing I say will make you feel better."

"Oh, that's fine. I know exactly how I feel," Kaden said with a huff of laughter, though he hardly felt like laughing. "I'm not ever, ever going to be the same. I don't have my feet—I can't walk properly, and I never will." He closed his eyes and pushed a hand against them to stop the tears from forming, but he could feel his eyes prickle. "I'm not sure about what I'm doing. I can only live in denial for so long. Without the armor, I'm just a hunk of meat to be pushed around or carried around or—"

Shun thankfully didn't speak, didn't try to say something inane and useless that would in no way help him. Kaden heard feet shuffling and felt a hand touch his shoulder followed by light lips on his neck. "We just need to get the armor back."

"You know it's not mine." Kaden voiced his greatest fear, even as he tipped his head back. "They'll take it away from me. Maybe not now, but eventually, the Army will want their hardware back. It's not like I can have it forever. No matter how compatible I am, there's a limit to the time I can stay an armored warrior."

"Funny you mention it." Shun lifted his head and breathed deeply. "What does happen to armored warriors who retire?"

Kaden had to collect himself and think on that. "Most die in combat, but some retire. If they have someone compatible, then the armor is fitted, but if not, then the Army has to wait."

"Is retirement voluntary?" Shun followed the question with a kiss to the corner of Kaden's mouth.

"Not really. There's an age limit and years of combat. Armor only works if you give it away, so they kind of... convince people it is the best thing to do." He knew it would take a lot of "convincing" for him to give away his armor.

"No age limit?" A hand on his upper thigh, warm and distracting.

"There's no real age limit for original armor. Hypothetically, you can't have sixty-year-olds struggling in armor but—" Kaden shook his head to clear his thoughts. "As long as you can operate the damn thing and there is no better, compatible person waiting in the ranks, then yeah, I think I have a better chance of keeping my armor than, say, Bradley." He tried hard to think about it, but most modified armor wearers had to retire quickly because lugging all that weight around never benefitted anyone.

"So the chances they'll find a compatible person for your armor?" Shun prodded. "I know all the other black armors are without matches, you said it yourself, so how likely is it that there'll be a match for yours? Unless you have a kid who'll grow up or—" To emphasize his point, he cupped Kaden's crotch.

"No kid of mine will ever be a warrior. If I ever have one, that is," Kaden said. "I mean, the armor I have—had—have was lying in storage for a long time, and it was just luck I could move it. There might be some kid from somewhere who will fit into it as well."

"Let's see about getting that armor back," Shun offered. "And I'll be there to help you with it."

Kaden ran a hand over Shun's head, leaned in, and placed a careful kiss on his lips. Kaden wondered just what was wrong with him. He was technically stranded in enemy territory without backup, with two girls he had to supervise, and he was considering a quickie with a guy who might not be on his side… and was probably pumping him for information. He wanted to believe otherwise, but he couldn't figure out why else Shun would be willing to have sex with him. But he also knew it was his way of trying to balance things—he was feeling useless, and sex always made him feel good.

He closed his eyes and listened hard. Dead cities were always quiet; he could hear the sea in the distance, some birdlife, but nothing else. "We do have some time," he said before Shun kissed him back. He reached down and worked at the waist of the underarmor. The waistband was still wet, but the heat of the day seemed to have left it damp, not dripping wet, and he'd hardly noticed it until then. "This isn't the most ideal setting for sex."

"I agree with you. This is a terrible idea," said Shun as he fumbled for his belt.

There was a reply to that, just finish what they had started… were starting. "I can lean back." Kaden demonstrated what he meant by tipping back, supporting his body weight on his elbows. "I want you to fuck me as fast as possible."

Shun didn't look any too pleased with the idea. "I don't have anything on me, not even oil."

"It's fine," Kaden blurted out.

"No it's not, you're going to feel it when you—"

"Walk," Kaden finished with a wry grin. "Hardly going to be a problem here."

"When you move around," Shun growled. "Stop putting words into my mouth."

"Ah, keep forgetting you're against violence," Kaden couldn't help saying a little bitterly. "But this isn't violence. It's perfectly consensual."

"Not if you don't enjoy it," Shun said as he pushed Kaden back to the table. He cleared his throat several times. "At least we have spit."

He pulled the lower part of the underarmor off, draped it over the side, and leaned in. He hesitated a little as he pulled at Kaden's legs and finally settled for placing his hands on the knees. He pushed up Kaden's legs, and suddenly Kaden felt a little exposed as Shun pushed his buttcheeks apart, but all he did was step between Kaden's legs and align his erection.

He paused, spit into his palms, which should not have been hot in any way, and proceeded to slather his dick with it before pulling Kaden closer. Kaden found the initial penetration painful but accepted it as his due. Pain helped him feel grounded at times, and pain tinged with pleasure helped him feel more alive for a change. If he could just concentrate right, he was sure he could break away from the fog of lethargy that surrounded him all the time.

The sex was hot and frenetic, both men aware there was little time for finesse. There was only the sound of Shun grunting, the table legs shaking a little, and the sound of flesh against flesh.

Kaden reached for his own erection and gave it a quick twist of his wrist, wishing they really had packed something for lubrication. His palms were callused and dry, hardly ideal for the job. Still, he felt his spine arch with pleasure, and he closed his eyes and went with the moment.

It was over quickly, neither of them trying to hold back but simply reach completion before someone walked in on them. Afterward there was a sticky mess on Kaden, and Shun was straightening his clothes, looking apologetic. The encounter was hardly comparable to the previous night; at least there had been a bed and candles, though the sentiments between them had hardly changed. But as Kaden looked around for something to clean himself with—he wasn't going to wipe himself down with his own clothes and then wear them—he wondered why it felt slightly hollow.

"Here," said Shun, handing over a wet wipe to Kaden, which made him snort.

"Essentials, huh?" he said as he cleaned himself to the best of his ability before pulling on his clothes. He let Shun watch as he got dressed. He and Shun had had sex before, but the conversation, the way Shun had handled Kaden sitting on the edge, had felt... nice. As if there were more. But the impromptu rutting had lacked—Kaden blinked as he thought it over—an emotional connection. He was surprised he'd even noticed it, given that he had existed on meaningless sex so far, and that unsettled him. Why did he want more from Shun, someone he wasn't even sure he trusted? Was it because Shun had seen him naked, with all the scars, and had still acted like he was a normal person? Kaden shook his head. He didn't want to think of any other possibilities; there was no way he was developing feelings for Shun, whom he'd just met.

His dissatisfaction must have reflected on his face because Shun paused and looked at him with a frown. "What is it?"

Kaden opened his mouth to dismiss Shun's inquiry with a word or two when he felt a prickle at the back of his mind. He sat up straighter and looked around for his chain while trying to pinpoint the feeling. "Someone's coming."

"Wayland?" Shun asked as he picked up a chair and turned toward the entrance to the floor. At least they were located on a floor with very few entry points.

Kaden shook his head, dropping down to the floor, onto his knees. He moved away from the cart, and Shun seemed to realize that Kaden was mobile and swore. "Where're you going?" he asked automatically, speaking in a low voice.

"Out of sight," Kaden said as he did just that, moving out of the direct line of sight from the entrance. It was a given that Shun hadn't gone through any military training, but surely he must have had some common sense if he'd survived to adulthood on his own. "Duck behind the table or something, you idiot, don't just stand there." He tensed, waiting as the itching at the back of his skull grew stronger.

"Are you sure there's someone coming?" Shun asked after a while in a normal voice. "I don't hear anything."

"Well, it's there, so shut up," Kaden snapped as he reached the wall. There was a sound of soft footsteps, and Bradley came into view. She paused at the entrance to the floor, took in the sight of them, and sighed.

"Where did my sister go this time?"

"She's doing a survey of the building," Kaden replied. "Before you say it, she's technically a warrior, and she's hardly a child. She should be able to do something that simple without any problem." And he had been the totally responsible adult, getting a quickie while she was out of the picture. Even he knew when his power of reasoning was compromised.

"Knowing her, I doubt it," Bradley said, looking unconvinced. She looked from Kaden to Shun, who was pushing aside a chair. "I'm thirsty. Is there water?"

"What did you find out?" Shun was the first to speak.

Kaden could see her hesitating to share her news before she looked at Kaden for permission. He knew where the conversation was heading. "It's his friend Roy, isn't it?" he asked.

"Is he dead?" Shun asked, quickly moving toward Bradley, looking worried.

"No, he's working with them," Kaden said before Bradley could speak. "Isn't that it?"

Bradley leveled an accusing gaze at Kaden. "How did you know?"

Kaden expected Shun to protest, but all he did was stand there, disbelief written on his face. "Because there's no struggle here, but Roy didn't leave in a hurry either. He'd closed up everything, gotten rid of all perishable food, and seemed to have left with the idea he'd be back but not for some time."

"That's no reason to assume he's siding with those people," Shun protested, though he didn't look as if he believed in what he was defending. "Roy isn't like that. He doesn't have any loyalty to anyone."

"Exactly," Kaden concluded. "He'd have jumped at the chance of working with the armors, no questions asked as to where they'd gotten them."

Shun growled in frustration and turned away from them, his head down. "He's not like that."

Shun's unwavering loyalty to Roy stung, as if Shun was being faithful to someone else... other than Kaden. "Why, because you were pumping me for all kinds of information so you could go back and tell your precious Roy?"

A flicker of pain flashed across Shun's features. "I didn't ask those questions for that." He stepped back and threw his hands up. "So what if I tell Roy about it? It's like a hobby; we both collect information on armors. He's into nonviolence, like me."

"You pacifists think not taking sides helps. Do you think doing nothing will stop the war and it will help people? Well, you're wrong. Every single one of you are spineless idiots who are too scared to fight, who think sitting back and spouting all that shit is going to make it better." Kaden felt a sudden frisson of pleasure at seeing Shun hurt. His ideals were being proved wrong: his so-called friend Roy wasn't all he was supposed to be. He wasn't jealous of the connection Shun had with Roy; he was simply... simply worried about how Shun was sticking up for Roy, even after being proved wrong.

Shun didn't look angry, he looked betrayed, as if he couldn't believe Kaden was attacking him. "I want the war to stop—doesn't mean I'm not fighting. I have killed people... well, not really... does 'almost' count? I've done... other things, so I'm not some coward."

"Really, this theological discussion is very interesting, but can we drop it?" Bradley said dryly as she headed over to where their supplies were. She opened a water bottle and proceeded to drink, her head tipped back.

"It's not theological," Shun objected. "I think that involves religion or something."

"Well, being in armor is as close to religion as it gets for me." Bradley moved toward a stack of furniture. "I'm going to sit down and take a breather. Do you think my sister's been gone long enough?"

"I suppose that's my cue to go look for her," said Shun without much amusement. He gave Kaden a flat look, which made him wince internally.

Kaden shifted a little, feeling the burn from their earlier activity, and hoped Shun would return in a better mood. He'd just said what needed to be said, though he supposed he could have worded it a little better.

"I need my sister in this room so I can tell her what I saw, so we can discuss the next step in our plan."

Shun walked toward the doorway, glaring at Kaden as he did. "I'll go bring back the kid."

Bradley put her drink down as soon as Shun had left the room, and walked to the doorway to check on Shun's retreat. She returned a couple of seconds later and sidled up to Kaden. "He went up. We're alone."

There was little time for small talk. "Tell me."

Bradley tried to give the report as quickly as possible, and Kaden could see her formal tone fighting with her attitude. "The group that ambushed us was there, along with a few other people. I'd say about fifteen in total. They had handguns, and probably semiautomatics, not good for closed spaces, but who knows if they know it. Plus, I noticed a variety of metal bars, chains... the usual."

"Is this the same building Wayland pointed out?"

"They're holed up in that building closer to the sea, the next one... I think in one of the rooms that overlooks the beach. It's secure, even the ducts. They're on the second floor up. It's more secure than the ground floor, I guess, with one staircase going in and out. I scaled the building next to it for a quick look."

"How did you get onto the floor in their building?"

"I didn't. They were moving the armor up the steps in pieces, and I don't think they expected anyone to be around, so I got a quick look."

"The armor... did you see the armor?"

"It's there, scattered around. Even mine's in pieces... even after Wayland said she saw someone wearing it. It makes sense. No one can move around in that for long." Bradley reached into the rag she had tied around her waist, and Kaden held out his hand.

"Throw it at me."

"You knew?"

"I could feel it," he said as she pulled out the piece of his armor she'd brought back with her. She threw it at him and he caught it in one hand and looked at it. A vambrace, nothing to be excited about, but still it was a part of his armor and he was glad to have it. He flicked it up with his hand and looked at Bradley, waiting for her to continue.

"Our armor was being taken to be examined by Shun's so-called friend, if we can trust him."

"Are you sure it was Roy?" Kaden didn't have any fondness for Shun's supposed friend, but he knew better than to jump to conclusions.

"Everyone called him Roy," Bradley offered.

Kaden nodded distractedly. They didn't have the luxury of believing in the coincidence that there were multiple people named Roy, in Compen, working with Captain Allen.

"He's probably got his hands in the guts of my armor as it's the easiest to examine," Bradley continued. "The original isn't so easily unfolded. The pieces were scattered around the place, and this was the only one I could snatch. I wanted to pick mine up, but even I'm not going to be able to take fifteen people head-on."

"We need a plan." Kaden fervently wished she'd picked up a boot piece even as he snapped the vambrace on.

"Fifteen people, upper floor, very secure, and scattered armor. Weapons—"

The vambrace came loose and fell onto Kaden's lap. Kaden looked at the fallen piece of armor with his heart in his mouth. It had happened. His armor had stopped responding to him. He was finally not compatible with it, and it was over. It was over for him.

"It's probably because it needs the rest of the parts to power it," Bradley offered as she drew near. She knelt a few feet away from Kaden, as if he were an animal that needed to be tamed. Her face, pale and drawn, contradicted her hopeful words.

"It's not that," said Kaden, picking up the piece with shaking hands. "I've walked around in my boots alone and left the rest of the pieces in my room."

"Maybe the other parts are just too far away."

"Maybe." But as he stood there, holding the vambrace that was looking less and less as if it fitted over his arm, Kaden wondered if it was really over. The unwritten rules about armor said that if a wearer lost focus or faith in their armor, the thoughts were picked up by the microcircuitry built into it, and that it would affect the compatibility level.

"Maybe you just need to try it on your other hand," Bradley suggested, though she didn't look at all confident in her advice. "It's not like there's a glove to fit, so it has to be interchangeable."

"It's so damn interchangeable right now I can wear it on my foot," Kaden snapped at her, before he realized it was true. He could wear it on his leg because it didn't look like a vambrace anymore: the metal—he always had assumed it was made of metal—was changing. With hands that shook more than they should, Kaden picked up the now-altered piece of armor and snapped it around the stump of his left foot.

Bradley inhaled sharply and drew back, her eyes wide and Kaden watched in surprise as the piece that had once covered his lower arm warped until it became his lower calf cover. The changing stopped once it tapered down to what Kaden could see was the same length as his other stump. There was no foot, but the way it fitted him made him wonder about the possibilities as he pushed himself up. Balancing on one "ankle" was not that easy, but his body compensated and his armor helped. He stood for a moment and felt his face—

"That's the first time I've seen you really smile," Bradley said, her voice shaky.

Kaden sat down with a weak laugh as he took off the piece. "It's not like I can walk around in this." But he felt the relief at the thought he hadn't lost compatibility with his armor—perhaps he was even more compatible. All of a sudden, he felt as if he could fly. "Thank you." He took it off and carefully tucked it underneath him.

"You're not going to tell your lover boy about it."

"Do you always talk to your instructors like that?"

"I'm stuck with you, what do you suppose?" Bradley said with a roll of her eyes. "Please tell me you two didn't send my sister to the roof to count birds or something so the two of you could fuck."

Kaden felt himself coloring in protest. "I didn't," he started and looked at her. "How can you tell?"

Bradley gave a small laugh. "Discarded wet wipes, Shun's clothes are a mess, and it's not like I wasn't looking for the signs."

"It wasn't anything like that. It wasn't much, just fooling around." Kaden felt half his age all of a sudden. Here he was discussing his sex life with a teenager who was offering him some of the sanest conversation he'd ever known.

"So it was fornication," Bradley said unimpressed. "Huh, that figures."

"How old are you, seventy?"

"Please, I was trained to kill people for the past—uh—three years, not very long when you think of it, but I was trained to believe I was going to be an armored warrior, and I had to grow up fast." She stood up and walked forward, holding out the last of the water to Kaden. "Unlike my sister, I know what we're about. We take orders, we go out and kill people or blow up things."

"Not win the border back." They turned around to see Shun walk in with Wayland.

"I suppose there's not much use in denying my bloodthirsty nature," said Bradley, looking at him coldly. "At least I'm doing something."

"There's Harian drones in the beach town," Wayland declared.

Kaden felt his body freeze as he sat straighter and looked at Bradley. "What? Are you sure?"

Bradley swore as she also wheeled around.

"The Harians couldn't have sent them—not without alerting the patrolling boats," Shun said firmly, looking the least ruffled of them all. He turned to Wayland and said, "I'm asking you again, are you sure? You said you saw them from the distance."

"I was watching for boats, but there weren't any," Wayland told Kaden, ignoring Shun completely. "Then I saw a movement to the north, and it was a Harian drone. I tell you, it's a drone."

"Well, we do have to think this over," Kaden said, settling down a little. "Wayland, you've never seen a drone in—"

"Not in real life, but I've seen pictures and films and models they use to teach us shooting and armor control. Really, how different are the real stuff from the models we have at camp?"

"Not much," Kaden admitted. "But they are inside the border, which shouldn't happen. I don't know how it happened or why but—"

"Are you sure about this?" Shun asked, still sounding unconvinced. "It makes no sense while there are peace talks going on. Why would anyone aggravate the situation?"

Bradley looked grim. "Because no one ever touches Compen Island and this surrounding area. We don't have troops there and—"

"Actually." Kaden could remember all the talks Vorani had subjected him to. "We don't have troops here because we don't consider the beach town important, and the island is considered a no-man's-land, just like the area between the two borders. Going there means WUC would impose an economic embargo on us, and we need the food to survive."

"But there are patrols," Bradley said even as realization dawned on her. "Of course, peace talks. They pulled back on the security or... or there are lesser patrol boats or something."

"Whatever it may be, we need the armor back," Kaden concluded.

"Are you crazy?" Shun snapped. "I don't know what you think you can do, storm the building and take it back?"

Wayland balled her fists and turned to face Shun. "What do you suggest we do?"

"Why don't you call headquarters and ask for backup or WUC or something?" Shun sounded reasonable. "This is obviously more than you can handle, I mean, I don't even know what to say, but this is not something you need to go barreling into."

Kaden shook his head. "We might not have the time for that. Those drones move pretty fast, and it could take days before we get through to headquarters and convince them to take action. We need to get the armor first. Bradley, can you get the armor out if we create a diversion outside? Something loud, that'll draw at least some of the people out."

Shun snapped his fingers as if struck by inspiration. "Speaking of people, did you see a lot of people outside—apart from the sorry lot Kaden beat up?"

"None," Wayland said, and even Bradley shook her head.

"That's kind of strange. This isn't exactly crowded, but the town center did have a somewhat decent population."

Kaden remembered what the gang told him. "Your friend and his gang are doing a systematic clearing of the town."

"Allen is a lot of things, but he won't—"

"Or maybe it's the drones," Wayland offered.

"But it might work to our advantage to get the armor back," Bradley said, dismissing the conversation and moving on to the next topic. "I don't think they noticed me when I went around the first time."

"I have my electric net with me," Wayland spoke up. "I saw a lot of dried stuff outside. Maybe we can start a big fire, light up one of the buildings next to it."

Kaden could see the benefits of such a plan. "We can actually—"

It was obvious Shun was not with the plan. "You are two and a half people, with no weapons and no backup, not even proper shoes, and you're going to attack a place... a...."

Kaden wondered when Shun had removed himself from their group. It wasn't as if Shun had been with them, but he had started to count it as a group of four, and all of a sudden Shun suddenly distancing himself from them shook him. He needed to think logically, step back, think of Shun as who he really was, not as—

"You were with us." Wayland sounded betrayed. "You agreed to help us. Look, if the Harian drones are in Compen, we need to go and stop them before they get on the island. That island is ours."

Shun did not seem to agree. "It's not anyone's. The first thing to do is warn the people inside the buildings that the drones are here. We should evacuate as much of the town as possible."

"We would lose the element of surprise," Kaden said with a wave of his hand. He knew the people Shun was referring to were Captain Allen and the crew who had taken their armors, and he didn't feel generous toward them.

"If you're not going to warn them, I will," Shun insisted, as if he had a choice in the matter.

Kaden looked at Bradley and inclined his head a little. He would have loved to do the next part, but he was unfortunately without a leg to stand on. There, wasn't that nice, he could still make self-effacing jokes to himself.

Bradley tried to reason with Shun. "But aren't you worried about what'll happen to our armor? We can't just leave it there with those people."

"I know it's bad, but won't you get hurt if you try to get it?" Shun persisted. "Roy is there. If you set fire to the building, won't he get hurt as well?"

"But he's a bad guy." Wayland glared. "Don't you see that? You're with us and—"

"Wayland." Kaden knew his voice was a little too loud. "That's enough. Shun's a civilian and he doesn't need to fight our battles. And what he says makes sense. We are outnumbered and we never expected to see someone take over Compen Beach Town."

Wayland looked far from convinced. "But—"

Bradley stepped forward and kept a hand on her sister's shoulder. "You can't force anyone who doesn't want to fight, to fight."

Shun nodded, looking relieved. "Finally, you're all getting it. I'm just going to warn—uh...." And he crumpled to the ground as Bradley's uppercut caught him under the chin. They watched Shun hit the floor, hard, stunned but probably not knocked out, and Kaden nodded to Wayland, smiling grimly.

"Get the chain and tie him up. We don't have time for this. We'll come back for him when we get the armor," he ordered. He felt under him, pulled out the piece of armor, and fitted it back onto his left leg. "Get me that iron bar. I might be able to move around with this."

"Did we really have to do that?" Wayland asked in a small voice.

"It's better for all of us and safer for him," Kaden told her. "I'm sure you'd have been able to convince him if we'd had time, but now it's not as if we have a lot of that."

"But weren't you and him… you know….," Wayland said hesitantly, making Kaden color.

Well, he supposed he should be grateful he was working with such observant people. "I have never behaved so unprofessionally in the field before," he admitted in a whisper. He was supposed to be Wayland's mentor anyway, even if he knew he wasn't exactly role model material.

"Well, there's a first time for everything," said Bradley, picking up the chain and then looking around.

"Chain him to the table," Kaden said, feeling a little tired. "Wayland, you and I have a building to set fire to."

# CHAPTER 10

"COULDN'T YOU change your shape, change the armor into a boomerang or something?" Wayland asked as she pulled out a piece of dried wood.

Kaden had assumed that starting the fire would be easier than descending to the ground floor and reaching the building they needed to burn. However, while the process of collecting firewood at the base of the building seemed to be taking forever, Bradley had moved faster than expected. "There seriously isn't enough wood to light up this place. We need something bigger."

"I agree," Kaden said, wishing it was less hot. Compen Beach Town had had a resort, which boasted of lots of white sand and plenty of sun. Kaden was getting the "plenty of sun" on his back and face, and it was, in his estimate, close to four in the afternoon.

"We should—" Kaden looked around and then sighed. He motioned Bradley to move closer. "Perhaps you should go and see how Shun is doing."

She didn't look too pleased, but she nodded. "You sure he's not going to be waiting for me at the top of the staircase with a metal crowbar?"

"He did swear off violence," Kaden drawled. "Thank you, Bradley. You know, if I"—*had legs*—"could move—"

"You still wouldn't be going to check on him, you coward," Bradley muttered but broke off, moving with a smoothness that Kaden knew he could never achieve.

"Well, I can see why she was so popular with the other instructors," Kaden told Wayland as he pulled at a piece of dry wood.

Wayland seemed to have missed the obvious sarcasm in his statement. "Senior Instructor Vorani likes her."

"Vorani likes everyone." He might have been a little sarcastic—not that Wayland understood him.

"Said Bradley reminded her of you."

"That's a—" Kaden broke off and tilted his head to the side.

"What is it?" Wayland asked, and Kaden signaled for her to be quiet and hit the ground. She complied quickly; thankfully that part of her training was complete.

Kaden was listening intently, and Wayland followed suit, her face scrunched in concentration. Then she placed her hands on the ground, flat, and he let her think it over.

"I can hear something, but it's not on the ground," she said in a low whisper. "But I... this feels familiar. Should I know this?"

"That's because it's floating," Kaden told her. "Or hovering." Now they could hear the familiar hum of a drone, an unmanned hoverdrone, armed to the gills. "You said you saw Harian drones in the town."

"Why would it come over here to this side of the border?" asked Wayland as she leaned toward him.

"As you pointed out, no one here is monitoring the city. Peace talks mean withdrawing troops, and if they are going to Compen Island, then they'd probably have a few drones watching the beach town to make sure it's uninhabited."

Kaden looked at Wayland, gauging her reactions. This was the first time she was seeing any action against the enemy (Shun really didn't count), and he was worried about how it would affect her. She looked calm but it could be because she hadn't really thought about what was about to happen.

He nodded at the electric net attached to her belt. "Think you can use that?"

"Of course!" She at least didn't sound scared or even excited. She looked—ready.

Kaden stared at her to see if she was going to freeze as she had done before.

"What?"

Kaden could hardly tell her he was waiting for her to go into battle shock. "Nothing."

"It's only people," she told him in a low voice. "I just don't want to hurt people."

Kaden wondered just how much of the government propaganda everyone believed in—that the other side used faceless, inhuman drones, while they used real people who threw themselves into danger, constantly, to keep the country safe. The truth was some of the unmanned drones weren't as unmanned as the publicists claimed. Kaden gave

Wayland one more look and nodded. "When that thing comes close, throw the net over it."

Wayland rolled her eyes, and Kaden decided to keep his mouth shut. Stating the obvious had never won anyone any points. Insubordination was something he'd have to live with.

There was a low hum, and for a moment Kaden wondered if he'd misjudged the distance of the drone, whether it was closer than he'd assumed, when it rounded the corner. He stared at it for a second, wondering why he'd expected it to look different. It was a drone; it looked threatening. Kaden remembered the first time he'd seen one in training. This was of a similar model, about three and a half feet in diameter, spherical, with multiple offensive weapons bristling out of it. But somehow, at the same time, it looked different, and he couldn't figure out why.

The drone turned toward him, and he realized it seemed to have only one operational camera, which was different from those that had fully functional, 360-degree mounted views. He pressed his hands to the ground, waiting for it to spot them, when Wayland moved. She sprang to her feet, all light, quick movements, snapping the net off her waist without any hesitation, and flung it over the drone.

The net wasn't large enough to fully cover the drone, but it did its job. When the cadets were being shown demos there were always sparks and smoke, but in reality, there was very little fuss. The net flashed once and the drone stilled; its light went out, and it fell to the ground with a dull thump. There were no additional movements, and Kaden looked at Wayland and smiled. "Well done."

She appeared stunned. "That's it? Don't I have to do something else?"

"Well, let's knock out its gyro controls," Kaden offered. "Do you know what that is?"

Wayland nodded. "It's what actually stabilizes the drone by spinning in two different directions."

Kaden wondered if she knew where to find them. "They should be on the left, under the black section. There's a control panel beneath that you might need to pull out."

She gave him a strange look. "You know a lot about this."

Cadets only learned about drones in theory class with a few simulation takedowns, and actual models were for the more advanced students. "It's a part of what you learn when you advance to level four," he told her. "We fight these drones so much we have to learn how to disable them."

Wayland knelt next to the drone, and then reached for the net and hesitated. "Is it all right if I pull the net off?"

"Better if you pull the corner up and deal with the control panel first."

"So, how did we learn so much about these drones?" she asked him as she pushed at the panel. Kaden was about to tell her to wait until Bradley came, since the panels had to be pushed open with great force, but it slid open without a sound.

"Huh?"

"What?"

"It's usually more difficult to open those," he said, then shrugged. "The net might have done some internal damage."

"Anyway, how do you know so much about this?"

"Because we have captured quite a number of those and have studied them," Kaden told her. "The second division has a storeroom or ten full of captured drones. I think they make improvements to the new armor based on what they find."

"Well, that's cool," said Wayland, reaching in for a fistful of wires and pulling them all out. "I guess that should do it."

"Yes, it should," said Kaden, looking at the drone for even a flicker of movement. "Let's see if we can—"

The second drone rounded the corner just as he looked up. There was a momentary pause as everyone and everything took in each other. The drone reacted before they did. The front port pushed open as the gun emerged, and a line of fire erupted at their feet. Wayland screamed, a high-pitched, girlish scream that startled Kaden more than the actual firing had. He jerked back, feeling his legs slip as he searched for a way to push himself up and failed. Wishful thinking had never grown back limbs, and he watched in horror as the drone turned to Wayland.

At least he had even stumps, thanks to the piece of armor, even if that was fucking useless. He rolled off the cart, fell to the ground, and pushed himself up.

The stump cradled by the armor didn't protest, but the longer stump screamed in agony as soon as he put his weight on it. The bone might as well have been exposed and grinding on the concrete from what he could feel, and he bit back a scream of pain as he threw himself at the drone. The drone turned to fire at him, but he was already behind it, cringing as he waited for the back port to start firing. But the drone either was malfunctioning or simply some new variety that didn't have back ports.

Kaden found a fingerhold just as the drone jerked up, and he was lifted clean off the ground with it. The drone wasn't the largest he'd seen, but it was close to four feet in diameter and strong enough to carry him without a problem. The front gun continued to fire, but luckily Wayland seemed to have enough sense to stop screaming and duck for cover. His right hand found another fingerhold in the drone, and he dug in deeper, trying to figure out if it had any form of structural weakness. They were all taught how to disable the drones, not disassemble them, and the best way to do that while in armor was to shoot it down or kick it to bits. How to grapple a drone while out of your armor was a class he'd missed out on.

The fingerhold didn't offer any additional support as the drone lifted up, then jerked down. Either his extra weight had taken it by surprise when it'd tried to rise, or the drone was programmed to shake off anything that was on it. The drone continued to make even more erratic moves, each of which ended with an abrupt jerk that would have had Kaden flying off if he hadn't worked on the strength of his upper arms for the past six months. He could feel his stumps hanging free as he tried to find a weak spot on the outer cover of the drone with his right hand. Any thought he had of capturing it flew out of his head as he tried to hang on.

The drone jerked up and down, reminding him of a bucking horse he'd once seen in a parade—a rather unpleasant thought—just as his right hand found a hole. It wasn't much—only the tips of his three longest fingers sank into the opening—but he dove right in, forcing the plating to part with as much strength as he could spare.

Just then, the drone rose up abruptly and pulled down so hard his hands jerked. His shoulder protested at the move, the left hand came free, and he found himself hanging from his right hand alone, the gap he'd forced his fingers into cutting his flesh. The drone did an odd circular move that had him hitting his head hard against the outer shell with a dull thud.

The drone again rose in the air, and this time Kaden felt his hand and shoulder pull in a way that made him think of letting go. He wasn't sure he could survive if he broke his arm as well—when the drone jerked back down with a vengeance. Kaden was reminded of the one time his parents had taken him for a Ferris wheel ride at a local carnival before the war reached them. It was a week before the unmanned drones had bombed their hometown while Kaden and his brother were away at school. The Ferris wheel had been hand powered. When the people who'd turned it went a little too fast on certain turns, the drop had been body numbing. He remembered screaming, clutching at his brother as he left his stomach behind at each turn.

The sensation was similar, and adult Kaden didn't seem to be handling it any better than he had as a child. As the drone plunged back, Kaden knew what was coming, but he didn't want to let go. It was a little too late—he didn't know how high it had risen, and letting go from an absurd height might break what remained of his legs. He closed his eyes as the plunge continued for what felt like forever before the drone came to an abrupt halt.

His entire body jerked and his right shoulder pulled so hard he screamed, and then the pressure across his shoulder relaxed as the panel he had been digging into tore off. The weight of his body combined with the jerk and structural weakness forced the panel to come open, throwing Kaden to the ground. The drone had suddenly stopped about a foot above the ground, but Kaden hadn't been expecting it, and he tensed as he hit the ground. His head rang as he lay there. A figure darted out, clutched at the exposed wires, and pulled. The drone did spark this time, before it died and fell to the ground.

Kaden lay there, breathing hard, head ringing, his stomach emptying of what little was in it as Wayland rushed to his side.

"Instructor Kaden, are you alright?" Cool hands cradled his head, feeling his body and trying to pull him to a sitting position. Apparently she hadn't heard of the first-aid classes where people were encouraged to lie still.

"I'm fine," he said as he kept his hands on the ground and pushed himself up, wincing as a bolt of pain ran through his right shoulder. He didn't think it was broken or dislocated, but he had pulled a muscle, and it was going to be a bitch to move around.

"I was so worried—"

"What the fuck is going on here?" Bradley demanded as she appeared at their side, breathing hard. She must have run all the way,

Kaden thought as he watched her pant for breath, sweat streaming down her face.

She looked at the two fallen drones and then at the two of them, and made a face of surprise. "Oh, did the two of you...?" She wheeled toward Kaden. "You were the one who told me to go and check up on Shun."

"I think Instructor Kaden is hurt," Wayland said under her breath.

"I pulled my shoulder," Kaden said as he pushed himself toward the corner, trying to ignore the flare of red-hot agony at every move.

There was the sound of more footsteps, and Shun rounded the corner as well, looking equally out of breath, and stopped at the sight of the fallen drones. "Is anyone hurt?"

Kaden stared at Bradley. "You set him free."

"Instructor Kaden's pulled a shoulder," Bradley said as she moved toward Wayland, ignoring Kaden's question. "Are you hurt?"

"No, I'm fine," Wayland said, looking at a drone lying on the ground. "I thought there was only one. I took it down with the net."

Shun approached Kaden slowly. "Do you want me to look at the shoulder?"

Kaden looked away, feeling his face flush as he realized just how he'd left Shun behind. "We need to move. We can't stay here. People will come to investigate the sound."

"I heard her scream all the way over there," Bradley told Kaden, confirming his worst fears. "Do you think there're more around?"

"Hardly likely they'll risk sneaking in a large number of drones into this place," Shun speculated.

"I say we move just to be on the safe side," Bradley said, picking up Kaden. The brisk way she pulled at his arms had him gritting his teeth, and once he was on her back, it didn't ease. He needed both arms to cling to her, but his right arm protested at the thought of putting any weight on his shoulder, and he almost cried out in agony. "Do we go back to the building?"

Kaden had never imagined what it would be like if he lost an arm as well. He'd been so focused on losing his legs, he'd never considered what he did have. Now the thought of becoming even more dependent on someone, since his arm was starting to stiffen, made him want to burst into tears.

He looked up from Bradley's shoulder to see Shun staring at him with large, concerned eyes, and Kaden looked away with a scowl. "I think I have an idea to get our armor back."

Bradley stopped so fast that Kaden bumped his nose on the back of her head. "How?"

"There will be people coming down to investigate the sound. What if we ambush them first to reduce their numbers? Then we blow up a drone to create an even bigger distraction, and while other people come to see what it is, sneak into the building and get our armor back."

"That's a bad plan," Shun muttered.

Kaden gave him an unimpressed look. "You need to keep quiet and sit still. Close your eyes if it bothers you."

"I don't think we have the manpower," Shun stated with more confidence. "Especially since you are barely mobile."

Kaden flushed at the implication, even if Shun was using we and not you. "I can still fight."

"I'll have to be the one to sneak in during the distraction to get the gear," Bradley said thoughtfully. "That leaves Instructor Kaden and Wayland on the ground and—"

"I'll help," Shun spoke up.

Kaden snorted. "Really."

"It wasn't right that they stole your armor," Shun pointed out. "And you need me for this. Anyway, I'd feel even worse if you kill yourself with an idiotic plan because I didn't help."

"Fine," said Kaden after a few seconds of consideration. He might have just knocked out Shun, but there was little else to do but hope Shun was willing to overlook that incident. "Let's just scout for a place and see if someone's going to come see what the sound was."


HALF AN hour later, Kaden was getting pins and needles in his nonexistent feet, and he could feel that the rest of the group was getting restless as well. Shun slid up to Kaden and touched his throbbing shoulder with the tips of his fingers. "You want me to take a look at that?"

They had decided the best place to wait for Captain Allen's crew was in an overgrown alleyway between the two buildings. Kaden and Shun chose to hide behind a pile of old filing cabinets at one end, while Bradley and Wayland headed for the other end to crouch under an upturned garbage bin. Though Kaden couldn't see the cadets, he could hear them very well. "Did you have to scream?" Bradley grumbled, not even bothering to be quiet.

"I'm fine," Kaden said stiffly.

"It just came around...." Wayland was louder than Bradley was—if that was even possible. They were supposed to be lying low.

Shun started to pull at the neck of his underarmor. "Let me just rub it a little. I wish we had a cold compress."

In the background, Bradley sounded frustrated and angry. "There's no need to shout now. Why the fuck did you scream when you saw the drone?"

Kaden shrugged off the probing fingers, though he acknowledged Shun's touch was soothing. "There's no need for that."

Wayland's whisper sounded very loud. "You know they told us to scream in self-defense class—"

Shun ran a hand over the shoulder and Kaden tried to relax into it. "Don't let it stiffen. Very little we can do now, but just try not to strain it." Kaden felt the brush of hot breath before Shun's lips touched his shoulder. He tensed a little, waiting for an indication that Shun was angry at what he'd done, an indication he was mad at Kaden for leaving him tied up in the building, but Shun seemed to be a regular saint.

Bradley's voice jerked him out of the moment. "That's when you want to startle someone—but the drone isn't exactly something you could startle with a scream. All you did was almost give me a heart attack."

The lips mapped a warm path across his shoulder, up his neck....

"For that, wouldn't you actually have to have a heart?" Wayland snarled.

Kaden tipped his head to the side, letting Shun find the pulse point, curling his fingers at the sensation.

"Oh, you little bitch, that all you've got?" Bradley reiterated in an equally cutting voice.

Bradley's voice, loud and grating, snapped Kaden back to himself. He jerked away from Shun and pulled at the neck of his underarmor. "That's it! We need to go to plan B." He refused to look at Shun as he moved toward the garbage bin, behind which the girls were hiding. His shoulder still ached, but his erection proved to be an equal distraction as he forced his stumps to bear his weight. The uncovered stump hurt despite the padding he'd improvised, and he wished for something more to cushion it with.

Seeing him approach, Bradley got to her feet. "Looks like they either didn't hear or didn't care."

Kaden nodded. "We can—" He sighed as he looked down at what remained of his legs. "Look, I hate to say this, but things have gotten beyond us."

"The drones," Bradley said with a nod.

"What are you talking about?" Wayland asked, sounding puzzled.

"The original plan we had didn't figure drones on our side of the border," Kaden told her. "And from the way the drone I latched on to reacted, I'd say there's a control unit close by."

"That's not good," Bradley said while Shun approached them slowly.

He looked as if he was thinking things over. "You will have to call for help."

"We don't have a way to communicate the situation to them. We'll have to walk all the way back to the main road, and that's a… seventeen-mile walk." Kaden thought it over. "We could split up, obviously. Leave me behind and—"

"Bad idea," Bradley said quickly.

"The day's almost over," Shun added. "There won't be many vehicles on a coastal road, going anywhere at night."

"What do we do?" Wayland asked, sounding a little petulant.

Bradley looked troubled and Kaden closed his eyes in frustration as he sat back down on the ground. He looked at the building where the armor was supposed to be kept and tried to think of something to do. His shoulder ached, his back ached, and he was the most immobile of the four of them.

"The only way," he said. "We shake the building from under them. At least that'll drive them out."

Wayland looked at the fallen drones. "I've heard they have fuel cells that explode when rigged just right, but I have no idea where."

Shun walked up behind him. "I can help."

Kaden wasn't sure why Shun was all for helping them when just an hour ago he'd been in favor of warning the people inside the building. He decided to go with it for the time being. "Good," said Kaden, looking at Wayland. "You have the net. It can bring a man down. Stick to Shun, and I want the two of you to move one drone to the side of the building and blow it up."

He knew from experience that those fuel containers blew big, but he also knew his team didn't have a huge weapon to trigger the explosions and would have to dig into the innards of the drone to find the much-needed parts. If the drones even had enough fuel to explode....

"Bradley and I will move the other drone to the other side of the building and blow it up there. Give yourself time to move away once you trigger the explosion, and Wayland, take down anyone who comes to investigate."

"What do I do?" Shun asked.

"Whatever it takes to keep Wayland safe." Kaden knew he could trust Shun with that. The man might be a pacifist, but he wasn't someone who would allow a person to be killed by his own inaction. He could see even Bradley seemed to find the plan agreeable.

"Let's do it," she said, approaching him. "I'll carry you up to the drones."

"When do you want us to blow that up?" Shun asking, indicating the drone with a thumb.

Kaden looked at Bradley for guidance. After all, she was the person who'd be moving around the drones and perhaps him as well.

She thought it over. "Five minutes." She knelt in front of Kaden, her back to him. "Last time I pulled you up, I hurt your shoulder."

Kaden had been hoping she hadn't noticed the wince. "Thank you," he said as he scrambled up her back, hating every moment of it.

"Bradley." It was Shun who looked at them. "Just don't do anything stupid."

Kaden knew whom that comment had been aimed at. "I'm not going to kill myself in the middle of an explosion, on purpose."

Bradley got to her feet, and they started to walk toward the lobby. "You really think an explosion will get them out?"

"All the screaming didn't," Kaden told her after some consideration.

"They have guns, big guns, and we have nothing." Bradley adjusted Kaden on her back. "Too bad we can't fly up there."

"Could we arm the fuel cores and throw them through the window?" Wayland held out a hand. "Hear me out. We could climb to the rooftop of a building of similar height and then aim it to—"

"Let's just do this," Kaden said, feeling a little tired. The plans were becoming even more absurd as time went on. Fuel cores were heavy and cumbersome; carrying them to the right floor would require far too much effort and time. Kaden didn't like any plan where he couldn't at least be involved in some way since he had an idea he would be left at ground level.

"Fine," said Shun, and they all walked to the fallen drones, which they took apart with much less finesse than before. Bradley used brute force, and it worked most of the time.

"Here," said Shun, giving a smooth portion of the outer hull to Kaden. "You could use this to move around, like on a sled." Kaden took it, and he had to admit it was better than the rusty cart they'd used before. "And these." Shun gave him a long metal bar, but Kaden shook his head.

"I only need one. Keep the other in case we need it for something else."

"I'll take it," Wayland said, holding out her hand. "I can use it as a walking stick."

Kaden watched as the group split up, Wayland and Shun moving to one side while Bradley hesitated next to him.

"Got your matches?" he asked her. He supposed he should be grateful for Shun's foresight in packing them along with the wet wipes.

"Yeah."

"Then go. I'll be fine here." She hesitated, but Kaden knew it was the correct thing to do; he would only slow her down. He also had an idea of what he should be doing next, and he didn't want an audience. He waited as everyone moved away, then started the long, painful process of pulling himself toward the building that housed the group of people who'd taken his armor. Pacifists, mercenaries, all those cowards, he thought with disgust. More like common thieves.

The explosions came as expected, rocking the ground and shaking the building. Several buildings lost what remained of their windows, and Kaden heard some of the wildlife flutter away. He didn't have to wait long for people to come out of the building. He stayed still for a while, his head low as the people walked by, looking up and around. Captain Allen wasn't stupid; he wasn't sending everyone out, just a select few.

He remembered they had talked about how the basic design of buildings had changed very little over time and decided he would enter through the fire escape at the back. He didn't think it'd be open anymore or unguarded, but he remembered a lot about buildings and knew the construction of those couldn't have been that different. He reached the back of the building and looked to see where the fire escape should be.

He should have expected it. The fire escape turned out to be a rusted mess of metal at the bottom of the building. The connecting door at the top looked rusted too, and even though it appeared to be easy to open, there was no way for him to reach it, unless he perfected the art of wall crawling.

"I can lift you to it." Kaden looked around, surprised by the sound of a voice, to see Shun standing behind him.

Kaden shrugged. "I was just looking."

"I think the platform will hold you, even if you probably weigh more than any of us." Shun crept up to Kaden, crouched low on the ground to avoid detection from above.

"That's not the kindest thing you've said," said Kaden, looking at the platform. He was heavily muscled, perhaps more than Bradley, and if he had his legs, he'd be the tallest in the group too. "Why do you want to help me now?"

Shun rolled his eyes as he came closer. "You really think I don't know anything about wanting to get back something that is mine?"

Kaden nodded and lifted his chin. "We don't have much time."

Shun reached for Kaden. "I hope I can do what Bradley can," he said as Kaden climbed onto his back and then onto his shoulders. He grunted and straightened with Kaden on his shoulders, and Kaden tightened his thighs to secure himself.

The platform came within reach, and Kaden reached up to grab the metal, hoping his shoulder would hold. The muscles protested, but he found the need to climb up was more than the pain—barely. "Don't move," he said as his fingers closed on the platform. He felt the arm protest then, but he ignored it in favor of trying to pull himself up. He had to remind himself that his body was much lighter since he'd lost his legs—by almost fifteen or sixteen pounds—though he struggled to lift his body. He slithered up on his belly, a piece of metal snagging the suit near his hip, tearing through and scratching his skin. He pushed himself farther back from the edge, not sure how the wall fastenings were going to be after years of open-sea air exposure, and found himself near a small window that doubled as a door and led into the building. He pushed the door open with his left hand and peered in to see if there was anyone around.

"Psst, Kaden."

Kaden looked down just in time to catch the metal rod Shun threw at him. He nodded his thanks before slinking inside, ignoring the various aches in his body. Kaden wasn't sure if the armors were even on the second floor, but this seemed to be his last chance to get his. The drones in Compen Beach Town were a sure indication that the Harians were taking advantage of the peace talks, and he wondered how long it would take for Joscal to make a move.

For all he knew, Vorani and the rest could be on their way, ready to save the day. But he also knew that should they see him without his armor—well, without his legs—they would simply take away the one thing that meant the world to him.

He was at the beginning of a dark corridor covered in dust. The dust had been disturbed a little, and the tracks Kaden left blended right in. He moved toward the center of the building inch by inch, holding the wall for balance, his unarmored stump becoming even more painful with each halting step he took. He stopped a little, taking the weight off it to rest on his armored stump, wondering why the hell he'd ever thought this was a good idea.

He looked over his shoulder to where he'd entered the building—he had moved just a couple of feet, and already his physical limitations were slowing him down. He remembered the days after the amputation at the hospital, sitting in bed listening to Dr. Lane telling him the dangers of contractures and what not, resulting in permanent shortening of his leg muscles. Telling him things like how to sit up, how to move, how to roll over in bed, how people who had been paralyzed below the waist had managed just fine, and how lucky he was to be alive.

Which had been about as relevant to him as—well, it had been too soon and he'd not been in the right mindset to deal with it, and Dr. Lane had had little time to spare for him with the stream of injured coming in through the doors of her hospital.

When the twenty-three-year-old who'd been in the bed next to him, minus an arm and a leg, had managed to kill herself with a smuggled handgun, Kaden had thought of following suit with his drip. He had lied about it later, said it had been an accident, but Dr. Lane might have seen the same desire in his eyes because she'd rolled his armor to his bed one day, suggesting that he might as well polish it a little. Kaden had picked it up, and it had wrapped itself around him, and in the end the armor had saved him.

Now he needed it back.

He reached the juncture where the corridor split into two long, narrower corridors, and he could see what seemed to be an endless line of doors along both of them. He could also hear the sound of hard soles against concrete; the distraction could work for only so long. He looked left then right, wondering which side he should duck into, when his armored leg pulled toward the left corridor. He braced against the metal rod he was using as a walking stick and lifted his leg again to see if it would happen. There seemed to be a faint pull toward the left, which he couldn't be very sure of. It could be wishful thinking on his part, though there was nothing else for Kaden to do. A faint pull was as good a reason for choosing a direction as any.

He'd started toward the left-hand corridor when footsteps came from close behind him. It spurred him to move faster, using his metal rod to pull himself forward. He felt like a man rowing a boat on dry land.

The pull seemed to feel stronger. He was sure his armor was somewhere on the corridor, but even as he stopped to feel, there was a cry of surprise behind him. Kaden looked over his shoulder and groaned—two people, one armed with a handgun. The only reason they hadn't shot him was probably because they had not been expecting him.

Kaden thought out his options and stopped completely, turned around, and shrugged. "So, what can I do for the two of you?"

He should have brought his chain with him; it would have given him more reach and compensated for his limited mobility. The men came toward him with confidence, but he wasn't stupid enough to try anything. He leaned against his rod, sat on his rump, and waited, letting them do all the work.

The men came to a halt near him, not so close he could touch them, but close enough that he could see the dirt on their boots. Sitting down, he could only see as high as their waists without tipping his head back, and he decided he didn't want to look up at them.

"Leave the rebar," one of the men said. Kaden kept it on the ground next to him.

"Kick it away."

Kaden shrugged. "Can't."

There was a long silence and then the sound of the safety being taken off the gun. "Come, we're taking you to meet the boss."

Kaden looked up quickly at that, assessing what they intended to do. One of them was brushing his hands, preparing to grab him, while the other had a gun trained on him.

"Where's your boss?" Kaden asked as he bent his knees.

"What's it to you?"

"In case you haven't noticed, I don't do stairs very well."

"If you made it to the second floor, another staircase up won't kill you," the man who was reaching for him said.

It took Kaden about three seconds to process: they were taking him upstairs, away from the armor he knew was on this floor. It was on the very corridor he was in. If he was taken up, there might not be a chance for him to regain it, and he might never see it again. He nodded, and as the man leaned in to help him up, he picked up the bar and hit him hard across the head.

The man jerked back, hurt but not unconscious or immobile. Kaden hadn't had the height or the force to complete a deadly swing, and anyway, he knew from experience people rarely fell unconscious when hit on the head. The man he'd hit reeled back, cursing, and Kaden tightened the grip on his bar to—

The gunshot reverberated through the corridor, making Kaden's eardrums protest. He felt the force of the bullet punch into him and push him back before he felt the pain. It was not a killing shot, he thought as he lay in the corridor, pain pulsing low on his chest. At least not straightaway.

He used the rod, still in his grip, to swing out and used the momentum to stand up. He pivoted on the armored leg to drive the metal bar right through the middle of the man who was holding the gun. The gun went off one more time before the man fell backward, leaving a hot streak of pain across Kaden's right cheek.

Kaden followed the falling man, a leap of desperation because he knew it was his only chance at survival. He grabbed the gun as the second man struggled to react, and shot him square in the forehead. Shooting had never been Kaden's specialty, but he wasn't going to miss a target three feet away.

He forced himself to move smoothly, despite the burning pain in his side and the feeling of hot blood soaking into the underarmor. He searched the fallen man for ammo (none) and considered frisking the other guy too, but time was short, and he could feel the insistent need for the armor. He wondered how long it would take for the rest of the people inside to react to the sound of the gunshot and come raging out.

Kaden didn't want to pull out the metal bar from where it was embedded in the guy's chest, so all he had was the gun. He studied it as he moved deeper into the corridor: a civilian model of a more commonly used Army gun. The military version of the gun he'd used was a 9 mm automatic that held up to thirty rounds. The one he was holding felt lighter, and there was no telling, but he assumed it carried less ammo in the magazine and was semiautomatic. Given that the previous owner had fired only twice, there might still be some ammo left in it.

Kaden was hoping that the group wasn't armed to the teeth; the display of armor-piercing rounds didn't mean they had enough of those launchers for everyone. Only one of the two men had had a gun: perhaps the group didn't even have enough weapons for everyone. There were plenty of military-grade weapons on the black market, but they were expensive. From what Kaden had seen of Captain Allen, he seemed the type to buy a few good weapons rather than splurge so that everyone in the gang had a subpar gun. Kaden hoped for the best as he kept the gun in hand and struggled toward the pull of the armor.

The next group of people rounded the corner: three this time—two women, one man—and Kaden had his gun firing before they had time to react. One of his shots hit a woman across her breast, and she reeled back, gasping, to be pulled back to safety by the other two. Kaden kept moving forward. He could feel the pull like a throbbing in his bones. His armor was close; he could taste the metal.

There was the sound of more footsteps behind him, more people, and Kaden didn't have time to slow down. He turned around, fired off two shots, and started forward, ignoring everything. Someone from the first group peered around the corner and emptied his weapon, and a sudden feeling of dizziness had Kaden slumping to the floor, saving him. Several shots, fired blindly by people who were a little scared of his gun, hit the floor and the walls of the corridor. A stray bullet flew by Kaden's scalp; he felt his hair shift. He assumed he hadn't been hit until something ran down from his head onto his eye, and when he wiped it off, his hand came away red. Kaden was chipped by flying pieces of plaster, and he had to wipe more blood so it wouldn't obscure his vision. He'd been shot twice, but his need to reach the armor kept him moving.

He fired back blindly, focusing on the pull. The armor was so close he could smell the oil he'd used to polish it. His strength began to falter, draining out of him like the blood pumping out of the bullet hole in his side. There was very little pain, but he knew he was bleeding badly. He started to crawl, leaving a trail of blood on the floor. The gun clicked empty, and he threw it away, using his now free hand to find grooves in the floor to pull himself forward.

Another bullet bit his upper thigh, but he was beyond caring as he reached for the door where he knew the pull was coming from. He looked at the door uncomprehendingly; it was locked and there was no way he could open it. He balled his fist in frustration and banged it against the door, feeling his armor inside but having no way to reach it. Blood blinded him in one eye. He could feel his side bleeding, and his thigh and shoulder joined it in screaming agony.

He was losing his vision, and he didn't know if he could do anything beyond what he had done. Kaden wondered if he was finally going to die, separated from his armor by a couple of inches of reinforced wood. He clawed at the door as the group behind him came into the corridor. He realized somewhere in the back of his mind that they had stopped shooting and were simply standing there watching him trying to open the door. He wondered why someone didn't just put a bullet to the back of his head and get it over with.

But he could also understand that human nature was cruel. He had killed some of them. They were going to relish the moment of his suffering before, hopefully, putting him out of his misery. Kaden wondered if he should turn around and just shout at them to shoot him, but to do so seemed to require more coordination than he possessed at that moment.

He started to bang his head against the door, a slow rhythmic bumping as he waited for his body to bleed out.

The door swung open. "What's with all the noise, I'm trying to work—"

All Kaden could see was a pair of skinny legs as he fell face-first into the room. He could hear the group in the corridor move then, but not too quickly since he was obviously beyond a threat, to get him out of the way. But Kaden didn't care. He was inside, and he could see his armor. He reached out to it, but it seemed as if he were underwater. He could feel his hand move, but it moved sluggishly, slowly, as if against an invisible force.

"Well, get him out of here," the person who opened the door exclaimed, and Kaden felt someone grip his right leg.

"Come," he shouted, or thought he shouted. His armor was so close, and all he needed was to… was to… put it on. His mind relaxed as the piece of armor on his leg tightened and then rolled off completely. He heard someone exclaim something, but by then Kaden was pushing himself up. The armor surged across the table it had been resting on, dragging with it parts that were on the floor and on top of shelves.

Kaden could see through his hazy vision as parts that had been pried apart tried to mold themselves as they came toward him, and he accepted them all. The armor closed around him like a welcoming hug, the weight, the balance, the feel—all right. It lifted him up like a puppet on a string, assembling around him like a giant cocoon. The helmet enveloped his head as the leg pieces fitted under him, giving him the last inches of height back.

People started firing then, but it was too late for them. The armor opened the laser port, and Kaden watched as a line of fire tore the people into pieces and dropped them like fresh meat. He turned toward the person who'd opened the door, a reedy young man who looked as if he could do with a few good meals. He wore loose brown trousers, an equally large T-shirt, untucked, and wire-rimmed glasses that actually suited him.

Kaden wondered if he should shoot him and get it over with, but he had an inkling that this would be Shun's friend, Roy, and Shun would be very angry if Kaden simply shot him because he was in the way. Kaden clenched his armored fist and punched the man hard enough to push him across the room. Pieces of armor scattered as the man fell, and Kaden recognized both Shun's and Wayland's as they rolled across the floor.

He looked at his options, wondering if he should leave them behind or just—a wave of dizziness had him struggling to find his balance, and he listed to the side. He pulled himself up and made a quick decision. Wayland's armor it was. She could use it; it was hers even if he was leaving behind the one they had initially set out to retrieve. They were in enemy territory, and the best option was to defend themselves and come back for Shun's armor later.

Giving back Shun's armor could mean he might turn against them—leave him, no, them—and that would be a bad outcome.

He thought about picking up the armor—and he was sure he attempted it—and though in a span of a few seconds he did have what seemed to be all of Wayland's armor in his hands, he really couldn't remember picking them up. He thought it best to regroup, to find Bradley and the rest.

As he stepped over the dead bodies, he could hear more people coming to investigate. He turned, just as an armor-piercing missile shot past him. He hadn't even heard it fire, so he had no idea how he'd reacted to it.

Kaden felt a punch across his abdomen, his plates locking, but the force still carried him up and away, and when he rolled and stood up, he could see someone wearing Bradley's armor advancing.

Kill him, he thought, but he had a feeling Bradley would be extremely pissed if he blew a hole in her armor. Instead he felt his body surge forward and kick the armor hard. The new armor, with its weight and reinforced plating, was heavy, and Kaden's physical status should have made it impossible for him to kick the damn thing over at all, but the force of the kick threw it through the wall and off the entire floor. Watching it fall, Kaden blinked, wondering if he was even in control of the armor.

What next?

He needed to get away from the building. Past experience had shown him that though the armor was self-repairing, he was going to need medical treatment to heal himself, and from the way he was unable to keep his thoughts in line, probably fast. He jumped out the hole in the wall after the fallen armor. He thought he saw the new armor lying in a crater in the ground and wondered if the wearer was dead. He didn't think so; those armors were technically designed to protect the wearer.

Kaden remembered he had once taken part in such a test with Vorani, to measure the plating strength or... what...? He really wasn't sure what he was thinking or why he was even moving when he couldn't even remember where he wanted to go.

It seemed a long way, but then again it seemed every time he opened his eyes, the surroundings had changed and he was moving. He was climbing something, and then... he heard voices. He was with people, people he knew, though he wasn't sure if he could name any of them. He could see light skin and blond hair and a hand on his shoulder, though he couldn't feel it, and thought... *Better let me go. I'm losing blood, and they might be able to stop it.*

His armor dropped him to his knees. Familiar clicks sounded as the plate fittings came off, and suddenly he was free, falling onto the floor. Hands caught him, and he looked at the dark girl with worried eyes, something about her armor, and then he was swallowed by the dark.

# CHAPTER 11

KADEN OPENED his eyes with difficulty. It was dark, almost night, and the only light in the room was from a candle. It felt as if someone had dropped a handful of sand into his eyes and glued them shut. His mouth felt so dry the inner lining of his cheek stuck to his teeth to the point he was sure they were crumbling.

He groaned as he struggled to sit up and felt someone approach him quickly. "Here," said Shun, helping him sit up. In one hand he held a canister of water with a straw inserted. "Drink this."

Kaden tried to lift a hand to grab it and found his body simply wasn't willing to move. Shun held the straw to his lips while supporting his body with one hand. He opened his mouth a little and sucked hard. The straw was dragged out forcefully. "Slowly," Shun said, pulling back the bottle, and Kaden found his hand did move as he tried to grab it back.

There was the familiar sound of armored feet on concrete, and Kaden whipped his head around in surprise. It was Bradley in her full armor, right down to the helmet. She smiled, all teeth, and Kaden had the idea she wasn't too pleased. "Well, you certainly shook up a lot of things," she said as she entered the room. "How are you feeling, Instructor Pace?"

Kaden closed his eyes and tried to get a handle on how he was feeling. It felt like someone else's pain, as if he were experiencing it from a distance. "Where did you get the painkiller from?" The words didn't leave his mouth clearly; he was still a little sluggish, and his tongue felt heavy.

"Well, at least we can confirm you didn't hit your head too hard," Shun said, sounding relieved.

"Not really sure about that," said Bradley as she walked up to him, the clank of each step echoing in the empty room, and finally Kaden felt the water he'd drunk reach his stomach and clear his mind. He looked around the room they were in—an empty office building by the looks of it, though it seemed to be somewhat clean....

"Where exactly are we?" he said, reaching for the water again. This time he finished it in one gulp and set the empty bottle on the floor, surprised to see his lower body was encased in his armor. He hadn't even noticed the usual stiffness where the armor plates overlapped. He ran a hand over his middle, reaching for the place where he'd been shot, and his hand encountered another armor plate. A second look confirmed it was his armor and not a piece of metal, and he pulled it off with a quick turn of his wrist. The bandage underneath was not as bulky as he'd expected it to be, and he grunted in surprise. "Where did we get medical supplies from?"

"Some questions can be answered more easily than others," Shun said with a wry smile. "We are in the enemy base, so to speak. After you caused havoc in their midst—" He rolled his eyes. "—and for the record, I didn't expect you to do something that stupid—they packed up and left."

"And your armor?" Kaden directed his question to Bradley.

"Believe it or not, there I was sneaking around the corner, and this guy wearing my armor just fell from the sky and landed at my feet." She didn't sound particularly pleased. "What were you thinking? You could have died."

Kaden looked down at the bandage on his side and sighed. He wasn't sure if he could explain to her what he was thinking, that if he hadn't been able to get his armor, he had been ready to die. "They left in a hurry," Shun said in the ensuing silence. "It's rather convenient for us, since they left a lot of their things behind, including some food and medical supplies." The hand on his shoulder was warm and comforting. "It was a good thing. You were rather badly hurt."

He felt, more than heard, the approach of the final member of their little group. Wayland, also in her armor, gave him a relieved smile. "It's good to see you awake, Instructor Kaden," she said, kneeling beside him. "I thought you were going to die when you took off the armor and all that blood came out."

Kaden looked at Bradley while tapping the chest plate. He was curious as to why they had replaced the plate after dressing his wound.

Bradley understood his unspoken question. "The chest plate was acting as a brace against your wound," she explained. "When you took it off, the bleeding started again."

"Your armor was able to halt the bleeding and keep you moving, so we thought it best to put it on," Shun explained. "That and the fact you're so fond of the damn thing."

Kaden sighed as he put the plate back on and folded his legs beneath him to stand up. The wave of dizziness caught him unprepared, and he fell back heavily.

"You lost a lot of blood." Shun stood, not offering a helping hand but looking prepared to steady him if needed. "None of us have any practice in giving an infusion, even if there was any way of doing it. The best we could do was patch up the bullet hole and grazes after making sure they were clean."

Kaden touched his side, the painkillers making it hard for him to figure out if he was hurt or not. "Did you get the bullet out?"

"The armor did that," Wayland said, sounding awed. "It was stuck to the inside of the armor—like a magnet or something."

"What about my leg—I got shot there as well."

"It seemed more like a flesh wound, not too deep, maybe a… ricochet," Shun said hesitantly. "It should hurt when you stand up."

That was something to look forward to. Kaden made a second attempt to stand and was able to do so with the help of Shun's hand on his lower back. "Damn," he said in a low voice as Kaden finally unfolded to his full height. "I'd forgotten how tall you were."

"It's good to see you back on your feet," Wayland said with a cheeky grin.

"No sudden moves," Bradley added as she watched him. "There's only so much medical glue can hold together."

Kaden nodded, feeling elated despite everything. A smile appeared on his face. He had his legs back. "What did I miss?"

"Dinner," Shun said before Bradley could speak. "You need to eat before you can make—"

"Where did the people here go?" Kaden had to ask. "Captain Allen and his lot?"

There was a reluctant silence. Wayland folded first. "To the island."

Kaden wondered if he'd misheard. "To what island?"

"Compen," Bradley said reluctantly. "They had a boat—we heard it, and they all got into it and went away. They took Shun's armor."

Kaden didn't bother correcting them. It wasn't Shun's armor, but arguing over something that simple wasn't worth it. "We need to get it back."

"Agreed," Bradley said. "But I don't think we can do it. We might be able to find a serviceable boat and go to the island, but we could be outnumbered, and we have no idea how many people they have in place already."

"How could they have crossed to the island when there are border patrols and all that?" Kaden asked. Then he realized the answer himself. "The peace talks—they withdrew everything."

That would mean Captain Allen and his crews were safe in a very defendable location with no way of anyone reaching them. If they were to discover some research secret from the lab, there could be a shift in the power balance. There was the additional risk of WUC stepping in and discovering Captain Allen and the crew along with a fully functional armor, which would mean Joscal might as well hand it over to the enemy.

"This is bad," Kaden said.

"We think so," Bradley replied. "We need help. Call home base and tell them what happened."

She was making sense. They were in no situation to go blazing into the unknown. "Fine," he said, taking a deep breath. He turned to Shun and grimaced. "I think it's time you left."

Everyone in the group looked taken aback. Shun had a stunned expression on his face. "What?"

"We came to get the armor back—we'll get it back—and there's no need for you to get involved."

"But...," Wayland started, then became silent when she realized what was being said. "Fine," she said with a nod.

Bradley looked to Kaden. "We don't have to do anything yet, do we? We have until morning. I say we get a couple of hours of rest and then head back toward central command."

Kaden didn't like the sound of that. "Perhaps one of us should stay behind to keep an eye on the island," he said after a couple of seconds, walking toward the low table where he could see some food rations.

Bradley rolled her eyes. "You think that needs to be you."

"Yes."

"Even with a bruised head, a hole in your side, and numerous... I don't even know what those are."

Kaden sighed. "I'm fine, and it's not like I'm going to swim across to Compen."

"I should certainly hope not," Wayland said, sounding older than her years.

"As you pointed out, I'm hurt," Kaden added. "I won't be able to move as fast as you. Go and call for help and come back with proper medical and...."

Bradley didn't look fully convinced but nodded, as if understanding him. "It wouldn't be nice to leave you all alone."

Something about that made Kaden pause. He could see the rest of his armor on the floor, a couple of shoulder pieces and the endpiece that made up his helmet. He looked at his boots, at where his legs should be, and tried to remember something he needed to tell Shun. "You know I'll slow you down."

Wayland sighed and looked at Bradley. "You'll have to go for help. I'll stay with Instructor Pace to watch over Compen. I don't think one person will do."

"I'm not going to throw myself off the ledge the moment you've gone." The moment Kaden said it, he realized just how wrong it sounded. He sighed as he took a bite of an energy bar, nudging the rest of his armor toward him with his foot and trying to ignore the pointed silence. "We don't have to decide anything just now," he added for good measure. The side of his head hurt with every bite he took, and his arm ached, deep and penetrating, which made him think his bone must have been bruised. He didn't think he'd be that energetic once the painkillers were gone from his system.

"We can't go stumbling around in the dark anyway," Shun said firmly, putting a halt to the conversation. "You might want to sit down again and perhaps get some rest."

Kaden conceded. "Do we have more painkillers on us?"

Shun nodded with a grimace, looking none too happy.

"Hey, I don't need it now, and it's not like I'm going to become an addict or anything," Kaden snapped, aware he was under the influence of the drug even before he'd finished the sentence. "Anyway, just checking." He flexed his right arm. "Doesn't feel broken but don't expect me to carry anything."

"It's late anyway," Bradley agreed, giving up on the argument. "Do we take turns keeping watch?"

Shun grimaced. "It was a long day for all of us. Can't we lock the door and sleep in the corners?"

Kaden knew he was in no condition to keep a lookout, and Shun probably had never been trained in that. Bradley had done enough lifting and running around that day to need a rest, and he really couldn't see Wayland being responsible enough. They were already drifting away to their own little worlds, prepared to sleep the night away.

"Let's just sleep," he said, tired and feeling the brief energy he'd received trickle out from him. He walked over to a corner of the room and slumped down, folding his feet beneath him.

"Are you going to sleep in your armor?"

Kaden looked up to see Shun settling down next to him. He seemed at ease with the arrangement as he indicated that Kaden should move over. "I got you some old newspaper—works great as padding."

Kaden removed his arm pieces and signaled for Shun to come closer. "You really are so practical."

"You mean because I'm willing to sit and talk to you after you tied me up?" Shun responded. "I wouldn't say that. I was damn angry, and maybe that's why I pushed you up the fire escape." He gave a dry laugh. "It was exactly because of that—I was so damn angry at you, and I thought that if you went inside, you might be able to tell the lot inside about the drones. I thought you'd meet Captain Allen and talk to him rationally, and—"

"Thank you."

Shun slapped the newspaper bundle on the ground hard enough to raise a cloud of dust. "It's nothing to thank me about. I almost got you killed."

Kaden let his head fall back against the wall. "I wanted it."

Shun looked at him without speaking for a couple of seconds. "I didn't. I'd have lost something important."

Kaden looked at him sharply and felt something well in his chest. It wasn't pain, and it certainly wasn't happiness, but it felt like relief. That someone was telling him what he wanted to hear.

"You know, this was a simple mission, but I screwed it up," Kaden told Shun without any animosity. "You stole the armor and then this— but I guess without it, I wouldn't know that the Harians were invading. Just, I keep making the wrong choices. I'm not ready to be in the field. I know it, Bradley knows it, and even Wayland knows it. I keep making the wrong choice, no matter what I do."

"But we're all here, in one piece."

And Kaden remembered what he'd wanted to tell Shun when he'd regained consciousness. "Your friend," Kaden queried as Shun looked away, as if to hide his expression. "Would he be tall, skinny with bad skin and large glasses?"

"That could be a lot of people," Shun said, but the way he looked at Kaden sharply confirmed his suspicion.

"Well, he wasn't their prisoner. He seemed to be working with them, calling the shots and all."

Shun looked shocked. "You can't be sure."

"A room to his own with all our armors, I'd say yes," Kaden told him.

Shun got to his feet then, looking none too pleased, head bent, eyes closed. "I didn't think he'd do it, give up on his principles."

"Maybe it was the lure of being able to study the armor," Kaden offered. "You did say that he was obsessed with them." He sounded pleasant to his own ears, which was not like him. Even Shun must have understood that Kaden was in a good mood.

"I suppose," Shun said with a faint smile. "When he got going, he did forget a lot of things."

"I'm more worried about what tomorrow morning will bring." Kaden patted the newspapers. "Sit, rest. Where are you going to walk off to?"

Shun snorted but didn't reply as he returned to his previous place, and Kaden sighed into the silence. The candle flickered in the faint breeze from the broken window, and the room slowly sank into darkness. He carefully put his good arm around Shun's shoulder, and Shun didn't pull away. Instead he leaned against Kaden, and Kaden found himself drifting to sleep.

KADEN WOKE up with a start and cursed as he pulled his injured shoulder and then his side in quick succession. The painkillers had finally run out, and it seemed he wasn't going to get any more sleep unless he found some more. Shun was fast asleep next to him, head to the side. His mouth was open, and he breathed out with a soft hiss that made his upper lip quiver. Kaden could see Shun's face in the faint light from the outside—he looked young, younger than he usually did when he was awake, and Kaden wondered just how old Shun was. He fought the urge to brush back Shun's hair and instead got up as silently as possible and felt his boots connect with the floor. He moved with care, feeling every injury with each small movement, toward the table in the middle where he knew Bradley had kept the painkillers.

Both Bradley and Wayland had chosen to sleep in other corners of the room, in direct view of each other. If they were attacked, at least they'd not be cornered in one place. He supposed it was strategy of sorts, but he really wished Bradley was within talking distance so he could find out where the pills were. He didn't seem to be bleeding, and he knew the medical glue used in the field was tough. It couldn't bond broken bones, but it could glue almost anything, even act as an anti-infection agent. But just to be sure, he plucked a couple of tablets of what they called "field cure-it-all" and dry swallowed them. He followed it with a couple of painkillers.

He tipped his head back, allowing the pills to slip down his throat, and while waiting for them to make their downward journey, he looked up at the ceiling of the room and wondered what the odd patches of mold were from. He supposed the painkillers would kick in eventually, but it would take a while, and he was feeling restless. He moved his stiffening shoulders several times to make sure his muscles hadn't atrophied, or whatever happened to strained muscles, and continued to do so as he walked around the room.

The metal plates on his boots clanged softly though he tried to be quiet. There wasn't much of anything to fill up the night. Kaden looked at the shadows dancing on the wall as he did his stretches. In the distance a bird hooted, and he found himself smiling. The world outside was empty: just the surf beating against the beach, no people, not many anyway, no vehicles, and definitely no moving lights.

Kaden snapped his head around and looked at the shadows he'd seen on the wall. The moving shadows. The candle was out—there should be no moving light source for the shadows on the wall to dance. He moved toward the boarded window as fast as he could and looked out. Nothing.

He looked over his shoulder. The shadows on the wall seemed still.

But he had seen them move. A cloud over the moon, perhaps, or....

Kaden had seen the shadows flicker and it had reminded him of lights on a moving vehicle. He pushed the window open and walked out onto the balcony. The building they were in faced the sea, and he could see Compen like a dark shadow across the ocean. He could hear the sea and smell the wet shore and.... Kaden leaned over the balcony to get a closer look at the beach.

It seemed so faraway and dark, and he couldn't even see anything, but surely he wasn't mistaken....

A hand around his waist pulled him back sharply, and he was spun around so fast he gasped. A hand pushed against his chest, pinning him to the wall, and he was able to make out Shun's face.

"Really, now you need to be watched all the time?" Shun snarled. "I thought you were over that phase."

"What...," Kaden stuttered in confusion. He was sure he'd seen something on the sea, headed toward Compen, and he was trying hard to figure out what it was. Then Shun's words penetrated the fog of thought, and he blinked in surprise. Kaden could feel Shun's hand on his shoulder, holding him in place with all his strength—

"Why are you smiling?" Shun demanded, sounding none too pleased.

Kaden found it hard to explain why he felt a strange warmth in his chest, a feeling of lightness. "Look, Shun, I wasn't going to... jump, I just thought I saw something on the horizon."

Shun didn't ease up. "Really."

"Really." Kaden let his head fall forward until their foreheads touched. "I wasn't even thinking of it right now, but thank you. I do appreciate that you thought I was going to jump...."

"It's no joke," Shun snarled. "I hate that you are like that. Do you know how scared I was when I found you were not there when I woke up? Then I find you on the balcony and your head hanging over the railing." Kaden tried to capture Shun's lips, but Shun turned away. "No, this is serious. Are you listening? I don't want to be with you, wondering if you are going to jump or kill yourself or... or I don't know what."

"Be with me?"

The two became silent as they realized just what had been said. "You know what I mean," said Shun, easing up. He stepped back and turned away, his back to Kaden.

"Maybe I don't," said Kaden, lowering his voice, wanting to preserve the moment. He didn't want Bradley to wake up and intrude on them. He walked behind Shun and slipped a hand around his waist, pulling him back. He was now tall enough to rest his chin on Shun's shoulder by slumping a little.

Shun didn't reply.

"You mean, you aren't averse to being with me on a longer basis?" Kaden murmured. "As in regularly—like a relationship."

Shun caught one of Kaden's hands and squeezed. "I think that is something that needs to be discussed in detail, but I'm not saying no. But we both know it's not going to happen. We'll be going in opposite directions tomorrow."

Kaden sighed. "I'll take what I can get. I appreciate the sentiment. I know I have issues—"

"You were right."

"I think you meant, I am right."

"No, I mean, look…," Shun said, pointing out to sea. "You were right, there are lights at the corner of the beach. There are people there."

And Kaden realized with a start what he was looking at. It wasn't a boat—it was too still—but it was over water, floating toward the island. He unclasped his hands from around Shun's waist and lunged forward to the balcony railing. There was no mistaking the light pattern, too steady but above the water, and now that he knew what he was looking for, he could make out the faint outline of the dark drone on the beach. A drone heading toward Compen Island, where Shun's armor was, following the shallow sandbar under the sea.

"Oh, this is bad," Shun said as he peered in the direction of the bobbing lights. "It'll be low tide soon, and then it might be able to cross over. Captain Allen…."

"Captain Allen could be selling what they got from our armor to the other side." And then Kaden realized something even more urgent, and his heart missed a beat at the thought of it. "Shit, they have your armor. They might pass it on."

Shun looked like he wanted to argue. "Okay," said Kaden, backtracking. "Even if they weren't planning on selling the armor, they might be overpowered and the armor taken."

Shun nodded, his face a mask of doubt. "So what do you suggest we do now? It's not like you can call head office somehow and tell them you need a force at Compen."

Kaden strode into the room with a shake of his head. "Bradley, Wayland," he called. "Wake up, we need to move."

There was a groan and Bradley opened her eyes, underarmor sliding over one shoulder. "Damn, is it already morning?" she said as she staggered to her feet.

"It's not morning," Kaden told her. "But we have drones going toward Compen."

Bradley blinked at him a couple of times and tilted her head. "Huh?"

"Compen is being invaded."

Bradley blinked a couple more times, sleepiness slowing her down as she stared at Kaden blankly before her mind finally kicked in. "Oh, shit," she said. "Shun's armor is there."

"Exactly," Kaden said. "You have to go and inform head office about it. Can you get Wayland to suit up and—"

"We don't have enough time," Bradley said quickly. "Going for help, even in armor, will take half a day." She kicked Wayland as she walked by. "Wake up, we have to move." Wayland stirred, rolled over, and went back to sleep.

Kaden hoped she'd eventually be weaned out of that habit, since it could get a person killed on the field. He looked at Shun. "There might be a few headed toward the sea, but there are some on the beach, and if we can stop them we might be able to save everything before it gets started."

"Wh-at's going...." Wayland yawned herself awake and looked at them in confusion, blinking the last of the sleep out of her eyes. "Come on, Brad, five more minutes."

"Suit up," Kaden told her without sparing a glance. "We have an invasion to stop."

KADEN HAD to make a couple of quick decisions, and in the end he did what he thought was right. He assigned Wayland to go call for help, with Shun escorting her until the edge of the town. Shun would act as her guide out of the city, and he knew from experience that Wayland was no fighter. There was no need to have her in danger. Then he assumed Shun was free to go wherever he wanted while Wayland would try to flag down a vehicle on the beach road. He and Bradley would stay behind and try to hold off the drones as much as possible. Kaden wasn't worried; he knew a person in full armor could hold off as many as... well, a couple of drones at once.

"You sure your injuries are all right?" Bradley whispered to him as they made their way to the beach.

Kaden nodded. He still hurt, and the painkillers he'd swallowed hardly seemed to matter, but he could feel the adrenaline flowing, keeping him upright and moving.

"I don't get it," Bradley said in frustration. "Why did the drones have to cross to Compen from our side of the beach? Wouldn't it have been safer to just cross over from their side?"

Kaden had figured out the answer to that; it had also been plaguing him. "It's the depth of the sea, and the tide. If I recall, even before Compen was blown up, the crossing was from this side because there's something wrong with the other side of the beach." Too deep, or some underwater current, or some shit.

Bradley slipped in the dark and cursed. "I remember the overland bridge was planned from here, something about the sea currents and the sandbar in the middle." She slipped again and sat down hard. "Damn, Instructor Pace. For someone with no feet, you haven't had one misstep."

"It's all in how you handle the armor," he said as his "feet" unerringly found the next foothold. He knew from where he was keeping his boots just how steady the ground was, but it was more than that. His armor did it all: balanced him, kept him from falling over, and compensated for his lack of real feet.

"Well, mine's about to crush me to death," Bradley said as they approached the beach. They stopped near the sand dunes, and she groaned quietly. "God, I hate this. I'm going to be bogged down by the sand. Don't even think about me going near the water—this armor's like a steel coffin for me."

"As if I'm going to swim in this thing," Kaden told her.

"From the way you walk, it looks like you can walk on water," she said, voice laced with admiration.

They reached the beach, which looked deceptively empty, and Kaden spoke without looking at Bradley. "I'm going to find the drones and attack. You don't have to do this."

"Are you joking? I joined the Army to kick some drone ass," she demanded, even as she slipped and sank into the sand.

He turned to tell her to step where he was stepping when he heard a crunch, crunch on the sand. Heavy footsteps of people who were stepping far too hurriedly to care about the noise, with no thought of concealment. The crunch of sand, similar to Bradley in her armor, which could mean they had reinforcements. People with no fear of being caught, which meant armored troops.

"Do you think it's Wayland?" Bradley asked as she also turned around. She tilted her head to the side and then pulled off her helmet.

"What—?" It probably blocked her hearing, even with the small sound-enhancing holes near her ears. The helmets were not designed for long-range hearing ability.

Then he shook his head and signaled for her to stay still. "Too many of them. Put your helmet on," he said, turning around. "I'm going to circle around."

"Just draw them out, Instructor Pace. I'll take care of them," she said, reminding him to stick to their original plan.

Kaden nodded as he shifted his shoulders, working out the kinks. He trusted Bradley to guard his back, something he hadn't been able to do before, not even with Vorani. He took a deep breath. "Take care."

The gunshot wound ached and his shoulder protested as he moved it, but it didn't affect his speed or his maneuverability as he threw himself toward the sound. The darkness would mask him, but he had an idea the followers knew they were there.

He felt more than saw Bradley merge into the darkness, and he smirked. His black armor was ideal for the job, and there wouldn't even be a glint of light to give away his position. He started to creep back into the shadows, letting the armor do the hard work of being quiet. He needed to get behind these people, whoever they might be, and disable them as fast as possible.

The slam of the heavy body took him by surprise, and he was rolling on the sand before he realized he was fighting another armored person. Someone who was wearing an offensive armor with hip weapons, which were rather familiar. Kaden knew who it was, but as he rolled, he activated his upper-arm lasers, which were probably depleted, and aimed them.

"Vorani," he called. "Is that you?"

They stopped rolling with Kaden on top, pinning Vorani down with his weight, his lasers pointed at her, her armor's double guns pressed against his middle, and he was sure he could feel the heat of them through the layers of protection.

"Is that a gun or are you happy to see me?" he quipped as he rolled off her, and Vorani snorted as she got to her feet.

"You're lucky your young student told us you were here," she said as she brushed aside his hand. "Call Bradley. I don't want to accidently shoot her."

"Bradley," Kaden called as he withdrew his weapons. "It's friendly. Come out." He turned toward Vorani. "What are you doing here?"

"We heard of a possible infiltration to Compen." She sounded far too calm and collected, as if unaware of the seriousness of the situation. "I also remembered your team was here and thought to see what you were up to."

"Really," said Kaden as he heard Bradley come up behind him. "Where's Wayland?"

"She and the prisoner are safe." Vorani gave him a quick look over. "Though Wayland doesn't seem very sure of that status. We didn't have time to debrief, but from what I understand, you still haven't retrieved the armor that you nearly caused an international incident over by entering this place."

Kaden was glad the darkness hid his face as he turned to face Bradley. "Go see to Wayland," he said to her, and for a change, Bradley didn't ask him what he was talking about. She nodded, obviously understanding his unspoken implication as she turned inland.

And he was left with Vorani. "What seems to be the problem?" he asked. Apart from the obvious. She seemed unusually pissed. Which was nothing new, really.

Vorani shrugged and indicated they should also turn inland. "We can't go to the island. There isn't any way to cross, and the international patrol is going to be heading this way soon. Better to clear out instead of causing some embarrassing event that'll take us years to clear up."

"But—"

"You really weren't cleared to go this far into Compen Beach Town." Her voice fell into steel. "You have no idea the nightmares I've had to endure to keep the incident out of everyone's eyes."

"But—"

"And nothing's changed, has it, Kaden?" she continued. "You didn't retrieve the armor and—"

"Will you let me speak?" he shouted in frustration.

"Not when I'm this mad at you. Kaden, what were you thinking? You could have cost us the next eight years in international funding, not to mention you just lost an armor. You should be grateful I took the time to come here and drag you out, you moron."

"About the armor...."

"You were letting that thief walk around free," Vorani said, and Kaden felt it was the end of the discussion. "We're heading back to HQ. Let's go. Transport is some distance away."

"What about the drones in the city?" Kaden asked as he started after her, knowing he'd already lost the argument.

"I came with plenty of manpower. We'll handle this with less bang and flash."

"And Shun—the prisoner?"

"Why don't you leave that for intelligence," she said shortly, and Kaden realized he was in for a world of trouble.

# CHAPTER 12

ONCE, AT his orphanage, there had been an entertainment show. He remembered the act vaguely—some parts stood out more than others—a comedy skit of a man who kept making mistakes. It started with the man ironing something when he received a call on the telephone. The man would put the iron on the side of his face, burning his cheek. Then he would run around looking for water, breaking the tap in the process and drenching the kitchen. While he was trying to get the water to stop, something on the kitchen stove would boil over, and he would rush toward that, tripping over the cord of the iron. Near the end, the iron would catch fire, and the act ended when the man poured water over the still-plugged-in iron, apparently electrocuting himself.

Kaden had hated that act. Everyone else had found it hilarious. Was it because a nice family had adopted his brother that day? A family who hadn't wanted Kaden—who had taken the last family Kaden had away from him. He could barely remember his brother, but he remembered the skit.

Kaden wondered if he hated the whole thing because every action the man took ended up creating bigger problems.


*Then, for four weeks, it seemed as if nothing happened....*

IT SEEMED nothing had changed. He was back where he'd started.

He still didn't have his legs.

He was not approved for field missions.

He had not even completed his one escort mission: it was a failure.

But a lot of things had changed, and Kaden didn't like any of them.

"I suspected there was something wrong with your legs when you didn't take your armor off," Vorani said.

He sat on the examination table, sans armor, watching the camp doctor study his stumps. He was grateful for the level of detachment Vorani was showing because that allowed him to shrug off the mind-numbing awkwardness of the situation, where a stranger was touching what was left of his legs.

"Just be glad I'm not calling Dr. Lane in for an inquiry for insubordination and withholding information."

"Don't you have enough inquiries going on, with Shun and all?" Kaden didn't bother to hide his bitterness. Vorani was personally in charge of grilling Shun over the stolen armor, and there was very little Kaden could do about it but cooperate with her and pretend everything was all right.

Vorani gave him an unimpressed look. "Yes, but I have enough time to make sure everyone gets what they deserve."

"Well, there you have it." Kaden pointed to himself in the hopes of distracting her. "You can't take me off the active list. I outperformed everyone out there."

"At least the bullet wound is healing nicely," she agreed. "How's the shoulder?"

"Fine," Kaden lied. His shoulder was taking longer to heal, and though the external indicators such as the swelling and the redness were long gone, he could feel the twinge when he moved. It was all in the torn ligaments, apparently, something he was hoping would eventually heal. He knew of people who were still suffering from muscle aches years after accidents, and he wondered if his shoulder would ever go back to normal.

"Good." Vorani did not look convinced. "But you might be more useful to Research and Development than in the field. They can study you, and if they find out what makes you so compatible with the armor, that would—"

"Out of the question," Kaden said as he called his armor to him. "R and D can keep their hands to themselves." There was a couple of seconds' delay, but he had his arms encased, and that called the rest to him. He rolled off the table and let the armor do the work as he stood up. "You know I have the highest compatibility here. You can't afford to waste me on the sidelines."

"I am being very tolerant here," Vorani warned him. "I know you have the highest compatibility, which is why I'm not pushing you for prosthetics." She gave him a thoughtful look. "Though this is the first time anyone's seen an armor move when the wearer is this injured. Any more than a couple of missing fingers and that part of the armor stops moving. Maybe we should try you with a fitting for one of your legs to see what would happen."

Kaden fought to keep his face blank. "I'm not willing to gamble on the chance I'll lose compatibility. You still need me in the field."

"I heard the water part of the course still gives you trouble."

"And I keep telling you it's the way to get across," Kaden told her with confidence. "No one can afford to take off their armor in a water fight."

"You can only fight for so long," Vorani said without a trace of anger. "You'll have to think of retiring, eventually."

Kaden looked at her and didn't say anything. He was afraid he might say something that would give away his true feelings about what retirement would be like. Without his legs, retirement should be in a coffin, not in some disabled veterans' center for poor husks like him. There had been a brief time when Kaden had not thought of it, when he'd been with Shun, and now even Shun was going to be taken away.

"Well, look at the bright side, then," he said as he started to walk toward the door. "I heard the peace talks just didn't work this time around."

"Maybe," Vorani agreed. "Why don't you get yourself measured for a prosthetic?"

"No, thanks," Kaden growled. He wasn't going to subject himself to that, of walking awkwardly on things that resembled badly formed stilts. To settle for that was admitting his armor days were over, that he was resigned to the life of a disabled soldier, only good for living off charity. "If there's anything else, maybe we can talk about it later at dinner."

"Not today," Vorani said after a pause. "I'm going to the fertility clinic."

"Found a poor soul to share your eggs with?" Kaden said, ignoring the odd feeling in his chest. He had assumed once, long ago, that he and Vorani would have a child together. That was before he realized the harsh realities that would entail and how unfair it would be to a child who would be bred for the specific purpose of getting into armor. After listening to Bradley's rant about how much she had disliked her life, he knew more than ever he could never do that to anyone with his genes.

He shook his head and smirked. "You know WUC said it was illegal to breed people just for war."

"Kaden," Vorani snapped. "You know I would never do that. I just think it's time I had a child, and I couldn't do that before with my busy lifestyle. I've been going there for some time now—which you would have known if you'd just stayed in touch with me."

Many people chose artificial insemination to get the child of their dreams, and should Vorani's child grow up with the idea of becoming an armored warrior, so what? It wasn't like other children hadn't grown up with their parents' ambitions.

"Tell me you at least know who the father is," Kaden told her softly. "You know how I feel about—"

"Which is why I didn't ask you," she retaliated. "Let it be, Kaden."

Kaden nodded as he walked to the door.

He could think of a few people who would make worse parents, and Vorani still came out on top in any argument. He didn't have the energy nor the time to argue with her.

He pulled open the door.

"Where're you going now?" she asked from behind him.

"Do you need me for something?" he asked from the doorway. He turned to the lab technician, the nurse, and the doctor who had been silent during the exchange. "You know all about doctor-patient confidentiality, don't you?"

The nurse snorted and looked away while the doctor simply seemed distracted.

"They won't tell," Vorani assured him.

As far as Kaden was concerned, far too many people knew of his disability: the hearing committee that had questioned them on what had happened on Compen Beach Town, the medical technicians, the doctor who had treated him for his bullet wounds and the damaged muscles in his shoulder, and the people who'd come to speak to him afterward… it was a long list. In fact, he was sure the whole camp knew now, though they were all acting otherwise.

"Well, then," he said as he walked out, feeling Vorani's stare between his shoulder blades like a knife thrust. He blinked at the sunlight, shrugged, and felt the pull of the muscles as he strode toward the building across the campground, when he heard a familiar voice call out to him.

"Instructor Pace!"

Kaden was back to being Instructor Pace after they returned to camp. He turned and inclined his head. "You know, you can simply call me Kaden," he said as he waited for Bradley to catch up to him.

The sisters had been able to graduate to the next level, despite not having completed their mission properly. The disciplinary committee at the camp had concluded that their actions had been reasonable, given the circumstances, and were enough to pass them to the next phase in training—well, given that their instructor was incompetent. And that they had been compromised by the presence of a third party—Shun. Kaden might have been able to accept his own bungling efforts, but he hadn't been ready to accept that Shun needed to be punished for it as well.

"It doesn't sit right," Bradley said, pushing her hair out of the way as she fell into step beside him. She was dressed in an off-duty one-piece fatigue and looked well rested. But her eyes were thoughtful, as if she was wrestling with some internal conflict. "You're going to the lockup, aren't you? I'll walk with you."

"Where's Wayland?"

"She's in training—weapons," Bradley said shortly.

Wayland was in the training room more and more since they returned. She had approached him the week after he'd been released from hospital, with a request for him to train her, and Kaden agreed. He needed the distraction to stop himself from worrying about Shun, and he felt he somehow owed Wayland after their time together. She was proving to be less of a whiner. She worked hard, and Kaden knew enough to recognize someone who was driven. She didn't look as if she was enjoying herself, but it wasn't his place to say anything.

It wasn't as if Shun was having a cushy time in the camp either.

"Well, if she trains for any longer, it'll be muscle memory and she'll just shoot everything in her sleep," he said only half jokingly. He had a feeling all the training was for just that. Wayland had approached him about tips on how to train in the armor, and he had done the best he could. He had even done some training-course runs with her, but it didn't feel enough. He wondered if he should say something about the issue, that no matter how hard people trained, real fighting was nothing like the imaginary enemy inside a training circuit, and those who froze up once always did.

"Well, she's thinking of going for some of the peacekeeping briefings," Bradley added. "It'll be good for her if it takes her…."

"Away from the fighting?" Kaden finished. "I agree. She might do better."

"But she still wants to fight," Bradley said in anger.

Kaden tactfully remained silent. He had an inkling that Wayland was trying to mimic her sister, to live up to the image Bradley had of a fighter, especially since the sisters' relationship had shifted from the start of the journey. He didn't think they were friends yet, but Wayland seemed more open to looking up to her sister, even if it bordered on hero worship.

"Well, perhaps I'll try to talk to her," he said, tapping his thigh. "Seeing action didn't do me any good."

Bradley didn't answer for a few seconds. "I... uh... wanted to talk to you about it."

"My legs?"

"About Compen," she corrected him. "You see, I was looking around some of Senior Instructor Vorani's documents, and there's been no mission to get the green armor back."

"You're her aide," Kaden reminded her. "Maybe you should speak to her about it, not me."

"I did," Bradley said through gritted teeth. "But apparently, doing anything like that would shake our chances of appearing as if we're in agreement with the neutral zone, and that would mean we lose international aid, and that would mean no milk powder for kids or something."

"Perhaps she's speaking sense," Kaden pointed out as they reached their destination, the detention center. He nodded to the guard on duty and ignored the feeling that Henry was simply staring at Kaden's armor-encased legs as he signed the visitor book.

Bradley also reached for her ID, and Henry pushed the sign-in book to her wordlessly. They were regulars, having been there nearly every day. Kaden paused as they walked through the double scanners and watched the second guard, whose name he didn't know, scowl at the armor.

"Henry, it's not like I'm carrying weapons," Kaden said as always. His weapons registered empty, and he showed the reading.

"Not when you're a walking weapon," the guard muttered but shrugged, letting Kaden enter first.

"Anyway," said Bradley, starting the conversation the moment they were out of hearing range. "I say the armor is still on Compen Island. There's no way they could have left, since the water is patrolled now.

The island is closed off, and there's no record of anything leaving it, especially not a small boat."

"Maybe the armor isn't intact," Kaden offered.

"I thought of that," Bradley admitted. "But that was before you got back our armors. They don't have any to spare, so I don't think they'll simply dismantle them, even if it were possible."

"Say I agree with you on that," said Kaden as they turned another corner in the corridor. "Vorani has already said she won't risk going after it, regardless."

"But you're her friend." Bradley, at least, was unaware of the tension between Vorani and Kaden since Shun's arrest. "Can't you ask her about it?"

"You're really overestimating our friendship," he said as they finally reached the large locked door, in front of which another bored-looking guard sat.

"What did you two do, take the scenic route?" he grumbled as he keyed the door open from his small control tower. "I got a call that you were in the building a while ago."

"We walked slowly," Kaden said, knowing the guard had monitored their progress from his station. "You know, with me not—"

Not having legs, he wanted to say.

"Is he here?" Bradley interrupted Kaden and walked past him into the open doorway.

Kaden followed, feeling his breath catch. He never thought about this part of the day, though he'd been doing the same for three of the four weeks he'd been back.

Not unexpectedly, Shun was not alone. At their entrance, Tracy Caramesh, Shun's military lawyer, looked up from the files she and Shun were studying and smiled. "Expert Pace, Cadet Bradley," she said, greeting them with a familiar nod. "We were waiting for you."

"I had a medical examination." Kaden pulled a chair to the left of Shun and sat down. Bradley sat to Kaden's left. Tracy glanced at Kaden's legs before looking up quickly.

At his voice, Shun turned his head and looked at him squarely. "Medical. Is anything wrong?"

Kaden didn't want to add to Shun's worries. "No, no. Just... things... uh, how's it going?"

"Well, I'm stuck in this place," Shun said without any bitterness. "And it's been the same for the last three weeks. We appeal for a hearing, and then we get it approved, and nothing."

"Was there a hearing today?" Kaden asked with a frown. "I didn't hear—"

"You know it only happens every other day," Shun said with a roll of his eyes as he slumped back into his chair. "But I did have an unofficial questioning."

Kaden's gaze snapped to Shun's wrists and was glad to see nothing but the old bruises from the restraining straps. They were from a much earlier questioning session. Kaden, then recovering in the infirmary, hadn't been there for the interrogation, but Tracy, who had been new to the job, had put her foot down at the treatment of the prisoner.

"It wasn't like I had anything new to tell them," Shun said, sliding farther down in the chair. "And in the end, there's nothing to do."

"I hate to get our hopes up, but I really think there might be something that'll help us," Tracy said after Shun vented.

"You found something that might help him?" Bradley sounded hopeful.

"I wouldn't say it would help us solve the glaringly obvious problem that he stole the armor—"

"And gave it to the enemy according to some," Shun muttered.

"But," Tracy continued. "I was able to get ahold of a friend over at Tienden, where the correspondence records are kept, and we finally did manage to find the letters Shun wrote, complaining about armored warrior MacCrave and asking for the Army to take action."

Kaden blinked. "That's good news, isn't it?"

"It is proof that Shun is not merely making up nonsense, and there are several of these letters and even a form of complaint. Someone simply swept them under the filing cabinet, so to speak. The Army does receive a lot of such requests...."

Bradley snorted in contempt. "Really."

"Not in the exact same nature, but complaints against other soldiers." Tracy gave Bradley a cold, tight smile, almost a snarl.

Bradley glared at her, sitting back and crossing her arms, apparently willing to keep her mouth shut for the time being. "Anyway, there is a committee that is supposed to investigate such reports, and this was totally neglected. For their excuse, they were understaffed and in a wartime situation, and it's impossible to investigate every complaint they receive. Who knows how many other legitimate complaints have been ignored."

"That's not an excuse." Kaden clenched his fists. No matter what, Tracy was an Army lawyer and she would always try to look at it from their point of view.

"No, it isn't," she agreed quickly. "What I'm saying is we have a case. We can make an argument that Shun was forced to do what he did because his attempts to do the right thing the right way didn't work. We can also add that he was under stress from the recent death of his mother and the circumstances that led to that. I've called for an official hearing this week, and I'm optimistic that we'll get a fair hearing."

Kaden looked to see if Shun was in any way responding to that, but his eyes were closed and he simply appeared defeated. Kaden felt a strange stirring in his chest as he stared at Shun; four weeks of confinement had meant he'd lost whatever color he had on him. His hair seemed longer, which is probably why he looked thinner, though Kaden suspected he wasn't eating enough. Shun was served three square meals a day but had claimed the food was unpalatable. Even sitting with his eyes closed, Shun looked tense; there were bags under his eyes, and the lines on his forehead hadn't been there when they'd first met.

"How long will it take?" Bradley asked. "This whole procedure, before we can clear his name?"

"Maybe a couple of months to get the formal hearing arranged. If we're lucky, we might be able to get a date within this month. However, we need to get an official hearing and shift the blame…. I'm working on it, but we'll get there."

"There's no way you can keep him locked up for that long." The thought was Kaden's, but it was Bradley who spoke.

"People have been locked up for much longer, for things much less severe than stealing an armor," Tracy argued back. "The armors are the lifeblood of the Army, and if they were to get into enemy hands, we would lose the war."

"I know people who have done more and have gotten away with it," Bradley retaliated. "What about that major who ordered the missile attack into a civilian population?"

"Those are not really what is on the table," Tracy interrupted. "And we will not be winning anyone to our side by pulling out such incidents."

Kaden couldn't see much point of the whole conversation. "So, what do we do, then?"

"There are two ways around this," Tracy continued. "We…."

She trailed off as the door to the room swung open and Wayland walked in, looking freshly showered and carrying a couple of apples in her hand.

"They took the bag and scanned the stuff," she said as she passed the apples to Shun. "I was going to come earlier, but the showers were occupied." She slid into the final chair between Shun and Tracy, smiled briefly at Kaden, and then turned to Bradley. "I found the information you wanted."

"We'll talk about it later," Bradley told her with a shake of her head. "Tracy was telling us about some options Shun has."

Wayland turned to Tracy, who cleared her throat before continuing. "Well, as I was saying, there are two options: we ask for a pardon based on emotional instability, or we promise that when we get the armor back, Shun will join the Army as a full-fledged soldier. He'll have to go through basic training and all, but we can hash out the details later."

"They're not going to trust me with the second option, even if I want it," Shun retorted, reaching for an apple. He nodded to Wayland before starting to eat it, and Kaden wished he'd thought of bringing something too. There was no finesse in how Shun ate; he ate like he was hungry. He swallowed hard before speaking. "Which I don't, unless I didn't make myself clear the last few times."

Tracy tried to be diplomatic. "It is understandable that you would have some residual bitterness toward the Army."

"Residual bitterness?" Shun snapped as he reached for the next apple. Kaden had rarely seen a person eat that fast. "Is that what you call years of pent-up anger?"

"That's hardly going to win you any points." Tracy pushed aside the stack of papers in front of her. "Think of it this way. The other option is you being locked up, and that's hardly going to help anyone."

"What about the pardon?" Wayland asked. "You said that was an option."

"It would be if we had the right connections." Tracy dismissed it out of hand. "But I don't know of anyone who is willing to step in and take a risk. Pardoning Shun would mean getting involved in the whole debacle, and anyway, I don't think any of you know someone who can vouch for good behavior."

"We have Instructor Pace," Wayland said, and Kaden snorted at her naivety.

"I really don't count as much," he said as Tracy got to her feet.

"That's it for today. I have another case." She gathered her files.

"We'll go with you," said Bradley, also standing up. "Wayland, you said you had something to tell me?"

Kaden felt he should be grateful the sisters were working together more smoothly than before. Together they were a formidable team, and he wondered what they were working on, but he sometimes worried about the outcome.

"I'll—" He looked at Shun for a sign whether he should stay or leave with them.

"The lockdown is not for another half an hour," Tracy said as she picked up her briefcase from under the chair. After Tracy had pressed the button to let the guard know she was done for the day (though Kaden supposed they were being observed by a camera), all the females in the room left—Wayland after a quick look over her shoulder at the two of them.

Shun and Kaden remained silent for a couple of seconds, just looking at each other.

Kaden stayed seated until the door lock engaged with a loud click, and then he turned to Shun who was staring at the apple cores a little despondently. Shun looked up and struggled to smile. "I think she knows."

"That I don't have any legs?" Kaden said before feeling foolish. "Oh, you mean about us."

"Well, I don't know if there's an us or not—I mean, we did spend some time, two days at most, just fumbling with each other, but really." Shun sighed and placed his head on the table. "I just don't know what I am to you. You don't need to come and see me every day. It's not like I'm treated badly or anything. The prisoner treatment has definitely improved from what I've heard of, and as much as I appreciate you coming, I'm sure you have other things to do."

"If you're being well taken care of, why the need for the apples?"

"The food here is crap. I mean, I don't think there's a lot of people locked up here besides me, so… do they cook that especially for us? I'm flattered they go through all the trouble to make something so inedible."

Kaden had to smile at that. "I think they feed you what they feed us."

"Really? That's vile," Shun said, his lips curling in disgust. "I asked Wayland to bring me something."

Kaden wondered if he had the right to feel jealous about something so small. "You could have told me."

"Uh… the food here is giving me constipation," Shun said, color blooming on his cheeks. "It was just not something I wanted to share with you."

Kaden nodded as he reached across the table. His armor retracted and exposed his hand, and Shun covered it with his.

"They have cameras on the wall."

"Let them watch," Kaden said, not giving a damn. If people hadn't figured out by now, then they were stupid. "You are not considered a dangerous criminal. They let you have unlimited visitors."

"From the camp," Shun pointed out. "And because they know I'm harmless. It's not like I can pick up another armor and run."

Kaden nodded, knowing it was true. Anyone who had become compatible with an original armor automatically became incompatible with any other original gear. And using a new armor wasn't as simple as being compatible with it, and it sometimes took weeks of training. With all the armored personnel on base, it was impossible for Shun to break out.

Kaden had entertained the thought of breaking out with Shun, but then, even if he was capable of fighting his way off the camp, there was the problem of living on the run inside an armor that could be tracked. The very armor that gave him mobility was what trapped him as well. He smiled ironically and shook his head at the thought.

Kaden had never been a diehard patriot, but he never thought he would be speculating about going against the Army. He knew it was only a fleeting fantasy, but there were so many things about his outlook that had changed since meeting Shun.

"What are you thinking of?"

"Nothing." Kaden squeezed Shun's hand. "Except I seem to have changed a lot since meeting you."

"I hope for the better." Shun gave a wry grin.

He was only joking, but Kaden smiled indulgently.

"I'll send you some fruit," Kaden promised as Shun got to his feet.

Once all visitors were gone, Shun would be escorted back to his cell. Kaden knew the procedure very well. Once Kaden had left through one door, another officer would come in from a second to scan Shun for hidden weapons.

They usually walked to the two doors on the opposite end of the room and would knock on them simultaneously. But instead of walking away from Kaden, Shun took a couple of steps toward him. "I know I didn't ask before but... how are you?"

"You did ask me that," Kaden said in surprise. "You even sent me get-well wishes with Wayland when I was in the infirmary."

"I don't mean that," Shun said in frustration, stepping closer. "I mean, how are you? Have you had any urges to eat a laser or stand too close to the edge of a balcony or—okay, I'm going to shut up now."

"I'm fine," Kaden sighed. The simple words didn't indicate how he felt, but it seemed stupid to even try and explain something he could barely understand. "No, I hadn't thought of falling on a sharp object either."

"Ah, missed that one." Shun nodded, and suddenly the next step brought him in contact with Kaden's chest. Kaden had his hands around Shun, pulling him closer even as his armor retracted around his chest, and Shun hugged him tightly.

"Just hold on," Kaden told him as he leaned in and kissed Shun's head. His hair smelled of the carbolic soap and disinfectant used in the cells. "We'll get you out."

He tried not to think too much about the affection Shun was showing him. After all, Shun had been trapped in a room with no one friendly to speak to for the past four weeks. It was a given he would cling to a familiar face. It could also be the confinement was draining Shun's resolve; he had been more collected and independent when they'd been at Compen Beach Town.

"I don't have anywhere else to go," Shun whispered. "Thank you. I look forward to this time of the day."

"So do I," Kaden admitted as he let go of Shun with reluctance. With the camera present, he didn't want to kiss Shun on the mouth or do anything intimate. Who knew what sort of pervert might be watching them?

"Maybe, tomorrow when you come, you can bring me some reading material. I'm getting fed up of reading about just how great the Army is."

"About that." Kaden hesitated, not wanting to give the bad news. "I have guard duty on a train tomorrow. I'm to travel up and down on a route. The attacks from the raiders have been more frequent, and having armored warriors on board seems to be the only way to deter them."

Shun smiled, though it didn't reach his eyes. "You are going out on field missions. Congratulations. Isn't that what you wanted?"

"Yes," said Kaden, surprising himself even as he completed the sentence. "But I wish I could wait until this whole thing is cleared up a little."

"When will you be back?" Shun looked up. Up close he seemed worried but at the same time hopeful. He gave a bark of laughter and glanced down. "Oh man, that sounds needy, doesn't it?"

"I'll be back in a couple of days, five at most," Kaden promised. "I think I have some books with me somewhere. I'll give them to Wayland before I go."

"At least they'll come tomorrow," Shun said and stepped back. "You have no idea how much it means to have someone to talk to." Then he gave a nervous laugh and looked away.

"Tomorrow," Kaden whispered as Shun turned around and dashed to the door.

Walking back to his room, Kaden thought about what Shun had said. It was true—he hadn't thought about killing himself in a while. It seemed his life was taken up by trying to get Shun out, working with Bradley and Tracy to find the missing documents, reading through numerous law books to see if there were loopholes—not that he really understood them—and finally, helping Wayland improve her fighting skills.

He was busy. More than that, he was working toward something, and that meant he could wake up every day, roll into his armor, and… look forward to seeing Shun. Something told him perhaps he shouldn't think too much about it. He was going to become dependent on Shun, who might decide that he didn't need Kaden after he was free.

But Kaden felt more centered. He thought about having a goal to achieve, and though he accepted he wasn't healed, he was feeling better. He needed to find something to eat, see about those books he'd promised Shun, and pack a few things for the short mission.

After all, a five-day mission meant at least a couple of changes of underwear.

# CHAPTER 13

KADEN WONDERED if it was possible he felt homesick—was it the feeling of needing to go back to someplace or someone? He had never felt that before, always accepting wherever he had been shuttled to, whether it was to the grand capital where the war hardly seemed to have touched or to the border towns where it looked like the entire population lived in bomb shelters.

It could possibly be because the border run he was doing was hardly worth opening his eyes for. Kaden had been paired with Finzer for the run, Claina having taken much-needed leave to visit her family. Guarding trains was a boring, time-consuming job. He and Finzer took turns patrolling up and down the train, Kaden sometimes walking on the roof to give himself a change of scenery.

The first day when they were changing shifts, he'd gone to their compartment and thrown himself onto the bunk, taking off his armor as he did. He had a feeling it was not going to be possible to hide his footless state on this trip, which was pretty much common knowledge by now, and somehow it seemed easiest to get it over with. He rolled over and looked to see Finzer staring at him with a blank expression. "What is it?" he asked as casually as possible.

"So the rumors were true," said Finzer, his gaze fixed on Kaden's stumps.

"I have no idea what those might be," he quipped.

"Well, it's my turn to make sure this thing stays on track," Finzer said with a smile. "I'll see you at dinner." And that had been that.

Kaden had lain there feeling oddly deflated that the revelation hadn't garnered much of a reaction. He supposed he didn't feel as self-conscious about showing his legs to anyone as he did before. It seemed people were more accepting about it than he'd expected. At least Finzer hadn't mentioned some poor bastard who was quadriplegic or had lost all four limbs or something. Kaden realized he had gotten off easier than some people, but he didn't want to be reminded of that—it didn't stop his very real feelings of loss.

As they came closer to their final day of this tour, Kaden felt himself tensing as he waited on the roof of the train, scanning the terrain. The train slowed down as it reached the station at Rayc, and he stood up, waiting. He could see Haria on the other side of the border. Unlike Koresa, there was no no-man's-land, and he could see the other side quite clearly half a mile away. The track went close to the border in places, something he was hardly comfortable with. He knew it was sheer stubbornness keeping the route where it was, and he wished the railway authorities were more considerate. He sighed as the train slid to a stop, waiting for the jolt when Finzer appeared at the window.

"There's someone here to meet you."

Kaden frowned as he scrambled down to the compartment, wondering who in the world would come to see him when a familiar armored figure turned around to greet him with a smile.

"Wayland," he blurted out, feeling a little cheated. Who had he been expecting, Shun? But at the same time, his mouth lifted into a totally natural smile as he leaned in for the hug she was offering.

Armor met armor with a clang but he softened his, retracting his chest plate, and she gave a gasp of amused laughter.

"I wish mine could do that."

"What are you doing here?"

"I went home for a holiday," she said as he stood back. "I thought I'd travel with you. Safer."

"I see you polished your armor."

"It's not self-polishing like yours," she said with a quick look around. "Can we talk? I have a plan. I think it's going to work."

"Plan for what?"

Wayland was young enough to get away with a small foot stamp to show her impatience. "For Shun."

"What is it?" he asked, then nodded.

"It was Bradley's idea really, but I got to be the messenger, since our parents listen to me more than her," Wayland said without any pretense. "We were thinking of a way of getting Shun out of the cell, at least until the hearing."

"I didn't think it could be done," Kaden remarked, feeling hope bloom in his chest.

The train lurched as it continued its journey, and he caught Wayland when she staggered. "You underestimate just how much influence my family has, and it doesn't hurt that two of their daughters are fighting for the country," Wayland continued.

For a moment Kaden looked at her and felt sad—she sounded so old and cynical, and no one her age should sound like that.

"What is it?" he asked to keep the conversation moving.

"Well, I told my father Shun helped us, and he has nothing to lose in helping him. I told him that if Shun's side of the story went public, it would reflect badly on the Army, and anyway, I still have some influence over him… and… guess what?"

Kaden cleared his throat. "Tell me."

"They agreed to talk to Tracy and see if he can be released into your custody, within the camp only. He can't leave or anything and will have limited access to buildings… maybe the barracks, and perhaps… I was thinking…." She trailed off, coloring a little.

"What?"

"Perhaps he can stay in your room."

"Oh." Kaden felt himself blushing and looked away to hide his expression. "I… think it's too soon to say that." He knew Wayland was suggesting that he share a room and not a bed with Shun, but he was worried about how it would affect their relationship. The Army didn't discourage same-sex partners, as long as they joined the breeding program and squeezed out a bunch of future cannon fodder.

According to some, same-sex partners were more reliable than heterosexual couples at producing offspring, since they wanted to keep the Army happy. But the military did frown on anyone sleeping with the enemy, and Shun, unfortunately, counted as one of those even if one of his parents was Joscalian. The fact that he was compatible with an armor he'd stolen just made it all more complicated.

Wayland didn't seem to understand his hesitancy. "But Bradley and Tracy are working on it even now. I got my father to call ahead. Maybe by the time we get back to camp, Shun will be free."

Kaden smiled as he glanced over her shoulder to the far end of the train, where a few bored passengers observed their conversation with apathetic stares. "Well, we have a couple of hours before this shift ends. Let's keep our fingers crossed that nothing comes our way."

THE REST of the journey was mercifully eventless, and Kaden found himself humming as he put the last of his things into a backpack.

Finzer looked amused. "I thought you didn't swing that way."

Kaden looked up and shook his head, thankful Wayland was off patrolling another compartment of the train. "Don't even go there. She's my student."

"And painfully young," Finzer agreed. "Is it the sister you're banging?"

"Bradley," Kaden shook his head. "That's... not even close."

"Well, I hear Jensen has his eye on her."

"Bradley?" Kaden exclaimed before he felt a wave of shame. Bradley was a nice girl, but he couldn't see her in a relationship with anyone simply because she came across as so standoffish. Even as he thought that, he wondered why he'd done so. Given a choice of all the women in the camp, he liked Bradley. Perhaps he wouldn't have minded getting to know her better if he wasn't already with Shun and if she'd been a little older.

"Jensen's a general tech," Finzer told him, as if that would explain everything. "He's the one who adjusts her armor."

"Oh," said Kaden, zipping up his bag. "Then he's doing a lousy job because that damn thing is eating into her body through the underarmor."

"You've seen it, then?" Finzer shuddered. "Those plates are so heavy I wonder how they do it. I don't know about Bradley, but I've seen Gareth's, and damn, there are grooves in his body."

"The—oh, shit, what?"

The train rocked and there was the crash of an impact, something heavy followed by the sound of people screaming. Kaden's eyes widened as the whole compartment tilted over. He saw Finzer, looking back with the same wide-eyed look of shock, and as one, they scrambled toward the doorway.

Kaden was faster as he started toward the sound. Obviously the train had derailed, but he couldn't figure out how—no smoke from a fire or an explosion. People were scrambling out the doors and pulling their belongings with them, some talking or calling out for others, but there were no outright screams of pain or fear anymore. Kaden tore open a side panel, creating a larger opening, and stepped out. He turned around and helped a couple of people who were struggling to get out but then ceased when he spotted the center of the derailment.

Something large had run into the train and pushed a couple of compartments sideways, which had then pulled the rest of the carriages off the tracks with them. But the shape of the dent looked familiar—

"I guess we didn't hit a stray cow." Finzer was deadly serious.

"You get the people to safety." Kaden flexed his knees. "I want to see where the drone went."

"Let the gray armor get everyone to safety," Finzer suggested. "I'm circling right. You circle left."

Kaden prayed Wayland was somewhere safe. The carriages had slid off the track without much force, and since Wayland had been in armor, he didn't think she'd be injured, but she could be anywhere in the mess. Kaden had to take care of the drone before he could check on her. He wondered why it had attacked the train in the first place. There had been an observer onboard, a civilian from the railway company, whose sole purpose was to keep an eye out for trouble. Kaden had never heard of a drone attacking a moving train before.

There had been a couple of railway tracks that had been blown up at the start of the war, but that was decades ago, and WUC frowned on the killing of civilians. But, Kaden thought as he searched for the drone, civilians always got caught in the cross fire. It was a given.

And who knew? Maybe the Harians were getting desperate.

He finally spotted the drone and frowned. It was hovering a couple of feet away from the train, doing small forward movements rather jerkily as it appeared to be trying to move away from the tracks. It was obviously the drone that had crashed; a side of it was crushed inward, and the impact must have damaged it.

It struggled to move a couple of feet, hit the ground, raised itself again, then moved forward. Kaden flexed his shoulders to engage his laser guns. People in the background were moving away from the drone but not quickly enough, and he didn't want to fire through them.

He inched forward cautiously, on the lookout for more surprises. Even as he moved closer, a blur of gray and green appeared at the corner of his eye.

Wayland streaked forward in her armor, a metal bar in hand.

Kaden almost shouted at her to stop, but he had no idea why he should do so. Someone had to deal with the drone. Wayland aimed the metal bar through the front, impaling it and stilling its movements. There wasn't even an explosion; it simply fell to the ground with a thud, slid a couple of feet, and stopped.

It was so anticlimactic that Kaden felt cheated.

Wayland turned to him, pushing her helmet back and smiling widely. "I did it," she said, jumping up and down in joy. "I didn't freeze. I did it."

Kaden winced internally at the display of emotion. "Yeah, yeah, you did," he agreed, but the smile didn't come. He wondered why it felt wrong. He should be happy. Wayland had finally mastered her reluctance to fight.

But all he felt was a sense of foreboding.


THE BRIEFING took so long that Kaden developed a case of pins and needles in his ass. It didn't help that the people questioning him kept glancing at his armor-encased legs.

"So, Instructor Pace, did you confirm if the dent in the train"—a flick of an eye toward his legs and then back up—"was the same shape as a drone?"

Kaden bit back a sigh. "Yes."

"Why did Cadet Wayland Olgesh reach the drone first?" Another quick look at his legs.

Kaden wondered if he should simply take off his armor. "Because I was surveying the area for further attacks."

He was sure his frustration carried through to the questioners. He hadn't seen Shun in close to a week, and he wanted to know if the request for his release was going to go through. Perhaps, if he hurried, he might be able to give Shun the good news himself. "We've been through this before. Can I go now?"

The questioner hesitated and finally nodded. "We might call you back if we need further clarification."

As Kaden stepped out of the main administrative building, he wondered why none of them had asked him if he was sure the drone was of Harian design. Perhaps that had already been confirmed. He was considering going back and asking them when he spotted Bradley.

He hurried down the last few steps to her. "Are you waiting for Wayland? I think they released her before me."

Bradley smiled broadly and shook her head. "Come quick. Father came through for a change. It seems Shun is being released into your custody."

Kaden blinked. At first he couldn't understand what she said; he'd visited Shun nearly every day in the cell for so long that it had become a habit. Then the enormity of the announcement hit him and his knees buckled. Hold me up, he thought to his armor as he stared at Bradley. "When?"

"Right now if you hurry. Tracy is waiting for you. But she has to be somewhere in half an hour and—"

Kaden broke into a run toward the holding cells.

Bradley laughed loudly as she joined him. "Slow down, Instructor Kaden! I can't keep up with you."

Kaden covered the distance of six hundred meters between the two buildings in less than a minute.

"I HEARD the train you were on got attacked," Shun said in greeting as soon as Kaden walked in. Shun was in ankle shackles but outside the detention cell, in the final briefing room.

"It was a single drone and no one was killed." Kaden did not want to discuss it with Shun out in the open. "Wayland took it out."

"That's nice," Shun said with a puzzled look, probably because Kaden sounded so negative about it.

Tracy handed Kaden the controller for the shackles. "Press that and they'll snap together. Won't be able to walk at all. Expert Maxis and Camp Master Brandon also have these. You'll be his direct guard. He can't leave the camp, and the list of buildings he can enter is mentioned here." She pushed a file at him. "It was easier than listing the buildings and places he doesn't have access to." She didn't smile. In fact, she looked downright angry.

Kaden didn't look at Shun in case his resolve to act professionally might weaken. He wanted to give him a hug or just touch him. "Anything else?"

"Don't even think of bending the rules," Tracy warned him. "You will be tempted, but it's not worth it."

"Right," said Kaden dismissively.

Tracy turned to Shun. "Senator Olgesh put a lot of faith in his daughters when he agreed to the request for your release. If you try to escape, you will not only discredit him, you will also get his daughters in trouble. They would be suspended and taken to trial along with you."

Kaden stepped up to Tracy. "Isn't Wayland a minor and... and Bradley didn't steal the armor."

Tracy shrugged. "Wayland is a level two cadet and therefore a member of the Army. A member of the Army, no matter the age, can be tried as an adult during wartime. That's in special section 45, subsection 9. As for Bradley, she agreed to this."

"But can't I be the one to take responsibility?" Kaden demanded.

Shun touched Kaden lightly on his armored shoulder. "I understand. I'm not going to do anything stupid."

Tracy turned to Kaden again. "Cadet Bradley moved an extra bed to your room. I wasn't sure of it, but short of having him return to the confinement cell at night, it seems the only solution."

"It's fine." Kaden could just think of the awkwardness of the situation it would create, but he was hardly going to let Shun return to the cell. And it was typical Bradley, taking charge of sleeping arrangements for both of them.

Tracy snapped her file shut. "If there's nothing else, I'll be going. Call me if anything comes up."

"When is the hearing?" Kaden asked as she got to her feet.

"The dates aren't confirmed yet, but we're hoping for the twentieth or the twenty-eighth of next month."

Kaden did some quick calculations in his head. "That's a lot of time—a little over a month. Anyway, if that's all?" He looked at Shun for the first time. "Shall we get going? It's almost time for lunch."

Shun did not look pleased at the prospect of camp food. "Yeah, I'll pass. I'm dying for a shower somewhere I'm not watched."

"Sure." Kaden didn't want to sit through an uncomfortable lunch with everyone.

"But I don't want to get in the way of your lunch."

Kaden rolled his eyes at that. "As you once pointed out, the food here isn't all that great."

Kaden stepped out of the detention center to bright sunlight and two eager faces he was coming to think of as friends.

"Shun," said Wayland with a smile and moved forward as if to hug him, then stopped, unsure.

"It seems I have you to thank for my release." Shun took in both of them. "Both of you." He made no move to hug them, but he smiled, the corners of his eyes crinkling.

Bradley grunted with her usual briskness. "Where to?"

"I'm going to shower," Shun told her apologetically. "I know lunch will be over by then but...."

"It's fine." Bradley looked disappointed but nodded in understanding. "I wanted to talk to you, but it can wait. Wayland and I have things to do."

"Yes," said Wayland wryly. "I have to go and write another report about the train incident."

"Were you also involved?" Shun asked even though Kaden had told him about it.

"Yes, I was the one who took out the drone."

"That's nice," Shun said with a proud look. He turned to Kaden with a slight frown. "She took out a drone alone?"

Kaden was aware that speaking about the incident out here wasn't the most advisable thing. He didn't know just how much information Shun, as a prisoner, was allowed access to. He didn't want him thrown back into the cell because Kaden couldn't keep his mouth shut. "Damaged from the impact with the train." Wayland open her mouth to protest, and Kaden turned away from her. He wished Shun would simply let go of the topic. "That's something I can't discuss with you in public. Shall we go to my room?"

Shun managed a weak smirk at that, and Kaden tried to put aside the unease he felt every time the drone incident was mentioned.

# CHAPTER 14

KADEN PICKED up his discarded clothes and pushed some furniture back into place to give the room a more spacious look—not that he could do anything about the actual size of the room. He spotted half his dirty clothes in a heap under the hastily put together folding bed that someone had pushed into his room. He should dust the whole place and sweep up the corners—at least there wasn't any decomposing food on the table, and he was sure there were some clean clothes in the cupboard.

The steady sound of water falling, of someone moving in the bathroom, was alien to him. Kaden couldn't remember a time he'd ever brought someone else to his room, not in any capacity that might lead to further contact.

He hastily opened the window to shake out a bedspread so the dust wouldn't fly all over the place. The dark brown curtains were threadbare and not capable of keeping the light out. Something dark crusted the edge of the windowpane; it had been a while since he'd cleaned anything. He suddenly remembered Shun's home—worn-out but with clean furniture, the well-scrubbed floor, the bathtub with the hot water—and he felt a flash of embarrassment at what he was seeing.

He was a slob. He should at least make some excuse for the state of his room. The bathroom door swung open and Kaden turned around, bedcover in hand. "Excuse the mess. I haven't been in here for some time."

He didn't know what else he could say.

Shun was dressed in Kaden's towel, which Kaden had used just recently and left out to dry on the hook. It should at least be dry, but he couldn't remember the last time he'd laundered it, which made him feel bad about letting Shun use it. Shun was still partially wet, his hair curling into ringlets and looking darker than it normally did. His skin was pink from scrubbing, with stray water droplets rolling down to soak into the low-riding towel.

"Uh," Kaden managed.

"Sorry, I had to borrow it. It was the only towel there, and I didn't want to dress in my old clothes."

"No... uh, yes," Kaden agreed. "I don't think that would be a good idea at all."

"Yes." Shun stood there as if waiting for something.

Kaden stared fascinated as another droplet of water rolled down Shun's flat abdomen. Shun wasn't as muscled as Kaden, and he had lost some mass during the time he was locked up, but he'd also gained the pale sheen that was probably part of his genetic heritage. The paleness, along with his lack of clothing, made Kaden feel tight in some places, and he understood why the media always blamed the Harians for their ability to stir up people. Shun looked like a model for a very adult calendar.

Shun looked at Kaden with wide eyes, as if unsure why Kaden was staring. "I was hoping you had something I could borrow."

"Clothes," said Kaden, feeling foolish. "Yes, it'll be good to cover yourself up." He felt himself color as he said it and turned away to hide his face. "It's a little cooler than the inside of your room."

"I guess it is," Shun agreed.

Kaden rooted around his meager belongings for something Shun could wear. Something that was clean and covered him up from top to bottom. He found an old T-shirt and a pair of knee-length shorts. He tossed them over his shoulder to Shun. "You... get dressed while I take a shower."

Preferably with cold water.

"Right," Shun said. Kaden grabbed the small stool on the side. "I left my clothes in the basin, but the corner of the bathroom is stacked with your clothes. There were a lot...."

"I didn't get to do the laundry before I left." Kaden thought his lie sounded extremely convincing. In reality, he hadn't been very interested in hygiene; he would drop his dirty clothes in a corner and hope the pile didn't grow too large.

"Yeah, you must have been busy with the debriefing and then coming to visit me." Shun seemed to buy the explanation, and from the looks of it, at least in part, felt responsible for the mess.

"After I take a shower, perhaps we can go down and do laundry." In fact, he'd never been too busy to do his laundry; he'd just had little motivation to do so. He'd slumped onto his bed after his daily activities, too drained to tackle anything too complicated.

"Can I dust the place until then?" Shun asked.

Kaden colored for an entirely different reason. He lived like a slob and Shun found it distasteful. "I think there are cleaning supplies in one of the closets in the corridor. They're for everyone on this floor."

Shun nodded, and Kaden ducked into the bathroom with a grimace. He pulled his stool with him as he did. After his experience at Koresa, he'd discovered it was easier to clean himself sitting down. He arranged his soap, shampoo, and all the other things in order near him before shucking off his armor.

After some trial and error, he found the best place for the stool so he wouldn't have to reach too far to open the shower. After the shower he shook himself clean—his towel was long gone—and reached for his underarmor, then paused.

It probably stank of sweat and dirt; he'd been wearing the same underarmor for the entire day. When he was with other warriors, no one really noticed, but after a fresh shower, his skin crawled at the thought of getting back into it. He looked over his shoulder at the bathroom door and hesitated for a second.

"Uh, Shun?" he called before his resolve could waver.

A couple of seconds later, Shun stuck his head in, duster in hand. He didn't seem fazed by the sight of Kaden naked. Kaden turned his back to the door; he was sitting on the stool, swinging his legs. "You called?"

"Can you pick me a spare underarmor from the pile? I forgot to bring one."

"Sure. Uh, do you want the towel as well? You seem to have only one."

Kaden nodded. "Thanks." Shun would have to step into the bathroom to give them to him, and Kaden faltered for a second. They'd had sex in the semidarkness once, and not counting that time in the lamplit bathtub, Kaden had practically been fully clothed the second time they'd had sex. This was probably the first time Shun was getting to see Kaden under a bright light, and it wasn't exactly a pretty sight. He was not Bradley, with a history of armor wearing traced on his body, but he did look as if he'd lost a couple of fights.

But Shun didn't comment or stare. He returned with the items in less than a minute. "You only have one clean… this thing," he said as he handed over the towel and put the underarmor on a hook. "Might need to do the washing tonight."

"Right," said Kaden, pointedly not looking at Shun. He raised the towel to dry his hair, wincing as his shoulder pulled.

Shun stepped close. "H-how's the shoulder?"

"Still hurts when I, uh—" He found himself struggling to remember what hurt. "—lift my hand over my head. I didn't think you'd remember."

"It wasn't as if I could forget. I was responsible for it."

"Is that how you feel?" Kaden asked. Shun's hand appeared over his shoulder and took the towel. He rubbed it over Kaden's hair vigorously. The feeling of Shun's hand brushing his scalp had Kaden closing his eyes. He basked in the warmth of Shun's hand on his shoulder followed by a warm body pressing against him from behind that made his fingers curl.

Kaden's blood pooled below his waist, and he was glad he was sitting down. Shun let out a shaky breath, and Kaden felt chapped lips brush against his neck. He leaned back more into Shun's firm hands, and Shun responded by running them down Kaden's side and over his healed gunshot wound. The scar had puckered into an ugly pink mass, and he had a similar mark on his upper thigh. He also had two new scars, though thankfully the one visible on his cheek was starting to fade.

Kaden tipped his head back for a kiss, but Shun stepped back. "Get dressed. You really need to do your laundry, and afterward get something to eat."

"Right," Kaden agreed, stunned, wondering what had just happened.

Had Shun come on to him, or had he gotten his signals wrong?

"I'm hungry, and you have green stuff growing on these tiles, and really, now that I've taken a closer look, your laundry pile has fungus growing from it."

Kaden looked straight in front of him, and his erection withered. He owed Shun an explanation, and it was a chance to redeem himself— he wasn't a slob; he'd just stopped caring.

"It was after I returned from the hospital," Kaden said as he took the damp towel from Shun's hand. He rubbed himself with quick, efficient movements and dropped it to the floor. He was going to have to wash that as well and see if Supply had extra towels for Shun. "I'm not making excuses or anything… or maybe I am."

Shun held up a hand, silencing him. "You don't owe me an explanation." He passed the clean underarmor to Kaden and turned to leave the bathroom.

"No, but I need to speak about it," Kaden insisted. "As I was saying, after I came back without my—" His resolve faltered as he tried to talk about his injury.

"I know what you mean." Shun turned around.

"I didn't really feel like doing anything. I would sit on the bed and stare at the window, thinking I should open it but not getting around to it. I didn't feel hungry, but I slept a lot. Sometimes, I slept for days on end because I didn't feel like getting out of bed."

It had been about a week and a half. He had been on medical leave, and no one had questioned him about it. In a way, it felt longer as each day passed and stretched before him endlessly, but at the same time, he'd lost track of days, of time altogether.

"What happened?" Shun picked up the towel. He looked around and Kaden pointed to the large blue plastic basin where Shun's prison clothes were.

"If you could move everything that needs to be washed into that, I'll take it to the laundry room on the ground floor."

Shun nodded and moved to do so. He didn't prompt Kaden to continue, but Kaden could tell he was waiting. There was no judgment in the way Shun regarded him.

"I don't think I washed for days, and then one day I was thinking about it... about a week, week and a half into my slump, when I heard the bell. There's a dorm bell downstairs for the new recruits, and...." Kaden wondered how to explain it to Shun. "I grew up in an orphanage and then a military compound. My life was a series of bells that told me what to do, keep time, and all that. So, when I heard the bell, I had to get up. I was trained for it, like those dogs that come for food when you blow a whistle.

"But it scared me," Kaden added in a small voice. "I felt that if I'd stayed in my bed any longer, I would have never gotten up from it. Like there was nothing for me to get up for. So I started to leave my room more."

Shun had reached the middle of the laundry pile, and Kaden could see him wrinkle his nose in distaste.

"Go on," Shun spoke in a soft voice, his words at odds with his expression. "What did you do afterward?"

"I just didn't come to my room much," Kaden confessed. "I went outside for food, came back only to change my clothes and run back out

of the room. Sometimes I didn't even return for that. Then I went to—"
He hesitated for a moment, then sighed and continued as he reached for
his armor. "There were a couple of prostitutes outside. I went to them.
It wasn't because I wanted the sex, but because I wanted to feel like I
existed."

Shun continued to shovel clothes. He looked at Kaden and nodded.
Though he wasn't exactly smiling, his face wasn't closed off. "No other
friends, this Vorani of yours or someone else?"

"Vorani was busy with the new recruits. She'd gotten a promotion,
and there was nothing I could do about it. It's not like I had a lot of
friends."

"So these prostitutes." So much for hoping he'd managed to avoid
the topic. "Did you... how did you do it? Did you do it standing?"

Kaden actually burst out laughing at that and Shun spun around.
"What? I just wanted to know because you were so against taking your
armor off when we first met. Don't tell me all those hookers just closed
their eyes."

"It wasn't sex." Kaden stood up and walked over to the basin. "It
was hand jobs and a few blow jobs. I didn't even come, most of the time.
It was things I could do without taking my armor off and... it didn't
mean much. I'm grateful they made me feel alive, but in the long run, it
was just a lot of expense for very little outcome."

Shun snorted. "Out-come."

Kaden's lips stretched into a small smile. "I realized I had to get a
field mission or just let go. I was thinking more and more about... killing
myself, and I knew I just had to get out of this place." He sighed heavily.
"It's water under the bridge, really."

"Can I ask you a couple of questions about that?"

"I...." Kaden shook his head. "I think that's all there is to say."

He knew there was more to say, but he wasn't ready, and he hoped
Shun understood. It had taken a lot of courage to reveal so much about
himself.

Shun nodded, straightening. He looked at the overflowing basin
and then at Kaden. "So, where's the laundry?"

Kaden hesitated. "How about lunch and then we split up? I'll grab
some cleaning supplies and some bedding for both of us. Then I'll do
the laundry while you work on the room." Because it looked like he was
getting the easy job, he added, "I'll help you with everything afterward."

Shun actually smiled at that. "It's fine. Cleaning will keep me moving instead of thinking too much. I like to put things in order when I have a problem."

KADEN HAD never imagined his room could look so clean. As he lay in bed looking at the ceiling—and he could imagine Shun scrubbing it—he wondered why he felt so much better about everything.

The room looked less dark, even though it was night.

Kaden had never had any wall hangings, and there had never been any pictures to put on the walls—all the pictures of his parents and siblings were faded memories in his head. There had been little left of their house in the aftermath of the bombing. But, Kaden thought as he looked over to Shun snoring softly in the next bed, it felt like home for a change.

He'd thought about sex, especially since Shun was sharing a room with him, but by the end of the day, they'd both been exhausted from the cleaning, and Kaden didn't think there'd be any point in even trying. Shun hadn't eaten much that day, complaining that the food was bland and stale; Kaden hadn't had the heart to tell him it was the usual camp fare.

He closed his eyes and tried to get back to sleep, but he was awake for the day and rolled off his bed reluctantly. After a shower in the newly clean bathroom, he donned his full armor. Perhaps the washing was dry and he could bring it up. They were running out of things to wear.

"Where're you going?" Shun was sitting up on the bed, in nothing but his sleep shorts. He looked wide-awake and curious.

"Going to grab the laundry." Kaden's gaze fixed on a spot just above Shun's left shoulder. "If you get dressed, we can get breakfast."

Though he was under camp arrest, Shun had been treated rather well by the other soldiers. His crime was not common knowledge, but everyone knew he was awaiting trial, and until then he was Kaden's responsibility. Shun's ankle bracelet made him stand out, but no one had been hostile toward him. Kaden knew letting him go for breakfast alone would be fine, but still the thought didn't sit right with him.

"Is breakfast going to be as bad as dinner?" Shun asked, standing.

"It's not going to be better," Kaden offered.

Shun stumbled into the bathroom.

Kaden's words proved to be true when they sat for breakfast half an hour later and were served a soggy yellow mess that looked as if it'd seen better days.

Shun's exclamation of revulsion was echoed by Bradley and Wayland, who had joined them that morning.

"How can you eat that stuff?" Wayland asked Kaden, who was shoveling food into his mouth with resignation.

"I grew up on this," he said with a wry grin. "I know it doesn't kill."

Shun swallowed hard and picked up the spoon. He opened his mouth, tried a taste, and let the spoon drop with a loud "Gah" that had some of the people at the next table snickering. "It can't be this bad all the time," he said in disbelief.

"There was a time when it was a little more palatable," Bradley said as she pushed her tray away. "But recently, even the decent cooks have been moved south with the bigwigs because they're expecting more fighting."

"I hadn't heard that," Kaden said in surprise, food forgotten.

"After the attack on the train," Wayland explained, "they really heightened the security, and we heard they've doubled the patrols heading to Compen Beach Town. The way we sneaked in—well, I don't think we can do that anymore."

"Really?" Kaden tried to act as if he was interested, but with Shun sitting next to him, nothing else mattered. "That's not good for the peace talks, is it?"

Bradley, at least, had things to talk about. "From what I heard, that came to a stop after the last drone attack on a civilian train. You should have seen Instructor Vorani. She was running all over the place, waiting for someone to call her. She really likes being on top of things."

"Well, she was like that when she was a student here—"

Shun got to his feet all of a sudden. Kaden wondered if he would make some loud announcement regarding the state of the peace talks. It wouldn't do for Shun to anger the soldiers; there was always an underlying tension when fighting was around the corner, piling up more bodies, and it wasn't in their best interest to instigate an argument.

"I want to speak to the chef."

Kaden had not expected that. "Huh?"

"I mean, this is inedible. I want to know what the hell this is made of."

Kaden opened his mouth to tell Shun that was not how things worked around the camp.

"I'll come with you," said Bradley, standing up. "I want to see this kitchen as well."

Kaden sat at the table, wondering just what had happened when Bradley and Shun walked away from them. He turned to Wayland, who was looking just as nonplussed. "How good are you at laundry duty?"

"I HEARD your… uh, prisoner… roommate… uh, boyfriend is cooking for us now," said Finzer as he gave Kaden the supplies.

"Must admit, the food is better." Kaden took the additional toothpaste and the soap, ignoring the implied question in the statement. "On Stores duty this week, then?"

Finzer took the avoidance with good grace. "Until tomorrow, then I'm heading to Livera. They need a couple of armors to suppress some civilian unrest or something like that."

"I haven't received any missions after the train attack," Kaden said in puzzlement; he took the clipboard with his requests written, signed the receipt, and gave it back. "Wonder what the holdup is this time."

"Knowing Vorani, she's saving you for something special." Finzer took back the forms. "Thank your boyfriend for me. I haven't eaten like this in a while."

Kaden thought it over as he walked back to their room, where to his surprise, Shun was seated on Kaden's bed. He hadn't seen much of Shun the past two days, given that Shun had taken it upon himself to teach the camp chefs how to cook. He'd been gone long before Kaden rolled out of bed and only came back late at night to drop into bed, exhausted.

"I didn't expect you back." Kaden dropped everything on the bed next to Shun. "I got extra toothpaste and toothbrushes."

"Any wet wipes?"

"Yes." They had not been free, unlike basic supplies, and the cost would be deducted from Kaden's salary, but it seemed a small thing to keep Shun in a good mood. "Finished your kitchen duty?"

"Not really. I'll keep ducking in once in a while, but the worst is over," Shun said with a wry grin, flopping back on the bed. "I showed them the basics, and well, everyone has common sense. Okay, not all of them, but some seemed to have been raised in houses with kitchens. I predict the quality of food will... at least be a little better from now on."

Kaden snorted. "Thanks for that."

"Please, I was also eating that slop." He looked up at Kaden, leered, and stretched. His shirt rode up, his trousers rode down, and Kaden felt his cheeks color. "Are you free now?"

And that put a damper on Kaden's mood. "Oh... not really. I have an appointment with the doctor."

"Why? Is anything wrong?" Shun sat up in an instant, his eyes flat and serious.

"No, just a checkup. Vorani made it so that I have to have one every week or so. I can't skip them."

"I'll come with you."

"No need for that. You said you were tired...." Kaden trailed off, a little unsure.

"Not that tired."

"Are you sure?"

"I don't mind," Shun said with a ready smile that looked natural. "Is it far? Are we leaving the compound?"

"No, it's the building next to Stores." On impulse, Kaden reached for Shun and gave him a peck on the cheek. "Finzer called you my boyfriend."

Shun didn't reply straightaway. "That's a big word," he said after a while. "At least you haven't gone for the hookers outside, have you?"

"What? No! Not since we came back from Compen. I told you, it was just something I needed to do to clear my head, not to.... Well, it's different."

"I shouldn't have brought that up. It's not like I have any say in—"

"No, it's fine," Kaden said quickly, wondering why he was feeling pleased that Shun had brought up his past sexual activities. Perhaps it was the tone Shun had used; no matter how casual he'd tried to sound, Kaden had heard the lingering undercurrent of—he hoped—jealousy. "It kept me centered."

"You mean fucking kept you sane," Shun said as he shepherded Kaden out the door. "You must be very centered these days."

"I didn't say that." Kaden turned and stopped when he saw the teasing smile on Shun's face.

It was rare to see Shun smile. He wondered what Shun would do after the trial. Or even what his fate would be. Kaden hadn't heard from Tracy in a while. Shouldn't they be coming up with a good defense by now?

Shun looked at him inquiringly. "You went somewhere all of a sudden."

"I just thought of something else. We haven't heard from Tracy in a while."

"You really think of a lot of things instead of answering my question." Kaden looked at him in surprise. Shun's voice was laced with heat as he spoke again. "Are you avoiding my question?"

"I didn't realize there was a question."

Shun had the grace to blush. "It was implied."

Kaden actually had to think back before he could form an answer. "You kind of implied I was… sleeping with someone else?"

"If you don't want to have a long-term relationship with me, it's fine. I did notice you didn't want to—We haven't… exactly… fucked since I came out of the detention center."

"I thought you'd need more time," Kaden defended. "And you seemed so tired every night. It just didn't seem right to push. As for Tracy, I was just wondering about when your trial was and how long you'd be here and what'd happen afterward."

Shun was silent for a couple of seconds while Kaden led him wordlessly toward the medical center. "You still haven't answered my question."

"I do want you around for a long time," Kaden admitted. "It's not that I'm avoiding your question." He slowed his pace a little so that Shun, who was shorter, could keep up with him. "But I don't know what the future will hold for you."

"Or for you," Shun pointed out.

"I'm not going to let go of my armor anytime soon," Kaden responded. "But you did say you wanted to get away from all this."

"My trial might not be up for another month or two," Shun offered.

Kaden felt his chest squeeze even as he shook his head. "That's too soon for me," he said with a weak smile. "I know I have problems, and they haven't gone away. But I haven't thought of jumping off a building in a while. I don't want to get used to having you around and find out that you're gone. I don't think I could take it."

Shun frowned but didn't argue as they reached the medical facility, which Kaden was starting to become far too familiar with.

The checkup went the same as always, with one notable difference being that Shun stood watching as Kaden was stripped of his armor, measured, and prodded.

"Nothing to say," the doctor said as Kaden pulled his armor toward him.

Both the nurse and the doctor watched in fascination as the armor snapped around him, almost before he guided the correct parts to his body, and in the end when he stood up, he felt as if he should take a bow for the applause that was sure to come. It was never as fast and smooth as the time he'd gotten his armor back after it was stolen, but it happened faster than for anyone else he'd ever observed.

The doctor cleared his throat and shuffled some papers. "Have you considered getting your leg—stump restructured?" The doctor was at least astute enough to pick up on Kaden's reluctance to talk about his stumps.

It wasn't exactly a new topic, and Kaden had heard variations of it on all his visits. "You mean trimming one to the size of the other." They both knew what the answer was going to be. "No."

The doctor was not willing to let it go. "Let me at least get you a brochure I picked up for a rehabilitation clinic, near the Galesh Beach Town. Pretty place with a nice—"

"No." This time his refusal was less polite.

"Why?" Shun asked suddenly.

"Why what?" Kaden snapped. He'd been annoyed since the beginning of the physical examination and hated to be probed and looked at. At the end of each examination he felt like a piece of meat.

"Why do you want to trim his stump down, what's wrong with having two of different sizes?"

"Shun, there's no need for that," Kaden barked as he moved to the door.

"Please." Shun's hand on his upper arm stopped him from moving. "It doesn't hurt to hear, does it?"

It might not be painful to Shun, but to Kaden it always felt as if he was being stabbed in the chest every time the doctor spoke of disability and prosthetics and moving on. It was the last thing Kaden wanted to hear, but Shun seemed unmoved, and the stubborn set of his jaw meant Kaden was bound to listen to the spiel as well. And he was a little curious as to whether the doctor had anything new to say.

"To start off with, you are one of the luckiest people I've seen."

Which was not a starting line Kaden was prepared for. "Really," he said coldly as he tried to move back, but Shun prevented him. He could have pushed Shun aside, but a part of him knew that if he were to do that, Shun would probably never forgive him.

"After your time at the hospital, you didn't have proper stump care, and you still managed to get away with no infections, no ulcers, and zero muscle problems."

"I don't think—"

"What exactly does proper stump care involve?" Shun asked quickly, and the doctor nodded as if pleased.

"I'll give you the reading material which is—"

Kaden had had enough. "No need."

"Thank you very much," Shun said at the same time.

The doctor continued. "The insides of the underarmor suits are designed to absorb sweat and water, so they probably absorbed a lot, but do you even dry properly after a shower? Don't answer that. It's just a rhetorical question. My point is, your armor has been adjusting for you, compensating for your muscle differences, and even cushioning your skin like some synthetic…. I've never seen anything like that."

"So, what else do I need?"

"To be fitted with prosthetics, you're going to need to be properly balanced. Otherwise one set of muscles will be used more than the other and your body will suffer." The doctor spoke quickly, apparently aware that he needed to say his piece before Kaden lost patience. "The normal procedure is to—"

"I don't want to hear this." Kaden abruptly turned away.

"Kaden, please," Shun said softly and placed a hand on his shoulder.

"No, that's it." Cold sweat rolled off Kaden as he thought of the possibility of losing his armor. "No, I don't want to talk about this."

"You can't be in the armor forever," the doctor said, as if he thought bluntness would get through to Kaden. "The sooner you get fitted, the sooner you can—"

Kaden almost tore off the door of the infirmary in his hurry to leave, and this time Shun didn't try to stop him.

Kaden charged through the front door and out into the bright sunlight with a curse, pushing people aside as he did. He stopped near the mess hall and looked around, wondering if Shun was trailing behind, perhaps running after him. He stood for a couple of seconds, composing himself. He turned around, ready to defend his actions, and realized there was no one. Shun was nowhere to be seen.

Kaden wondered if Shun was looking for him, but he just wasn't in the mood to go back inside the infirmary. Instead, he turned around and walked toward the training ditches, where a group of cadets was crawling through a mud pit. He stood for a second catching his breath, when someone came and stood next to him.

Finally. "I'm sorry I—" He stopped short. "Wayland, aren't you on office duty right now?"

She looked at him with her head tilted to the side. "And aren't you supposed to be in Medical?"

"It finished early."

"So did my shift." Wayland didn't look too pleased about the idea. "Tracy and Vorani are in some form of discussion in the office. I think it's about Shun's trial, but when I tried to listen, Vorani told me to come out here and supervise."

Kaden watched a cadet stand up, slip, and then fall back into the mud. He couldn't figure out who they were since they were covered in a layer of mud. He opened his mouth to ask about Shun's impending trial but discovered he wasn't even close to accepting what would happen next. "Want to spar? I'll go easy on you."

Wayland looked at Kaden for a moment and then nodded. "I'm not going to go easy on you," she warned him with a quick grin.

"Hope your armor's self-cleaning, because you're going to be wearing mud," he warned her, trying to work up a smile. He liked Bradley and relied on her, but Wayland was still learning, and he enjoyed teaching her. He was glad he was needed and looked up to—it did wonders for his confidence.

In an effort to keep himself moving, Kaden trained Wayland for much longer than needed, in fact for most of the day, until the cadets were long gone and the sun was starting to set. Finally he decided he was pleased with the progress they'd made. He watched her move in the armor and nodded in satisfaction: she was moving smoother, faster, her punches were powerful—

"Sloppy," Bradley growled from where she stood next to Kaden's shoulder. "That girl has no killer instinct."

"Isn't that good?" he asked as Wayland went around an obstacle, jumped over a cutout of a man, and finally hit the water course.

"You think?"

"She's not cut out to be a killer. Let her be," he said softly, watching Wayland slip out of her armor and throw it to the ground. Then she crawled out of the pit, grabbed the armor by the shoulder piece, and started to put it on piece by piece in a painfully slow process that made him wince. "But she does need to get into that faster."

Bradley snorted. "That might look slow to you, but have you seen how long it takes me to get into mine? And mine doesn't have easy clasps. I need to strap some of those things on step-by-step."

Kaden looked sideways at Bradley, who was dressed in off-duty fatigues, looking invincible. "You sound more and more as if you don't like your armor."

"Well, got to make the most of it, I guess." Bradley sounded tired. "I've probably got a couple of years, maybe a decade or so before I slow down and they give mine to someone else." There was no talk of stepping down or passing it on now.

Kaden placed a hand on Bradley's shoulder. New armor, unlike the original, did not rely on soldier compatibility and willingness to give away the armor. When the wearer was too slow, it was stripped away and handed to the next person with the same body stats, with a few adjustments where needed. With the wear and tear the new armor had on the wearers, they didn't have much of a life after their duty was done either.

"How many hours of practice do you put in each day?"

"Six hours."

Kaden sighed. The regulations said six was the maximum number a new warrior could practice in armor, but it varied during wartime. In the field, they all had to be in their armors. It wasn't as if they could take a break while everyone was shooting at them. Kaden knew of people who'd lived in their armor for days and days, just stopping at charging stations to restock their weapons and then move on. "They say the back is the first to go."

"My back is still fine," Bradley admitted. "It's the shoulders that're killing me." She smiled wryly as Wayland reached the end of the course. "But I'm not dead yet, and I'm hanging on to my deathtrap with all I've got."

"I don't know about you, but they do pull armors off us as well," Kaden said, referring to the original armor he was wearing.

"With your black armor, at the compatibility rate you've got, I don't think anyone else can fit into it."

Bradley said it without any special meaning behind it, not looking at Kaden at all. She helped Wayland pull off her armor, which was dripping mud with each step. Kaden stood rooted to the spot, feeling the words reverberate through him. He had never felt very reassured by those words, but as she walked away, a reluctant smile grazed his lips. Let the sisters have their alone time. He needed to pick up Shun.

He checked in a couple of places, but he guessed Shun might have returned to their room, and it turned out to be true. Shun lay sprawled on his bed, his hand flung over his eyes, fast asleep. Kaden softened his gaze as he took in the clean lines of Shun's relaxed body and wondered if he should catch up on his sleep as well. It was tempting to crawl into bed beside him, even if he wasn't sure if there was room enough for two, when he saw a flash of color under Shun's outflung arm.

He moved carefully and plucked the item off the bed. It turned out to be a medical pamphlet he'd seen before—Amputation and Recovery—and he fought the first impulse, which was to crumple the thing and throw it away, as he had done to a hundred other pamphlets he'd been bombarded with. He let it drop to the floor and moved back to his bed, not wanting to be even near the thing.

His bed was unmade and his covers were in disarray. If he had been in the cadet dorm, it would have meant a day of yard cleaning. As he automatically straightened the covers, he banged against the bedframe, making it rattle. He looked up to see if he'd woken Shun and saw that he was being observed through half-open eyes. "Sorry."

"I was just resting my eyes anyway. Not the time to sleep," Shun said with a yawn, sitting up and brushing his hair off his eyes. "Where'd you run off to?"

"I went to the training course and met up with the sisters."

"I see."

"I'm not going to give up my armor anytime soon."

"No one asked you to." Shun held out his hands.

Kaden backed up a little. "What?"

"Take off that armor of yours and get in here. I haven't touched you since I came out of the prison, and I miss holding you."

"I shouldn't do that." Kaden pulled off his chest piece, belying his words.

"Why not?"

"Because I'm going to die in my armor, and you're going to walk away once the trial is over."

"Provided the trial is going to save me," Shun said as he shifted back and opened his legs. "Who knows, they might lock me up for good."

Kaden knelt between Shun's thighs; the bottom half of his armor fell off. He kept his hands on Shun's shoulders for balance while the rest of his armor fell aside. "Not if we have anything to say about it."

"Thank you."

"But either way, we have different needs." Kaden kept his head on Shun's shoulder. "I respect that, but… but…."

"I don't want you to fight," Shun whispered. "I don't want you to die in this damn metal—"

"It's my life."

"It shouldn't be," Shun snapped.

Kaden was leaning in more to Shun, and his eyes started to prickle as he spoke. "If you make me cry, that's going to be the end of this," he warned.

Shun, in reply, started to shuffle them awkwardly backward until they were both lying on the bed, Kaden mostly on top of him. "Let me just hold you for a bit," he said without raising his voice. "I also want to talk to you a little, and this seems to be the only way."

"About the prosthetics?" Kaden asked, stiffening.

"No… yes. I'm not really sure. It's like you're avoiding your problem."

"If I accept it, will my legs grow back?"

"Don't be like that," Shun protested, though there wasn't any heat in his voice. "Just, I know this is not what you want to hear, but to me, it doesn't matter. I know you can survive without your armor. You're more than that."

Kaden didn't bother opening his eyes as he shifted around until he was comfortable. "That's so cliché."

"But true."

"I should get up and storm away, but right now I just want to sleep," he said with a tired yawn. "Let's just—" He nuzzled Shun's ear, feeling the warmth seep through his underclothes. "I don't want to talk about this."

"Thank you." Shun kissed Kaden's forehead, a soft brush of lips. "And before you ask, that's because you were willing to listen to me at all."

# CHAPTER 15

VORANI AMBUSHED them at breakfast the next morning. Ambush was a strong word, but Kaden had just finished swallowing the last of the food when Vorani placed her tray next to him, cutting off his escape.

"I hear I have to thank you for the quality of food," she said, looking at Shun over Kaden's shoulder.

Shun didn't look particularly alarmed by the appearance of Vorani, but he didn't look all that pleased either. "I'm happy to help in any way I can."

"Still not convinced enough to join us, though," she said as she pulled up a chair and sat down.

Shun shrugged. "I didn't know the Army needed more cooks."

Vorani had never been one to beat around the bush. "No, we need more men to fight." She turned around as if looking for someone. "Where're Bradley and Wayland?"

"Somewhere in the back," Kaden spoke for the first time. "Eating with their dorm mates." He took a deep breath. "What do you want, Vorani?"

"To get back the armor Shun lost."

Shun flinched, which solidified Kaden's annoyance to plain dislike. "Have you tried whistling for it?" he asked. He placed a hand on Shun's knee to calm him down. Vorani would have missed nothing about their interaction, but he didn't care—it was a well-known secret anyway.

"I wish it were that easy," she said as Wayland and Bradley appeared as if they had been silently summoned. "Pull up a chair, you two, we need to talk."

"Shouldn't we do this in an office somewhere?" Bradley said. She turned around and easily picked up two heavy metal chairs and brought them over.

Vorani looked around and Kaden followed her gaze. Breakfast was almost over, and apart from a few stragglers, most had gone to their assigned posts. There was hardly anyone around, and those that were seemed immersed in their own conversations. And it wasn't too odd to see people discuss work over a meal.

"So what do you have in mind?" He leaned back and crossed his arms over his chest, not giving a hoot as to how his body language would be read.

"First of all, let me explain the current situation in simple terms." Vorani pulled herself straight. She looked down at her uneaten plate of food and then with a grimace pushed it aside. For someone who had just complimented Shun's food, it seemed a tad insulting, and Kaden frowned at the implied slight. "WUC is finally taking action after the last drone attack on a civilian train, but they're doing something we didn't expect. They want to make Compen Island into a dead zone."

"You mean obliterate everything and shut it down?" Shun looked stunned. "Damn, I live there."

"Well, actually, we think that'll open Compen Beach Town to the people again if they're willing to live close to the island." Vorani corrected him, looking annoyed at the interruption. "But the point is, for that, they're evacuating Compen Island... soon. As soon as the end of the month, from what we know."

Kaden could see where the conversation was heading. "And those people who took Shun's armor are still there on the island."

"Exactly." Vorani looked up with a smile. "I spoke to Shun's lawyer, Tracy. We can talk about dropping his charges if we get back the armor."

"A small team, sneak into the island, get it back," Bradley joined in. She looked at Vorani with something akin to respect. "Is that what you have in mind?"

Vorani nodded and her features relaxed. "Yes."

"And if you're telling everyone here, we must be the team," Bradley surmised.

"Including me?" Shun sounded surprised.

"Easier to wear an armor out than carry it." Kaden could see the logic of the plan. "We know the terrain and we'll be going in prepared. The correct firepower, something to cross the sea, and technically we should be able to do it."

"We don't need to cross the sea." Wayland almost shouted in her eagerness to join in the conversation. "Senior Instructor Vorani had me studying the tidal maps. There'll be low tide around the island for a couple of days. At its lowest, you can walk across the sandbar that appears."

Both Kaden and Bradley shook their heads in unison.

"Boat," Kaden stated, leaving no room for argument. "The sandbar's like walking in a line, inviting people to shoot us."

Vorani cut through their small talk. "We can talk strategy later and fine-tune everything, but the question is will you do it? If WUC evacuates the island, the armor could fall into their hands, and that's the last thing we want. This will give Shun a chance to redeem himself, and it's a mission three armored warriors should be able to complete."

"How are we going to get close to Compen Island?" Bradley demanded. "It's going to have WUC checkpoints all the way. You surely don't intend to air-drop us?"

"That is why I'm still the senior instructor and you're my underling." Vorani smirked, but there was a fondness in her eyes, and Kaden had an inkling who Vorani was grooming to take over after her. Now that she had an administrative position, he didn't think she'd have a lot of time for field missions.

"I... I have a suggestion," Shun offered after a slight hesitation. "Perhaps if Wayland were to stay behind...."

"She proved herself on the train," Vorani said with a dismissive wave of her hand. "She is able to fight, and without her, it'll be just the two main fighters. Take another person as backup. Anyway, from what I hear, Shun isn't much of a fighter, and without his armor, he'll need someone to babysit him."

If Shun was angry at the dig about his nonfighting status, he didn't show it, but Kaden felt it was his duty to defend him. "Then why don't you come with us? We can always use another trained warrior."

"Because for one, you'll be leading this team, and you know how I feel about following some of your orders," she said with a small secretive smile. "But most importantly, if you must know"—she patted her middle—"my morning sickness will slow me down."

And looking at Vorani's smug smile, Kaden remembered that she always got what she wanted.


"WE HAVE three hours more to go," Shun said in the dark.

"I thought you were asleep," Kaden said, rolling over to lie on his back and look at the familiar ceiling of his room.

"Can't sleep."

"Nervous about the mission?" Kaden pushed aside a sweat-dampened curl of hair off his forehead. He had been dreaming, something not very pleasant, but as usual he couldn't remember. "Or did I move around too much?"

"You don't move when you sleep." Shun surprised him by understanding what he was implying. "You kind of twitch a little, but that's it. It'd have been easier if you'd shouted or moved, because then I'd know if you were having a nightmare."

"Don't remember them much. Can't be anything really interesting," he said dismissively, rolling to his side and bracing his longer leg on the bed. The doctor had said he was using that leg more than the other, but it wasn't much. People probably used their dominant leg more all the time. He snorted at that and completed his roll to find himself face-to-face with Shun, whom he hadn't been aware was so close to him. Which should be no surprise, since even with the beds pushed together, there was very little space.

He studied Shun's face in the semidarkness—floodlights pierced through the thin material he used as a curtain. "From what Vorani told us, this time should be smoother than last time."

"I should hope so," Shun muttered under his breath, and Kaden realized with a jolt that he was just not used to fighting, to action, the way Kaden was.

"I'll take care of you." Kaden was going to keep his word no matter what. "Nothing will happen to you as long as I live."

"That's a big promise," Shun said after a couple of beats.

"I mean it."

"I know." Shun smiled a little and shuffled forward. "Thank you."

The kiss was soft, a simple thank-you with no pressure to it, but Kaden pressed forward, chasing the elusive taste that was uniquely Shun. Shun didn't pull away when Kaden rolled him over until he was on top, even as he continued the kiss.

"Wait," said Shun after a second, breaking off the kiss and wriggling away.

Kaden watched, half-aroused, half-amused, as Shun pulled open a drawer and pulled out a couple of condoms and a tube of lube. "What?"

"I spoke to the doctor after you left," Shun said as he threw a condom at Kaden. "He gave me these."

Kaden nodded, took the condom, and hesitated. "My tests were negative. I got tested as part of my routine checkup two weeks ago, and I haven't been with anyone since then. Actually, the last person I was with was you."

Shun hesitated as well, then nodded, putting the lube aside, absentmindedly. He looked as if he understood the implications of what Kaden was saying. "I got a clean bill of health as well. They tested me after they locked me up, and well, it wasn't like I have anyone to even look at."

"Good," said Kaden firmly. He continued the kiss from where they'd stopped, and Shun joined in enthusiastically. Kaden pulled away from Shun's lips, which looked swollen already, and trailed down the jawline, feeling the faint hint of stubble on the tip of his tongue. Shun tilted his head back, inviting more, and Kaden found himself sucking the exposed skin, aware he was leaving marks that would be obvious to anyone who saw them. Moving downward, he reached the juncture of Shun's collarbone and throat, and encouraged by Shun's enthusiastic moans, he sucked a little harder.

Kaden looked up to see Shun stare back at him, lips swollen and half-open, his eyes blazing with need. Kaden let Shun feel for and find the zipper for the ratty top he wore to bed, and he tried to shrug it off while he continued exploring Shun's chest. Their times before had been hasty and a little exposed, but Kaden was secure in his room, aware it was at least soundproof. The rooms on either side of him were separated by bathrooms, and the window opened onto a courtyard. They were free to make as much noise as they wanted, and Kaden wanted to take advantage of that as much as possible.

Shun tugged at Kaden, eyes blown with lust, lower lip caught between his teeth, urging him to continue, and Kaden complied without hesitation. They'd been living in close quarters, keeping their lust in check, and now it was finally being let loose. Kaden was rusty, but he'd had lovers before, and he dug deep inside himself to bring up all his experience to satisfy Shun.

Shun pulled Kaden up for another kiss, while clawing at the top that was probably getting even more stretched out of shape by the insistent tugging. Kaden broke off long enough to shuck it off and throw it into parts unknown while stroking a hand down Shun's spine. He pressed along the center, and much to his delight, discovered Shun was sensitive at certain pressure points—perhaps he could offer him a back massage later.

Shun pulled him down for another kiss, his body undulating, and Kaden balanced his weight on his knees between Shun's spread legs. Shun pulled him down harder, and Kaden cautiously lowered himself until he was lying on him, pinning him with his weight. He broke off immediately and gasped out, "Am I too heavy?"

Shun grunted a short no and at the same time ground his hips up forcefully. Their erections brushed together, separated by cloth but still very prominent, and Kaden gasped. Shun used the moment to roll him over until Shun was on top, and with a smirk he leaned in for another kiss. His hands were roaming well past Kaden's waistline, inside his sleeping shorts, and Kaden found himself doing the same with Shun. He reached cupped Shun's erection through the sweatpants he wore to bed, and decided he liked having time to mess around.

It was different from the quick tumbles they'd had, but the way Shun gasped and moaned made him aware that perhaps going slowly had its benefits. He couldn't remember the last time he'd had the luxury to do anything similar—perhaps never. Kaden didn't worry too much about his lack of recent experience. He had Shun to go by, and he knew that they were at least enough at ease with each other that anything that would make them uncomfortable would be discussed up front.

"Let me know if I'm hurting you," he said to Shun, who was wriggling on top of him insistently.

"The only pain I have now is you talking," Shun snapped, his voice shaky and breathless.

Kaden laughed as he flipped them over and tweaked Shun's nipple as he pushed him down. He found out that Shun had sensitive nipples and liked it when Kaden played with them, first with his fingers and then with his mouth, sucking them, then blowing. Shun moaned and tugged at Kaden's hair as if he was getting a blow job, which made Kaden snort in amusement.

Kaden's remaining clothes were uncomfortable, and Shun's felt a little wet in the front. "Do you think we should switch on the light?" Kaden reached to make sure of the wet spot forming on the front of Shun's tented sweatpants.

"No," squeaked Shun—his voice went up an octave and then cut off abruptly. "What are you doing?"

"Trying to figure out if you're wet or—"

"Shut up," Shun said, and even in the faint light, Kaden could see that his face was an interesting shade of red.

"At least let me…." Kaden sat back on his knees, balancing himself carefully so he wouldn't fall over. Without feet to keep himself steady, he had to rely on Shun's hands on his hips as he slowly pulled down the fabric of the sweatpants. Shun lay perfectly still, breathing a little too hard for someone who had been doing nothing, as his last piece of clothing was stripped off him inch by inch.

"I wish we had more light," Kaden mentioned, eyeing Shun's erection bobbing up, free of the confinement of the clothes, looking angry-pink and glistening, even in the faint light.

"No, we don't need it." Shun sounded contrary even while he lifted his hips so the sweatpants could be removed.

Shun lay there as Kaden studied him, wanting to memorize every detail.

Kaden couldn't remember the last time he'd given a blow job; he had been at the receiving end of a few, which he'd paid for, but that was probably not a good idea to mention just then. He wondered if he could give Shun a blow job or at least try. The science of it was simple: lean forward, open his mouth, and suck.

"Don't…," Shun gasped, shimmying away from Kaden on his back. "You have to first take your clothes off, since… you get to see mine."

"Fine." Kaden struggled to remove his shorts, a little unsure as he fought to balance himself. He let himself roll until he was kneeling. Shun also sat up a little and helped him with his shorts. Kaden felt a little self-conscious as his stumps were exposed in bed. He wished he'd worn the stump socks the doctor had given him for the mission, but he had packed everything and hadn't felt the need for them while getting ready for bed.

Shun didn't even blink at them as he leaned in for a kiss. Kaden kissed back and then pushed him down onto the bed, silently indicating he wanted to get on with what he had been doing. He touched Shun's erection, feeling him shudder at the simple contact. Then he scooted back a little to find a comfortable angle and leaned in.

"What are you doing!"

"If you can't tell, then maybe I'm not doing it right. Let me take care of that." Kaden finally, finally closed his lips around Shun's penis. It was not something he was familiar with; he knew he had to keep his teeth away, but he was more concerned about not making it a total mess. He tongued the tip, prodded gently, and was satisfied with the moan he drew; he decided to try for something a little more daring. He tilted his head and found the underside of Shun's erection, soft and warm, and traced it down, leaving a slick trail of saliva in his wake. He came back up to swallow the tip, taking care not to take in too much. He was no expert, but gagging at this point would probably not be a positive outcome.

He continued to slowly take in as much of his cock as possible, careful with his teeth until he slipped a little, and Shun shuddered in a very good way. Kaden slowed down but let his teeth graze Shun again, and Shun bucked up; it seemed Shun wasn't averse to a little danger. Kaden wasn't really good at taking the whole length, and he didn't want to choke, so he settled for wrapping his fingers around what he couldn't fit into his mouth.

Then he hollowed out his cheeks and—

"Oh, fuck, shit... nnh," Shun moaned, thrusting up involuntarily.

Kaden kept a hand on Shun's hip and held him down so Kaden wouldn't be forced to try deep-throating. Shun responded by putting a hand on Kaden's hair and tugging wildly, spreading his legs even farther. Kaden remembered to hum a little, and Shun responded with another moan that ended in a yelp. His other hand fisted the bedspread, knuckles white as his legs spasmed uncontrollably.

Shun started to tug at his hair insistently, and Kaden was tempted to just let Shun come. However, he wanted to make the most of the time they had, and he withdrew slowly, letting the hard-on slip free of his lips, leaving a trail of saliva and precome connecting it to him.

"I'm close," Shun told him, and Kaden was very, very tempted. He leaned in again, this time surer as he closed his mouth on its target and then sucked hard. Kaden could feel Shun's thighs tremble, his stomach muscles clench, and the way his breath came in loud gasps. "Damn you... if I come in your mouth... I'm going to turn around and go to sleep," Shun shouted, his voice broken with sobs of pleasure.

Kaden gave a few more experimental sucks until he was sure Shun was on the brink and then withdrew abruptly, tightening his hold at the base of his cock. Shun practically screeched in frustration, opened his eyes, and Kaden noticed a trickle of saliva down the side of his mouth.

"You fucker," Shun cursed, so unlike himself that Kaden burst out laughing.

"Where did you leave that lube?"

"In the… uh… on the table."

Kaden sighed as he looked at the table that was in the far end of the room. "Go get it, I'm not going to crawl over there."

"You've got to be kidding me," Shun grumbled as he sat up with great difficulty, his cock bobbing with each move. "You have to appreciate how young I am. I could have died of a heart attack just now." He kept his feet on the floor and stood up slowly, shuffled to his feet none too steadily, and lurched toward the table.

"How old are you?" Kaden asked as he watched Shun root around the table for the lube, pushing aside a bundle of pamphlets in his hurry.

"Don't know." Shun pushed aside a few more objects on the table. "Damn, where is it?"

"Don't know?" Kaden was enjoying the sight of Shun's rounded behind. He gave his cock an experimental tug and smirked as Shun slammed his fist down on the table.

"I don't know where it is," he snapped. "And I don't know how old I am because I wasn't born in a hospital. My mother wasn't exactly herself, and I was never registered. Border village, no doctors… damn, no lube!"

Then he seemed to remember something and turned around. He rushed to the corner of the room where the bags they had packed the previous day in readiness for their mission stood. He opened a side pocket and pulled out the tube of lube triumphantly. "I had a spare."

"Planning something?"

"Yes, greasing the wheels of your wheelchair." Shun threw the lube at Kaden, who had to catch it quickly before it struck his face. "Quick, fuck me."

Shun practically jumped to the bed and tackled Kaden. "Kiss me, then fuck me."

Kaden didn't know Shun could be that way. He grinned as he complied with the first part of the request, knowing Shun would taste himself on Kaden's lips. Shun broke off quickly, lying back with his legs spread. He hooked a pillow from above and lifted his hips to slip it under him. Then he allowed his legs to fall open unashamedly.

"Perhaps I should take a picture."

Shun blushed but held his gaze as he kicked Kaden. "Hurry up. I don't think we have a lot of time."

Kaden pushed open the lube top and took a generous amount on his finger. He kept his eyes on Shun even as he slipped a finger inside Shun and waited for him to relax enough to accept two more. He gave a couple of experimental thrusts and wriggled his fingers a little, but Shun made an impatient sound.

Kaden withdrew his fingers and wiped them on the edge of the bedspread before reaching for more lube. He slathered his cock before pressing into Shun's entrance carefully. He knew Shun wasn't a virgin and might be used to rough handling, but he wanted to continue with the theme of being gentle or at least thoughtful of Shun's needs.

"Will you just hurry up." Shun practically shouted, and Kaden complied by pushing in inch by inch. He paused a little to let Shun get used to him, and when he was finally seated to the hilt, he stopped, letting them both adjust. Shun gave another impatient growl and wriggled his butt a little, but Kaden held him steady for a couple of seconds longer. It wasn't just for Shun's benefit—Kaden was afraid he would come if he moved too fast.

"Are you okay?"

"Will you fucking just move," Shun said.

Kaden found he was able to move. He didn't want to spare any time starting slow and steady and building up a rhythm, hoping he wasn't hurting Shun. But he needn't have worried too much, since Shun reached for him with the enthusiasm of a—Kaden had no idea; he'd never really experienced such a thing before. Shun wrapped his legs around Kaden's waist and pulled him farther in. His blunt fingernails dug deep into Kaden's back as he moved up into each of his thrusts, his mouth open, gasping as he did so.

Kaden had seen porn and experienced sex before, and he'd been sure all the sounds porn stars made couldn't be real. He could understand making some noise, but the string of curses and repetitive words spat out during porn had to be fake. But it turned out that Shun was a screamer, and when he wasn't shouting stuff, he was moaning and grabbing Kaden... almost painfully.

Kaden knew neither of them would last, and the sounds Shun was making further fueled Kaden's desire. He started to thrust erratically, aware he was close, and Shun hung on to him, screaming his name over and over again. A part of Kaden wondered just how soundproof his room was as he spilled into Shun and helped him reach his climax by giving his neglected cock a couple of squeezes.

They lay in a heap, gasping for breath until Kaden rolled over, and Shun gave a bark of laughter.

"That was... amazing."

"Well, I'm happy to please."

"It did seem as if it was more about me... as if you were going out of the way to make me feel comfortable," Shun said after a short while.

"Nothing wrong with that. You deserve it."

"Next time it'll be your turn."

Kaden considered the next time they could possibly have sex. "I have a feeling neither of us will get a turn, with what Vorani has planned."

The reminder of the mission dampened their spirits, and they fell silent as they thought of what was to come.

"Well, at least we had one for the road," Shun quipped, and Kaden managed a dry laugh as he reached for his armor.

# CHAPTER 16

KADEN HAD to give credit where it was due, and it was obvious Vorani's plan had merit. The plan was to stick as close to the truth as possible.

There was apparently a doctor, Dr. Sajiv, who specialized in prosthetics and had retired after some injury. He lived close to the beach and ran a small clinic, but apparently didn't do crowds too well. It coincidentally turned out that the prosthetic clinic and workshop he ran was on a nice part of the beach close to Compen Beach Town. Not too near, but enough that they were told to anticipate a couple of WUC checkpoints as they approached their destination.

Kaden was an injured armored warrior who had the right connections with the Olgesh family—he dated one of the daughters, Bradley, who was in the same unit as him, and finally wrangled an invite to meet Dr. Sajiv. The military IDs got them through the WUC roadblocks easily enough. It helped that Vorani had contacted Dr. Sajiv about Kaden's unique situation, and he in turn had been delighted to get a chance to meet Kaden.

Kaden didn't know just how much of the last part of the story was fabricated and how much of it was real. He wasn't sure if Dr. Sajiv even specialized in armors, but knowing Vorani, she might have transplanted some doctor who did have that particular specialization into a convenient beach location just so her plan would work.

It had been harder for them to find a reason for Wayland to fit in, so they'd finally settled for the angle that she'd snuck into the group uninvited because she wanted to rain on her older sister's parade. It seemed somewhat believable in the long run.

"We might have to leave her behind," Vorani said, much to Kaden's relief. "I can't think of fitting her in convincingly."

"Well, then, it means just the three of us." Bradley didn't sound relieved, but she did seem a little too quick to agree.

"But that would mean I'll have to get someone else in on this," Vorani said with a frown. "Bradley can keep an eye on Shun once he gets his armor back, but I don't know if she can keep up with him if he runs."

Bradley gave Vorani a flat, unimpressed look. "We have Instructor Kaden."

Vorani returned the look. "Who is currently sleeping with Shun."

"I mean, if it's a problem of having me traveling with the group, I can get there by myself," Wayland offered. "Or I can just be the annoying younger sister who's hanging on to the older sister, cockblocking her all the way."

"I see you're learning a lot of new words in the barracks," Vorani said, making Wayland blush.

According to their cover story, Kaden was Bradley's fiancé. "I think my lack of feet does that."

Vorani paused to consider. "The problem is your armor. If you travel with it, it would look like a lot of firepower."

Wayland shrugged, unimpressed. "I can hide it."

"You might be able to stow it somewhere in the van, but there will be metal detectors and…."

"I can hide it," Wayland repeated flatly. "My armor's base ability is that, metal manipulation."

Vorani looked at her thoughtfully, then seemed to soften a little. "I need you to demonstrate this ability of yours. I want to see if it would actually work when you're in a van."

The van they traveled in was small but not too bad. The first day of traveling involved very few roadblocks, all of which were Joscalian manned, so there was no need to even get out of the van. Their military IDs got them through them without any problem. Their overnight accommodations proved to be slightly problematic when they stopped at the place Vorani had picked for them, and there turned out to be no wheelchair ramp.

Kaden found out just how much he hated being out of the armor and strapped into a wheelchair as time progressed. He was helpless, more so than when he'd been at Compen Beach Town when people had simply pulled him along. Perhaps time had softened his memories, but Kaden thought he'd contributed more to that expedition than sitting on his butt.

The innkeeper, an elderly man, was apologetic as he pulled out a wooden ramp.

"I keep meaning to put a permanent one in," he said as Bradley opened the van door and Shun maneuvered the wheelchair out carefully.

The owner, wringing his hands in genuine distress, seemed not to notice that the disabled soldier's caretaker had blue eyes. Shun had taken to using the hair dye, but the contact lenses had made his eyes water, and even Vorani had to admit it was easier to explain away the blue eyes rather than the red swollen ones in a health caretaker. Dark hair on Shun looked strange but striking at the same time, with his pale skin looking fairer than normal.

"I was asked to keep two rooms for you," the owner said, looking at the group of four, all in their civilian clothes.

"Yeah." Kaden made no attempt to hide the frustration in his voice. "I'll take one room with Shun, and my fiancé and her sister will stay in the other."

The owner looked at them and then nodded silently. "Dinner at seven."

"Can you make that room service?" Shun asked as he pushed Kaden inside. "We're a little tired from the traveling."

In their room, Shun helped Kaden shower and change for bed without a single slipup. Shun rose to the task of caretaker, exercising Kaden's limbs, washing, drying, and dressing his stumps as if it was really his job.

"You don't have to do that," Kaden said when Shun knelt in front of his chair to check his stumps for signs of abrasions. "You're taking your role a little too seriously."

"I don't mind." Shun reached for the little socklike covers and slipped them over the stumps. "Let me know if it hurts or you feel something isn't right."

"You shouldn't believe everything you read in those pamphlets."

"I'll take the risk of being too careful." Shun pushed Kaden's wheelchair next to the bed.

Kaden had practiced transferring to and from the wheelchair often enough that he was able to get into bed on his own.

Shun walked over to the second bed.

"Aren't you going to join me?"

Shun hesitated for a second. "Just for sleeping. We have a long day of traveling ahead, and I want to be awake for it."

Bradley and Shun were to take turns driving.

"Fair enough." Kaden nodded. A full day of being trapped in a wheelchair had killed his libido, and he didn't really feel like trying to revive it. He was just glad the journey was only two and a half days long.

Vorani had planned for the most efficient route that had helped them skip a couple of key roadblocks, but the second day turned out to be even more roadblocks as they started to enter WUC territory along the beach road.

Everyone who looked at Wayland's sweating countenance assumed she was coming down with a fever. She was, in fact, using her armor's ability to mask her and Bradley's gear, which they'd hidden in various crevices in the van.

A physical inspection could have meant something else, but the WUC soldiers were sympathetic toward an injured solider who was suffering from the heat and fatigue.

"We're really sorry to trouble you like this," the soldier who searched their van told Kaden.

Kaden managed to squeeze out a small smile at her.

Her face was scarred, and she was missing part of her nose and left ear. She didn't seem to care that Wayland kept staring at her with wide eyes while she ran the scanner over them.

"Whose armor is this?" the soldier asked as she looked at the black armor piled on the floor.

"Mine," Kaden said shortly. It would have strained Wayland far too much to hide all three at once. "I can't move in it since I lost my…."

The soldier looked at her fellow uncomfortably and then sighed. "I… I'm sorry, but we need to make sure it's yours."

Kaden looked to Shun. "Go, bring me an arm piece."

Shun complied quietly but the soldier stopped him. "We need to test the others," she said to Kaden, "not you, to see if they're compatible with the armor."

Kaden almost sagged with relief but fought to keep his face blank. "Is this going to take long?"

Again the uncomfortable, guilty looks of having to make a disabled person go through more trouble than needed. "No, but your caretaker will have to stay behind."

Kaden hesitated at the thought of leaving Shun there.

The soldier forced a smile that was more of a grimace. "Would you like to come and sit in the shade?"

Kaden was used to seeing pity in the eyes of other people, and there were some who would look at his legs and stare, but for the most part, he was simply accepted in this group. But the entire day of being helpless meant he was becoming more and more aware of his situation and questioning his choices. An older WUC soldier, probably from one of the far-north countries if his red hair was anything to go by, looked at Kaden's injuries and asked, "Land mine?"

"No, it was a building falling on me and then gangrene," Kaden said shortly. He expected the man to back away after such an answer, but the guy nodded while handing Kaden a cup of cold water. He had only three fingers on his left hand. Kaden had forgotten just how many people had been injured in the war.

"I know your paper says you're going to this doctor who's going to put you in the field, but perhaps you need to regroup yourself."

Kaden looked up hard at that, wishing Shun was with him. "The last thing I need is to sit and be an old relic."

"No, I mean talk to a couple of people who went through the same thing," the older guy continued. "I know how hard it can be to sit with people who are whole. There are places where people who have been hurt on duty can share experiences. It helps to simply talk."

"Why are you telling me this?"

"Because you've got a lot of anger in you. And I know that look in your eye."

Kaden looked away and turned his attention to the paper cup, which was starting to buckle under his grip.

The female soldier who had searched them entered to tell Kaden they were cleared to go. As he wheeled himself out, the older soldier kept a hand on his shoulder. "Don't do anything stupid."

Kaden remained silent as they reached their stop, a slightly better inn than the one they'd stayed at the previous night. He let Shun take charge, who took him to the room and directed him to undress. Kaden was getting used to having someone care for him, taking the time to inquire about his comfort. He hadn't had anyone go out of the way to look after him since his mother died.

"What are you thinking of?" Shun asked, kneeling by the bed to dry Kaden's stumps.

"Nothing, really, and everything." Kaden was aware he was deliberately being unhelpful. "Just, is it worth it... all this?"

Kaden was trying to get Shun's armor back, allowing Shun to walk free. Shun had no reason to stay with him. All of a sudden, Kaden saw his life stretching before him, bleak and empty. Mission after mission, getting battered inside his armor, only to return to bad food and an empty room. It wasn't just the missing feet; if Shun were to go, he'd lose an even bigger part of his life, and he wasn't sure he'd survive that.

"Hey," Shun snapped, dropping the soft cloth he'd been using to wipe Kaden's legs. "Don't you do that to me."

"What?"

"The reason I'm going with this harebrained plan is because of you."

"That's not fair," Kaden protested as he pulled Shun up to his level.

Shun stood and followed until he was leaning against Kaden's knees. "Want me to give you a lap dance?"

"Just sit down," Kaden insisted, eager to keep the original conversation going. "Why do you have to sound as if it's my fault that you have to follow this plan? You were planning on stealing armors just fine before you met me. You don't need me. Once you're free of these charges, you can go back to your life outside. The only reason you're with me is because you don't have a choice."

"What would I do after I'm freed?" Shun leaned in for balance. His breath smelled of toothpaste. "I get the armor and then what—my life's dream is complete? Before I met you, I lived in an old house by the beach in an abandoned town. It wasn't as if I had a lot to live for."

"Oh, quit being dramatic," Kaden said seriously.

"The reason I want this armor back is because I want to be a free person. I mean, even if you're in the Army, you can still visit me from time to time, right? I'm not giving up on you that easily, you idiot."

Kaden froze as he realized what Shun was saying, what he was offering. He was giving Kaden a life outside the Army, a place to go to away from the camp. "Damn you for doing this to me," he snarled and pulled Shun in for a kiss, and Shun leaned in smoothly. "You'd better plan on staying up all night."

THEY SPENT most of their night in a sweaty pile of sex that was not as discreet as they wanted it to be, and Kaden found himself feeling sore and wrung out by the time they were ready to leave.

Bradley and Wayland were both up, bright-eyed and freshly showered, looking far too optimistic for the responsibilities thrust upon them.

"Sleep well?" Kaden asked as Bradley, playing the obligatory fiancée, came to give him a peck on the cheek.

"Not really," she whispered. "The bed frame in the next room kept knocking against the wall."

"Ah." Both Kaden and Shun colored before Kaden remembered a corridor separated their rooms.

"Clever of you," Shun said with a smile at Bradley, acknowledging her teasing as he slid open the back of the van and pulled down the wheelchair ramp. Kaden rolled up and locked his chair into place while everyone else got in.

"We have a couple of hours before the final checkpoint," Bradley warned. "Get ready, everyone."

"Just let me know before we reach it," Wayland, who was riding shotgun, told her.

"One more time," Bradley said, shifting gears. "Then we'll be in the clear."

They reached the checkpoint an hour and a half later. Kaden assumed even Bradley was feeling nervous, as she'd been driving a little faster than called for.

The WUC soldiers were relaxed, not expecting an attack, and the nature of Kaden's group helped them relax even more. Shun was the only male who looked to be a threat, and even he was too preoccupied with Kaden to do more than glance at them. As Bradley spoke to the soldier who came to check their registration, Wayland smiled at them while activating her armor.

The trick was to hide the armors from the soldiers while making sure other things, such as Kaden's wheelchair or even the van itself, didn't disappear from the scanners. The soldiers made a cursory check under the van and around it, even moving the seats a little, but as Vorani predicted, asking an injured soldier to dismount seemed a little harsh. The dogs sniffed the van, searching for explosives and, finding none, retired with their handlers.

"Well, no more checkpoints," said Bradley when they were waved clear. None of them relaxed until the van slid through the narrow opening between the barbed wires, and they were finally through.

"This is it," said Bradley. She started to accelerate. "We'll be at the doctor's in half an hour."

DR. SAJIV was an older man with salt-and-pepper hair, who looked as if he had seen a lot of action. He had a large burn mark on his face and restless eyes that scanned everything. It was the look of someone who was waiting for the next explosion. When they shook hands, Kaden recognized the tattoo on his wrist: a symbol of protection for field medics. Dr. Sajiv's office-slash-house was located close to the beach, with a large sprawling garden that ended in a jetty. An open terrace, with comfortable deck chairs and a small barbecue grill, spanned the beach. The house was oddly peaceful, and Kaden could imagine people spending the day looking at the beach or simply relaxing on the porch.

"I expected more people," Shun said, looking around. "Do you live here alone?"

"Just my maid, who's off for the day, and me." Dr. Sajiv greeted them cordially. "My working office is in the town you must have driven by, which is about half an hour on foot. I walk to work to keep myself active, and I meet my patients there. But to tell you the truth, I've been seeing less and less people since the Army decided my ideas were too radical."

"What were your ideas?" Shun asked, head to the side.

"I published a paper on how the armor you use isn't really armor, and after that, and my injury, I fell out of favor."

"You're Dr. Francis Sajiv," Shun exclaimed. "I thought you were a woman—sorry. You published that paper on how armor was actually meant to be hostile-environment wear for space pioneers, and that the Army changed the original design because they wanted to win the war."

"Oh, you've read it, then?" Dr. Sajiv looked pleased. "I didn't think it was a popular piece to read."

"It wasn't me, really," Shun said with a faint blush. "I have a friend who's interested in all things armor, and he showed it to me when…." He trailed off with a look to the other three, who were listening with varying degrees of interest. "I'm sorry, maybe we can discuss that later."

"Of course," Dr. Sajiv agreed quickly. "Perhaps you would like to freshen up. We have time until sundown." Their instructions were to set off at night when the people who were on the island would set up some form of distraction. He turned his attention to Kaden. "Senior Instructor Vorani promised me that I'd be interested in your injury and the way the armor is compensating for that. Can I take a peek?"

"I really didn't come here for a medical," Kaden refused politely. "I suppose you have better things to do than examine people like me."

"On the contrary, I enjoy feeling useful," Dr. Sajiv said as he looked at Kaden, who was seated in his wheelchair to keep up appearances. "I was told you have remarkable compatibility with your armor. Is there any way I can witness that firsthand?" He indicated the armor. "I'd like to see your legs first, and then maybe how mobile you are with your armor on. We can go inside my office, and I'll close the curtains. No one will see it. I do occasionally examine a patient that way, so it won't be anything new."

They walked to Dr. Sajiv's office, which was located in the back of the house, and everyone apart from Kaden found somewhere to sit. Kaden was uncomfortable about being examined in the presence of Bradley and Wayland, but he tried hard to ignore their presence. Shun, of course, wasn't exactly a stranger to Kaden's anatomy.

"No one else has done that," Kaden said as he stood in place while the doctor measured him to see if he was balanced in his armor.

"They should have done this," Dr. Sajiv said, putting aside his tape. "I suppose they all want you to get your stump trimmed and move to prosthetics."

"Yes," Kaden said in surprise.

"Well, that is usually the solution," Dr. Sajiv said, his tone indicating the exact opposite.

"What do you mean?" Shun had been quiet in the background, watching the proceedings with narrowed eyes.

"Most of my colleagues do not want to see anything but the obvious," he said as he walked around Kaden. "Can you jump? Yes… a little. Stand on one leg…. Hm, do you feel a strain at your hip, any pain? Do it with your other leg now, thank you, and…." He looked at Shun and smiled. "How efficient are you when you move in it? Are you faster now or was it easier to walk, before?"

"I never thought about it," Kaden admitted.

"This armor is an example of a solution to a problem. It seamlessly replaces the missing limb, and the user does not even seem to realize it." He looked at Kaden and smiled to show that there was no malice in his words. "I would like to ask you some questions about the sensations you have, if that's all right."

Kaden shrugged. It wasn't as if he had a lot to do before nightfall, and this doctor didn't seem to want him out of the armor.

"See." Dr. Sajiv continued talking to Kaden. "The problem is, we cannot replicate the original armors, and there will eventually be a time when they will run out of those. I was studying the possibility of the armor forming a neural connection with the wearer, and this confirms it...."

"What stopped you?" Kaden asked. "I mean, from completing the research."

"It was before my convoy was caught in a shell attack, and afterward I was asked to retire."

"You don't seem very hurt," Shun noted.

"Broke my right hand in two places. I'm a surgeon—don't have that precision anymore. And I've developed a bit of a problem at the sight of blood, a very bad thing if you're a doctor where there's blood everywhere."

He looked at them and smiled. "I wish I had access to a lab and a little more time to study everything. This is very interesting. I'm now just a consultant on prosthetics. I don't get to do much hands-on practice. But after this thing you have going on tonight is over, if you feel like dropping by, I'd love to see about transferring some of the armor capabilities into prosthetics."

"What exactly does that entail?" Shun sounded interested.

"See, if we can get prosthetics to form connections like your armor is doing now, imagine the possibilities."

"It's not that I haven't thought of it." Kaden hadn't wanted to think of such a possibility, but he'd found himself doing it anyway. "I just assumed it wasn't possible to reproduce the armor. You just said it yourself two seconds ago."

"Well, nothing is impossible." Dr. Sajiv sounded optimistic. He turned to Shun. "Can you pick up a couple of things off the table? And as for you"—he turned back to Kaden—"I'm going to blindfold you. Then I'm going to place some objects on the ground... see if you can recognize what they are by stepping on them."

Wayland yawned loudly and stood up. "Are we going to be doing this until nightfall?"

Bradley stood up as well. "Dr. Sajiv, is it all right if I go and check out the boat?"

"If you want. I did go over it before you came, and it is operational."

"Just to make myself feel better," she told him. "After all, we're all going to be depending on it tonight."

# CHAPTER 17

THOUGH THERE wasn't a lot of space, the boat was fast, and the engine surprisingly quiet. Still, Kaden made sure they circled the island at a slightly wider angle than Vorani had suggested, not wanting to invite trouble. The distraction from the island was going as planned, if the light column of smoke was anything to go by, and they landed without any problem at all. The patrol boats were more invested in guarding the possible on-foot connector between the island and the mainland.

Kaden had always been told that if things were going too well, then it must mean that everything was about to go wrong. But he was just grateful for the way events were proceeding smoothly, and he knew enough about Vorani to trust her planning. And not to ask too many questions.

"How did you get people on Compen?" he asked the first time he heard the plan.

"We've always had a couple of people in Compen and the beach town," Vorani stated, as if she hadn't just revealed a potential war crime.

Kaden could see he wasn't getting any more out of her. "Would have been useful to know the first time around."

"Don't be stupid, Kaden. They're not the helping type. Just a few stragglers and deserters we got back on our payroll so they'd keep us informed—if they feel like it."

Shun jerked upright in his chair as he thought of something. "How do they keep you informed? Radio? We could have really used a radio when we were there."

"Well, this is going to be a silent operation. We equip you with the armor detector, but nothing fancy. Won't work long distance."

"How will the people on the island know when to make a distraction?" Bradley asked suddenly.

"That's my problem."

Kaden could see that Vorani was ready to move past the question. "Look, unless you have a regular-as-clockwork firework show on the island, there had better be a more believable explanation as to how you're going to communicate with the people there."

"When the tide was low, some people moved to the island and they took the radio with them. I will transmit the instructions to them—it'll be a quick, short message WUC will overlook since there are a few military transmissions in the area around there anyway."

Kaden wondered just how reliable these people were. "How do we know they'll do it?"

"Because I said they would, and that's all you need to know," Vorani snapped. "Anyway, they're going to be evacuated soon, and when they come to the mainland, they're going to need some help settling in." She pointed to the map spread out on the table between them. "Can we please go back to discussing the layout of the island?"

Kaden helped Shun off the boat, not that Shun needed the help, and looked to see if the other two had gotten off safely. He didn't insult Bradley by offering her a hand. If she needed help, she would tell him. "I'm going to scout ahead."

"The locator says the armor is in the building there." Wayland pointed in front of them.

"That's so random," Bradley said, walking past her. "What did I tell you about the proper way of relaying information in the Army?"

"You have no hope of telling me what to do," Wayland quipped as she swept past Bradley in her lighter armor.

"Not many people around," Bradley added. "Instructor Pace—"

"Why did I become Instructor Pace all of a sudden?" Kaden joked. He was starting to relax a little, which was not a good thing. Going on a mission with his close friends wasn't a picnic.

"The building also seems to be empty. Two or three people and—"

"Show me the scanner." Kaden leaned in for a look. It was a small screen, with the humans showing up as red heat dots inside the building. The scanner was only meant to work in close quarters, but for what they needed, it was good enough. "Hmm, not many. I can take them out." Then he frowned and tapped the screen.

Wayland edged closer. "What?"

"Seems a little too still."

"Maybe they're sleeping. It is night."

"Could be." Kaden was unconvinced, though people didn't expect attacks in the middle of the night, especially when on an island. Still, he didn't express too much surprise when the building the armor was stashed in turned out to be a two-story structure with one side completely obliterated. Every building on the island had suffered damage from the bomb, but some of the damage here looked new. There wasn't much to search; he came across the heat signatures quite easily and found two guards who were in the process of dying, lying in pools of blood that looked black in the night.

"We're not alone here." Kaden turned over the guard to see if he could recognize him—or what was left of him.

The man was a complete stranger. Kaden leaned in and closed the sightless eyes with his armored hand, then pushed the body aside carefully. He indicated to Bradley that he needed to look at the scanner. Now that he knew what he was seeing, the heat signatures were weak, and he assumed the people on the scanner were simply fading away even as he watched.

Captain Allen's crew were all dead or dying.

"The armor is still there," Bradley told him, and Kaden nodded.

He looked over his shoulder at Wayland, who was sticking close to Shun. He hoped the two of them were doing all right. It wouldn't do for Wayland to break down or run away at the sight of death. Although quiet, so far she seemed to be handling the bodies scattered on the floor with aplomb, even steering Shun over a couple of places where the floor was crumbling.

"Which way?"

Bradley pointed silently. Kaden walked over to the room where the armor was, his lasers ready since he was wary of what was on the other side of the door. The last thing he needed to do was step on some hidden explosive or trigger a trap.

The door didn't open fully, coming to rest against a pile of metal stacked high on the inside of the room. On one of the small metal piles sat the tall, lanky man from the Compen Beach Town mission, his wire-rimmed glasses held together by tape and wool.

*Roy*, Kaden thought, but he didn't say it aloud.

Roy was dressed in heat-camouflage gear from head to toe, which explained why he'd remained undetected. Roy looked up from fiddling with a metal shaft to look at Kaden; he blinked without any sign of fear. "Was wondering how long it'd take you to get here."

Kaden tensed, waiting for the other shoe to drop.

"No, no." Roy jumped to his feet, clearly alarmed at Kaden's stance. "I didn't mean it's a trap, just that we've been playing with government property for a while, and there's only so much time before the rightful owners want it back." He looked to Shun, who appeared at the doorway, and Roy's façade of calm dropped like a stone. "Hello, stranger," he whispered in a gruff voice, eyes watering.

"Really, Roy, I thought you were better than siding with these people." Shun might have protested to Kaden that he didn't believe Roy had sold out, but he probably hadn't believed in Roy as much as he wanted to either.

"They offered me a chance to study the armor," Roy protested, arms open as if to embrace Shun. "How was I to turn down such an opportunity?"

"With Captain Allen and his... mercenaries?"

"I wasn't going to let him hurt anyone," Roy stated in a lofty tone. "I told him the armors would stop working if the wearer was killed.... He didn't hurt anyone."

"What did he want the armor for?" Kaden asked, aborting the conversation before it became a full-fledged argument.

"To fit his people with them, what else?" Roy sounded surprisingly blasé about something so serious. "But I suppose most of his men are dead now, so who knows what happened to Allen."

Kaden had assumed as much. "Who attacked you, and did Allen escape to the mainland?" Kaden hadn't seen Captain Allen's body anywhere; it could be buried under the rubble.

"Who knows? If anyone could have, it would have been Allen. He had more lives than a cockroach."

"Who attacked you?" Kaden repeated.

Roy shrugged. "You did."

Bradley snorted. "Don't be ridiculous! We just got here."

"Well, the people who attacked us were certainly dressed like Joscalian soldiers."

Kaden felt disgusted at Roy, who had to be lying through his teeth. "Don't speak if you can't tell the truth."

"I am telling the truth," Roy shouted at them, spit flying out of his mouth. "Don't pretend you're not the cleanup crew. Why else would they leave the armor and me?"

Whoever had attacked Captain Allen's group must have heard their approach and left. "Whatever, we don't have time for this. We need to move."

Roy approached Shun. "Don't tell me you joined up with them."

Shun pushed him aside to walk farther into the room. "I came to get my armor back."

"It's here. I didn't take it apart, though I was tempted to. I'm not that careless."

"Well, do we kill this guy?" Bradley asked, coming into view.

Kaden knew she wasn't being serious; it was just her way of speaking. At the sight of her, Roy's eyes grew wide in surprise, and he gasped.

"The new armor isn't self-supporting. The number of females who are able to bear the weight of all that armor plating must be...." He trailed off and looked at her appreciatively. "You must be very strong." Then what she'd asked seemed to sink in. "I don't see why you wouldn't kill me. After all, you did kill everyone else."

Bradley looked him up and down, assessing him. "Yes, I'm strong, and no, we didn't kill anyone here."

"That arsenal you carry on you must be worth the weight."

Bradley didn't answer. She turned to Kaden. "There seems to be some activity toward the other end of the island."

"We leave the way we came," Kaden ordered. "We get into the boat and we sail out. No one plays the hero."

"I want to come with you," Roy said. "You must be planning on leveling the island with some attack after this. I can't stay here."

Bradley shook her head. "We can't take him."

"We have to take him." Kaden spoke at the same time. "He's been studying the armor, and if he's as intelligent as Shun says he is, we can't leave anything behind." He turned to Wayland. "You're on guard duty. Make sure he gets to the boat in one piece."

"What about me?" Shun asked a split second later.

"Get into your armor," Kaden ordered. "Bradley, see if there's anyone around and if we need to pick up anything from this pile of rubbish."

"I'm on it." Then she looked at the room. "This is going to take some time. Can't we simply blow it up?"

Kaden shook his head. "At least collect the computer memory chips and the written material." He supposed he could ask what was important, but he didn't trust Roy. He turned to Wayland. "Go ahead and secure the landing site and wait for us." He supposed it would take some time to go back to the boat with an unarmed civilian.

Shun didn't even spare a glance toward Roy as he approached his armor and started to put it on.

"Wait—" Kaden walked up to Shun and tapped the arm piece to get a reading of Shun's compatibility level. "—57 percent, not bad."

"What do you mean?" Shun asked as he picked up his chest piece.

"If you really hate that armor and were ready to give it up, your compatibility with it would have dropped."

"You mean being born into it isn't enough?" He reached for the next piece. "Do I have to take off my shoes to fit the boots on?"

"Isn't that what you did the last time?" Kaden moved to the door and looked out to see if there was any change in their surroundings. "You might not want to fight, but you do want that armor."

"What's that supposed to mean?" As fun as it was to watch Shun struggle into his armor, Kaden felt the need to move, and the conversation was going nowhere. He looked at Bradley, who tapped her scanner, and he held out his hand. "What do you see?"

"Something I don't really like," she said, giving it over to him. She pointed to the left-hand corner of the tiny screen. "Is it me or do those patterns look like—"

"Drone thrusters," Kaden finished. "Well, good news is they don't seem to be on the same side as Wayland or where the boat is." He looked to Shun, who, unaware of the conversation, had slipped off his shoes and was struggling into his boots. "Help him—then move to the boat. Get ready to leave. We sail in five." He didn't want to linger.

"On it." Bradley nodded. "Here, take the scanner."

Kaden shook his head. "I can't fight with that thing strapped to my arm." He didn't know what sort of weapons Shun had, but he knew Bradley's was a better offensive armor. However, he needed at least one person whom he could trust to guard the others, and it was Bradley. His black armor was excellent for stealth, and he could move quickly if required.

They needed all the help they could get.

"Be safe," Bradley muttered as Kaden gave the scanner one last look and handed it over to her.

He was outside in a couple of seconds. He could feel the plates lock and release as his body moved, preparing for battle. The armor moved as fast as the body inside could keep up. Kaden realized with a start that perhaps Dr. Sajiv was correct: the reason he could move at the speeds he did was because he didn't have feet. He gave up the need to control them completely, trusted the armor to do it for him, and the armor took over seamlessly. There were no conflicting information feeds. Kaden's feet and part of his legs didn't exist, and most horrifyingly, he had a feeling that if he'd lost more body parts, he'd have been able to move even faster. But it was probably just Kaden's armor that would do this. The black armor was the hardest to control because it expected the person inside to trust it completely. No other armor operated that way.

He finally got to field test his newly increased compatibility. Kaden jumped from the second floor neatly and landed between two drones that actually jerked back as if startled by his appearance.

Kaden took a deep breath and activated the lasers. Clean bolts of light cut into the hulls of the drones, but even as he did so, the drones fired. A dual antiarmor missile salvo would have been something he'd have trouble walking away from, even if he'd been in defensive blue armor. So he turned and threw himself flat as he fired over his shoulders, and strangely enough the drones didn't follow. Instead they turned toward the pier, and Kaden cursed.

He'd hoped they were not heading toward their landing site. He fired again, once again scoring a hit, and the drone closest to him fell. Moving quickly, Kaden tore off the control panels and pulled out a handful of wires from its innards, before jumping back, just in time to avoid another missile.

He ducked to the side, rolled, came up, and fired, hoping he could hold them off until Bradley and Shun made it to the boat. Wayland and Roy should be there already.

The missile caught him squarely in the back, threw him in the air, and slammed him down so hard Kaden saw stars behind his eyes. His body rattled inside the armor, and his teeth closed painfully over the tip of his tongue. His back screamed in delayed pain as he struggled to roll over, spitting up blood as he did so.

He had to stumble to his knees before he was hit with another shot of—something. The armor plating on his back gave, not really exposing him but still making it crack. The weakness in the plating was like a hole in the back of his head, and Kaden knew a third shot would kill him. He needed to move... move now, and... move.

The armor moved, twisting his body to the side. The human body was not meant to turn like that, not that fast and not at that angle. He was slammed to the ground again in a painfully stunning moment as the armor tried to compensate for the hole in the back, by exposing his other side to the next shot from the drone.

The missile hit Kaden under his right arm; his ribs cracked and breath escaped his mouth with a gasp. Dark spots danced in front of his eyes as he fired his laser, and this time he caught the third drone. The second staggered into view, and he managed to wing it from his position, lying awkwardly on the ground.

He struggled to stand, knowing the three people he'd come to the island with would never leave without him. He had a group to go back to, he had Shun waiting for him, and they had to exchange Shun's armor for his freedom.

Consciousness surged back to his body and he lurched upright, ignoring the aches and the blood, firing as he moved. The second drone fell from the sky, and Kaden made sure to disintegrate its middle and everything that helped it fly.

He just needed to—He cursed under his breath as he looked around. There were five new drones, circling him. They were of various sizes and models; an egg-shaped one from a decade ago flew next to a more recent one that was pear-shaped. Some of the smaller ones were getting ready to fire and—

He moved. He might be in pain, but his armor was still functional and he was running so fast the ground blurred around him. He punched through the first drone he came across: his arm drilled through the body, and he closed his fist around the midsection, swung his hand, and flung it toward the next one, which hopped back in midair to avoid the collision. Kaden was left with a handful of loose wiring.

He stepped back and considered his predicament. There were far too many of them. He could run to the boat, but there was the danger he'd lead the rest of the drones to it, and the last thing he wanted to do was put the rest of the team at risk.

He braced himself to go down fighting. Four drones against one was far too poor odds.

They were going to have to peel the armor off his dead body but—

I don't want to die, Kaden thought in surprise as he set his legs for balance.

Thoughts churned as he braced himself for the last attack. People had told him their entire lives flashed before them when they'd assumed they were about to die, and Kaden wondered if what he was experiencing was something similar.

*I'm not ready to die. I was finally coming into myself. I have friends. I have a lover and maybe a doctor who will look at my legs objectively.*

He directed all remaining power into the lasers for one last burst, when everything changed.

The smaller drone flung up into the sky, got caught in a metal net, and slammed back down onto the ground.

Kaden looked up in surprise as Wayland appeared next to him, smiling and holding a metal pike. "I just have to spear them through, right? Like I did at the train?"

"Yes… but watch out!"

The smaller drone fired and Kaden began to pull Wayland down, but Bradley appeared between them and the drone. She staggered under the missile attack but stood her ground.

"All the armor plating I have has to be good for something," Bradley gritted out as she fired at the smaller drone. "Well, three more to go."

"I have this one," said Wayland, rushing forward and impaling it, leaving Bradley free to veer toward the next one.

Feeling a little redundant, Kaden shrugged and took the second one, still vibrating on the ground, out of action. The two cadets were leveling the enemy without breaking a sweat—all of Wayland's training had done her some good.

Wayland ran toward the last drone. It moved as if to dodge her attack—but not fast enough. Slightly larger than the rest—probably a signal relay drone, from what Kaden had learned. When Wayland thrust her metal spike through it, it jerked wildly, then sagged a little, its thrusters losing power but still tenaciously trying to stay in the air. It struggled to float backward.

Kaden tried to move forward and stopped, his ribs protesting, and he cursed as he tasted more blood on his lips. He hoped it was his tongue and not a punctured lung… it certainly hurt enough to be that, though.

Bradley jumped onto the final, large drone, and together the sisters brought it down with a slam. Kaden smiled as he stepped back, letting them have their moment of triumph. "Well done. Let's hurry back to the boat."

"Shun will be worried," Bradley agreed as Wayland pulled her pike out of the drone. "Let's—"

"Bradley," Wayland said slowly.

Her voice made Kaden freeze, and he turned to look at her. Her tone screamed louder than words that something bad had happened, the sound of a woman who'd just discovered a hole in the middle of her body. She looked unharmed, there was no blood on her, and her armor was intact, but there was a chance she'd been injured. Had one of the drones gotten to her?

She held up her weapon. "There's blood on the pike."

Kaden could see the reddish tint at the edge, obvious even in the semidarkness.

"Could be oil," Bradley said in a low voice, sounding desperate.

Kaden could see Wayland struggling, wanting to believe that, but not convinced. He moved to the drone calmly, expecting the worse but keeping his face blank. It was a simple job for him to hook his right arm under the hole made by Wayland's pike, and pull.

The plating opened, and Kaden peeled the drone apart as easily as a person peeled an orange, one-handed. Then Bradley was next to him with her strength, helping him reveal the inside of the large drone. It was not the contents that made Kaden pause—it was the unexpectedness of it.

The interior was hollowed out, and in the small space there lay, curled up around an array of control panels, a small woman with dark hair and dark skin. The pike had pierced her in the middle, and blood bubbled from her lips, staining her teeth a dark hue in the waning light. She snarled at them, a gasp that turned to a groan of pain and a gush of more blood. She looked at them all with hatred and then held out her hand. A grenade lay in her palm. She reached for the pin.

"Shit." Kaden fired his laser and neatly severed her hand at the wrist. The grenade fell to her lap. Gasping, lips drawn back from her teeth in a snarl, she picked up the grenade with her other hand.

Bradley shot her dead with a bolt between the eyes.

A couple of seconds of silence, and Wayland reeled away, falling to her knees. "You killed her," she told Bradley in a small voice.

"She was going to blow us up." Bradley's voice was expressionless.

"She was dying anyway." Kaden understood that this might have been the first kill for both of them. "We need to move. More cadets… uh, drones might come, and Shun and Roy have been left unarmed."

He didn't say the obvious thing that everyone must have noticed. The dead woman had been wearing civilian clothing, but her coloring was similar to theirs: dark hair, dark eyes, dark skin. And the grenade she'd tried to toss at them was Army issued.

"I…," Wayland said as she stood smoothly and brushed at some dirt on her knees. "I don't feel anything. Shouldn't I feel something after killing someone?"

"I need you not to feel anything right now." Kaden pointed toward the boat. He wanted her to feel nothing as long as possible because the other option, having her break down, just wasn't an option. The Army didn't offer counseling to people who killed others in a war situation unless they requested it, but Wayland could get all the help she needed once they were on the mainland.

He took a deep breath and turned to Bradley, who was standing relatively still, looking at the dead woman. "Let's go."

"She was one of ours," she said in her flat voice, as if she was announcing the weather. "Why would she try to kill us?"

There were so many ways in which the woman could be a Harian. She could have been from a family who had Joscalian roots, like Shun; she could have stolen the grenade or bought it on the black markets. They all spoke variations of the same language and—"We'll deal with that later."

The urgency rose inside him, and Kaden turned and started to run toward the boat at a slightly slower pace than his top speed. The sisters kept up with him on either side, and he smiled grimly to himself. They could still make it.

Kaden's armor had tightened under his arm to compress his broken ribs in place, and the pain was negligible. His "feet" found the best places to step, and he kept a steady pace, even if he didn't voice the need to hurry back to the boat. The portion of the island they were on had never been developed, and the lack of buildings meant he felt exposed, even in his black armor. He desperately wished he'd told Shun to keep a low profile, to try to hide the boat or duck behind a bush or something, so no one on the lookout would spot them.

When he reached the landing place, Shun was standing by the boat with Roy sitting on it. The water lapped the beach in dark waves. The beaches on that side of the island had never been popular, small and sandless, and the ocean floor dropped sharply a couple of steps in, into a sea with treacherous undercurrents. It was ideal for bringing a boat in without any danger of breaching the hull, but not an ideal spot for swimming or relaxing.

"Push it into the water," Kaden shouted as he reached the boat, and Bradley joined Shun in pushing it into the sea.

Kaden turned his back to the boat to keep a lookout for pursuers.

"I can see your back," Shun called. "You're burned pretty badly."

"Start the engine," Kaden snapped. He pulled Wayland and threw her into the boat. "Bradley, Shun, get in."

Bradley paused to refer to the scanner she was carrying. "We have drones coming from all sides."

She scrambled on, and Kaden jumped aboard just as Shun got the engine started.

"We're not hanging around for them," Kaden said with confidence as the boat jumped forward, clearing the beach in a sudden burst of speed. "Head for the middle, away from the shore. Drones can't travel on deep water, and there are no convenient sandbars, but they have some range in their missiles." Shun complied silently as he aimed toward the sea, and Kaden felt his shoulders relax. They were going to make it—

The shot from the drone hit the engine squarely.

The boat was airborne for a couple of seconds, and then it smacked the water with a thud, still facing the right way up. Roy screamed and Shun cursed, but Kaden had very little time for that as Bradley lost her grip and flipped over the side of the boat.

"Everyone stay low. Shun, can we steer? We're too exposed in the open."

The other option was to order everyone into the water in case there was another missile attack; the boat was simply drifting now that the engine was dead. They were sitting in the middle of the sea, in range of the drones. They might as well have put up a sign that said "Shoot us."

"The water isn't too deep. We can get back to shore." Kaden turned to see if Bradley needed help getting back into the boat and realized she had yet to surface. He cursed under his breath. Her armor weighed the most and was the least suitable for a water scenario, and he didn't even know if she could swim in deep water. Kaden thought over his options, but the boat didn't come with any equipment useful to find an armor under the sea.

There was very little time or choices to consider, and Kaden wouldn't ask Wayland to follow her sister into the water.

He threw himself off the side of the boat and the water closed over him like a cold fist. What little air he'd collected in his lungs escaped in a gasp. The water was close to freezing, probably one of the undercurrents he'd read about in Vorani's report. Fully encased in armor, Kaden was far too heavy to be swept away, and he considered it a blessing in this whole nightmarish scenario. The water was deeper than he'd anticipated, and by the time his feet had struck the bottom, he was in over his head.

The only luck for them seemed to be the false daybreak; the beach faced east. It was barely anything to go by, but Kaden had seen where Bradley went over the side, and her armor, being even heavier than his, would surely be in the same place. He struggled to move forward in the water, pulled down by mud, aware he had very little air to spare. The armor, aware of his urgency, pushed forward, and it seemed to Kaden that the armor was driving him forward rather than the other way around.

Kaden felt the vibration of another attack and looked up to see the others hit the water just seconds before the boat exploded. He paused, torn between going back to help them and going toward Bradley. But everyone had exited the boat closer to the shore, and as Shun, the tallest of the three, touched bottom, his armor extended a breathing tube out of the water. Shun held out a hand to Wayland, holding her head above water until she latched onto a piece of driftwood—a part of the boat—and Roy, of course, swam like a river rat.

Their boat was a total loss. So much for our escape route, Kaden thought, even as he came across Bradley a couple of feet in front of him, struggling to get upright. She was having trouble standing up—even her strength was no match against a waterlogged armor. Kaden held out a hand to her and pulled, but that made him sink farther into the mud and silt on the ocean floor, and he let go hastily. Bradley pulled herself up to a crouch as bubbles of air escaped from her suit. She started to undo the chest clasps.

Kaden understood what she was doing. There was no way she was going to get to her feet in that damn armor, and she wasn't about to drown in it either. He could feel his lungs burning with the need for air and could only imagine that Bradley, who'd fallen into the water first, unprepared, was in a worse situation.

She was not going to be able to get that armor off in time.

He could not crouch down and help her; he just didn't have that much air to spare. He looked at where the clasps in her plating would be and asked his armor for the correct aim.

Kaden had never fired underwater. He didn't even know if he was capable of it—an oversight in training he intended to correct—but the armor didn't find it a shortcoming. Clean bolts of light sliced through Bradley's side clasps and most of the upper and lower body pieces fell to the sea bottom. Lightened from her burden, Bradley made quick work of her arm pieces and boots and swam to the surface like an eel. Kaden turned around, heading back toward the island; there was no other dry land. He wasn't able to swim ashore; he didn't think anyone would be capable of it either.

A single drone hovered in sight by the shoreline, but Kaden didn't worry too much about it; it was within range. He fired his final laser burst, burning a neat hole in its middle, and the drone collapsed as he and Bradley reached the step in the continental shelf. His armor was heavy, but it compensated for the water, locking its plates and draining water out of the joints. Even though he had been the farthest out, Kaden reached the stepped shelf on the beach first. He held out a hand to help Shun and Roy, who were struggling up as well, and looked around for Wayland.

Bradley was barely walking, coughing up water and bile, and Wayland was struggling to climb up onto the beach farther down. Her piece of driftwood had pushed her a couple of feet away from them, toward a slightly better-looking patch of the beach. Kaden tried to walk over to help her, but his plates relaxed. For a second it felt as if he'd been stabbed, and the next instant he was on his knees, coughing up blood. Pulling up Bradley had strained his ribs to the point that one of the broken edges had shifted. He was definitely looking at some internal injury.

"Shit, that doesn't look too good," Shun exclaimed and rushed to his side.

But Kaden's gaze was fixed on Wayland, who'd slipped back into the water. "Shun…," he gasped. "Wayland needs… no…."

Even as he watched, Wayland did the usual maneuver for getting out of a water situation. She took off her armor, put it onto dry land, and pulled herself up, reaching for the armor as she cleared the water. It was something she had practiced on the obstacle course again and again, a move she could complete in ten seconds.

"No," Kaden tried to shout as he shook Shun off, but it was too late.

The enemy fire caught her across the chest, obliterated her right shoulder, blew chunks off her arm, and flung her back into the water, staining it black even as she fell. It had taken less than three seconds.

Kaden moved in an instant, clutching her lower body before it could sink. He dragged it up, aware she was as good as dead. The line of fire had caught her side; her ribs were exposed and her arm just didn't exist, but the wound was neatly cauterized by the lasers and there was almost no additional bleeding. Her arm was nowhere to be seen, lost for good, but she was alive, conscious, breathing shallowly.

Wayland slowly lifted her head and looked to her nonexistent shoulder, an eerie smile on her face. "I don't think I'm going to be able to wear that armor anymore."

She looked… happy.

Three large drones lined up into view, hovering threateningly. It was the end for all of them. He could let go of Wayland and attack the drones, but there was no way he would get them all; he was the only person wearing battle-ready armor.

The drones aimed at Wayland, and Kaden couldn't leave her, even if she was dying. The plating on his back hadn't finished mending, but it was all he had. He grabbed Wayland's limp body and curled around her, trying to protect as much of her as possible as the drones fired. He was out of ammo, his power was low, and he was coughing up blood. Maybe the armor would prefer he be paralyzed below the neck because his body was slowing him down. Kaden's ribs couldn't keep up with the speed he needed to move at.

All he could do was pray the other two could get away to safety while he distracted the drones. Shun was no fighter—he wasn't going to fight in that armor—and a gas attack wouldn't work against the drones.

A soft hiss and the drones fell from the sky. Kaden opened his eyes and looked around to see…

The back of Shun's green armor, standing in front of them. Shun's arms were open and his head was tipped back. Beyond him, the ground smoked and the drones were melting.

"What do you know? Acid attack—just took me a while to figure it out," Shun said as he dropped down beside Kaden. "Is she... dead?"

"Not yet." Kaden gritted his teeth in pain. "Did your radio survive?"

"No, but maybe one of the drones still has one." Shun got to his feet.

"Try the large one. There's going to be people inside them, though."

Shun looked at him sharply and nodded. "Don't worry, I can kill when needed. I'm apparently not as stuck to my ideals as I thought myself to be."

Kaden wondered if they had enough time. There could be more drones coming, and Shun alone was in no way a solid defense.

Then he heard the sound of armor plates locking in place one by one, the soft click of self-automated guiding, and he flipped his headpiece open to see Bradley picking up Wayland's discarded armor. Her face was strangely calm as she donned the family armor, piece by piece. She was probably aware she was being watched. She turned around and smiled at Kaden. Her eyes were gleaming with manic intensity. "What do you know," she said in an eerie voice. "It's all in the head."

Kaden nodded in understanding and turned to Shun. "Good. Then call for help on the WUC frequency. The people who are shooting at us are actually on our side. We need outside help."

# CHAPTER 18

THEN THERE was the recovery period....

"Someone had to take the fall," Vorani said as she leaned back into the straight-backed chair.

She was still slim and her stomach flat, but Kaden couldn't help but look at her for a second before his gaze flicked away. It seemed wrong to lock away a pregnant woman, no matter what.

Vorani didn't seem to notice. "It's going to be me taking all the blame, but I tell you, I wasn't the only one in on it. Do you think an operation of that scale was something I could have planned and executed? There are people way above me who supported and funded that plan, but in the end, I'm the person important enough but not high up enough on the food chain who has to take the fall."

Kaden decided to let that statement be. There was little chance of finding out who the people at the top were. "Sending us to Compen Island," he said instead. "Why?"

"We needed a distraction," she admitted. "But we also needed the armors—yours and Shun's."

"Mine because I was damaged, and Shun's because he wasn't a fighter," Kaden concluded. "And also because neither of us would give them up 100 percent, and that would cause compatibility issues. But why didn't you simply kill us here while we were at the camp?"

"And the problems that would cause," Vorani said with a roll of her eyes. "But realistically, not possible. Black armors hardly ever break connections, and you were always in it. Kill you in your armor and it would have frozen for another hundred years or self-destructed or something. As for Shun's armor, we needed to get it back before we broke his connection with it. What if someone else who was not a part of the Army was compatible with it and wore it once we broke the connection from here? But more importantly, you were coming up as mentally unstable, and after the accident, we needed a new operator for that armor."

Kaden wondered what she'd do if he told her of what he suspected: if they disabled the preexisting armored warriors, their compatibility would improve. He was glad he hadn't suggested that because there were people crazy enough to try it.

"I'll buy that for now," Kaden said after some consideration. "But Bradley and Wayland?"

"Bradley's armor can be—could be—" A reminder that it was still at the bottom of the ocean. "—worn by anyone with the right build and the strength, and she had at best another five years. The toll on her body was too much. As for Wayland, we didn't anticipate her fighting… or even joining the mission when we thought it up. And in the end, it was easier to have you all there than come up with explanations. If she had run back to her father, we would have had problems." Kaden filed that away as information for later—Senator Olgesh was clean. "The deciding factor was when the group on the island reported that their cover was blown, that you'd seen one of our people inside a drone. Knew we couldn't let you leave."

Kaden grimaced. "I was actually not sure about that."

"Really, Kaden, you were always so bad with people. That woman was from our camp."

"Oh."

"Anyway, the girls also tended to search for information where not needed. Easier to get rid of them than keep them. That metal affinity armor is easy to match, and there are others from that family who will eventually be old enough to try it on."

"Fine," Kaden said, used to the cold-blooded way in which the Army decided who wore which armor. "But all those drones on Compen to take us out?"

"Oh, don't flatter yourself. They weren't for you," Vorani snapped. "They were drones we recovered and repaired from the war. Our tech department is better at that than replicating armor tech. We smuggled them into Compen during the cease-fire—you must have run into a few during your time near Compen Beach."

"You were searching the island for anything valuable from the Orche labs before WUC closed it down for good," Kaden said, realization dawning on him. "You used our people inside Harian drones, so even if they were caught, we wouldn't be blamed." He felt like an idiot as he figured it out. "No wonder the drones were from different series—they're the ones we've collected over time."

"We tried so hard to keep the fight going, but WUC is not backing down, and we're losing international aid," Vorani said softly, and she clenched her shackled fists.

"The drone attack on the train," Kaden realized. "It was you... us... the Army, to try and keep the war going."

"We can't stop this now," Vorani said, eyes blazing, spit flying. "We've lost people, good people and time and money. We have to win this war, not give up and shake hands with them. We need to kill them all, even if it takes another ten, twelve years. After all this time, we can't just walk away."

Kaden leaned back in his chair and looked at her. "You always saw the big picture, not the individuals," he concluded. "What's a life here or there in the grand scheme of things?"

"You could say that."

"But what about my armor?" he asked after a couple of seconds. "You tried to break my connection, but to find someone to wear it is next to impossible."

"I can wait." She smiled smugly at him. "Why do you think I asked to speak only to you? Well, it's because we worked together for a while, so I don't have to explain the basics to you—it gets so tiring—but also because we already have a connection."

And because Vorani was still Vorani and knew the information she'd given out had already been figured out by the intelligence committee.

"Shun did say something to that effect," Kaden said, getting up. "So let me be clear, how long are you willing to wait before my armor is operational?"

Vorani's hand traced a circle over her stomach. "We're thinking of reducing the recruitment age to ten."

Kaden spoke in a slow, measured tone that belied his anger. "If that child is mine, I'm going to fight you for it. You're not going to raise it as a weapon."

"So you and the little peace lover can raise it as a cook?" Vorani smirked.

"If that's what they want." Kaden turned away. He looked at the one-way glass and nodded, letting the people outside know he was ready to exit. Then he turned around and smiled at her. "You know, it was all for nothing."

"What do you mean?"

"WUC stepped in. There's no more fighting. The armored warriors will always have a place, in peacekeeping all over the world. The agreement is going to be that they'll be neutral troops to maintain borders and stop skirmishes—and fight crime. The terms are being settled now, but it is happening."

"And you're going to the front line."

Kaden shook his head. "I will always be a fighter, but I'm going to be working with Dr. Sajiv to see if we can replicate my armor's properties in prosthetic limbs. Might take a couple of years, but he and Roy are positive that it can be done. Roy's going to serve his probation working under him. And in the meantime, if called, Shun and I will go and fight, but as peacekeepers."

"So he did join the Army in the end."

Kaden shook his head again. "He joined the peace force. As did Bradley."

"There's always going to be fighting," Vorani screamed at him. "And people like me, people who want to see the results of all the sacrifice, not some pat on the head and a good-bye."

"But this time we're trying to stop it." Kaden could hear the pleading tone in his voice, begging Vorani to understand. "Don't you get tired of all this? All the bodies piling up? We're going to join with the WUC forces, both sides to define the border and build a no-man's-land throughout. As for Compen, well, we're not touching it for a long time."

"What makes you think either side will keep their word?" Vorani grated.

"Each side has agreed to send a couple of their important people as peace envoys to the other."

"Hostages," Vorani snorted. "How cliché. I suppose it'll be people who mean something but are not very important."

"The president of Haria is sending his son as well as some other people who are interested in seeing how things work from this end. They're calling it a youth exchange, sending the young people over."

"And who are we sending? Our president's kids are grown-up."

"But he has grandkids," Kaden said. "And there have been volunteers."

"Why are you telling me this, Kaden?" Vorani smirked at him. "I'm locked up. All this is useless to me."

"Because we were friends once," he said, almost thinking out loud. "We fought together side by side for over twenty years." In a way, Vorani had manipulated him because she knew him so well. "You were my family."

"Then you decided that Harian bastard was worth more than our friendship." Perhaps she wasn't as calm as she pretended to be. "Now I'll be raising my own family, and you can sit and watch."

He looked at her middle. "I'm also supporting the changes so no one has to grow up to be a soldier anymore. Don't you think we've been through enough?"

"This is my legacy," Vorani patted her middle. "Could have been yours as well. Don't you get it, Kaden? I never lost. I might have lost a battle, but not the war."

Kaden knew he had to leave. He got to his feet and stepped back.

"Reality is, Kaden, we wouldn't know what to do if we stopped this war."

"Maybe you don't." He didn't feel angry, just tired and defeated. There was truth in what she said, and it scared him.

"Doesn't matter if you run, I have what I need from you." Vorani had one last parting shot.

He nodded to Vorani and stepped out of the room, where Shun stood waiting patiently beside Tracy. Shun's green armor looked as if it belonged on him, and he smiled warmly at the sight of Kaden.

"Don't tell me I told you so," Kaden said as he leaned into his embrace. "Talking to her is like talking to a wall." He needed to say something about the baby, but he wasn't sure how Shun would react to the news.

"But she's your friend. You had to try," Shun said. "Let's go, or we'll be late."

They hurried to the exit, where Bradley stood by the jeep. Kaden smiled as he saluted her. The eye patch from a training accident made her look rakish. Just because she was in an original armor didn't mean she was invincible.

Bradley rolled her eye. "I heard you two are going to relax at Dr. Sajiv's beach house for a while. I'm flying to Nagaho in a couple of hours. They need help evacuating people after an earthquake, and I have a feeling this armor is going to be extremely useful at finding people trapped under the rubble."

"I'm being deployed in two weeks to inspect the border from Koresa to Gastin," Shun told her. "Six months, with two days of leave per month, or something like that. WUC works their people hard, you know?"

Kaden shrugged. "I'll just relax and see what makes my armor tick." He smiled at her. "I'll give Roy your love."

"That man's never seen a woman in a new armor," Bradley scoffed as they walked up to the gate, and as they did, he could feel their mood becoming sober. "It's not like he's over Astrid, and all I hear is about how she walked when she found him siding with Captain Allen." She stilled as they came to the convoy of blue WUC vehicles and forced a smile as Wayland came tottering out of one of them.

They celebrated Wayland's sixteenth birthday gathered around her bed, in the hospital. Shun had baked a cake, which Wayland declared was the best she'd ever eaten. Balancing the plate on her knees, fork in her remaining hand, she chattered away excitedly, telling them something a fellow patient had told her. Then she laid her fork down and said seriously, "I'm thinking of joining the youth exchange program."

Bradley sat up straighter with a muted protest. "Wayland, that's—"

"No, hear me out," she said, picking up her fork and waving it for emphasis. "I can't sit back and do nothing. It's not like I've lost my mind or something."

"Maybe we can figure a way to transfer the armor back to you," Bradley pleaded.

She wasn't in her family armor just then, but everyone knew she was training in it. The more time someone spent in an original armor, the more it grew with the user. "The leg piece has stretched, but that can shrink back and...."

Wayland shuddered. "I don't think I want it even if I could. Don't think you were the only person who hated it."

"I... didn't hate it," Bradley said in a small voice. "I was... scared of it. Of what it would do to me if I were compatible. By the time I realized just how much easier life would have been for you, it was too late."

"I was the one who hated the armor," Shun added when the silence between them became far too awkward. "And I guess even I've gotten over it."

"To think I hated you when I first saw you on that train." Bradley's comment startled everyone, including Kaden, who was simply sitting there, watching everyone interact. "You were free, you could go where you wanted, you could do whatever you felt like… I wanted to be that."

"I wasn't as free as I looked."

Bradley picked up a fork and a paper plate. "I know. I guess we all have responsibilities."

"So, what do you think?" Wayland demanded. "About my idea to sign up for the exchange."

Kaden finally decided to join in the conversation. "I thought you were simply telling us about your decision, not asking permission. Was it Casper who spoke to you about it?" He'd seen the resident WUC representative speak to Shun as well, and he wanted to know what the man had said. Shun had been pretty closemouthed about the encounter.

Wayland smiled through a mouthful of cake. "He says I can make a change. I want to do that."

"He told me the same thing," Shun said, surprising them all. "Said I might as well use everything I have."

"He hasn't gotten around to speaking to me yet." Bradley served herself a piece of cake.

"Please don't snap at him," Wayland told Bradley, gesturing with her fork for another piece. "We owe him for getting us off Compen."

"I'm not stupid." Bradley handed the plate with a frosted piece of cake to Kaden. "I'll be polite." She turned to Shun. "What are you going to do with that armor?"

Shun shrugged and moved to sit by Kaden on the window ledge. "There are options where I don't have to fight. I'm considering them. I think that's why my compatibility level hasn't fallen."

"It's all in the head," Wayland said cheerfully, and this time Bradley did not even glance at her.

The conversation helped Kaden figure out a couple of things. "It is. I think I know why I became compatible with the black armor—it was because I really wanted one. Genetics helps, but you have to want it and for me, then, it was either match up or go back to the orphanage for another couple of years."

"I wanted to save us all." Bradley stabbed at her cake a little too forcefully. "That's why I was able to put our armor on."

Everyone nodded. An armor accepting someone whom it had previously rejected was unheard of.

Kaden took a bite of the cake, and although he wasn't exactly a fan of sweet things, he had to admit Shun baked the best cake. "You did look after us," he said to Bradley when it became evident she was waiting for them to say something. "Back at the beach town when we lost the armor, here at camp when we came back." He was referring to her part in finding evidence against Vorani and getting Shun pardoned—after the great embarrassment of having troops on a closed-off section, it seemed the least the Army could do. "You didn't need the armor for that."

"Maybe, but I still need it." Bradley sighed. She turned to Wayland with a forced smile. "So, tell me more about the exchange program before our parents show up."

Wayland was waiting for them in her new Peace Exchange uniform, hopping from one foot to the other, peering through the group of well-wishers. She spoke as soon as she saw them. "I thought you'd never come to see me off. We're leaving in another few minutes."

In the end, the person who'd proved to be the strongest of them all had been Wayland. The shot that had almost killed her had taken off her shoulder and the top of her lung. The reconstructive surgery had not helped make her body even. The lack of her arm was obvious as was the pull of her face muscles where the neck tendons had been damaged. She could no longer wear the armor. As she bounced toward them, she looked happier, and Kaden felt an answering smile form on his lips. She was by far the most resilient person he'd ever met.

When Kaden had mentioned to Vorani that volunteers were to be exchanged as peace ambassadors, he had meant people like Wayland. She was no longer an armored warrior, but she was still Senator Olgesh's daughter, and it counted as something. Plus, with her kind nature, she wasn't cut out to fight, but she had always wanted to make a change. This was her way of contributing to it, unlike Vorani, who, from the background, had tried to manipulate them all. As with the stories she told the new recruits, Vorani had twisted the truth so only what she wanted was visible.

The reason he agreed to work with Dr. Sajiv was not just for him but for all the other people who might benefit from it. "You can still stay if you want to," he said, meaning it.

Wayland shook her head. "It's fine. I want to do this. I don't feel like a fake this way. I'm helping people without killing anyone."

"Then good luck." Kaden stepped into a one-armed hug. "I'll come visit you next month. Coming with Dr. Sajiv for the international research symposium there."

"Maybe we can all meet up there," Wayland said forcefully, and Kaden nodded before stepping back to let Shun say his good-byes.

"You're not going to stop fighting," Bradley observed as she stood next to him in her armor. It suited her very well.

"No, but the Army agreed to let me work with Dr. Sajiv for a couple of months," Kaden observed. "Plus, I'll be helping with the land-mine defusion on the beach side. It's not like I'm going to be sitting on his table the whole day."

"Good." Bradley nodded warmly, and Shun returned to their side.

Letting Bradley and Wayland have their good-byes, Shun and Kaden moved away. "We have two weeks before we split up," Kaden told him under his breath. "We should go and make the most of it."

"It's not like I'm dead." Shun didn't sound as pleased to hear that as Kaden expected. "I'm not leaving you. A couple of more years and we can settle together. Your thirty years of service will come up eventually, and you can retire and—"

By then Kaden hoped the prosthetics would be perfected. Even if they weren't, he realized he had other things to look forward to, more things than just worry about his legs. "That lawyer of yours still around?"

"Should be." Shun looked at him through narrowed eyes. "What do you need to ask?"

Kaden looked at Shun for a moment, then sighed. "You were right—I think the kid Vorani is expecting is mine, and I'm going to fight for it."

Shun didn't look shocked, but he didn't sound completely convinced either. "What if the kid isn't yours?"

Kaden thought it over for a second. "Doesn't matter. Vorani can't raise it in prison."

"That's for sure," Shun agreed.

Kaden was struck by the enormity of the undertaking he was planning. "I can't do it alone, but even if you say no, I'm going to try to do it by myself. Vorani won't be out for a while, so they might place the kid in an Army orphanage, and I'm not stupid enough to think they'll let those compatible with armors walk away. But I'm a mess, still a mess…. I have issues and…."

"Yes." Shun smiled. His entire face lit up and he looked radiant. "You don't need to overthink it, Kaden. The answer is yes. I know it's a lifetime commitment, but yes, I'll raise your kid with you."

Kaden blinked.

"I always thought it was kind of sad, all those houses by Compen Beach Town, empty, with those rotting swings. I'm not exactly thinking of that ghost town, but I've always liked beaches and… that is what you mean, right?"

Kaden could see Shun wanted it, and it didn't seem like a bad idea. He'd imagined an occasional babysitting favor with maybe sex thrown in if Shun wanted to. He had no idea whether he could raise a kid while fighting, whether the Army would let him keep the armor if he retired, but… but… he had a feeling there might be loopholes. He could come to some form of arrangement. Maybe use the armor until the prosthetics were prepared, or offer to remove the weapons and… and there were ways. And he knew of families where both parents worked in the Army and had kids. They could do it. He could get maternity leave or something.

Was that only for women? He had never paid any attention to such things because it was the last position he imagined himself in.

He looked over to see Shun looking at him anxiously.

"I didn't mean to shove that at you." Shun shuffled his feet and looked down, embarrassed. "I mean… er…."

"No, it's okay." Kaden hurried to salvage the situation. "I was just thinking I'll have to buy you a ring."

Then, as Shun stood there openmouthed, Kaden turned to the sisters and called out, "Shun just agreed to marry me."

Amidst the cheering and hugs, Kaden hugged all those who meant so much to him. This was his family, no matter where in the world they might end up, and that was all that mattered.

*Stay tuned for an excerpt from*

# Bound by Guilt

By Sandra Bard

Kit Mason works at Eddy's, a boutique where the clothes are chic, the paycheck's weak, and Kit has no qualms about snagging rich older men looking to pay for play. When Cory St. James walks in, he checks all Kit's boxes: he's middle-aged, the entrepreneur of a pharmaceutical company, and already has a kept boy at home—what's one more? Kit sets out to seduce Cory and bulldozes through his denials, but when Cory finally gives in, his lover, Sasha, catches them with their pants down.

Sasha isn't the pampered toy Kit expected. In fact, Kit may have misjudged him. And the consequences that ensue when Sasha catches Kit and Cory together leave him alone. Unwilling to be weighed down by guilt, Kit decides to look after Sasha himself, even if Sasha can't stand the sight of him and there are a few things about Kit's past he doesn't want Sasha to know. But Kit isn't willing to do all the work when it comes to forcing Sasha to rebuild his life. It's a slow process of growing trust and learning to stand on their own—and together.

## www.dreamspinnerpress.com

# PROLOGUE

KIT HATED funerals and had sworn he'd never attend another after suffering through his mother's at the age of seven. But here he was, head bowed with shame and guilt, wearing mismatching clothes, wishing he'd never set eyes on Cory. Dr. St. James, he reminded himself sarcastically as he tried hard not to squirm at the feel of the sweat running down between his shoulder blades. He didn't think he'd be able to return the shirt with sweat-stained armpits, and hoped fervently that Eddy would leave stocktaking for some other week.

Not that Eddy would fire him or anything, Kit thought. He had been at Eddy's shop, called Eddy's for obvious reasons, for two years, and he'd been very careful in keeping his social life and work separate—until now. The pay at Eddy's wasn't great, but it was enough to get by, and the working hours were manageable. Kit usually supplemented his income by snagging a few lovers in his off time. He preferred his lovers male, mature, and rich—single, married, or otherwise attached. In fact, he preferred them attached. That way he did not have to drag the relationship on for long. Just because Kit's lovers were rich enough to pick up his tab, didn't mean they were good in bed, and Kit liked it short and sweet. Long-time relationships with rich lovers led to complications, and Kit wasn't looking for some fairy-tale romance where his mark fell in love with him and declared undying love.

Kit's longest relationship had been with an accountant, and that had lasted three months. By that time the guy had been on wife number four, and Kit had quit (his john, not Eddy's) when the accountant started adding up his alimony bills while in bed with Kit.

Cory, dear, dead Cory, had been something of an accident for Kit, since he had not been looking for anyone—actively searching, that is—when Kit had run into him.

# CHAPTER ONE

KIT MET Cory during a dry spell in between "boyfriends." Kit didn't do any outright hooking, and one-night stands made him feel cheap. Most of the time, they expected Kit to pay for his drink and room, and Kit was not in the mood for another month of budget balancing. He had been on the lookout for someone new to support him for a bit, and in walked the perfect guy.

The first time Kit ran into Cory was at the store, as he was arranging the racks in the summer-wear collection. He had heard the door open, accompanied by the tinkle of the chimes indicating a customer, as a draft swept through the interior. It had been a particularly slow day with a grand total of five customers. Only two of the previous customers had bought anything, and Kit had been feeling lethargic from boredom.

"Can I help you, sir?" Eddy called out from behind the cash register, where he had been reading a paperback, and Kit rolled his eyes. Apparently the slow spell was getting to Eddy as well if he was accosting customers before they made it past the doorway. Or maybe Eddy was just worried he might not be able to pay the rent on the shop at the end of the month if the sales fell off too much.

"I'm just browsing." The voice made Kit pause, but he did not turn around. It was a slightly more cultured voice than he was used to hearing in the shop. "I was passing by on my way to lunch, and the green shirt on the display caught my eye."

"Christopher," Eddy called out, pretending as usual that their shop was much larger and Kit was at the far end instead of two racks away. "Can you bring up the summer collection—hunter-green number eight, please?"

Kit had to bite his lower lip to stop himself from laughing out loud. Eddy's was at best a trivial shop that sold clothes from small-timers— some unique designs but nothing to boast about. They certainly didn't have numbers for their shirts, and green was green—what the fuck was hunter green? Eddy was trying to look good because he knew Kit was listening in on the conversation and knew exactly which shirt the customer was referring to, since Kit had done the shop display in the morning.

Kit was debating the wisdom of informing Eddy that they only had one green shirt in the entire shop, and it was currently on display on their one and only unisex model, when the customer spoke. "It's all right," he said. "I'll just walk around and take a look—browse to see if something catches my eye."

Interesting voice, but might not be an interesting guy, Kit surmised as he finished arranging the blue pinafore the best he could on the mirrored drapery. He scooted down to arrange the hem in a way the lace would catch the light, and found a pair of well-polished shoes in his line of sight.

Kit looked up slowly, up the well-pressed, dark-blue dress pants, cream dress shirt, and dark-blue tie with a hint of gold stripes, held in place with a gold tie pin. Working at Eddy's meant Kit knew how to assess the value of clothes when he saw them, and this guy screamed money. Probably from the law firm across the street, by the looks of it.

As he stood slowly, brushing his hands on his clean but faded jeans, Kit realized the guy was old—well, older than he had first expected. The green shirt on display was for someone young; this guy, Kit assessed quickly, was around fifty or thereabouts, with gray at his temples and lines around his eyes and mouth. He was, however, rather good looking, and the expensive cologne he wore was enticing.

"You must be Christopher," the customer said, and his eyes smiled.

"Yes, sir," Kit answered, snapping into his sales assistant mode. The guy was just his type, rich and not young, but that did not mean Kit was stupid enough to press his luck.

"Then perhaps you can help me out," the potential mark said, appearing slightly thoughtful. "I'm looking for some light wear—for a friend… a young man about your age, perhaps a little older. I'm told I have no sense of fashion, so perhaps you could help me out."

Even as the customer spoke, his gaze roamed over Kit's body in an almost unconscious gesture that had Kit smiling to himself. He had already made an assessment about the guy—one, he was rich, and two, he was old. Three, he had a younger male "friend" for whom he was buying clothes—that screamed younger lover. A son, nephew, or brother would have been specifically mentioned as such, and the way the guy was looking at Kit said he liked what he saw. No one looked at sales assistants as though they were on sale unless interested.

"Certainly, sir," Kit said chirpily. "But perhaps, if you could bring your friend over, maybe he can pick out—"

The customer smiled and shook his head, and to Kit, it seemed that he was sad. "Sasha doesn't go out much," he said.

Oh! Well, Kit could work on such a person. Apparently Sasha didn't go out much and his lover was unhappy about it. The relationship was on rocky ground, and this gave Kit the confidence he needed. He knew from experience that any weakness could be exploited for his benefit. Anyway, Sasha sounded like a name more for an exotic dog than a person. "What does your friend look like?" Kit asked breezily as he walked over to the left side of the store, where most of the men's clothes were. "Blond? Dark haired…?"

"Sasha's a blond." The customer hesitated. "He's got these red highlights, though, and—" Kit flicked his eyes up to see the old guy blush slightly, and he made a mental note to get some highlights the next time he went for a haircut. "—perhaps a couple of shades lighter than yours…." And bleach his hair a bit—this kind of guy always went for the same type of twinks, Kit knew from experience. "A little taller than you and somewhat slimmer."

A model, then, Kit thought. Kit was proud of how his body looked. Slender, not overly muscled—not many older lovers liked bulky twinks with more muscles than they had—and he preferred to wear loose clothing to appear slimmer. For Sasha to be slimmer, he must be fucking anorexic or bulimic, Kit thought savagely.

Just as Kit was about to open his mouth to make a smart-assed remark, he saw Eddy making frantic gestures behind the customer's back.

"See if any of these will suit your Sasha," he said, pulling out a select few shirts and placing them on the dress he had been arranging. "The purple is my favorite, and this blue one looks good with almost everything." He turned smoothly as the customer perused through the selection of shirts. "Excuse me a moment, sir," he said, and strolled toward Eddy.

Eddy all but grabbed him by the collar and pulled him over the counter. "Do you know who that is?" he whispered into Kit's ear, spittle flying in his eagerness.

"No," Kit said in surprise. Not many things got Eddy this excited—unless it had four legs and a tail and was running on a race track. "Should I?"

"You should read something other than the comics," Eddy retorted, and Kit bit back the reply that he read the personal-ad section in the paper. He didn't want to abandon a potential customer for long in case he lost interest. Kit's paycheck always included a little bonus if the monthly sales went up, and he knew a buyer when he saw one. "He's Dr. Cory St. James," Eddy replied. "You know, scientist turned businessman, he owns St. James Pharmaceuticals down the road."

"You've been reading the gossip column, I see," Kit joked as he drew back. "Don't worry, I'll treat him like royalty."

He walked back to the customer, St. James, who was looking at him with an amused expression. "Problem?" St. James asked, and Kit laughed.

"Not at all," he replied. "My manager just informed me that you're rich and prestigious and if I make a sale, I'll get a bonus."

St. James laughed as well, and Kit could see Eddy cringing visibly in the corner. "I like your style, Christopher," St. James said, smiling. "So, what else do you have that might interest me?"

"I'm always willing to show you more, Mr. St. James," Kit said, tilting his head down and gazing from under his lashes suggestively. "My friends call me Kit." Eddy had said the man was a doctor, but he didn't look like any doctor Kit had seen, and anyway, it was too late to go back to calling him Dr. St. James. Kit moved to the next rack and bent down instead of squatting on his heels as he usually did to move aside the small stool in the way. It was good to show off what was being offered. Then Kit was all professional, knowing he had just about pushed his limit for the day, and switched to his sales-assistant mode perfectly.

He managed to sell five shirts, seven trousers, jeans, and enough odd ends to double his monthly check, and decided that even if St. James did not come back, he should be happy with what he had.

But St. James was back two days later with most of the clothes he had bought. It was Eddy's off day and Kit was at the store alone, which was just as well, since Eddy would have been heartbroken.

"Sasha didn't like this," St. James said, pulling out the purple shirt. "Or this…." The blue shirt. "Said it made him look like an old man…."

Fussy little bitch throwing a hissy fit, Kit thought through gritted teeth as he tried to smile. "We can't reimburse you, Mr. St. James, but we can exchange these for something else—of equal value."

"Cory, please," St. James said with a smile. "Calling me St. James makes me feel old, not that I am not." A wry grin.

Kit laughed at the joke and didn't try to guess St. James's age. "Cory it is, then," he said, letting the name drag in his mouth just to see a reaction. "Tell you what, sir, we'll be getting a new shipment next week, and you can pick out something from that. Until then, leave these here, and I'll write up a receipt for you."

"I think that's an excellent idea," Cory replied as he pulled out a business card. "My home number is on the back, my office number is at the bottom. Just give me a call when you get new stock."

Kit decided to give it a try again, just so he could get a feel for the competition. "If you could bring Sasha with you, though...," he said, letting the suggestion hang.

"Sasha is a little busy at the gym these days," Cory replied, and again there was a shadow of sadness in his face. "The pool and the gym are just about the only places he goes... so...."

Kit smiled to himself and did a little dance inside his head. Here was a guy crying for attention, and Kit was going to lavish him from head to toes. But Kit knew how to play his cards. He held back, writing receipts and smiling politely at St. James—no, Cory.

The new stock came on Monday. Kit waited until Wednesday afternoon to call up St. James. Thursday was Eddy's off day, and Kit wanted the shop to himself. Kit dialed the home number, and someone picked it up on the fourth ring.

"Hello." The voice was chocolate and honey melted together. If this was Sasha, Kit was in for a long trial. "St. James residence."

"Hi, I'm Kit from Eddy's... boutique." The voice had thrown Kit off balance, and he did not know what to say. Three words, and that voice had him panting—no wonder St. James was mad over this Sasha guy, even if he was such a bitchy little thing. "I just wanted to tell Dr. St. James"—there, Kit had rehearsed that line several times, so he knew what to say—"that the new stock he ordered is here. If he could drop by tomorrow to—"

"I'll tell him." The voice said, sounding cold, forcing Kit to speculate that his mere existence had won him the wrath of Sasha. "Anything else?"

"Uh...," said Kit, still off balance. "No, but...." He was listening to the dial tone. Stupid Sasha had hung up on him. Now he wasn't even sure if his message had gotten through.

But St. James showed up the next day late in the afternoon, just when Kit was about to give up, and was more than happy to go over the new stock with Kit. As Kit was totaling up the bill after the sales, he glanced at the wall clock and smiled. "I'm about to close up for the day, Mr. St. Ja… Cory. Care for a cup of tea?"

St. James appeared surprised but pleased. "Yes, I…." He looked at his watch and grimaced. "I'm sorry, but Sasha has an appointment—I promised to drive him there, and…."

"Just a cup of tea," Kit said, smiling invitingly. This was his first test to see if Sasha had an absolute grasp on Cory, or if Kit had a chance. "Please, I've been here the whole day without a lunch break, and I hate eating alone."

"I suppose." Cory seemed to hesitate. "Well, I guess a cup of coffee won't hurt, just give me a minute to call up James."

"James?"

"My chauffeur," Cory said as he pulled out his cell phone. "He can take Sasha to his appointment."

Success, thought Kit, as Cory took Kit to a local coffee shop. The place wasn't so flashy that Kit in his jeans and T-shirt would feel out of place, but not too grubby either. Kit's new patron paid for everything with his credit card. Kit didn't leave with Cory, knowing anything too obvious might drive him away. Cory was far too well bred to be taken in by someone who came on to him like a ton of bricks.

Instead, Kit stood on the pavement outside the café and watched Cory walk to where he had parked his car, when the waiter who had served them came to the door. "Here," the waiter said, handing over to Kit an off-white calling card. "Your friend dropped this when he paid."

"Uh," said Kit, nonplussed as he took it. "Thanks." He turned it over and frowned. The card was embossed in gold and looked expensive, and on it was a long word followed by the word "clinic." The long word did not make sense, but the clinic bit did. So did the name underneath the title, Dr. Henry Hausser—some sort of medical card. Whatever, Kit thought as he pocketed it. He'd give it to Cory the next time he dropped into the shop—and Kit was sure he would come back.

SANDRA BARD grew up traveling the world from Africa to Asia and, though she now lectures full-time at a university, dreams of having a job that won't tie her down to one place. She also volunteers for an animal rescue organization and works with students from improvised schools to improve their education.

She enjoys reading, watching anime, and occasionally visiting a fanfiction site. She also dabbles in tai chi and yoga in the hope they will keep her flexible and help her lose weight. She lives with her pets (fish, cats, and dogs)—yes, she's single and has been all her life. She would love to hear from her readers.

Tumblr: sandrabard.tumblr.com
E-mail: sandrabard123@gmail.com

www.ingramcontent.com/pod-product-compliance
Lightning Source LLC
Chambersburg PA
CBHW070053030726

47506CB00002B/453